Erinsmore

by
Julia Blake

Sele Books
www.selebooks.com

www.juliablakeauthor.co.uk

ISBN: 9798630506665

Erinsmore is written in British English and has
an estimated UK cinema rating of PG
containing mild fantasy violence and flirtatious behaviour

Erinsmore is an Authors Alike accredited book

~ Dedication ~

To Francesca
my very own Cassandra!
You always said you wanted to see Erinsmore
published as a proper book,
with your name in the front.
Well, here it is.

Thanks for all your patience and understanding,
and for all the help with technical stuff
when I didn't understand

Love
Mum

~ Acknowledgements ~

Thank you needs to be said to so many people.

To my editor, Dani, as ever thank you. For your patience with this stubborn author who thought she knew best. Thank you for sometimes letting me have my head, but for keeping a firm hand on the reins.

Then my pair of diligent and eagle-eyed beta readers K.M. Allan, Ruth Miranda, and Rachel Churcher. Thank you, my lovelies, for picking through all my words, finding the bad ones, and letting me know of any other bits that weren't quite right. Both amazingly talented authors and bloggers, you can find them at:

Instagram.com/k.m.allan_writer
amazon.com/author/ruthmiranda
tallerbooks.com/battleground

And a huge thanks to Becky Wright at the wonderful Platform House Publishing for all your help with formatting. Your patience, friendship and support over these years have saved my life more times than I care to remember, and without you, I doubt I'd ever have got this writing lark off the ground.

Becky and the crew at Platform House Publishing are also responsible for the awesome cover, and for all your publishing needs why not contact them at:

www.platformhousepublishing.co.uk

And finally, a massive thank you to my wonderful daughter, who not only helped me with all the illustrations and the technical bits I didn't understand but also made the fabulous map.

~ A Note for the Reader ~

Erinsmore popped into my head, almost fully formed, when I was on my way back from London, having been to see the Lord of the Rings stage show, many years ago.

I've always had a deep and abiding love for fantasy and other world stories, beginning, of course, with the Narnia books by C.S. Lewis and working through the superb Dark is Rising series by Susan Cooper and the darkly brilliant books of Alan Garner. All coming to fruition in Erinsmore, my tale of far-away lands, magic, myth, and dragons.

I hope you enjoy the adventures of Cassie and Ruby, and, as ever, appreciate comments, thoughts or maybe even simple shout-outs on my Facebook page, Julia Blake – Author.

You can also follow me on Instagram @juliablakeauthor and on Goodreads. And why not sign up to read my humorous blogs about life, parenthood and writing on "A Little Bit of Blake"

https://juliablakeauthor.home.blog/

Finally, there's my website for information about me, as well as background on all my books and free tasters.

www.juliablakeauthor.co.uk

All the best
Julia Blake

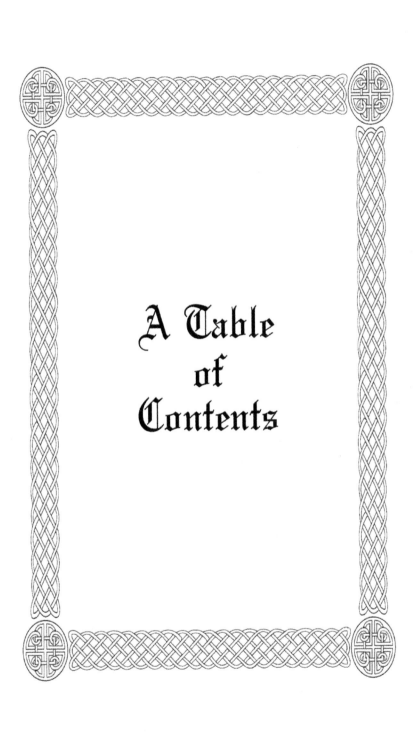

A Table
of
Contents

Prophecy
Rhyme of the Four Treasures
Map of Erinsmore
Dramatis Personae
Creatures of Erinsmore

Prophecy

When darkness has descended
And evil stalks the land
Two shall come amongst us
With sacred stone in hand

One a precious treasure
One a warrior maid
Innocence is destruction
And Erinsmore betrayed

Two shall fight for freedom
Defend the dragon's throne
Two shall walk the dark path
And one return alone

{traditional Erinsmore prophecy,
source unknown}

Rhyme of the Four Treasures

Earth, water, air and fire,
Mark well these omens of might.
Kept apart for millennia,
Since the dragon's final flight.

From earth the stone of prophecy,
Its message clearly writ.
From water the heart of crystal,
Its guardian the Sleskeritt.

From air the golden griffin,
Crafted by elfish hand.
From fire the D'raiqwq,
'Neath the centre of this land.

Torn apart by warfare,
Two and two did journey long.
Reunited by a gemstone
And a dragon's new-born song.

{traditional Erinsmore rhyme,
source unknown}

~ Dramatis Personae ~

Erinsmore ~ long ago

Lady Ninniane	Immortal Member of the Mage Council
Samson	Her manservant
Lady Ansianda	Immortal member of the Mage Council
Lord Lorcan	Immortal member of the Mage Council
Lady Gwnhyfar	Orphaned Princess of the Far Isles

London

Ruby Markson	14-year-old dreamer and wisher
Cassie Markson	Her sarcastic and feisty older sister
Mr Markson	Their Father
Mrs Markson	Their Mother
Mick Smith	Owner of disreputable East End gym
Shop Keeper	Tintagel Gift Shop Keeper

Erinsmore

Colwyn	Heir Apparent to the Dragon Throne
Delmar	Colwyn's Mage
Reutghar	Colwyn's Father and Rightful Heir to The Dragon Throne
Lord Darius	Captain of the Erinsmore Guard
Siminus	Lord Reutghar's Mage
Garth	Lord Reutghar's Bodyguard
Gilmesh Leader	Evil Head of the Gilmesh
Lord Barnabus	Erinsmore nobleman
Lady Melinda	Erinsmore Lady
Gretchen	Head Cook at Dragonswell
Moll	Lady Ninniane's Gentlewoman
Wilfric	Young Erinsmore Soldier
Gunther	Erinsmore Soldier – friend of Wilfric
Nerrisa	Ruby's maid and friend
Merric	Lorcan's slave
Hobbs	Serving Lad at Dragonswell
Edwin	Erinsmore Man-at-Arms
Adam	Serving Lad at Dragonswell
The Guardian	Keeper of the Dark Path

~ Creatures of Erinsmore ~

Wild Hind	Inhabits the Sacred Forest. Good eating
Bella	Colwyn's horse
Wild Boar	Savage and unpredictable wild pigs
Skraelings	(Skray-lings) Evil hellhounds released by Lorcan
Cora	Sacred Raven and Lady Ninniane's familiar
The Pale Ones	Creatures of Lake Minwarn – benign and gentle, hive minds capable of telepathy
Sleskeritt	(Sless-ker-ritt) Mindless vicious creature. Guardian of the Crystal Heart
Gilmesh	Evil, undead skeletal creatures in league with Lorcan
The Golden Griffin	One of the Four Treasures
Irridian	A dragon
The D'raiqwq	(Dray-Q) One of the Four Treasures
Iliana	A baby dragon
Kroneals	Brutish creatures from the dawn of time
Indrina	A dragon

Chapter One

The Prophecy Stone

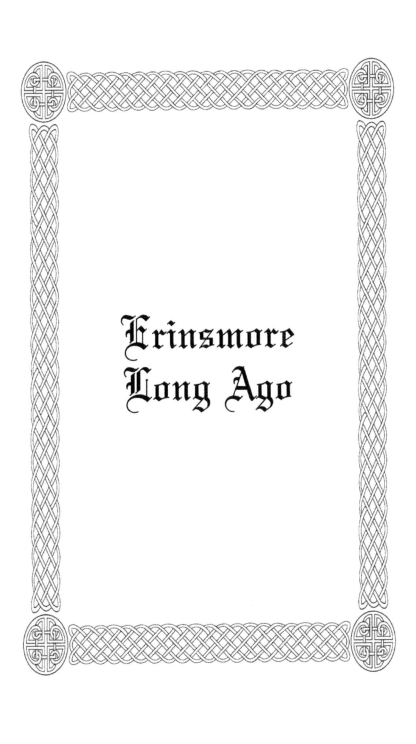

Erinsmore
Long Ago

eath she was familiar with; knew its many faces. This was new. The multitude of voices that cried out in her head, then were horribly silent. She waited until they came to her with the news, sitting by the dying embers of the fire as the first thin rays of dawn passed over her face, drying her tears.

"My lady." Samson's expression was like stone.

She knew the tidings he carried.

"Are they all dead?" she murmured.

His face changed, and for an instant, she saw through his implacable resolve to the young man he had been, the man who loved her.

When her abilities singled her out, Samson had become her servant. A valued one, true, but so much less than he'd hoped for.

"Ninniane," he began helplessly, wishing to spare her pain. "The Lady Alys..."

Ninniane closed her eyes at the mention of her former, much-loved lady-in-waiting.

"She, the Lord Valarian, and the nobles of their court, all have perished."

"How did it happen?" she asked, quietly.

"You do not know, my lady?"

"No," she shook her head. "I felt the outcry as hundreds of souls were ripped untimely from their bodies. It shook the foundations of the world. I felt them die, I do not know from what."

"It was a monstrous tidal wave. Survivors say it stood three times as high as the tallest turret. It engulfed the castle. All who slept on the seaward side were lost."

"The child also?" Ninniane asked, imagining the last despairing moments of those poor souls as this freakish event of nature unleashed itself upon the sleeping castle.

"No, my lady."

Samson's face brightened at the scant good news.

"The child is teething. The nursemaid had taken her to her own room to allow Lady Alys a night's rest..."

His voice trailed away at the thought that now she would have nothing but endless rest.

"Where are the survivors?"

"In the great hall, my lady. Lady Ansianda requests your presence."

Wrapped in a warm cloak against the chill of the early morning, Ninniane hurried down stone steps to the welcoming warmth of the great hall where fires already blazed brightly.

The kitchen staff were handing out steaming goblets of mulled wine to the dazed and exhausted survivors who milled around in confusion, clutching blankets to themselves like lifelines.

"Ninniane."

She turned at the quiet voice which rang with a tone of authority and crossed to where Ansianda awaited her.

Surveying her normally placid fellow council member, Ninniane gathered from the hastily pinned up hair, and the dishevelment of attire, that Ansianda had been caught unawares by the news.

How could that be, she wondered.

How could she not have sensed them die; heard them cry out in anguished horror?

Maybe Lorcan was right – we are much stronger in our ability than they are. Shaking off such treacherous thoughts, Ninniane reached Ansianda's side, and the older woman clutched at her in despair.

"What a disaster," she gasped. "I have never known of its equal. All those poor people lost forever to the sea."

"I am told Lorcan brought back the survivors using a portal stone?" Ninniane was unable to keep the concern from her voice.

"Yes. It seemed … best."

Ansianda fell silent in the face of Ninniane's unspoken criticism.

"I know what you are thinking," she continued. "The victims could not be left there, and it would have taken too long to bring them all back individually."

Logically, Ninniane could see the wisdom of the argument. Even council members could only transport four at a time.

It made sense to have used a portal stone, and yet...

And yet...

"I thought we agreed they should never be used again," she couldn't help murmuring.

"I know," Ansianda flushed, defensively "Under the circumstances ... After all, it was an emergency. Surely it will not hurt to use them one more time."

No, it will not, thought Ninniane, but there would always be one more time and one more time.

Each time the stones were used their power unravelled more of the fabric of existence.

Across the room, she caught sight of Lorcan, his strength and vigour making the breath catch in her throat. He raised his head and locked gazes with her.

She felt his power but could read nothing behind his eyes.

Lately, she had sensed he was keeping much hidden from her.

No longer could she read his soul and it bothered her...

...The secrets she sensed he kept.

Samson ushered forward a serving woman dressed in the grey livery of the household of the Lords of the Far Isles, a squirming white bundle clutched to her breast.

Holding back her emotions, Ninniane reached for the bundle, gently taking the eight-month-old babe of Alys into her arms. Softly, she parted the folds of the shawl and looked in the face of the girl child she had promised Alys she would always protect.

The child moved; tiny fingers clutching at the shawl.

Ninniane felt the world tilt as dark lashes swept upwards to reveal eyes of the clearest green, regarding her calmly, knowingly, almost as if the babe were aware of all that had occurred.

The ability surged within Ninniane.

A tide of prophecy as strong as that which had destroyed the child's home, flowed free.

Her voice rang with power.

All stopped to listen.

"This child," she declared. "This child, Gwnhyfar, will change the fates of two worlds. Her importance cannot be underestimated. She will unite two royal bloodlines. Her legacy will pass down through generations."

In a trance, Ninniane's gaze passed over them all, seeing a strong and steady blaze of light. It burnt like truth around Samson and many others in the hall, over some there hovered a grey cloud.

She saw it, recognised it for what it was – death.

Desperately, she turned to her fellow council members and saw the spectre of death hovering over Ansianda's gentle face.

As for Lorcan...

She could not look at him.

It hurt too much.

Reeling from his shrewd, almost mocking gaze, she uttered a soft cry, and Samson hastily seized the child from her mere seconds before Ninniane crumpled to the ground in a dead faint.

Kneeling by the side of his beloved lady, Samson held the babe too tightly and the child opened her mouth and began to bawl. Her thin, high cries added to the confusion and consternation in the hall, as all rushed to aid Lady Ninniane lying still and white on the cold stone floor.

London

2008

hen did it begin, thought Ruby, this need, this longing to escape? Perhaps that sense of expectation had always been there. That her whole life had been spent waiting for something. What, she didn't know. But those dreams of other worlds were merely shadows of a real longing, a hunger so vivid she could almost taste it, which started on the day it all ended, or began, or perhaps both.

It was the Easter holidays and they had been shopping for the day. She and Mum and even Cassie had come, her normal sulky, teenage angst put briefly aside to make her the fun sister she used to be.

Both girls needed summer uniforms ready for school, so they did that first. Then lunch in a restaurant so posh Ruby swallowed down fits of nervous giggles each time a waiter minced over to refill her water glass, or pick up the massive, snowy white napkin that somehow kept slithering off her lap onto the floor.

Flushed from two glasses of wine, Mum then took them shopping. Reckless with the moment, the number of bags they carried had grown until even Cassie murmured that perhaps it was time to go home. Still Mum persisted, gold credit card flashing.

Finally, they went home, buoyed on a wave of feminine giggles. Mum was opening a bottle of wine, pouring Cassie a glass, even promising Ruby a taste, when the back door opened. Dad walked in, and everything changed.

He was carrying a huge rubber plant. Ruby recognised it as the one from his office. His face, ashen beside the vivid greenness of its leaves, looked somehow beaten, older as if he had lived years since Ruby had seen him that morning.

He talked.

Ruby watched the whiteness of her mother's knuckles as they clutched the stem of her wine glass so tightly, that she feared it would surely snap. Finally, what he was saying began to sink in, and she understood.

It was over, all of it. Dad's job, the one that made this life possible, was gone. The salary and bonuses that paid for a new car and three holidays a year, private schooling, the lovely house, and the beautiful life they lived, were all gone.

It was all gone.

Looking back on that day when everything changed, Ruby's memories were vague and disjointed. All she could clearly remember was the gold of Mum's credit cards sparkling under the bright store lights, and her father's chalk-white face above the rubber plant, clutched to his chest as if it were all he had left to him.

After that, life turned ugly.

Dad looked for another job, of course, without success. There were no jobs; none that Dad could do anyway. It turned out they didn't own anything they had, so the house had to go.

Luckily, given the housing market, they managed to sell it after dropping the price so much Dad's face turned even greyer, and Mum, when she thought Ruby and Cassie couldn't hear, shrieked continuously at Dad about houses of cards, and houses built on sand.

After they lost the beautiful house where Ruby had lived all her life, they moved to a three-bedroom semi on an estate. Ruby and Cassie had to leave their nice, civilised, all-girls, private school where everyone was polite and friendly, to attend the local state school. Ruby didn't mind so much losing the house but having to move schools came very hard.

Cassie covered up her misery with an aggressive façade of frustrated rage and became a complete and utter bitch, withdrawing any degree of support from Ruby at a time when she needed her older sister the most.

In a way, her superior, sarcastic manner served her well, carrying her into the hostile regime of a new school on a wave of indifference. Her arrogance and complete disregard for school protocol and rules afforded her a degree of instant acceptance in the eyes of the other students.

For poor Ruby, it was a very different story. Only fourteen and forced to leave behind everything she knew – Ruby spent her days in a bewildered daze. She was aware that others thought her stuck up and snobby, but she was too shy and insecure to correct them or attempt to make new friends.

Too ashamed of their reduced circumstances to contact her old friends, Ruby was cast adrift in a sea of loneliness, the longing growing until it threatened to drown her.

Mum managed to get a job in a local call centre, her meagre wages the only income they had, apart from benefits. Mouth tight with martyred fury, she told Dad he'd have to manage the house – the cleaner had gone, of course.

He tried, he really did, but didn't know how to. None of them did. Ruby tried to help him after school, miserably aware of their inadequacies.

And so, it went on. Mum got more and more tired. Voice shrilling with bitter fear and disappointment, she railed at Dad until he shouted back.

Then Ruby would run away to her tiny bedroom, now her only sanctuary, covering her ears against the hateful, hurtful words, the bruised exhaustion in Mum's eyes and the hopelessness on Dad's face.

Life dragged on, weeks and months until the holidays arrived, and life was a little easier. No longer having to go to school, Ruby spent most of her days either trying to help Dad in the house or absorbed between the covers of a book, desperate to travel to distant worlds; to a life as far removed from her own as possible.

Then Mum's supervisor at work, a kindly woman – aware of the difficulties they'd suffered as a family – offered them free use of her holiday home in Cornwall for two weeks. Dad argued they couldn't afford to go, but Mum insisted. She desperately needed a break. They were going, that was that.

So, they went.

It was not like holidays in the past – holidays in exclusive resorts abroad when money was no object and meals were cooked by someone else, where kids' clubs were fun and kept Ruby occupied, and where Mum and Dad could relax and enjoy themselves.

Credit crunch holidays were horrible, thought Ruby grumpily. A holiday with parents who hardly had two polite words to say to each other, even more so.

Add a sarcastic, bored sister who didn't want to be there and was missing her boyfriend into the mix, well, that made for the worst holiday of all.

Ruby wished her parents could like each other again. It seemed adversity had ripped them apart, making her mother cruel in her attack, and her father hostile in his defence. They would say things, horrid, hurtful things, in low, tightly controlled voices, as if she and Cassie couldn't hear them; couldn't understand.

When they went into one, Cassie would plug herself into her music, rolling her eyes in disgust, escaping out with friends or her precious Sean.

Ruby was interested in boys too. After all, she was fourteen. It was just that with her head stuffed full of romantic heroes from ancient myths and legends, the spotty, silly little boys at school couldn't match up.

Sometimes, Ruby listened in on her sister's phone calls with her new best mate Lisa, a tall, dark girl whose catty attitude was matched only by Cassie's own.

She didn't mean to eavesdrop, not exactly, but when you're only fourteen nobody will tell you anything. Sometimes, the only way to find out stuff was to stand quietly outside doors and listen.

Cassie talked a lot of junk over the phone, mostly stuff about Sean and how amazing he was. Ruby couldn't help feeling Cassie was laying it on so thick to lord it over Lisa, whose gaunt hatchet features, and nasty mouth rendered her chances of having a boyfriend almost zero. Sometimes, Ruby wondered if that was why Cassie had chosen her to be her best friend.

Ruby supposed Cassie was pretty, she knew others thought so, but it's hard to see your family the way others did. Cassie was tall and slim, her long, straight hair currently dyed a deeply false plum colour which had made Mum shout a bit more, and Dad accuse Mum of completely losing all control.

So, when she listened at doors, Ruby overheard a lot of girl rubbish – mean things about people at school, and of course tons of slop about Sean – but sometimes, just sometimes, she overheard important stuff too.

Like before the holiday, Ruby overheard her on the phone with Lisa. She didn't want to go, she moaned. Imagine it, two whole weeks with the brat and the bickering parents. Lisa asked something at this point because Cassie sighed.

Yeah, she complained, they were still at it. Why didn't they get a divorce and do everyone a favour?

Ruby crept back to her room stunned, feeling small and cold inside. Divorce? Mum and Dad?

Surely, things weren't that bad?

Were they?

Over the next few days, Ruby watched her parents closely as they prepared for the holiday. The last holiday they'd probably all have together, Mum exclaimed brightly, seeing as Cassie would be off to university in September.

And now the holiday was almost over. Ruby had the feeling the holiday had been a kind of last chance for her parents. She also felt that whatever expectations they'd had, it hadn't worked. The holiday had been a complete disaster.

Two very long weeks cooped up in a small fisherman's cottage with bickering parents, forced to spend long periods together because they couldn't afford expensive, touristy attractions. The agony of watching Mum, who hated cooking with a passion, forced to struggle in the tiny kitchen every night because eating out was also impossible.

The weather hadn't helped. Long, cold, rainy days made sightseeing a damp nightmare. Enforced exposure to each other in the car and the cramped cottage had caused tempers to fray and self-control to snap.

It was a shame, Ruby thought, because she had ached to go to Cornwall. It fascinated her, the birthplace of Arthur, Ruby's favourite legend. The lure of Cornwall had long called to her.

On their last day, following Ruby's repeated requests, they piled into the car and went to Tintagel where they climbed the millions of steps down, and up, to reach the breath-taking ancient ruins.

She blanked out her parents' exhausted, heavy breathing, and her sister's non-stop moaning. Did she never shut up? Ruby wandered in a delighted daze, running her hands over rough stone walls, hearing the wild sea pound at the land below.

All too soon her mother insisted they leave, wanting a sit-down and a cup of tea before returning to the holiday home where the arduous task of packing up the past two weeks of their lives awaited them.

They wandered through the village, her parents brightening at the sight of the tearoom, readily agreeing to meet back at the car in half an hour, leaving Ruby and Cassie free to roam. Cassie plonked herself on a wall and pulled out her mobile.

"Beat it, brat," she ordered Ruby. "I want to call Sean."

"We're supposed to stay together," began Ruby, only to be silenced by Cassie's scornful expression.

"How old are you?" she demanded in disgust. "Don't be such a child. Just don't accept sweeties from strangers and look both ways before crossing the road. Now, get lost. Come back in twenty-five minutes and we'll go to the car together."

Ruby got lost. On reflection, she'd rather look around the village by herself than trail along behind Cassie, listening to her moaning.

The village was, disappointingly, nothing but touristy shops, all selling Arthurian rubbish, and Ruby held tight to her purse seeing nothing that tempted her to buy.

As she leant against a wall, a watery and insubstantial sun broke through the cloud cover doing its best to cheer her. A wave of absolute misery engulfed Ruby – that now-familiar yearning to escape, to get away, to be free of it all – welling in her heart.

She longed to be somewhere, anywhere, but here. Tears blurred her vision. Angrily, she dashed a hand across her eyes, drawing herself determinedly upright.

Things would get better, they had to. At least, they couldn't get any worse, could they?

Finally, she reached the last shop in the village. A tiny, dingy-looking place set back from the rest of the buildings, almost as if they didn't want to stand too close to it. The Dragon's Throne, the sign above the door read. Ruby peered through its grimy windows trying to see if it was worth going in.

She glanced at her watch – fifteen minutes before she had to interrupt Cassie's silly phone call to Sean. She decided to kill ten of them in the shop.

The door stuck, as if reluctant to open, and Ruby had to push on it quite firmly before it finally flew open and she stumbled down the steps into the dim, dusty interior. Slowly, she wandered around the shop, its breathless silence making her uncomfortable.

It was like being in a church, with that same sense of reverence and hushed awe. Ruby browsed through the shelves, quickly realising there was nothing there beyond the usual Pendragon tea towels and tacky Celtic jewellery.

She turned to go and saw … It.

A flat stone. It looked ordinary. As Ruby ran her hands along its smooth, conker brown surface, it rippled under her touch.

She blinked and stepped back. Irresistibly drawn to it again, she placed her palm over its flat, cool face. There was a tingling in her hand, heat, and a sense of recognition.

She swayed, the room buzzing around her, the silence so thick she could almost hear it. Dragging her hand away from the stone she saw to her amazement that where it had been blank, there was now writing – small, flowing script.

Curiously, Ruby picked up the stone and gazed at the writing. Disappointingly, it was in some strange language she had never seen before. It wasn't French or German, she was certain of that. She was pretty sure it wasn't any real language at all.

"Are you interested in that?"

The voice made her jump. Spinning around, clutching the stone tightly to her chest, Ruby peered into the darkness at the back of the shop. A man stepped forward. A tiny, wizened, frail-looking man, dressed in something flowing and grey.

"Oh!" Ruby exclaimed, startled. "I'm sorry; I didn't know there was anyone here."

Her voice trailed away as the man's eyes, surprisingly bright and sparkling with intelligence, fixed on the stone she was still clutching in her hand.

"Are you interested in that?" he asked again.

"The stone?" Ruby glanced down at it. "What is it?"

"Very ancient and special. It is Erinsmore's prophecy stone."

"Erinsmore?" repeated Ruby.

It was the strangest thing, but she'd heard the name before, somewhere, sometime, maybe in a dream? And her heart, why had her heart missed a beat in excited anticipation?

"What is Erinsmore?"

"Erinsmore, the lost Midnight Land."

"The Midnight Land?"

Again, memory nagged at the back of Ruby's mind. Something, there was something she had to remember, something wonderful.

"What does it say? I can't read it."

"Can't you?"

"No, it's in some strange language. I can't make it out."

"Look again."

Puzzled, Ruby looked back at the stone and nearly dropped it in surprise. Before her eyes, the writing was writhing, changing. She watched, eyes wide with wonder, as it transformed into words she could understand.

The writing was still spidery and looked very old, yet Ruby could just about make out the words.

"But ... I don't understand," Ruby looked at the shop owner in shock. "I couldn't read it before. What's happened to it? Why can I understand it now?"

"Perhaps you were looking at it the wrong way," suggested the man, an oddly intense gleam in his eyes.

"How could I have been looking at it the wrong way?" asked Ruby, puzzled. "Surely there's only one way to look at something?"

"Oh no," replied the man. "There are many ways to look at things. Wrong ways, right ways, and sometimes different ways. Tell me, child, what is your name?"

"R-Ruby," she stuttered.

"Ruby," mused the man, thoughtfully. "A very precious treasure indeed."

"Um, yes," agreed Ruby in a worried voice, edging towards the door. "I'm sorry, I must be going. My sister will be waiting for me."

"Tell me," began the man. "Is your sister a warrior?"

"A what?"

"A warrior?"

"Well, she likes to argue a lot if that's what you mean."

Ruby was beginning to feel scared and was trying to remember how far behind her the shop door was.

"That is not what I mean, Ruby. Is your sister strong in courage and spirit?"

Ruby paused to think. Cassie was never slow at sticking up for herself, or for others if she thought someone was being picked on. And there had been that time last term when Cassie had stood up to Linda Stokes who'd been bullying Ruby.

"I guess she is," she replied, slowly, "Sometimes."

"You must buy the stone, Ruby," the man edged closer, and Ruby swallowed nervously. "It has been waiting here for you. It is your destiny to own the stone."

"H-how much is it?" Ruby asked anxiously. "I mean, I only have £4 left."

"Then it is indeed fortunate, the stone costs precisely £4."

"Oh, well, okay then."

Without taking her eyes off the man, Ruby fumbled in her purse, placing four, pound coins on the nearby table.

"Thank you very much," she mumbled, backing away so far that she bumped into the door handle. "I must go. My parents will be wondering where I am. Goodbye..."

Thankfully fleeing from the shop, she stuffed the stone into her backpack and rushed to where Cassie was impatiently waiting.

"Come on," she snapped, as Ruby rounded the corner. "Where on earth have you been? We don't want to give them something else to have a go about, do we?"

"Sorry," gasped Ruby. "I lost track of time."

Cassie snorted but said nothing.

Silently, Ruby followed her to the car feeling the weight of the stone in her backpack. As they joined their parents, she wondered why she didn't show them the stone. Something stopped her.

For some reason, it felt like a secret.

Dad got the car started and they pulled away. Ruby, realising they would drive past the shop, excitedly craned her neck to see the strange place where she'd had the oddest adventure. They turned the corner and there it was.

Ruby gasped with shock.

"What's the matter with you?" Cassie snapped.

"Nothing," replied Ruby quickly, and pressed her nose against the window as they drove slowly past the ramshackle, partially fallen-down building, which only five minutes before had been a fully intact shop.

Ruby stared at its tumbled-down walls, broken windows and splintered door half hanging off its hinges. Had she imagined it? Perhaps she had sat down somewhere, nodded off for a while and dreamt the whole weird experience.

No, it was real.

Slipping a hand into her backpack, Ruby softly caressed the stone's warm, smooth surface. What had happened to the shop she couldn't begin to imagine.

It was all very strange.

As the car pulled away up the hill, Ruby had the oddest feeling something was beginning.

Later that evening, after dinner, and after Mum and Dad had had a row about the route home, Ruby finally escaped to her tiny attic room. At last, she could pull the stone from her bag and examine it in the warm glow of the bedside lamp.

All evening she had been aware of it, had almost been able to feel its warm, smooth surface under her fingertips. She ached to touch it, hold it, to try to read the mysterious words. Ruby tipped the stone in the light, and carefully whispered them out loud.

When darkness has descended
And evil stalks the land
Two shall come amongst us
With sacred stone in hand

One a precious treasure
One a warrior maid
Innocence is destruction
And Erinsmore betrayed

Two shall fight for freedom
Defend the dragon's throne
Two shall walk the dark path
And one return alone

Ruby let the stone slither into her lap and stared at it. The silence in the room swelled all around, pressing against her eardrums, as if the world were holding its breath, waiting, hoping, for something to happen.

She sighed, what did it all mean? Where was Erinsmore? The man in the shop had said it was the lost Midnight Land, yet what did that mean? Ruby had never heard of it but somehow, she knew the name; could feel a faint throb of recognition deep within, as if old, long-buried memories had been awoken.

Sacred stone? Ruby picked up the stone and examined it, turning it over, feeling the now-familiar tingle in her fingers. Was this the sacred stone?

What was it the man in the shop had said when she told him her name was Ruby – that it was a precious treasure indeed; then he asked whether Cassie was a warrior maid – it was all so mysterious, Ruby wondered if ... a creak on the stairs outside warned to quickly drop a book over the stone as the door nudged open and Mum popped her head around it.

"Time for lights out, Ruby," she declared. "We've got a long journey tomorrow."

"Okay," Ruby agreed, and carefully slid the book and stone into her backpack. "Mum," she called out. Her mother paused, turning back.

"Is everything okay?" Ruby asked. "I mean, with you and Dad."

"Oh Ruby," replied Mum, a look of absolute sadness settling on her face. For a wild instant, Ruby wondered if her mother was going to confide in her. Then the moment passed, and she plastered on the usual, too bright, smile.

"Everything's fine, Ruby," she reassured. "Now go to sleep, I'll call you in the morning when it's time for breakfast."

When Ruby finally fell asleep, the oddest dreams chased her through the confines of her mind. A strange, tree-filled land, and a flawlessly beautiful woman with long, black hair who was trying to explain something to her, but Ruby couldn't quite hear the words. The more she strained to make them out, the sadder the woman looked until finally she threw her hands up and vanished.

Left on her own, stumbling through vast forests of unfamiliar, giant trees, Ruby's heart pounded with the fear of being alone. Suddenly, Cassie was there with a man – a young, handsome man with long dark hair, dressed in strange, almost medieval-looking, clothes.

They were calling her name, searching for her, but didn't seem to see her even when Ruby touched her sister on the arm.

Ruby turned away from their worried faces and saw him.

Older than the first man, he was tall, with a thick mane of pure white hair which contrasted starkly with his eyes of jet black, glowing with malevolence. He stood, watching her, his thinly cruel face twisting with amusement as if her lonely, vulnerable state pleased him.

"Who are you?" Ruby cried out, her voice high and anxious.

"Your destiny."

"What? I don't understand. Where am I? What is this place?"

"This is Erinsmore," he replied. "And you are going to help me destroy it."

"No!" cried Ruby.

"You have no choice," he retorted, his black cloak billowing in the sudden piercing wind which swept through the trees.

"There's always a choice."

Ruby's heart pounded with fear, but she stood her ground, lifting her chin as she faced the evil madness in his eyes.

"You have no choice," he repeated, "Tis the prophecy." He strode purposely towards her. Ruby fell back, stumbling over a tree root.

She tripped, crashing to the forest floor...

... and sat bolt upright in bed, gasping with fear, heart thudding, panicked breathing loud in the small, still room.

With fingers that shook, she quickly fumbled on the lamp, its warm glow banishing the shadows to the corners of the room. Glancing at her clock she saw it was twelve o'clock.

Midnight exactly.

Chapter Two

Into the
Midnight Forest

n the bright sunshine of morning the dream retreated to the furthest corners of her mind, but Ruby was unable to shake it completely from her thoughts. She wondered what it meant.

Slipping her hand into her backpack, feeling the stone's warmth, she wondered if it had somehow triggered it.

Tempers frayed when it took forever to pack the car, Dad contributing little to the proceedings other than to criticise Mum's packing.

Finally, they were off, chugging up streets so narrow if Ruby reached out, she could have picked flowers from the houses' window boxes.

Almost immediately her parents began to row, voices low and sharp. Mum wanted to go straight home, thinking of the piles of dirty washing. The sheer volume of unpacking it would be her job to tackle.

Dad argued as it was unlikely that they'd be in this part of the country again anytime soon, they should visit a couple of places on the way back.

At last, her mother subsided, turning her head away to stare pointedly out of her window. Sitting behind her Ruby saw her mouth tighten, her eyes blinking furiously, warding off angry tears.

They stopped at Stonehenge.

As Ruby wandered about the prehistoric site, the stone in her backpack burnt between her shoulder blades, calling to the ancient stones.

Back in the car, Mum again tried to persuade Dad to head for home, but like a dog with a bone, he insisted they go to Glastonbury, have lunch, and visit the abbey and the Tor.

They got stuck in traffic. Ruby could feel Mum's simmering resentment as she cast reproachful looks at her husband. Beside her on the back seat, Cassie huffed with barely concealed disgust, plugged herself into her iPod and pulled out her phone, texting silently and furiously about her annoyance with the whole situation.

Having lost her phone in Truro three days earlier, Ruby had no such escape.

Closing her eyes, she found herself being drawn irresistibly back into the dream, lost among great looming trees, and the strange woman who'd tried so hard to tell her something.

Then he was there – the white-haired man.

Darkly malicious gaze burning into her, his cruelly handsome face loomed closer until it changed into a snarling, red-eyed beast, snapping huge, jagged teeth. It threw its head back and uttered a long keening howl which had Ruby gasping herself awake in the car.

"Had a little nap, did we?" Cassie enquired with mock, sisterly sweetness. Ruby ignored her and turned her face towards the window.

Finally, they reached Glastonbury only to find all restaurants and pubs had finished serving. Miserably munching a Big Mac, watching rain trickle in depressing rivulets down the windows of the car, Ruby reflected how things couldn't get any worse.

They visited the abbey, Mum's frustrated annoyance and Dad's over-the-top enthusiasm their guide as they wandered about the sacred building.

They climbed the Tor, well Ruby and Dad did. Mum planted herself in the car announcing her intention to stay there. Cassie also took one look at the hill and hunched determinedly into the back seat.

Reaching the summit, Ruby gazed in wonder at the panorama of Somerset laid out at their feet and turned shining eyes towards Dad, for a perfect moment in complete harmony with at least one of her parents.

"What a view, hey Ruby," Dad exclaimed, throwing his arms wide. "Look at it, magnificent! Did you know the Tor used to be almost an island? Long ago, this whole landscape flooded during winter. It's why Somerset is called that because you used to only be able to set foot on it during the summer. Isn't that interesting?"

Ruby already knew that but was so happy her dad was happy, she simply nodded and stared at the view, watching as the surrounding countryside disappeared underwater and great trees sprang up all around...

Ruby blinked, great trees?

A strange feeling swept over her.

She swayed.

Dad was talking, his voice telescoping away, getting smaller and smaller as another land, another view, began to crowd Ruby's vision.

"Something's coming."

The words sounded in her head. Ruby looked up, startled, as Dad stopped talking, turning to stare at her, and Ruby realised she'd spoken out loud.

"What? What was that Ruby?"

"N-nothing."

Ruby shook herself back into reality, flashing him a smile. Raindrops slid down her face, soaking the hair escaping the hood of her raincoat.

"I suppose we'd better go back," she continued.

Dad's face fell as if he too was reluctant to leave this place, this moment, and go back to the grim reality which awaited them.

"I suppose so," he agreed.

Carefully, they picked their way down the Tor to the car and the rest of their waiting family.

An accident on the motorway caused forever tailbacks. Each slumped in their corner of the car, boredom and driving fatigue draining them of energy and life.

Fed up, Dad inched his way off the motorway and tossed the atlas at Mum, curtly ordering her to find another route. He was sick of motorways. Going cross country was a much better idea.

Knowing their mum's map-reading abilities, Ruby and Cassie exchanged worried glances. Ruby opened her mouth to speak, but Cassie rolled her eyes and shook her head, so Ruby shut it again.

An hour later they were well and truly lost. Gloomy, rain-drenched dusk had fallen early, and now they were driving in complete darkness through some forest or other that Mum insisted was not on the map. They hadn't passed another car for ages.

Abruptly, Dad pulled over and turned to Mum in exasperation.

"Give me the map," he demanded.

Mum flapped it disdainfully onto his lap. "Here," she snorted. "If you think you can do any better."

"Right." Dad's finger traced their route. "We left the motorway here, turned left at this town, bypassed that one, so we should be … That's odd" he muttered, gazing at the never-ending swathes of trees. "There shouldn't be a forest here, not one so thick.

"You see?" demanded Mum, voice shrill. "That's what I've been trying to tell you. We're nowhere on the map. This place doesn't exist."

A chill danced down Ruby's spine and she shifted across the seat. Bumping thighs with Cassie, she realised her sister had also moved away from her door.

"Well," Dad declared, after studying the map in puzzled silence for several long minutes. "Nothing for it, I'll turn the car around and we'll go back."

He turned the key. The car gave a coughing, gasping groan, and stopped.

Dad tried again. Nothing.

Then the lights on the dash winked out, plunging them into almost total darkness. Dad cursed, freely and loudly, desperately turning the key again and again.

"What's wrong?" Ruby heard the edge of fear in Mum's voice.

"I don't know," Dad snapped, an edge in his voice too. "Perhaps I should lift the bonnet, take a look at the engine."

"What good would that do?" Mum demanded. "You know nothing about cars and it's as black as a coal mine out there. Even if you did know what you were looking for, you wouldn't be able to see it. Why don't we phone the breakdown service?"

"They should be able to find us," Dad brightened at her suggestion. "I think they can pinpoint your location via the mobile signal." He fished his phone out of his pocket. "I've got no signal," he turned to Mum. "What about you?"

Sighing, Mum rummaged in her bag and drew out her phone, peering uncertainly at its small, illuminated face.

"No," she conceded reluctantly. "I've no signal either."

They both looked at Cassie, who shrugged and pulled her phone from her pocket.

"Neither have I," she announced, then slid a malicious, sisterly smirk at Ruby. "No point asking if you've got a signal, is there?"

"What do we do now?" Ruby quickly asked, scowling furiously at Cassie.

"There's nothing we can do," said Dad. "We'll have to sleep in the car until dawn, then I'll walk to get help."

"It's getting cold," Cassie shivered.

Ruby realised her arms had gone to goosebumps, although whether from the rapidly falling temperature or fear, she wasn't sure.

Mum opened her car door and the night rushed in.

"Where are you going?" demanded Dad.

"To get jumpers," snapped Mum. "Do you want yours?"

"Oh." Dad subsided, sheepishly. "Yes, thank you, I can't believe how the temperature has dropped. You'd never know it's July."

The car dipped as Mum slammed the boot down and climbed back in, tossing jumpers over the back which Ruby and Cassie gratefully pulled on.

Time passed.

No one spoke, each sunk in their thoughts, silenced by the weight of the night bearing down oppressively on the car roof, lapping with dark malice at the windows.

Cassie fell asleep. Ruby watched her sister's face relax, her usual bored expression softened by sleep and moonlight. Maybe she was pretty after all. Perhaps even beautiful.

Ruby realised how much she missed her.

Not the sarcastic, superior, frighteningly grown-up person Cassie had become, the old, fun-loving, kindly sister of Ruby's past.

Mum and Dad fell asleep, Mum's even breathing reassuring in the gloom, Dad's snuffling snores making Ruby smile as her eyes grew heavy and her head fell forward, sleep pulling her under.

"*Ruby-y-y...*"

Ruby opened her eyes.

Who was calling her?

Groggily, she struggled up, rubbing at gritty eyes which yawned their reluctance to open. Everyone else was asleep. Ruby's head lolled heavily back on the seat as she wondered what had awoken her.

Cassie's phone lay on the seat between them. Ruby picked it up, squinting at the small square of light, struggling to make sense of the numbers. Her eyes focused, time clicked over ... 11:59 ... 12:00 ... it was midnight, exactly.

Slowly, Ruby turned to stare out into the oppressively dark trees.

"Something's coming..." she whispered.

Beside her, Cassie shifted uneasily, muttering something in her sleep.

A light, faint and twinkling through the trees.

Holding her breath, Ruby silently opened the door, and taking her backpack with her, slipped from the car. In a daze, she drifted across the narrow grass verge until she stood amongst the trees.

Quickly, she followed the light. It danced and beckoned. Feeling her way through trees, which seemed to grow as she pushed amongst them, Ruby looked around, unsurprised, as they morphed into the trees of her dream. Stately and massive they loomed above her, leaves rustling in the slight breeze.

Moonlight flooded the forest.

Ruby stopped, confused, looking around. She could no longer see the light. Reality drenched her in a cold sweat. She turned to go back to the safety of the car and her family, realising to her dismay that she didn't know which way to go.

She was lost.

Fear snapped her from the strange, dream-like trance she'd been in. Her heart juddered in panic, clutching with fear, as a howl rent the night air, distant and menacing.

The hairs on the back of Ruby's neck stood to attention as the wolf-like baying was joined by others, and she realised it was the beast from her dream.

Maybe she was dreaming now.

Maybe she was still safely curled up in the car having a weird dream.

Ruby stretched out a hand, touched the rough bark of a tree and shivered.

This was no dream.

She whimpered in fear, only to scream in genuine terror as a hand clamped down on her shoulder.

"Ruby! Shut up!"

"Cassie!" Ruby cried. "What are you doing here?"

"Something woke me," explained Cassie. "I opened my eyes in time to see you disappearing into the trees, so I followed you."

"We have to get back," gasped Ruby. "Did you hear that howling?"

"Howling?" In the moonlight, Ruby saw Cassie frown, "No, what howling?"

"There was ..." Ruby's voice trailed away. "Nothing..."

"We'd better get back." Cassie shivered and glanced around. "It's spooky out here. Besides, if the folks wake and find us gone, we'll be in big trouble. Come on."

She held out her hand. Ruby gratefully took it; thankful for her comforting presence, knowing when the chips were down her feisty sister would always defend her.

A warrior, the man in the shop had called her. Strangely Ruby supposed Cassie was.

They walked, silently and carefully, amongst the trees, Cassie confidently leading the way. Ruby hoped her confidence wasn't just for show. Another baying howl split the night sky.

Cassie froze, turning startled eyes skywards.

"I heard that!" she exclaimed. "What on earth was it? It sounded like a wolf, but there are no wolves in England."

"What do you think it is then?" Ruby asked.

"Don't know," Cassie shrugged. "Maybe we're near a zoo or a safari park." She brightened at the thought. "Yeah," she continued. "That's probably it. This whole forest is some sort of wildlife park," she swallowed hard. "I think we should get a move on Ruby. If wild animals are roaming around, we don't want to come face to face with any of them."

Her grip on Ruby's hand tightened. They resumed walking, their pace quicker.

It was several minutes before Ruby dared voice the thought. "Shouldn't we have got back by now?"

Cassie stopped, looking around.

The trees loomed even bigger. Ruby saw her sister's eyes widen as if realising the sheer scale of them for the first time.

Desperately, Cassie turned to her, and Ruby knew from the look on her face that they were lost and alone in this strange, otherworldly, giant forest.

Far away, a chorus of howls rang out. Ruby's heart skipped a beat with fear. Well, she corrected herself, not completely alone.

She shivered, fear turning into utter and complete terror, and huddled into Cassie as the howls rose, then abruptly stopped.

"Did that sound closer?" Cassie demanded, turning on Ruby worriedly.

In the darkness Ruby shrugged, struggling not to panic. "I don't know."

The moon once again sailed out from behind a cloud, drenching the forest with its eerie, white light.

"The moon," Cassie muttered. "When we walked from the car, was the moon behind or in front of us? Can you remember?"

Ruby considered.

She'd been so intent on following the twinkling light she'd not paid any attention to the moon. She did remember her shadow stretching before her in the forest, long and spiky. It meant the moon must have been behind her.

"It was behind us," she declared firmly.

"Yes," Cassie agreed. "So, if we walk towards the moon, we should be going in the general direction of the road, right?"

Ruby shrugged again.

It was not much of a plan, but Ruby couldn't think of a better one. Without a word, she allowed Cassie to lead them toward the moon.

Carefully picking their way across exposed roots which thrust themselves deliberately into their path, they walked for ages without finding anything even remotely resembling a road.

Cassie froze, and Ruby squeaked as Cassie's grip on her hand tightened painfully.

"Sshh," hissed Cassie. "Listen."

Ruby listened.

All she could hear was her breathing. Then she heard it, a soft nicker and a low, breathy, grunting noise. The sound was familiar. Ruby struggled to place it before it came again, followed by a jingle of metal, and she realised somewhere up ahead, not too distant, there was a horse.

Silently, stealthily, Cassie crept through the forest. Ruby followed; her hand clasped firmly in Cassie's slightly damp grasp.

When they'd gone a few feet, Cassie stopped, sank behind a clump of shrubs, pulling Ruby down and placing her finger to her lips as Ruby's mouth opened to form a question.

Carefully, quietly, Cassie pulled aside the foliage. Both girls peered through into a small, moonlit clearing, where a dark horse busily cropped at the sparse vegetation, its bridle quietly jingling every time it moved its head.

A campfire glowed, its welcoming warmth beckoning the sisters as they shivered in the chill night air. Over the fire, a hunk of meat was roasting on a crude spit. It smelt delicious. Ruby's stomach rumbled. The Big Mac seemed ages ago and she was starving.

Beside the fire, a man crouched. As he settled back into a more comfortable position, firelight played over his features and Ruby nearly gasped in shock.

He was the young man from her dream, the man who had been searching for her with Cassie.

His hair was long and dark, mostly loose, with two rough braids holding it back from his face. His features were wild and strong, as if he belonged here in this dense forest of freakishly giant trees, far away from any other human habitation.

Tall and rangy, he wore a rough leather jerkin, and well-worn leather trousers tucked into sturdy, knee-length boots. A dark cloak encompassed him from neck to mid-calf.

As he leant forward to turn the spit, Ruby saw a short, thick sword sitting low and easy on his hip. At the same time, she noted the quiver of arrows propped against a rock and the bow beside it.

Another cacophony of howls rent the night, yip yipping away into silence.

The man froze.

Ruby saw his hand had automatically gone to his sword. It hovered there, ready to pull the blade free should the need arise. No more howls sounded. Gradually, the man relaxed, settling back onto the flat rock behind him.

"Tis a dark and lonely night."

Ruby jumped at the low, rich tone of the man's voice. He didn't turn his head, but she knew he was aware of exactly where they were.

"On such a night as this," he continued, his voice casual, a ring of steel beneath the words, "fellow travellers should come together, perhaps to share hot meat and wine, and exchange tidings. Will you not join me by the fire?"

Ruby looked at Cassie who shook her head.

"If you bear me no ill will, you have my word of honour no harm shall come to you whilst you share my campfire."

He paused, then continued, his tone firm and uncompromising.

"If you choose to steal away like a thief in the night, I shall have no choice but to consider you my foe."

Chapter Three

Colwyn

he man stood and looked straight at their hiding place, hand resting on his sword hilt. Ruby swallowed nervously. If they were to make a run for it, he could easily outrun them with his long legs and probable superior knowledge of the forest.

She glanced at Cassie, who squeezed her hand encouragingly. Nervously, the girls stood and stepped into the clearing, walking slowly towards the welcoming warmth of the campfire.

The man's eyes widened. "Why, tis a pair of young maids. I pray thee, why do you wander abroad on such a night as this? Are you alone?"

"No," Cassie raised her chin bravely to look him square in the eyes. "Our parents are back there."

"I was not aware woodcutters came so deep within the sacred forest."

The man frowned, studying them intently in the firelight. Ruby realised he was younger than she first supposed, possibly only five or six years older than Cassie, and that it was his nonchalant, confident manner that made him seem older.

"Our parents aren't woodcutters," retorted Cassie. "We were travelling home and we kind of got lost."

"Travellers?" questioned the man in disbelief. "What manner of fool would travel the sacred forest without a guide? Your parents should have known better."

"Well, where's your guide?" Ruby blurted out.

"I need no guide, little maid." The man's face relaxed into a grim smile. "This is the land of my birth. I would know my way through these trees blindfolded."

"How convenient," drawled Cassie dryly.

The man stared at her in baffled silence, then threw his head back and laughed.

"Your words are strange," he said. "Yet I see the humour behind them and do not believe you mean me any harm. Come, sit, my fair young maids, rest for a moment, then I will lead you back to your parents, mayhap guide them out of the forest for tis certain they will never find their way out alone."

Cautiously, Ruby eased herself down before the fire, ignoring the furious glare Cassie shot her. She couldn't explain it, but she believed they could trust this strange young man.

Anyway, she was cold and tired, her feet were hurting, and where on earth did Cassie think they could run to?

Reluctantly, Cassie sat next to Ruby. The man settled himself back onto his rock, poking expertly at the sizzling lump of meat.

"Are you hungry?" he enquired casually.

"Yes," blurted out Ruby.

"No," declared Cassie defiantly, frowning at Ruby.

The man merely shrugged, took the spit off the fire, and used another stick to pull the meat off onto a wooden platter which he placed on the ground before them.

From the saddlebags at his feet, he took out a rough, dark-coloured loaf, and tore chunks off it. This he also piled onto the plate.

Finally, he pulled a water flagon from his belt and took a generous swig, before handing it to Ruby.

She took it, her reluctance to drink being overridden by an overwhelming thirst. She tipped the flagon to her mouth and choked in disbelief at the rough red wine which slipped down her throat, instead of the water she'd been expecting. Coughing and spluttering, she wiped at watering eyes.

Cassie snatched the flagon away, sniffing it in disbelief.

"Alcohol?" she demanded, turning furious eyes on the man who was grinning at Ruby's discomfort. "You gave her alcohol? Do you have no brains?"

The grin dropped away from the man's face. His body stiffened.

"You would do well to refrain from insulting your host," he remarked, tone tipped with steel. Cassie shrank back, abruptly aware of their vulnerable position.

"It is unsafe to drink the water in many parts of the sacred forest," he continued. "This is one such part, hence the wine."

"You keep calling it the sacred forest," began Cassie angrily. "Where exactly are we? There was no forest on the map. I think if there was anywhere like this in England, we'd know about it. Is this some sort of military enclosure, or a private wildlife park? Is that it? I mean, we heard those wolves howling..."

"Those were not wolves," retorted the man.

Cassie's eyes narrowed. "What were they then?"

"They were skraelings..."

"Skraelings?" echoed Cassie in disbelief. "What on earth are skraelings?"

"Lorcan's hounds of death. Since ancient times they have been unable to enter the sacred forest. Now, with such dark times come upon us, I am unsure how long the old rules will hold if indeed they have not already been broken."

"Oh, well that explains it then," Cassie retorted, sarcasm dripping from every word. "Please stop talking rubbish and answer my question. Where are we?"

"Why fair maid, do you seriously mean you do not know? You are in the sacred forest which covers almost the whole southwest province of the land of Erinsmore."

"What? But that's ..." began Cassie, as Ruby exclaimed.

"Erinsmore? The Midnight Land?"

The man looked in surprise at Ruby.

"It has sometimes been referred to as thus in ancient stories and legends. I wonder at a young maid such as you, knowing of it."

"I know from this," explained Ruby, pulling the stone from her backpack, and laying it on the ground before them. The stone's smooth surface winked in the firelight, and the words glowed brightly as if lit from within.

"The prophecy stone," gasped the man, reverently reaching out a hand and picking up the stone, twisting it to read the words. "I have heard of it, but never did I think to ever see it, and certainly not in the possession of a pair of young maids."

"Will you stop calling us that," erupted Cassie, Ruby heard fear in her angry words. "No one talks like that anymore, no one. My name is Cassie, and this is my sister Ruby."

"Ruby?" The man turned thoughtful eyes on them. "A precious treasure indeed," he murmured, looking at Cassie puzzled. "What manner of a name is ... Cassie?" He stumbled a little over the word as if it were unfamiliar to him.

Cassie flushed. "It's short for Cassandra," she mumbled.

The man's face brightened. "Cassandra," he repeated. "Truly a name fit for a queen."

Cassie flushed even more and flounced angrily away from him.

~35~

"Tell me, Lady Cassandra," Cassie's face flamed beetroot red in the firelight and Ruby smirked, enjoying watching her usually cynical sister being completely flummoxed by the strange, handsome young man.

"How is it you came to possess the prophecy stone, a thing so rare, so valuable, many believe it to be merely a legend?"

"That's a very good question," responded Cassie grimly, turning steely eyes onto her sister, "Ruby?"

Ruby swallowed nervously under her sister's accusing glare, then quickly told them the story of the shop and its strange keeper.

How he called Erinsmore, the Midnight Land, and persuaded her to buy the stone. How their car had stopped in the middle of nowhere and they had both, somehow, found their way to the clearing.

When she stopped talking the man was frowning, and Cassie was staring at Ruby as if she was a total stranger.

"Many of your words are unfamiliar to me," he began slowly, "yet they bear the ring of truth. It is spoken of another land, lost in the mists of time. A land once easily accessible from this one, where folk traded, even married across the borders. And then long ago it began to be harder to cross, the ways being closed to all but a few until finally there were no more crossings."

Cassie snorted in disbelief, but Ruby leant closer, hanging onto every word, hearing an answering echo of recognition deep within her. Yes, she thought, yes, that's how it was.

"Many believe these tales to be merely that," the man continued. "Stories invented aeons ago to amuse children at bedtime. But someone very wise and dear to me once told me there was more than a grain of truth to the tales, that someday the ancient crossings would be reopened, and the prophecy fulfilled."

"So, what are you trying to say?" demanded Cassie shrilly. "That we've somehow crossed into a magical world? We're now in this Erinsmore place?"

"You are indeed in Erinsmore, Lady Cassandra." A chill wind swept abruptly across the clearing, tossing the man's hair back from his face. The sisters stared at him in dismay. "As to where you have come from, truly, only you know the truth of that."

"We've come from England. We're still in England," insisted Cassie, Ruby knew she was close to tears. "I won't believe anything else. It's simply not true. It can't be!"

"As you wish, my Lady," the man replied, his face concerned.

Ruby knew he was someone who could be trusted; someone who would place truth and honour above everything.

"It's not true I tell you," Cassie's voice rose, as she hammered her point home.

"It is, Cass," Ruby insisted quietly. Cassie turned wild eyes upon her. "It has to be," Ruby continued. "It's the only explanation that fits – the stone, the trees, those weird howling things, him," she nodded towards the man. "What is your name, by the way?" she asked curiously.

The man smiled gently. "As you have honoured me with your names, I shall return your trust and will give you mine. I am Colwyn, the eldest son, and successor to Reutghar, Lord and rightful heir of the Dragon's Throne of Erinsmore."

This was delivered in a grand, even slightly pompous tone as if Colwyn expected it to mean something to them, and he looked vaguely annoyed when the girls merely blinked at him, then grinned good-naturedly and gestured towards the plate of food.

"Let us eat," he exclaimed, "before our meal grows too cold."

Cautiously, Ruby reached for a piece of bread and a generous hunk of meat. The bread was tough, it's slightly nutty-tasting chewy inside satisfyingly filling. As for the meat, Ruby rolled her eyes in delight.

"Oh Cassie," she exclaimed, tearing into a second bite. "You've got to try this. It's like the best tasting meat ever."

Carefully, Cassie picked up some food and gingerly ate a little, resolve melting away as the juicy flavours exploded onto her taste buds.

"What kind of animal is this?" she asked, around a mouthful of bread and meat.

"It is the hind that runs freely in this forest," replied Colwyn, seemingly delighted at their enthusiasm. "I was fortunate enough to happen upon an injured one and hence could despatch it with an arrow. Normally, they are so swift of pace even a skilled bowman would be lucky indeed to bring one down."

"A hind?" asked Cassie, wrinkling her nose. "That's, like, a deer or something, isn't it?"

"It is a female deer," confirmed Colwyn, looking at the girls in wonder. "Are such things so rare in your world then? That you are unfamiliar with their kind?"

"There are deer in our world, lots of them, I guess," explained Cassie.

Ruby noted with satisfaction that Cassie now seemed to completely accept the fact they had somehow crossed over to another world; that they were in Erinsmore.

Ruby hugged herself with glee.

Another world.

She knew she should probably be afraid, and it was true a delicious thrill of fear was tingling down her spine, yet at the same time, she couldn't help feeling excited. It was as if her desperate wish for escape had somehow, magically, been answered.

At that moment, sitting in the cosy clearing by the warm fire, eating delicious meat, and talking to Colwyn, she didn't feel in danger. Instead, Ruby felt alive. Looking up at the clear heavens and the bright stars which seemed closer than those back home, even the far-off keening of the skraelings couldn't dampen her spirits.

Cassie was explaining to Colwyn that even though deer roamed freely in their land, she had never actually seen any because they lived in a city.

Then she had to explain the whole concept of a city, Colwyn informing the girls the largest town in the whole of Erinsmore, Dragonswell, only contained a few thousand souls. Although, on special feast days or when a new heir was declared, the town swelled to nigh on three times that amount as visitors flocked to the land's capital.

Looking down at the plate, Ruby realised they'd finished the meat and bread and gave a little sigh of regret. Smiling at her, Colwyn reached into his saddlebag and brought out a handful of small, wizened apples. When Ruby bit into one, it exploded in tart, fresh juiciness in her mouth.

Colwyn handed round the flagon again.

This time Ruby sipped more cautiously, feeling the warmth of the wine trickle down her throat. Cassie took a sip, frowning at the unfamiliar rawness of the wine.

"Now that we have eaten and drunk our fill, mayhap it is time to make plans."

"Plans?" Cassie looked at Colwyn startled. "What sort of plans?"

"Do you think it mere chance you found your way through an ancient crossing into this land? No, it was meant you should cross my path. The sacred forest covers hundreds of hectares. It cannot be happenstance that put me here, ready to aid and assist you."

"Oh, well, maybe not," stuttered Cassie.

Ruby watched with interest as firelight flickered over Colwyn's ruggedly handsome face, and her sister looked down at her lap as if unable to look at him anymore.

"What do you suggest then?" she mumbled, twisting at a button on her jumper.

"Tonight, we rest, at first light, continue on our way."

"Go with you?" Cassie's head shot up, staring at Colwyn in dismay. "No, we can't, I mean, you promised to help us find our parents."

"Sweet Lady Cassandra," Colwyn's expression softened as he gazed into Cassie's flushed and angry face. "I fear, woodsman though I am, where your parents are it is beyond my skill to lead you."

"Are you trying to tell me we're stuck here?" Cassie's voice rose, shrill with fear.

Ruby stared at Colwyn, wide-eyed, as the reality of their situation struck hard, the thought of never being able to go home driving away her previous excitement.

"We have to go back!" demanded Cassie. "You must take us back to this crossing place. We must go home. Our parents – they'll be going frantic with worry."

"I am sorry for your parents' suffering," began Colwyn, frown deepening. "Believe me, Lady Cassandra, I would do anything within my power to assist you, but I fear it is beyond my skill. I am no mage. I barely possess basic ability."

"What?" Cassie stared blankly, but Ruby wiggled with renewed excitement.

"A mage?" she squeaked. "Do you mean that magic exists here in Erinsmore?"

"Ruby," chided Cassie, then turned a superior smile on Colwyn. "Ignore her, she's completely gone on stuff like that, you know, Harry Potter, Narnia, I'm afraid sometimes Ruby doesn't know where fantasy ends, and reality starts."

"Lady Ruby is correct, although I marvel at her question, Is your world so different then? Is there truly no magic there?"

"No," Ruby shook her head sadly. "Although, I think there may have been, long ago, nobody believes in it anymore except children."

"Mayhap that is why the crossings ceased, for I believe it would not be possible to pass from one world to another without the aid of magic."

"So, let me get this straight," drawled Cassie in a sarcastic tone, which made Ruby wince and Colwyn frown. "You're trying to tell me that you can do magic?"

"On a very basic level. Every child in Erinsmore is tested for the ability before their fifth birthday. Most are like me, proficient at only rudimentary skills. Some possess higher levels, and these dedicate their lives to the people, aiding them as township mages. Then, every generation, one is born with the true ability, and these are linked to the dragon's throne, honour bound to serve the heir."

The girls sat silently, trying to digest this sea of information. Cassie frowned as a sudden thought struck her.

"You said the rightful heir is your father?"

"That is correct."

"And that the rightful heir sits on the dragon throne?"

"Yes."

"That must mean your father is the king?"

"That is one of my father's titles, although he prefers to view himself as protector of the people of Erinsmore."

"So, if your father is the king," pressed on Cassie regardless, "that must mean that you're a prince."

"I do bear that honour, yes, Lady Cassandra."

"Oh," mumbled Cassie, blushing again.

"Then what are you doing here?" asked Ruby, eyes wide with wonder. "Why aren't you at Dragonswell helping your father to rule the land?"

"Dark times have come upon Erinsmore, Lady Ruby. Lorcan has escaped from his confines. Once again, he stalks the land bringing death and destruction in his wake."

Far away, the skraelings set up a chorus of baying howls. They all shivered. Colwyn tossed more wood onto the fire, the sisters inching themselves closer to its warming glow.

"Who is Lorcan?"

"The dark one. Long ago, Erinsmore was ruled by a council of six wise mages, the Lords Drufus, Cassion, and Lorcan, and the Ladies Ansianda, Melia and Ninniane. It was a golden age, a time of peace and prosperity when stories of crossings between our worlds were most prevalent. Then one of the mages, Lorcan, became dissatisfied with sharing power with his compatriots. Slowly, this worm of discontent festered and grew. Finally, he murdered four of the council and assumed control of Erinsmore, creating his fearsome hounds of death, the skraelings. The land was ravaged, the people scattered, and it was feared Lorcan's evil rule would extend through the crossings into other worlds."

"Other worlds?" asked Cassie, as she hung, spellbound, on his every word.

"Yes. Legend states there are many other worlds where such creatures as elves and the like still exist."

"Elves," breathed Ruby, and Colwyn smiled at her.

"Do such legends persist in your world then?"

"Oh yes," said Ruby, "In fairy stories and children's tales."

"Much as it is in Erinsmore," continued Colwyn.

"What happened?" demanded Cassie, "Was Lorcan stopped?"

"A young warrior lord, Arturius, heir to the dragon lords, rallied all the forces for good, including soldiers from your world. With the help of the last member of the mage council, the Lady Ninniane, he defeated Lorcan, imprisoning him forever with chains of pure good, so repulsive to what Lorcan had become it was impossible for him to even touch them."

Ruby had been listening to the tale with mounting enthusiasm, and as Colwyn fell silent burst out excitedly. "Arturius? Lord of the dragons? That means it's true, all of it, it's true!"

"What? Ruby, what are you talking about? What's true?"

"Arturius lord of the dragons ... Arthur Pendragon. They must be the same person," she turned on Colwyn. "You say soldiers from our world fought too?"

"Many valiant warriors from your world made the crossing."

"What happened to them? Did they stay here or go back?"

"It was a long and fierce battle. Many fell before the tide of Lorcan's evil minions." Colwyn frowned. "Though legend tells of a magnificent banquet Arturius held in honour of the men from your world, before those who chose to return made the crossing."

"They took the story back with them. Over time it's grown, been added to, but the basic elements of the tale stayed the same." Ruby's face glowed, and she hugged her knees fiercely. "I knew he must have existed."

"So, what went wrong?" asked Cassie quietly.

"My lady?"

"If these chains were so strong, how has he managed to escape? Why are those things," she broke off and shivered, "those skraelings, roaming around again?"

"I do not know," Colwyn's face grew serious. "Four moons ago we noticed omens of disaster – herds of cattle lying slain in fields, crops failing, children born dead. My father's mage, Siminus, and my mage, Delmar, spent many long hours in consultation before it was decided that Delmar would travel to the sacred forest to seek the counsel of the Lady Ninniane..."

"Lady Ninniane?" interrupted Cassie, incredulously. "You mean, she's still alive?"

"Why yes," replied Colwyn. "As Lorcan cannot die, neither can Lady Ninniane. So," he continued, "it was decided. Delmar would make haste to the Lady's Sanctuary to ensure her well-being, and to consult with her as to what these omens foretold."

"And had anything happened to the Lady?" asked Ruby.

"Delmar never returned. As the weeks passed, I feared for them both. I know he still lives; our link lets me know that much, but I could not reach him. I gathered enough supplies for a lengthy journey and set out on my quest to the sacred forest."

"Link?" Cassie wrinkled her brow in confusion. "What do you mean, your link?"

"Each generation, a mage is born destined to be linked to the rightful heir. A link so powerful, heir and mage have knowledge of each other's well-being and whereabouts. Thus, I feel Delmar lives, yet something prevents me from feeling more. A barrier is around him. I know he is here, within the sacred forest. As I travel deeper into its heart, his presence pulls me onwards."

"That's where you're going now?" enquired Ruby.

Colwyn nodded. "It is, Lady Ruby, and you and the fair Lady Cassandra would honour me with your company. Mayhap, when we discover Delmar and Lady Ninniane, she may be able to assist your crossing back to your world."

Ruby glanced at Cassie.

It didn't sound very hopeful, but they didn't have much choice. If they left Colwyn, what hope would they have of surviving in the forest? They'd wander until they died, not even knowing which water was poisoned, and which was all right to drink. Cassie reached the same conclusion.

"Thank you," she said solemnly. "If we could stay with you, at least until we reach the Lady's Sanctuary, maybe she'll be able to help us."

Colwyn dipped his head in agreement. Then, with eyes sparkling in merriment, he reached out a hand and playfully tapped Cassie's hair.

"I am curious, Lady Cassandra. Is purple hair a common feature in your world?"

Ruby grinned; Cassie spluttered and blushed furiously, all laughter dying as another chorus of howls erupted, still distant, but sounding closer than before. Ruby caught Colwyn's look of alarm.

"I think the skraelings have finally breached the forest's perimeters," he said.

"Will they catch us?" Cassie asked in alarm.

"They are many days' journey behind us," Colwyn reassured. "And tis only two days more to the Sanctuary. Have no fear, my lady; we shall reach safety before they find us. No, what concerns me is they should not have been able to enter the forest at all. Ancient laws strictly forbid all evil from entering sacred places."

"Weren't the skraelings destroyed when Lorcan was imprisoned?" asked Ruby.

"They were, Lady Ruby," agreed Colwyn. "But seven days ago, as I entered the sacred forest, a great pall of darkness fell over the land. It seemed the heavens split open and rained down a torrent that burnt the land outside the forest. That night, I heard the skraelings for the first time. They have not been heard outside of imagination for aeons, still, I knew what they were."

"You think Lorcan has escaped then?" stated Cassie.

"I believe he has, Lady Cassandra," agreed Colwyn soberly. "And I am greatly concerned for the well-being of my people. Before, it took the combined forces of both our worlds to defeat him. Now, Erinsmore stands alone. If Lorcan has escaped, it could mean the end for us all."

Chapter Four

Journey to
the Sanctuary

ext morning, Ruby awoke early and lay back staring up through the canopy hι of feet above her head, marvelling at the sheer scale of the trees.

She shifted uncomfortably, thinking how the reality of sleeping outside was not as much fun as it sounded. Her body ached from contact with the hard ground, and even though Colwyn had covered them with his cloak, Ruby shivered in the cold morning air.

Cassie was still asleep, and Colwyn was poking at the dying embers of the fire. Every time Ruby had opened her eyes during the night Colwyn had been awake, sitting on his rock, eyes glittering in the moonlight as he kept watch, and Ruby had drifted off to sleep again feeling safe under his protection.

"Good morning, Lady Ruby. I trust you slept well." Colwyn spoke softly, without turning his head and Ruby wondered how he had known she was awake. Perhaps by magic? Grinning, she struggled to sit up, groaning as her back complained at a night spent on hard ground.

"Not particularly," she answered.

Colwyn flashed a grin over his shoulder. "Tis plain you are unused to sleeping under the stars, Lady Ruby. I will try to make the going today as gentle as possible but fear I need to set a fast pace. It is necessary to reach the Sanctuary as speedily as possible."

"To find Delmar and Lady Ninniane," agreed Ruby.

Colwyn nodded. "That and ..." his voice trailed away, and he cast an anxious glance through the trees. "I fear the skraelings will not be long in picking up my trail, and three walking cannot go as fast as one riding."

"You think they might catch us?" asked Ruby, alarmed.

"I am sure we shall reach the Sanctuary in time," reassured Colwyn. "But it would be as well if we did not tarry."

Ruby nodded, becoming aware of another, more pressing problem. "Erm, Colwyn?"

"Yes, Lady Ruby?"

"I need to ... well, that is ... umm ... what do we do when we have to go?"

"Go, Lady Ruby? Go where?" Colwyn looked puzzled, then comprehension crossed his face as he observed her embarrassed squirms. "Oh, I see."

Reaching into his saddle bag Colwyn took out a ball of sturdy-looking twine which he handed to Ruby, who looked at it in alarm.

"Tie one end to a tree at the edge of a clearing, pay it out behind you until you reach a suitable place. When you have finished, follow the twine back to the camp site. You must promise, Lady Ruby, not to wander off alone. The ways of the forest are bewitching. They will all too easily trap unwary travellers."

"I promise," replied Ruby, and took the ball of twine. Carefully, she tied the free end around a sturdy shrub on the edge of the clearing and walked someway into the forest, vigilantly feeding it out behind her until she felt private enough.

Quickly, Ruby attended to her needs, imagining a thousand forest eyes were upon her, feeling nervous and skittish until she had rewound all the twine and was stepping into the clearing where Cassie was anxiously waiting.

"There you are," she exclaimed, relief making her voice shrill. "You've been gone ages, my turn." She took the twine from Ruby, paying it out behind her as she disappeared into the forest.

Ruby watched as Colwyn kicked dirt over the remains of the fire, gently whistling to his horse as he rubbed it down. He poured a little water from a pouch into a wooden bowl, which the horse drank thirstily. Colwyn lifted the saddle onto its back, fastening the bulging saddle bags on each side.

"What's his name?" Ruby asked shyly, edging closer to the frighteningly large animal, and risking a quick pat on its shoulder, which it completely ignored.

"He is a mare, and her name is Bella. It means..."

"Beauty," interrupted Ruby. "It means that in my world too." They stared at each other, pleased with the connection; then leapt as a terrified scream ripped through the forest, scattering birds from trees, and causing Bella to stamp in alarm.

"Cassie!" yelled Ruby and ran heedlessly towards the start of the twine.

"Lady Ruby wait!" called Colwyn. Ruby ignored him and ran through the forest as fast as she could go and still follow the twine. Crashing sounds erupted in front of her as Cassie charged around a tree.

"Run Ruby!" she screamed, eyes wide with terror, chest heaving with exertion. "Run!"

Ruby turned tail and ran, knowing by the look on Cassie's face they were running from something very scary indeed. Behind, she could hear the savage grunts and heavy breathing of their pursuer. Whatever it was, it sounded big and angry.

It was difficult trying to run while following the twine. Terror dragged them on though, as they crashed through the undergrowth, swerving to avoid the massive trunks. Ruby risked a glance over her shoulder, desperate to see if it was gaining on them.

A tree root viciously thrust its way out of the ground from nowhere, her foot tangled and she fell, sprawling, onto the forest floor. The shock of the fall jarred the breath from her body, and her ankle twisted painfully on the gnarled root.

"Ruby!" screamed Cassie, skidding to a halt, and falling to her knees as she tried to pull Ruby to her feet. There was a snuffling, snorting, tearing noise, and a thing burst from the bushes. Something that looked like a giant, many-tusked pig – with razor-sharp teeth lining its slobbering jaws, and large, strong hooves.

It stopped and looked at them, fierce malevolence in its small, darkly glittering eyes, and lowered its head ready to charge.

Twang! An arrow soared overheard. Thud! It slammed into the boar's shoulder, knocking it to the ground. It squealed horribly, struggling to get up, and Colwyn leapt over the two girls where they lay, frozen with fear.

Colwyn reached the beast, sword already drawn. He twirled it expertly, blade blazing in a shaft of the early morning sun. Bracing it with both hands he stabbed it deep into the animal's heart. There was an agonised scream, curdling the blood in Ruby's veins, and the animal lay still. Colwyn pulled his sword from the body, wiped it on the beast and re-sheathed it, before turning to them.

"Cassandra, I mean, my Lady, are you unharmed? Are you both all right?"

"Yes," Cassie shakily got to her feet, helping Ruby to hers. "What was that thing?"

"It is a wild boar, a very dangerous and unpredictable animal. I have never heard of one penetrating this far into the sacred forest. Mayhap the forest animals are fleeing before the skraelings, for they are indiscriminate killers and will slaughter anything unfortunate enough to get in their path."

"How long before they pick up our trail?"

Cassie stared directly at Colwyn until he dropped his eyes, busying himself with pulling his arrow from the boar's shoulder and slotting it back into the quiver, which Ruby saw rested diagonally across his back.

"In truth, I do not know, my Lady. It is as I was explaining to Lady Ruby, I believe we will reach Sanctuary in time, but it would be as well if we made haste."

"Right then," stated Cassie, giving the dead boar one last look and shuddering. "I suppose we'd better get on."

"Follow the twine to camp," ordered Colwyn. "In the top of one of my saddlebags, you will find bread and berries. They will suffice for your breakfast. There is something I must do first."

"What?" demanded Cassie, "What do you need to do?"

"Fresh meat is a scarcity in the sacred forest," explained Colwyn. "Boar's meat, whilst not as succulent as a hind's, will nevertheless provide many meals. We are unable to carry the whole animal so must take only what we can carry. I fear it will be an unpleasant job, one I am sure you would rather not witness."

Cassie swallowed hard and nodded, putting an arm around Ruby's shoulder. The girls turned to follow the twine back to camp. As they left, Ruby saw Colwyn pull his knife from his belt and kneel beside the dead boar. Quickly, she turned her eyes forward until they safely reached camp.

They sat on rocks, munching the bread and dried berries, which were tart and full of pips, but better than nothing. Silently, they sipped at the wine, waiting for Colwyn to return and their strange journey to begin.

"Do you trust him?" Cassie's voice broke the silence.

"Who?"

"Colwyn."

"Of course, don't you?"

"I suppose," Cassie stopped to consider. "Not that we have much choice. He certainly saved our lives. That boar wanted to kill us. You could see it in its eyes."

"Hmm," agreed Ruby, casting a sly look at Cassie. "He's very handsome, isn't he? Much more than Sean."

"Who? Oh, yes, Colwyn's a man, Sean's a little boy. I mean, can you imagine Sean coming face to face with that boar?"

Ruby laughed at the thought of slender Sean, with his floppy fringe and jeans halfway down his bum, going one on one with a wild pig, and marvelled at how quickly Cassie dismissed the boy she had been nuts over for months.

There was a disturbance at the edge of the clearing and Colwyn strode in, a makeshift parcel of leaves clutched to his chest. He drew a sack from one of the saddle bags, hastily shoved the parcel in, and tied it onto the saddle.

"It is time to go," he said.

By the time they stopped to make camp that evening, Ruby had gone beyond exhaustion to a state where every bone in her body ached. Groaning with pain, she dropped to the ground beside Cassie, also white-faced with tiredness. She watched through half-closed eyes as Colwyn quickly gathered firewood and laid it within a circle of stones.

Next instant, Ruby sat bolt upright, aches and pains forgotten, exchanging a shocked glance with Cassie.

"How ... how did you do that?" Cassie stuttered. Surprised, Colwyn looked around from the roaring, well-established fire.

"My Lady Cassandra?"

"The fire?" Cassie pointed a shaking finger at the crackling flames. "How did you get it alight so fast?"

"The ability, I told you I have basic skills, not much more."

"And fire lighting is one of those skills?"

"Yes, tis the first skill learnt as a child, and the last skill lost in old age."

"Oh, I see," said Cassie weakly.

The girls watched Colwyn thread chunks of pork onto a skewer and place it on the spit over the fire. Then he unsaddled and rubbed down Bella, tying on a nosebag which she munched and rattled with evident satisfaction. Finally, he strode around the perimeter of the clearing, gathering up armfuls of firewood and placing them beside the fire.

When he sat down with no sign it was a relief to do so, Ruby thought how being a member of the royal family in this strange world was no guarantee of a soft life.

Halfway through the next day, as Ruby was wearily placing one foot in front of the other, she became aware that the ground was sloping upwards and that the spaces between the trees were becoming wider.

For the rest of the afternoon the incline grew steeper, the spaces greater, until finally, as Ruby was beginning to think longingly of stopping to make camp, they broke free of the forest into a vast meadow which stretched away up the slopes of a low range of hills, and there before them was Lady Ninniane's Sanctuary.

Both girls stopped, gaping with astonishment. Not knowing what they had been expecting, the vast, multi-turreted fairy tale castle sparkling a shiny white in the bright afternoon sun was a complete surprise.

"It's beautiful," gasped Cassie.

Colwyn stopped Bella, turning to smile at them.

"Lady Ninniane is famed for her love of grace and beauty. Each year, towns vie to produce the most outstanding works of art to be sent to the Lady as tribute. It is considered a great honour if a local craftsman produces something worthy enough to be selected."

Now the girls had something to aim for their spirits rose and their pace increased for a couple of hours. When the sun began to set, it became obvious as tantalisingly close as the Sanctuary looked, it was too distant to be reached that night.

Colwyn readied the campsite, preparing a stew comprised of pork, apples, and fresh greens which he had picked from the meadow as they passed through it. As they hungrily ate, Ruby noticed Colwyn glancing apprehensively back towards the forest, and knew he was thinking about the skraelings.

The next morning, Colwyn shook them awake before dawn. Thinking longingly about a warm shower and hot, buttered toast, Ruby wearily pulled her shoes on as Cassie leaned against her pulling on her own, muttering sourly about the lack of coffee.

Insisting that they eat breakfast on the move, Colwyn silently handed them round, flat cakes made from rendered down pork fat stuffed with dried fruits, berries, and nuts. At first, Ruby found the greasiness of the food made her stomach churn uneasily but realised the cakes seemed to boost her flagging energy levels and ate them hungrily.

The pace Colwyn set now was fast, and the girls stumbled along in his and Bella's wake, desperately trying to keep up.

When the sun stood directly above them in the sky, they found a small, tumbling brook whose waters splashed crystal clear in the sunlight. Ruby hadn't realised how thirsty she was until she saw that beautiful, bright liquid. She looked longingly at Colwyn as he halted Bella on the riverbank.

"Is it safe to drink?" called Cassie, pitching her words over the roaring water.

"The water this close to the Sanctuary is supposed to be pure, but I will check," replied Colwyn, and held out his hand palm down over the brook. A glowing light formed under his palm. It was almost instantly answered by a pure, white light which danced on the water's surface, and then vanished.

"It is safe," he announced, letting his hand drop to his side.

"How would you have known if it wasn't?" Ruby asked.

"The light would have been black," he answered simply, and led Bella forward to drink her fill. Both girls lay flat on the bank, scooping up water in the simple wooden cup Colwyn passed them, then watched as he filled both water flagons to the brim.

He allowed them ten minutes to rest before leading Bella back up the slope. With heavy sighs, both girls followed, turning their faces towards the shining beacon of the Sanctuary.

They walked for the rest of the day.

Eventually, Ruby gave up looking at the Sanctuary. It seemed never to come any closer. Instead, she watched her own feet plodding along; one in front of the other, in a never-ending march.

At mid-afternoon, Colwyn allowed them another ten-minute break, during which they had a mouthful of water and one of the pork and fruit cakes each. As the girls collapsed in heaps on the ground, Colwyn climbed up a small pile of rocks to stare in concern back the way they'd come.

He jumped down and landed beside them, his dusty boots thudding barely a foot away from Ruby's head.

"Come," he ordered. "We must leave now. Hurry."

"What's the rush?" asked Cassie lazily, squinting up at him as he stood silhouetted darkly against the bright sky. "Can't we camp here tonight and get there tomorrow?"

"No," he snapped grimly, hauling her almost roughly to her feet. "We must leave now and go as fast as we can."

Ruby scrambled to her feet in alarm, the tight worry in his voice and the steely set to his jaw sending chills down her spine.

"What is it?" she asked quickly. "What's the matter?"

"Skraelings," he replied, tersely. "Not more than half a mile behind us." Ruby gasped and looked at Cassie in fear, as Cassie grabbed hold of Colwyn's arm and gazed pleadingly into his face.

"Will we make it in time?" she demanded.

"I vow to you, my Lady Cassandra ... to you both," his gaze flicked to Ruby, and she swallowed at the iron resolve on his face, "that I will defend you to the best of my abilities, and the last beat of my heart. On that, you have my word."

Cassie's eyes grew wide and solemn; then she nodded and released his arm. Colwyn caught hold of Bella's bridle and led her over to them.

"You are exhausted. We will make better time if you ride."

"Neither of us have ever been on a horse in our lives," protested Cassie.

"It will not matter, Bella is gentle, she will look after you. I will lead her. All you must do is hang on." Before Cassie could open her mouth to argue, he picked her up bodily and threw her into the saddle, where she gasped and slithered around, frantically clutching at Bella's mane.

"Lady Ruby," said Colwyn. Silently, Ruby held up her arms and he picked her up, placing her on the saddle behind Cassie.

"Now, hold tight," he commanded. Taking Bella's bridle, he led her quickly across the meadow towards the Sanctuary.

From her vantage point behind Cassie, Ruby twisted to look back down the steep meadow, surprised how far they'd come, her stomach twisting as she saw, far below, at least a dozen squat, black shapes, loping swiftly after them.

"They're coming," she murmured into Cassie's ear and her sister's body stiffened with fear. Neither girl complained when Colwyn clicked to Bella, who broke into a trot, Colwyn jogging easily by her side.

The climb grew steeper, both girls leaning forward in the saddle, desperately trying to hang on as Bella climbed ever closer to the castle. Colwyn glanced back; Ruby saw the keen worry on his face, and the way his hand kept straying to his sword hilt. Although, if the skraelings did catch up a sword wouldn't prove much of a weapon against them.

Finally, Bella scrambled over a steep incline onto a flat, flower-strewn plateau, and there before them, glorious in its magnificence, was Lady Ninniane's Sanctuary.

"Just a little further," declared Colwyn. He indicated two towering pillars of stone no more than half a mile away. "The guardian stones mark the boundary of the Sanctuary. None of evil intent may travel beyond them. Once we pass them, the skraelings will be unable to follow."

His words injected fresh hope in the girls, and they straightened weary bodies in the saddle, staring hungrily at the pillars still so achingly far away. Howls erupted, followed by a furious scrabbling on the rocks below, and Ruby's heart clenched with fear.

The skraelings had caught up with them.

"Go," ordered Colwyn. "I will hold them off to give you time to reach the pillars."

"No!" yelled Cassie. "We won't leave you."

"It has been an honour and a privilege to have served you, my Lady," replied Colwyn. He took Cassie's hand and pressed a quick kiss to it. "Now you must go." He slapped Bella hard on the rump. She took off like a rocket heading straight for the pillars, the girls clutching desperately at saddle, mane, reins, anything to hang on.

"Colwyn!"

Cassie's scream echoed back. Ruby desperately wanted to turn to see what was happening to him but knew if she did, she'd fall off and the skraelings would be on her in an instant.

They passed between the pillars. Ruby felt time split into infinity, as if every second of every minute, in every world, was being held in that one space. Then they were through, and Cassie was hauling on Bella's reins, sobbing, struggling to pull the big horse to a halt.

"Ruby, get down!" she ordered, falling to the ground in her haste to dismount, pulling Ruby bodily off the horse when her sister simply sat, blinking stupidly at her. Cassie gathered up

Bella's reins, tied them into a loose knot on the saddle and led her towards the pillars.

"Go back," she screamed, slapping Bella on the rump as Colwyn had done. "Go back for him, go back for Colwyn." Whether it was the sound of her master's name, the slap on the rump, or simply the fact she wanted to escape the screaming, mad woman, Bella charged through the pillars.

"Come on," shouted Cassie, dragging Ruby towards one of the pillars in which were carved rough stone steps leading up to a look-out post halfway up the pillar.

Tripping, skinning shins and knees on roughly hewn rocks, they stumbled up the stairs until they reached the platform. Finally, they could see down the incline to where one man ran, his pace fast and smooth.

As the girls watched, the huge, shaggy beasts lolloped after him, jaws gaping as they slowly but surely gained on him. It was obvious he wasn't going to make it, and they clutched at each other in despair.

Glancing back, Colwyn reached the same conclusion and veered to the left to a tumbled-down pile of rocks. Quickly, he scrambled up them and drew his bow, releasing arrow after arrow into the pack, each one finding its mark, but making no difference to the numbers or pace. Finally, he tossed his bow aside, and stood, sword lightly in hand, awaiting his doom.

"Oh no, I can't look," moaned Cassie, burying her head in Ruby's shoulder.

An instant later they were upon him, scrabbling up rocks, attempting to reach him. Valiantly, Colwyn defended himself, slashing and stabbing at each shaggy beast that hauled itself over the rim of his mini stone fortress. Ruby saw, with a thrill of disbelief, that he was holding his own.

"Look, Cassie, look!" she shrieked. "He's holding them off, they can't reach him, they can only attack one at a time and he's holding them off!"

Cassie raised her head and stared with mingled horror and hope. Colwyn thrust his sword through the breast of the final skraeling, collapsing to his knees in exhaustion, the animal's death wail floating up to their vantage point.

"He did it!" yelled Ruby.

"No," replied Cassie, quietly. "Oh no, look, Ruby, look!"

Ruby looked and saw.

The pack of a dozen or so which had attacked Colwyn must have merely been an advance party. Ruby heard herself give a great cry of wordless shock at the hundreds of skraelings which scrabbled, slobbering, and snarling, over the lip of the plateau, and began pouring up the incline towards Colwyn.

Sobbing in horror, she watched Colwyn raise his head, her heart clenching with pity as he wearily dragged himself to his feet, prepared to fight.

"He doesn't stand a chance," cried Cassie in despair. "Not against that many, they'll rip him to shreds. Oh, Ruby, there must be something we can do!"

Ruby shook her head. Movement caught the corner of her eye, and she turned to see Bella galloping over the brow of the hill, mane flying, eyes wide and panicked.

Colwyn saw her at the same time. A whistle, loud and piercing, rang out in the still afternoon air pulling the mare to her master. Quickly, Colwyn leapt from the rocks and threw himself onto Bella's back. Wheeling her sharply around, he headed full pelt for the pillars.

Both girls screamed encouragement, as behind him streamed hundreds of skraelings, their scampering pace closing the gap between them and the racing horse.

Colwyn glanced behind him, bent low over Bella's back, urging her forward with his whole body. A vicious howl sounded. The horse's ear flicked back, and her pace increased as if she knew what was on her heels and wanted no part of it.

Closer and closer they came, narrower and narrower grew the gap between him and the pack. Then he passed below them, and they saw him, suspended for an instant in the Sanctuary's barrier.

Frantically, the pack hurled itself at the invisible wall, howling their frustrated disbelief as it repelled them, throwing them roughly back onto the grass. Again, and again the skraelings tried, only to be repulsed each time.

Slipping on the stairs, Ruby and Cassie made their way down to the courtyard where Colwyn was pulling Bella to an exhausted, shuddering halt. They were in time to catch him as he slid bonelessly off her back.

Chest heaving with exertion, brow slicked with sweat, blood splattered on his hands and clothing, they clung to him, relief at his survival leaving them breathlessly dizzy.

"You sent Bella back," Colwyn declared as soon as he was capable of speech.

"Cassie did," Ruby informed him. "She did it, I never thought..."

"Lady Cassandra," Colwyn interrupted. "I am indeed indebted to you. By your action, you saved my life. Henceforth, I am your bondsman, yours to command as you see fit."

"Oh, don't be so daft," sobbed Cassie, swiping at tears with her jumper sleeve. "If it hadn't been for us, you wouldn't have been in danger in the first place."

"Nevertheless," declared Colwyn, "I am your man, my Lady Cassandra." With shaking hands, he unclasped a chain and pendant made of what looked like gold from around his neck and passed it to Cassie.

"This is the sign of the house of the dragon lords. Wherever you go in my world, this will show you are under my protection and may ask for whatever assistance you desire."

Eyes wide, Cassie looked down at the pendant in her hand. Ruby stared curiously at the dragon pendant. Its wide-spread wings glittered like gold in the late afternoon sun, and its serpentine body curled around itself.

She glanced at Cassie and Colwyn who were still staring at each other and decided the mushy stuff had gone on quite long enough.

"So, what do we do now?" she asked.

Her words broke the spell and they looked at her, Ruby saw the flush on her sister's face, then forgot it and everything else as she became aware of their surroundings, and her mouth gaped in astonishment.

Chapter Five

The World
between Worlds

uby's first thought was, "How like Cinderella's castle is this?" Her second, "Is nothing in this world normal size?" Lady Ninniane's Sanctuary was massive. Ruby gazed in stunned awe at the myriad of towers and turrets soaring up and up into the blue sky and thought how the whole castle looked like some colossal wedding cake fit for giants.

The courtyard they were laying in was paved with slabs of beautiful creamy marble, shot through with veins of sapphire blue. At its heart was a huge, ornate stone fountain, out of which shot a plume of sparkling, crystal water that danced and dazzled. Looking around, Ruby realised her local football stadium, the biggest place she had ever been in, could easily fit into the courtyard at least three times over.

Colwyn rose to his feet and helped both girls to theirs.

"This is amazing," murmured Cassie, turning slowly in a circle as she tried to see everything at once.

"My mother died when I was young," stated Colwyn. "So, I spent a great deal of my childhood here."

"On your own?" asked Cassie, sympathetically.

"No, indeed not, Lady Cassandra," replied Colwyn. "I had many playmates. It is customary for the children of Erinsmore nobility to be sent to Lady Ninniane for training. During my childhood, there were at least a dozen other children here..."

"Of which my Lord was the leader, and never ceased to create havoc and chaos wherever he went."

The three turned sharply at the dryly sardonic voice. A tall stick of a man stood at the foot of the wide-sweeping staircase leading to the castle's entrance. His face was craggy and forbidding, an enormous hook of a nose overhanging his pursed lips. Ruby saw blue eyes twinkling above it and instinctively knew she had nothing to fear from him.

"Samson!" cried Colwyn, and dashed to greet the man, clutching him in a fierce hug of greeting, which Samson didn't return. Watching carefully, Ruby saw his face soften for a moment, his eyes blinking his pleasure at Colwyn's presence.

"Samson, it is good to see you again after all these years."

"Indeed, my Lord."

Samson released himself from Colwyn's embrace, stepping back to study him intently.

"I see before me the man who has fulfilled all the promise of the youth. Your presence gladdens my heart, my Lord, for these are very grave times indeed."

"I know, Samson. We were pursued by skraelings to the Sanctuary's boundaries. We barely escaped with our lives. I thought they were forbidden to enter the sacred forest?"

"As I said, my Lord, these are very grave times. Now there is no time to lose, I must take you to my Lady."

"Of course, but first ... Samson, these ladies have travelled far, mayhap they could be offered rest and refreshment."

"My Lady's orders. You are all to be taken immediately to her."

"How did she know we'd be coming?" Cassie asked, puzzled.

"This is Lady Cassandra," introduced Colwyn. Samson inclined his head gravely in Cassie's direction.

"My Lady," he murmured. "All things will be made clear, please follow me ..." His beetle black brows shot up as Ruby stepped forward. "Lady Gwnhyfar ..." he murmured.

Ruby frowned in confusion. "No, I'm Ruby," she explained, fascinated as Samson visibly regained his composure, face smoothing into its usual impassive mask.

"Of course," he replied. "Welcome, Lady Ruby. Please, would you all follow me?"

Still wondering, Ruby fell in behind Colwyn and Cassie as they followed Samson's poker straight back up the great steps and into the castle itself. It was stunning, and Ruby's eyes darted around trying to drink it all in, thinking she'd never seen so much that was beautiful gathered in one place.

They passed through corridors, rooms, and courtyards, each more dazzling than the last, filled with gorgeous treasures and works of art all arranged in a seemingly random style that somehow never failed to please the eye.

Samson stopped at a pair of ornately carved wooden doors. On one door twined a dragon, instantly recognisable as the dragon from Colwyn's pendant. On the other was a great black bird, its impressive wingspan filling the entire door.

"What type of bird is that?" asked Cassie.

"It's a raven," replied Ruby, then flushed when Samson turned enquiring eyes upon her. "I think," she finished lamely.

"You are correct, my Lady," he confirmed. "It is indeed a raven, the most sacred bird in Erinsmore, and a living symbol of Lady Ninniane's strength and wisdom." He pushed open the doors, gestured for them to enter the room, and Ruby felt his thoughtful gaze rest briefly upon her.

As they had come to expect by now, the room they entered was massive, with great banks of twenty-foot-high windows lining each wall. Daylight flooded the room, forcing them to squint against its glare until their eyes adjusted.

At the far end of the room was a raised area. Ruby realised the whole room was some sort of throne room, except on the dais where there should have stood a throne, was a shimmering wall of dense white energy. It crackled and fizzed with life, and Ruby found herself being inexplicably drawn toward it.

Ruby-y-y...

It was the same voice she'd heard calling her in the car, a voice so strangely familiar it nagged at the very edges of her memory. Ruby glanced around. The others were talking amongst themselves, their voices quick and urgent.

"How long has Lady Ninniane been in there?" Colwyn asked.

"Almost five moons," was Samson's concerned reply. "We cannot pass through its walls, although many have tried. It repels all. All, that is, except your young mage."

"Delmar?" enquired Colwyn, anxiously. "Do you mean he is in there too?"

"When he arrived, we all hoped he might be able to unlock the enchantment encircling Lady Ninniane. As soon as he entered the room he walked straight to the barrier and was permitted to pass through. That was weeks ago. Neither has been seen since."

"Ruby!" Cassie's terrified voice broke into Ruby's dreamy wander towards the barrier. She paused, frowning, glancing back down the long room as Cassie began to rush towards her. How slowly she moved, Ruby thought, almost as if in slow motion.

Ruby-y-y...

The voice pulled at her. Ruby had to obey. She had no choice.

"Ruby, no..."

She stepped through the barrier. Her sister's voice stopped, mid-sentence. Rather like turning off a radio, Ruby thought in amusement, and looked with interest at the strange world she found herself in.

It was peaceful, so peaceful. Silent, but for the gentle murmur of a light summer breeze caressing the slender branches of the small grove of saplings Ruby stood in. Curiously, she looked at them; ash, rowan, willow, birch, as well as others she didn't recognise but instinctively knew were from other times, other worlds. With pleasure, she let her hand touch the nearest, a slim silver birch, its white trunk shining in the sunlight.

It was odd, Ruby thought, wandering from the grove into a flower-strewn meadow. She had no fear, no apprehension that any harm could come to her in this peculiarly quiet world.

She turned. A strange woman stood behind her, head to one side, watching Ruby with calm, kindly eyes. Her beautiful long red hair rippled in the breeze, her sumptuous dress rustling as she stepped forward.

"Hello, Ruby," she said.

"Umm, hello," responded Ruby, uncertainly. "My Lady," she tacked on hastily, noticing the slim golden circlet around the woman's brow.

"We have little time, Ruby," continued the lady. "Strictly speaking I should not be here, but due to the gravity of the situation the rules have been slightly bent to allow us to meet."

"Oh," said Ruby. "Where exactly is here, please?"

"It is the World Between Worlds," stated the lady, in her soft lilting voice. "A place where time is fluid and flexible, where those gifted in the ability may step from world to world and from time to time. More importantly, it is a place whose purity cannot be tainted with evil. Should any with malevolence in their heart even attempt to enter, they would be torn into a million pieces and scattered throughout all eternity."

"Wow," said Ruby, unable to think of any other response to such a statement.

"I know this must seem very confusing, Ruby," the lady smiled gently. "You must put all questions from your mind. The time I have is short. Attend closely to what I tell you and mark it well, for one day it will save your life and that of your sister."

"Oh," said Ruby, again.

"You must carry close to you a gift that appears nothing yet is given freely by a dark friend who is not human. For a time will come when all seems lost, and you face the grim enemy alone with nothing behind you. Then must you put your faith in the magic of friendship and take that step into the abyss."

"What does it mean?" Ruby asked in confusion when the lady stopped talking and looked at Ruby almost expectantly.

"That I cannot tell you. Only you alone will know when that time has come. Repeat the words back to me."

Ruby did her best, stumbling, forgetting some. Frowning, the lady made her repeat them until satisfied Ruby was remembering them correctly.

The breeze which had been gently caressing their cheeks gusted, twisting the lady's long flaming locks around her shoulders. She shivered, glancing around uneasily.

"I do not have much longer," she stated. "Now, heed this warning for your sister. A pledge made in exchange for a life saved will one day return the deed. Always keep the winged serpent close to your heart for it is an ancient and potent symbol. Its magic is as old as time and it has the power to reawaken long forgotten memories, even those buried deep within the blood of generations."

Again, the lady made Ruby repeat the warning, then her own, until finally, the lady sighed in frustration. "Not perfect," she stated, "but I believe the heart of each will be retained. Hopefully, it will be enough for you both to remember when the time comes."

"Couldn't you tell me, in plain English, what they mean?" demanded Ruby, slightly put out by all the fancy doubletalk and confusing metaphors.

"Oh Ruby," chided the lady mildly, green eyes flashing mischievously. "Even I could not break the rules so completely, not even for you. And now, I must depart. Fare thee well, Ruby, remember what I have told you..."

"Wait," cried Ruby, as the lady shimmered and began to disappear. "Who are you? Where did you come from? I don't even know your name."

"Gwnhyfar ..." sighed the breeze, and Ruby was alone amongst the flowers.

For three days she wandered that beautiful land, seeing not one living thing. No birds darted in its clear skies, no animals roamed its pretty forests, and no insects hummed in its flower-strewn meadows. Idly, she wondered how the flowers came to be so prevalent with no insects or butterflies, deciding rules of pollination must not apply in this World Between Worlds.

During those days, Ruby travelled ever inwards, instinctively feeling the world was circular and that she was slowly, inevitably, working her way towards its epicentre. At night she lay down where she was, sleeping a deep slumber of rich dreamlessness as if snoozing on the most comfortable feather bed.

When she was thirsty, she drank from one of the many streams which splashed and danced. When hungry, there was always a fruit tree nearby which amply satisfied her needs.

On the morning of the fourth day, Ruby awoke as usual and breakfasted on the pale, yellow-fleshed, sweet fruit which had rapidly become her favourite, then crouched by the edge of a brook to drink and wash her face.

As she sat back on her heels, water clouding her vision, a flash of black made her blink in sudden panic. She wiped away the water with her hands as a huge dark bird landed on the opposite shore.

Ruby and the bird gazed at each other for long, silent moments, the bird unblinking, surveying her through dark eyes alive with intelligence. Ruby realised it was a raven, like the one carved into the doors of Lady Ninniane's chamber.

Yes, that is correct.

The words formed themselves in her mind, and Ruby fell back in surprise. "W-what?" she stuttered. "Was that you? Can you talk?"

A confusing mixture of thoughts, impressions, pictures, and random words flooded her mind, and Ruby ground the heels of her hands into her forehead in pain.

"Stop. Please, stop." she cried in panic. "You're hurting me." There was silence as the raven surveyed her sheepishly. Then a picture was placed gently into Ruby's mind of it hanging its head in shame, and its sorrowful regret.

"That's okay," replied Ruby. "Try again, only, more carefully this time. Please don't try to send me too much at once."

The raven blinked in agreement, flew over the brook, and landed beside Ruby, with a rustle of jet-black wings. Close to, Ruby was taken aback by how big the bird was. Her fear must have transmitted to the bird for it looked as concerned as a bird can, and an image formed in Ruby's mind of the bird lying in Ruby's lap, Ruby gently stroking its glossy feathers.

"I understand," murmured Ruby. "You're telling me not to be scared, you won't hurt me, you're my friend." Seemingly delighted, the raven did a little dance, then settled down and stared intently at Ruby again.

Slowly, another image formed of the lady from Ruby's dreams, long, dark hair as glossily black as the raven's wings; her large eyes that wonderful shade of blue which can only be seen in the sky on a clear winter's day, when snow sparkles on the ground and bleaches the sky to the palest blue it can go and still be one shade above white.

"Lady Ninniane?" enquired Ruby; and sensed the raven's agreement. "You're a friend of Lady Ninniane's?" she asked. Again, the raven agreed, putting a picture in Ruby's mind of it flying and Ruby following, along with the single word.

Come.

Scrambling to her feet, Ruby followed as the raven took off, circled twice, anxiously checking to see she was following, before flying off slowly, Ruby trailing behind.

They walked for many hours, the raven constantly checking its flight to enable Ruby to catch up. Once, it put an image in Ruby's mind of cool water and led them both to the banks of a stream, landing beside her as Ruby gratefully drank its refreshing water.

Finally, the raven wheeled down, vanishing into a clump of rowan. Anxiously, Ruby pushed her way amongst their slender trunks, their leaves brushing over her face in a friendly fashion as she broke into a small clearing at their heart.

At the centre of the clearing burnt a small, bright fire, its flames releasing some sort of aromatic incense. Seated on either side of it, postures stiff and unyielding, skin and faces still and marble white, were the black-haired lady from her dream, and a man, well, a boy really, Ruby corrected herself.

He was young, looked kind, but was nowhere near as rugged or as handsome, as Colwyn. Dressed in a long, dark blue robe with an upstanding collar and flowing sleeves, his shoulder-length blond hair was tied back from his face with a short, leather thong. Ruby walked closer and looked at his expressionless, still features, thinking this must be Delmar.

With a flapping of wings, the raven landed and cawed loudly. As if waking from a deep sleep, Lady Ninniane looked up, her pale blue eyes lighting on Ruby in recognition.

"There you are, Ruby," she exclaimed, gently. "Did you bring the stone?"

"Oh, yes," replied Ruby, slipping her backpack off, and pulling the almost forgotten stone from its depths. "Do you need it?"

"Yes," replied the Lady easily. "It is necessary."

Ruby placed the stone gently in the Lady's lap. Her hands gripped it tightly. Ruby watched, fascinated, as light radiated from the stone, spreading up the Lady's arms, bringing life to their cold, marble-like appearance. Warmth travelled all over the Lady's body until finally, she arose, her movements fluid, to stand before Ruby.

Much to her surprise, Ruby realised Lady Ninniane was tiny, only as tall as she, yet power and energy seemed to flow from her, and Ruby could sense her life force snapping and crackling in an aura all around her body.

"And now for Delmar," said the Lady. She laid a hand gently on top of his head. For a second, nothing happened, then, as with the Lady, life and warmth flowed through his body. Ruby could see his veins thaw and the blood begin to flow. A few moments later he looked up, his gentle brown eyes wide and concerned.

"My Lady," he exclaimed. "Were we successful? Did it work?" He spotted Ruby and his mouth widened into an infectious grin. "Lady Ruby," he breathed. "You are here. Did you bring the stone?"

"Yes," agreed Ruby weakly. Her knees gave way and she slithered to the ground with a thump, feeling faintly ridiculous as tears of exhaustion and incomprehension sprang to her eyes. Instantly, the raven was by her side, cawing indignantly at the Lady who bowed her head as if being chastised.

"You are right," she agreed, softly. "As usual, I am grateful for your wise counsel my dear Cora." Gently, she placed a cool hand on Ruby's poor, aching head. "Sleep, child," she ordered. "All will be explained when you have rested. For now, sleep."

"I'm not sleepy," protested Ruby. "I want to know how..." The rest of her sentence went unspoken, exhaustion pulling her instantly into a dreamless slumber.

When Ruby opened her eyes, what could have been mere moments or long hours later, it was to find the raven, Cora, watching her intently. As Ruby looked at her, she gave a little jump of joy. Instantly, a jumble of images flooded Ruby's mind.

"Slow down, slow down," laughed Ruby, clutching her head. "I can't understand, you go so fast." Contritely, the raven did a little hop. An image formed of Ruby asleep. "Yes," agreed Ruby. "I do feel much better for my sleep, thank you."

Satisfied, Cora took off and landed on Lady Ninniane's shoulder as she sat in conference with Delmar by the fireside. Cora rubbed her beak lovingly over the Lady's cheek and cawed softly. Lady Ninniane turned to look at Ruby, her ageless, timeless face lighting in a smile as she saw Ruby struggling to sit up.

"Come," she exclaimed, stretching out a hand towards her. "Come, Ruby, sit by us, for there is much we need to discuss, and time is pressing."

"How long have I slept?" enquired Ruby, surprised at how refreshed she was.

"A few hours," replied Lady Ninniane. "Cora was right, it was necessary you slept. You are so young, despite the burden placed upon you, Bearer of the sacred stone."

Puzzled, Ruby sat beside Delmar who grinned delightedly at her. It struck Ruby he was the most unlikely magician she'd ever imagined – no long flowing Dumbledore-like beard; no swirling cloak covered with mystical symbols. He was a boy, no more than eighteen or so, with no signs, at least not outwardly, that he had any magical powers at all.

"Drink this, child," Lady Ninniane gently pressed a wooden cup on her, filled to the brim with yellow-coloured liquid.

"What is it?" enquired Ruby, sniffing at it suspiciously.

"A drink made from fruit juices only," explained the Lady, with a twinkle. "It will refresh and revive you, no more."

"Thank you," replied Ruby, and sipped at it, finding it was juice made from the yellow-fleshed fruit which had been her staple diet over the last three days.

"Now," began the Lady. "I know you have many questions. They will be answered in good time, for now, you must trust us, Ruby. You must believe we had no choice but to bring you and your sister here. Lorcan has escaped his bonds. The very existence of Erinsmore is threatened."

"You brought us here?" interrupted Ruby in excitement. "How did you know anything about us? I mean, I didn't know anything about Erinsmore until a few days ago when I went into that shop in Tintagel and bought the stone."

"Oh Ruby," sighed the Lady, fondly. "I have appeared in your life many times, guiding you in the right direction so you would take the path which would enable you to arrive here, at this point, with an open mind and a heart ready to believe. For if you had been closed to the idea of magic then Erinsmore would indeed be lost."

"I … I don't understand," stuttered Ruby, in confusion.

"Think back," urged the Lady, placing a hand gently over Ruby's forehead, her eyes pulsing a vivid blue. "Remember …"

Ruby closed her eyes as a flood of memories engulfed her. She saw … the supply teacher she had at the age of seven who first introduced Ruby to the magic of the Arthurian legends and sparked a lifelong interest in them…

She saw … the temporary librarian who helped Ruby when she shyly asked for books about Arthur and stuff like that. Interesting and informative, the librarian had suggested a list of books on the subject, which broadened Ruby's knowledge of ancient times and legends, and further deepened her interest…

She saw … the Sunday school teacher who encouraged her charges to have open minds and believe in their abilities. Finally, she saw the man in the shop in Tintagel.

And somehow, behind them all, she saw the Lady and knew she had been all those people and more. That she had always been a part of her life, controlling and dictating the choices she had made and the life she had lived, until finally, inevitably, Ruby fulfilled her destiny and made the crossing into Erinsmore.

Chapter Six

Gwnhyfar

uby gasped, "You." Her eyes flew open, and she glared into the intelligent, calm gaze of Lady Ninniane.

"You," she continued, stunned. "You were all those people? All my life, I've been led along ... manipulated, so when the time came, I'd be ready to believe in Erinsmore because I so badly wanted it to be true."

Ruby remembered her eager and complete acceptance when they first arrived and was angry at being so used and controlled. The Lady's eyes clouded sympathetically, and Cora ruffled her feathers, uttering a low menacing caw in the back of her throat.

"Believe me, Ruby," murmured Lady Ninniane. "I am sorry for interfering in your life. Had it not been necessary I would never have contemplated such a thing." She paused, her expression becoming steely.

"Desperate times call for desperate action," she continued. "I had no choice. It was with great reluctance that Delmar and I decided there was nothing else we could do and entered the great trance together. I needed his strength to anchor me here, at this moment, so I could voyage back through the time span of your life, enter it at key points, and guide you to the prophecy stone."

Ruby glanced at Delmar sceptically. From his appearance, he didn't look strong enough to anchor a toy sailing boat, let alone anything else.

"And now," declared the Lady, arising to her feet. "It is time."

"Time?" enquired Ruby nervously, "Time for what?"

"Time to return, and for the quest to begin," Delmar said.

The Lady held out her hands. Delmar took the right one, and they both looked expectantly at Ruby.

Swallowing hard, she stepped forward and placed her trembling hand on the Lady's left. The Lady drew in a light breath, closed her eyes, and led them back through the barrier into the throne room.

"... wait!"

Cassie finally finished the sentence Ruby heard her begin three days earlier, stumbling back in surprise at their sudden appearance before her.

"My Lady," said Samson, tonelessly. "It is good to see you safely returned."

"Thank you, Samson," replied Lady Ninniane, sweeping down off the platform. "Please ready rooms and refreshments for our guests and instruct the kitchen to prepare a feast for this evening for they have far to travel on the morrow."

"Wait a minute," demanded Cassie. "What's going on? What was behind that wall thing?"

She gestured towards the platform, gaping in astonishment as the barrier dwindled and vanished.

"Cassandra," murmured the Lady, placing both hands on either side of Cassie's face. "So brave and true. So staunch to defend what you believe in, but so doubtful of your abilities. Have faith in yourself, child."

Cassie shook her head in confusion as if trying to remember something, something from long ago.

Colwyn crossed to Delmar.

"My Lord?" exclaimed Delmar in surprise. "Tis good to see you, yet I must confess to being surprised by your presence."

"When you did not return, I grew concerned," explained Colwyn. "And when I could not reach you through our link, decided to travel after you. Along the way, I met the Ladies Ruby and Cassandra."

"Luckily," exclaimed Cassie. "If you hadn't, those skraeling things would have caught us and made mincemeat out of us."

"Skraelings?" Delmar looked anxiously at the Lady. "Have things gone so far then?"

"I am afraid so," replied the Lady gravely. "We will speak of all these matters and more tonight. For now, let us rest, refresh ourselves."

She inclined her head gracefully towards the sisters. "Samson will show you to your rooms, I look forward to your company this evening."

With that, she gathered up her skirts and left the room, Cora circling above her head uttering breathy little caws.

An image was placed into Ruby's mind of a sumptuous banqueting table spread with an unimaginable feast, with Ruby seated before it and Cora sitting on the back of her chair.

Ruby smiled and sent back a picture of herself feeding Cora grapes.

For a split second, Ruby perceived the surprise that emanated from both Cora and Lady Ninniane, then they were gone, and Samson was gesturing for them to follow him to their rooms.

Ruby settled back in her chair, pushing away a plate littered with the remains of the most delicious meal she had ever eaten. Sighing in contentment, she smoothed a hand over the full skirts of her beautiful silk dress and thought with pleasure of the sumptuous rooms assigned to Cassie and herself.

Gaping with awe at the sheer splendour of the rooms, both girls thankfully slid into the hot, fragrant baths strategically placed before the fire, soaking for an hour before languidly wrapping themselves in huge, soft towels.

Serving girls had discreetly entered bearing gifts from the Lady of jewelled slippers, necklaces of sparkling gemstones, and best of all, gorgeous silk gowns. Ruby's the colour of damp moss, Cassie's a stunning shade of sky blue.

Now, Ruby watched in delight as musicians began to play and couples left their tables to dance in the large, central space, their steps precise and well-practised.

Cassie sighed at the lovely sight, and Colwyn smiled at her.

"Mayhap, Lady Cassandra would honour me with a dance?"

"Me?" Cassie turned startled eyes up to his laughing, blue ones. "Oh no, I can't dance, I mean, of course, I dance back home in clubs and at parties, but not like this. Don't get me wrong, it's lovely, but I wouldn't have a clue. I'm sorry."

"'Tis a shame," stated Colwyn and laid a hand over Cassie's where it rested on the table. "Maybe there will be time for me to teach you, for I believe you would be an apt pupil."

"Well," replied Cassie, breathlessly. "I guess we'll be going home soon."

"Ah yes," Colwyn's face clouded, and he removed his hand. "Of course, you will be returning to your world. I had forgotten."

Cassie flushed and looked away, biting her lip. Ruby wondered what on earth was up with them. Beside her, Delmar cleared his throat.

Thankfully, Ruby turned to him, eager to learn more about this magician who looked so young and awkward yet was the most powerful mage of his generation.

"Do you look forward to beginning our quest, Lady Ruby?"

"I'm not sure," Ruby admitted. "After all, we don't know where we're going, or what we must do when we get there. I must admit it will be great to sleep in a proper bed tonight, and it was wonderful to have a bath."

Delmar smiled, as Ruby laughed. "I can't remember the last time I had a bath. I usually shower. It's quicker."

"Shower?" Delmar looked puzzled.

Ruby tried to explain the intricacies of showers to him as music played, the lords and ladies of the castle danced, and Cassie and Colwyn sat side by side studiously ignoring each other.

"Remarkable," exclaimed Delmar. "Hot water at the touch of a button. How advanced your world is, how backward we must appear to you."

"No," Ruby hastened to correct him. "Erinsmore isn't backward, it's different. After all, you still have magic which my world has almost completely lost. So, in that respect, we're the backward ones."

"Perhaps," agreed Delmar. "It is all a matter of perspective, is it not, my Lady? Sometimes a familiar thing can look different when viewed from an unlikely angle."

"Oh, yes, I suppose so," agreed Ruby, slightly bemused.

There was a loud caw. Cora landed gracefully on the table before them and inclined her head. Delmar returned the gesture, and Ruby sent a thought to Cora of how happy she was to see her, asking if she'd had plenty to eat.

Cora put her head to one side, studied Ruby intently through coal-black eyes and put a picture in Ruby's mind of fat, juicy grapes. Laughing, Ruby pulled a bowlful towards her and began plucking them from their stalks, passing them to Cora who gobbled them greedily from her palm.

"How did you know she wanted grapes?" Cassie asked, watching in trepidation as the gigantic black bird stabbed its beak into her sister's hand.

"She told me," replied Ruby.

"Lady Ruby," exclaimed Delmar, in excitement. "Do you mean you understand her?"

"Of course, I can," answered Ruby, surprised. "Can't you?"

"No, I cannot," replied Delmar. "Nobody can communicate with the great raven except Lady Ninniane." He stared at Ruby in awe. "You are fortunate, Lady Ruby, Cora has bestowed a great honour upon you."

"Oh," said Ruby, looking at Cora who winked saucily back and did a most undignified little dance on the table.

There was a dry cough and Samson appeared before them, tall and implacable, his craggy face shadowy in the candlelight.

"Lady Ninniane sends her compliments and requests the pleasure of your company in her chamber."

He stalked away, giving the others no choice but to scramble hastily to their feet and follow him.

The room Samson showed them to was small, by the castle's standards, and cosy. Its book-lined walls reflected the firelight which danced and played in a pretty, marble fireplace. As they entered, Lady Ninniane looked up from where she was reclining gracefully on a large, red velvet settle.

"Thank you for attending so promptly," she began, in her birdsong voice. "Please, sit, there is much we need to discuss."

Quickly, they all found seats, four pairs of eyes fixed anxiously on the Lady, wondering what was coming next.

Samson took up position by the door, stern and aloof, his face impassive as he too waited for the Lady to speak.

"As you are aware, the unthinkable has happened. Lorcan has broken free from his prison to once again threaten Erinsmore."

"How did he do that?" interrupted Ruby.

"I am unsure," the Lady frowned. "I fear the only way is that he had help."

"A traitor?" breathed Colwyn, incredulously. "Who?"

"Who indeed?" replied the Lady. "It is not widely known that during his reign of terror Lorcan had believers. Those who followed him not only because they feared for their own lives and those of their families, or because he had clouded their reason with potent magic; but because they hoped he would grant them riches and power, and make them rulers under him, of Erinsmore," she shook her head.

"I had believed all such followers perished during the last battle when Arturius captured Lorcan. Mayhap some escaped to start a line of secret followers, all dedicated to awaiting the right moment to aid his escape."

"Oh great," murmured Cassie under her breath. "Mr Evil has mates." Colwyn glanced at her in surprise. Cassie flushed and looked away.

"So, if he's so powerful, has all this magic at his fingertips," began Ruby, "what on earth can we do to stop him?"

"I have long considered the problem," began the Lady. "Ever since I felt the first stirrings and realised Lorcan was attempting to break free, I have fought to slow his escape and to weaken his abilities, to buy us some time.

That time is now running out, I cannot hold out against him much longer. Soon his power will reach full potency. We must act swiftly if we are to have any chance of prevailing."

"Tell us what needs to be done, my Lady, and we shall endeavour to succeed at our tasks or die in the attempt."

Cassie raised her eyebrows at Colwyn's statement.

"Speak for yourself," she muttered, so quietly only Ruby heard.

"I have concluded," continued Lady Ninniane. "It is necessary the four treasures of Erinsmore be brought together once again."

"The treasures?" gasped Colwyn. "Surely, they are but merely a myth?"

"No, indeed they are not," the Lady shook her head.

"What are these treasures?" asked Ruby curiously. Next to her, Delmar began to chant as if reciting something learnt by heart.

"Earth, water, air and fire, mark well these omens of might.
Kept apart for millennia since the dragon's final flight.
From earth the stone of prophecy, its message clearly writ.
From water the heart of crystal, its guardian the Sleskeritt.
From air the golden griffin, crafted by elfish hand.
From fire the D'raiqwq, 'neath the centre of this land.
Torn apart by warfare, two and two did journey long.
Reunited by a gemstone and a dragon's new-born song."

"What does it mean?" asked Ruby, feeling her heart quicken and her breath catch, as if it was something she had once known, long ago, something important which had been forgotten.

"The four treasures of Erinsmore," replied the Lady. "Originally, legend says, one powerful tool of magic. It was divided and hidden millennia ago to prevent it from ever falling into the wrong hands. However, joined and used correctly, it could stop Lorcan once and for all."

"How do we go about finding them?" asked Cassie. "I mean, if there's four of them and they're scattered all over the place it could take ages. By then Lorcan could have destroyed Erinsmore."

"One of the treasures has already been found and brought safely to Sanctuary," began the Lady, smiling at Ruby who beamed with sudden understanding.

"Of course," she breathed. "The prophecy stone, but I don't understand. Why was one of the four treasures in our world? How did the stone end up in Tintagel?"

"Gwnhyfar took it with her when she made the crossing," replied the Lady. Ruby stared at her. The fog created in her mind whilst in the World Between Worlds cleared and she remembered.

"Who was Gwnhyfar?" asked Cassie, struggling with the awkward pronunciation.

"To tell the story of Gwnhyfar, I must start at the very beginning," stated the Lady. As one, they all gathered closer to the firelight, listening spellbound as Lady Ninniane wove her tale of love and loyalty in the flickering flames.

"Long ago," she began, in soft, lilting tones. "I had a lady-in-waiting who was very dear to me. An orphan, Alys was as gentle as she was beautiful and caught the attention of Lord Valarian of the Far Isles. Although he was a good man, a loyal subject, he was a widower considerably older than Alys and I wondered at the wisdom of such a match. But Alys was determined in her quiet way, so eventually, I agreed, and she moved to the Isles where in time she was blessed with a child, a daughter they named Gwnhyfar."

Lady Ninniane paused as the name echoed softly in the room. Ruby saw Samson's lips move, repeating the name under his breath.

"Alys asked me to honour the child by standing as her guardian. I agreed, never dreaming within eight months both Alys and Lord Valarian would be dead, killed in a tragic freak tidal wave that destroyed part of the castle. Luckily, Gwnhyfar was spared. She came to live at the Sanctuary, where she was tested according to the customs of our land and found to be blessed with an abundance of ability. Also, according to custom, Gwnhyfar was betrothed to a young lord a few years older than her. He was the rightful heir to the dragon throne, named Arturius."

"Arturius?" Ruby's head snapped up in excitement. "Then, Gwnhyfar was Guinevere."

"I believe that is the name by which she is most commonly known in your world," smiled the Lady, in gentle agreement. "As Arturius and Gwnhyfar grew up together, I came to see a great fondness existed between them, but it concerned me there was no spark of passion, no promise of love."

Out of the corner of her eye, Ruby saw Cassie shoot a quick, intense glance at Colwyn, only to look hurriedly away, twin spots of colour burning on her cheeks when he smiled lazily at her.

"Then, the madness that was Lorcan erupted onto our land and there was no time for such things as love. It was a long and fierce war, the most savage battle being that to defend the castle. During the fighting, Arturius's horse was slain and Lorcan moved in to deliver the killing blow. However, as Arturius lay trapped under his dead mount, a brave young king from your world named Mark attacked Lorcan, distracting him long enough for Arturius to free himself, and using a sword charged with magic that I had given him, capture Lorcan. But King Mark was mortally injured, and it was feared he would not recover from his wounds."

Lady Ninniane paused, swallowing delicately. Instantly, Samson was by her side pouring crystal clear water into a rose-tinted goblet and handing it to her. The Lady sipped, then continued her tale.

"Arturius was beside himself with grief; Mark was a trusted and beloved friend and had saved Arturius's life. Should he die before Arturius could return the deed in kind, honour would not be satisfied. He pleaded with Gwnhyfar to help, for she was a most gifted healer, the only one who could save Mark."

"Did she save him?" Ruby asked.

"Indeed, she did," the Lady continued with a gently wistful smile. "As she laboured long hours to save the noble and handsome king, Gwnhyfar's untouched heart shaped itself into love and she knew no other would ever have such a claim over her as he would. Likewise, when Mark opened his eyes and saw Gwnhyfar sitting by his bedside, her beauty and goodness swept over him, and he fell deeply in love with her."

"But ..." began Cassie confused. "I thought Guinevere married Arthur, that's what all the legends say. She married him, then betrayed him with Lancelot."

"The legends lie," stated the Lady, her beautiful face stern with anger. "Mark and Gwnhyfar loved each other with a depth of unsurpassed passion. Out of their regard for Arturius and their honour, neither stated their feelings to the other and Arturius remained unaware as preparations for his marriage to Gwnhyfar went ahead." The Lady sighed, remembering.

"Knowing Gwnhyfar and Mark were destined to be together, I put the truth into Arturius's dreams. Unbelieving, he confronted Gwnhyfar. He knew instantly from her denials that she loved Mark. Confronting Mark, he realised her love was returned. Arturius further understood that out of honour, Mark would return to your world alone, Gwnhyfar would marry him, and they would both be miserable for the rest of their lives."

"Was he angry when he found out?" asked Ruby, caught up in the romantic drama.

"No, on the contrary. Arturius was a good man, true to his friends, and appreciative of the loyalty shown to him by others. Although truly fond of Gwnhyfar, she did not hold his heart. Furthermore, he was delighted he could repay his honour debt to Mark. Thus, it was that during a magnificent banquet hosted by Arturius to pay tribute to the warriors who had fought in the battle to save Erinsmore, Gwnhyfar and Mark married. When Mark returned to your world, Gwnhyfar accompanied him as his wife and queen."

"And took the stone with her," concluded Ruby.

"And took the stone with her," agreed the Lady. "Mark was king of the West Country, and their castle was the mighty fortress of Tintagel. The stone has rested there ever since, until the time came for you to carry it back to Erinsmore, Ruby."

"What happened to Gwnhyfar and Mark after they went back?" asked Cassie.

"They had many children," continued the Lady. "The heirs to their bloodline are still scattered throughout your world," she paused, glancing at Samson as if she had more to say but was unsure of the wisdom of saying it.

"She's so beautiful," mused Ruby dreamily, "That gorgeous long red hair and those amazing green eyes..."

There was a shocked silence in the room. Startled eyes were turned onto each other, then onto Ruby.

The Lady straightened. "What are you saying, Ruby?" she enquired, almost sharply. "You talk as if you have met her."

"I have," began Ruby slowly, a frown creasing her brow. "In that place, the World Between Worlds, when I first got there. It had faded from my mind, but talking about her, well, it's made me remember."

"Quickly, Ruby," demanded the Lady, voice sharply urgent. "You must tell me all that transpired between you and Gwnhyfar. Everything. Do not forget a single detail.

Hesitantly, Ruby related the entire short incident, the strange forecasts for herself and Cassie. As the Lady listened intently, she waved her hands and a scroll appeared, which she handed to Ruby.

"Are these the words as close as you can remember?"

"Yes," replied Ruby, hastily reading the now remembered rhymes. "That's it."

"What do they mean?" Cassie asked curiously, taking the scroll from Ruby, and reading it with interest.

"Well, winged serpent is an old expression for a dragon," explained Colwyn, reading the scroll over Cassie's shoulder. "As I am from the line of the dragon lords, mayhap I am the one you should keep close to your heart."

"What I don't understand though," continued Ruby, taking the scroll back from a flustered-looking Cassie, "is why did Gwnhyfar look so much like me?"

"Truly, bloodlines are powerful and mysterious things," replied the Lady, with a small smile. "Both Gwnhyfar and Mark came from ancient royal families, the echo of which would travel far through the generations. Now and then, descendants are born who carry the mark of such a noble pair."

"What?" began Cassie, confused.

"It's us, isn't it?" Ruby squeaked. "We're descended from Gwnhyfar and Mark. We've got Erinsmore blood in us. Is that why we were able to cross?"

Lady Ninniane looked at her for a long still moment, then smiled gently at the hopeful expression on Ruby's face.

"You look so like her," she mused. "Do you not agree, Samson?"

"Indeed, I do, my Lady," he agreed dryly. "I thought so from the first moment I laid eyes on Lady Ruby."

"And you, dear Cassandra," the Lady turned her smile onto Cassie. "I see so much of Mark in you, his strength and courage, his skill in all aspects of battle. Already, you are remembering."

"I don't understand," murmured Cassie confused. "What have I remembered?"

"When you sent Colwyn's horse back to him, how did you know to knot the reins so the horse would not catch a foot in them?"

"I don't know," said Cassie. "I just knew, somehow."

"Merely by being here, breathing Erinsmore air, memories are stirring deep within you. You are beginning to remember."

"That's ridiculous," insisted Cassie. "You can't remember things that happened to other people, even if they are dim and distant ancestors."

"Can't you?" enquired Lady Ninniane mildly. Before her quietly knowing air, Cassie subsided into mutters.

"It is truly amazing," said Delmar in awe. "Descendants of Lord Arturius and Lady Gwnhyfar, brought together to fight the evil one again."

"Indeed," agreed Colwyn. "What is our next step, my Lady? What is the next treasure, and where is it to be found?"

"You must find the crystal heart which has rested many long years in a cave on the banks of Lake Minwarn, high in the Carnethen Mountains. You must be wary though, for it is guarded by a fearsome creature, the Sleskeritt, whose sole purpose is to keep the heart from being taken from its hiding place."

"How far away are these mountains?" asked Cassie. "How do we get there?"

"The mountains are many weeks travel. Delmar," the young mage snapped to attention. "You will have to use your skills to travel as close to the Sleskeritt's cavern as you can."

"What is the Sleskeritt?" Ruby asked, half afraid of the answer she would get.

"An ancient and strong creature," replied the Lady, soberly. "Long ago it had a modicum of intelligence. Now long millennia of solitude have driven the poor creature insane. It cannot be reasoned with, nor will it show mercy. Its entire existence is based around the crystal heart. It would kill you in a heartbeat to prevent its removal."

Ruby and Cassie glanced at each other in alarm.

"Now, I suggest you go to bed," continued the Lady. "For tomorrow will be a long day, and who knows when the next chance to sleep will present itself."

Chapter Seven

Lake Minwarn

ext morning, the sisters awoke feeling revived and refreshed and climbed reluctantly back into their normal clothes, which had been freshly laundered and mended. Pulling on her jeans, Ruby sighed over the beautiful silk dress before joining the others for a hearty breakfast.

Afterwards, they were summoned to Lady Ninniane's chamber. She was absent at breakfast and Ruby was alarmed to see how exhausted the Lady looked, her perfect face showing signs of strain.

"My Lady," ventured Ruby, hesitantly. "Are you unwell?"

Lady Ninniane gave Ruby a sad smile. "I thank you for the concern, Ruby, and must confess the drain on my power from the constant battle I am waging with Lorcan is beginning to weary me greatly."

"Is there anything we can do?" asked Ruby, anxiously.

"You are already doing more than enough," replied the Lady, reassuringly, then turned to address the others. "May fortune smile on your endeavours," she murmured. "I pray I shall soon see you all safely returned, bearing the crystal heart." She nodded at Delmar, who ushered them into a tight circle.

"It is easier if we're all together," he explained, bowing his head. Ruby watched with intense curiosity, only to recoil in shock when Delmar's head snapped back to reveal a face taut and whitened with strain. His gentle brown eyes glowed, changing to a fierce deep blue that pulsed with energy and force.

Ruby closed her eyes as the room tilted, and nausea swept over her. Desperately, she grasped Cassie's hand, comforted by her sister's rock-steady grip as a wailing moaning howl filled her ears, and then they were somewhere else.

Ruby staggered, opening her eyes. Cold blustery wind gusted, nearly blowing her off her feet. Even though Ruby had been expecting to be magically transported to a mountain range, it was still a shock to open her eyes and find herself standing on rocky slopes; to look around, see no sign of the Sanctuary anywhere, and know they'd instantly travelled hundreds of miles.

"The Carnethen Mountains," declared Delmar, with evident satisfaction. "Although, I am afraid we still have two days to travel before we reach Lake Minwarn."

"Why couldn't you take us right to it?" asked Cassie, slightly put out at the thought of yet more walking.

"There is a protective barrier around the crystal heart preventing transportation into, or out of, the area. It was designed thus so the treasure could not simply be removed by magic," explained Delmar patiently.

"And the Sleskeritt was placed as its guardian," murmured Colwyn, eyes scanning the horizon. Ruby noticed his hand straying to his sword hilt.

"Do you think we'll be able to defeat it?" she asked anxiously.

"I have no doubt we will prevail, Lady Ruby," Colwyn reassured her. "Yet, I cannot help but wish we had more knowledge of the precise nature of the beast."

Quickly, he and Delmar divided out the backpacks of supplies. Ruby saw how both men were careful to ensure they carried the lion's share. She thought their concerns were sweet but knew by the tightening of Cassie's lips as Colwyn helped her on with a backpack half the size of his that Cassie didn't share her opinion.

"Which way do we go?" was all Cassie said, though. Ruby was glad she'd decided not to make a scene and thought how much her argumentative sister had changed in the few days they'd been in Erinsmore.

"Towards the sun," replied Delmar. "I can feel the pull of the crystal heart. Its presence is causing a disturbance, which makes it easy to follow."

They commenced walking. By the time they stopped for a break at midday, Ruby was extremely thankful both men had been so chivalrous when it came to carrying supplies.

Hopelessly out of condition, the sisters were struggling to keep up, their inadequate trainers slipping uselessly over the rocky terrain until Delmar pointed his hand at their feet, muttered something under his breath, and the girls found their shoes gripped and held like proper climbing boots.

Colwyn was completely unfazed by the hard going, jogging ahead to climb up small inclines and scan the surrounding area, always ready to assist the girls over difficult patches, although Cassie flinched, each time he offered her his hand and Ruby wished she'd stop acting like such a child.

As for Delmar, he was treating the quest as a great adventure, scrambling up and down the steep inclines in his long robe, as sure-footed as a mountain goat. His boundless enthusiasm lifted Ruby's spirits, and she found herself liking the young mage more and more.

They walked all afternoon, steadily climbing upwards, the brisk, ever-present wind blowing down off the mountains straight into their faces, stinging their eyes and making them squint against it and the bright glare of the sun.

Finally, shadows began to lengthen, and Colwyn declared they would camp for the evening. Both girls groaned with relief as he and Delmar looked around for a suitable camp site.

They found one in a small fold of land where a slice of cliff arose on one side offering partial relief from the wind. As the others gathered firewood from the stunted bushes which grew all around, Delmar, with a wink at Ruby, muttered some words. To her delight, two stout tents appeared, both equipped with thickly padded sleeping platforms and warm covers.

Colwyn roasted hunks of meat over the roaring fire, and they all moved closer to its warming flames as the sun set, and the temperature dropped dramatically.

"Tell me more about your world, Lady Ruby," requested Delmar, after they'd eaten and were relaxing by the fire under stars which shone in strange constellations.

So, Ruby talked. She told him about cars and cities, television and aeroplanes, animals and people, families, and schools. With Cassie contributing the odd remark, she jumped randomly from subject to subject, Delmar questioning and exclaiming, seemingly fascinated by everything she said.

"What do young people do?" he asked, "when not being educated?"

"Well," Ruby considered. "They spend time with friends. They go to the cinema and hang out around the shops. They listen to music and go clubbing. I'm not old enough to do that yet, but Cassie is."

"Clubbing?" asked Colwyn, puzzled. "Is that a form of hunting activity?"

"No," laughed Cassie then frowned. "At least, not the kind of hunting you mean. No, it's where people go to meet. They drink and talk, dance to music, very loud music."

"Ah," exclaimed Colwyn nodding. "You mean it is a banquet, like last night?"

"Not really," Cassie shook her head. "The music is like nothing you have here, I don't think you'd like it, and the dancing is not so formal. I mean, people get on the dance floor and sort of do their own thing."

"Do their own thing?" repeated Colwyn, exchanging a baffled look with Delmar.

"Mostly, people go there to meet someone," explained Cassie.

"Yeah," stated Ruby, unthinkingly. "Cassie met Sean in a club."

"Sean?" Colwyn asked, with casual indifference.

"Ruby," hissed Cassie, but it was too late.

"Cassie's boyfriend," replied Ruby.

"Your boyfriend?" repeated Colwyn, looking at Cassie, Ruby saw understanding flash in his eyes. "Oh, I see," he stated, getting to his feet, and stalking off to the side of the clearing to get more wood.

Cassie shot Ruby a furious look. Ruby looked down in consternation, biting her lip, realising she'd put her foot in it this time. There was silence around the fire before Delmar, glancing sympathetically at Ruby, enquired.

"In truth, are you betrothed, Lady Cassandra?"

"What?" Cassie snapped, eyes blazing. "Oh, for heaven's sake," she exclaimed. "What is it with this world? No, I am not betrothed, engaged, promised, whatever. It's different in our world. People are free to make their own decisions, choose their partners."

"As they are in our world," interrupted Delmar quietly.

"Whatever," Cassie was building up a head of steam. Ruby hoped she wouldn't say anything too stupid. "In our world, people don't get married at seventeen, at least, they're not supposed to. We wait until we've been to college, got careers sorted out, and decided what the hell it is we want from life."

"What if you already know?" The voice in the darkness made them jump. Colwyn stood there with an armful of wood. "What if you have always known," he continued brusquely, dropping it by the fire with a clatter. "Known, and accepted, what your role in life must be. What about if you have no choice?"

Cassie stared at him. Long minutes dragged out in silence before she rose, all anger gone from her face.

"There's always a choice," she said quietly and entered her tent without saying another word.

The next morning, the tension from the night before was still there. During their silent breakfast, Ruby exchanged a pained expression with Delmar as the distance between Cassie and Colwyn grew.

Breaking camp, Delmar vanished the tents with a wave of his hand, and they set off once more into the mountains, climbing, always climbing upwards. Hours later they crested a ridge of rock, and, found themselves gazing in wonder at the placid blue waters of a great lake.

"Lake Minwarn," breathed Delmar. "I never thought to see it. Truly, it is a most remarkable sight."

"It's beautiful," agreed Cassie. "So, where do you think this Sleskeritt hangs out then?"

Delmar briefly closed his eyes, as if trying to home in on a signal, then pointed across the lake. "Over there," he replied. "See, there is an entrance to a cave."

Shading her eyes against the sun's glare, Ruby saw, far away across the lake's vast expanse, a dark opening at the base of the cliff. Carefully, feet dislodging showers of small stones, they slid down the slope until they were standing on a rocky beach which ringed the entire lake.

Slowly, they began to walk along the shore, the going made treacherous by sharp stones which twisted beneath their feet. Almost an hour later, Colwyn decided they would stop and make camp.

"We're so close," complained Cassie, reluctant to sleep another night under the stars. "Another hour and we'll be there. We could get the heart and be on our way back."

"We do not know what manner of a beast the Sleskeritt is," explained Colwyn, patiently. "Nor how far into the caves we must travel. I would rather not venture into them in the dark and risk us possibly having to make a speedy escape through the mountains in the dark. No, we will camp here tonight."

Cassie opened her mouth to argue, thought about what he'd said, appreciated the sense of it, and closed her mouth again.

They fell into their usual camp-making routines, and Ruby realised how quickly they'd become used to this strange life.

Dinner comprised of roasted meat, supplemented with bread, fruit, and cheese, which Colwyn produced from his pack. Dusk fell as they finished their meal, and Ruby gazed at the flat placid waters of the lake, now turning a sinister black in the gathering gloom.

"Why is it called Lake Minwarn?" she asked curiously.

"I am unsure," replied Delmar. "In the ancient language, it means pale ones. There are many legends connected with the lake. People do not come here. It is practically inaccessible. No crops will grow here, and there is no grazing for animals."

"We need more water," stated Colwyn, holding up an empty water flagon.

"I'll go," Ruby jumped eagerly to her feet and took the flagon, picking her way carefully down the stony beach to crouch at the still, dark, water's edge.

"Lady Ruby seems to be enjoying her adventure thus far," Delmar smiled.

Cassie snorted. "Ruby's always been nuts on anything to do with lost worlds, fantasy, Arthur, dragons," she cast a sarcastic glance at Colwyn. "Dashing men with swords dangling from their belts." He grinned mockingly. "Back home she's always got her nose in some book or other about Arthur. If ever there's anything on telly about him, she must watch it."

"And what about you, my Lady?" enquired Colwyn, casually. "Are you also ... how did you put it ... nuts about dashing men with swords dangling from their belts?"

"That depends," replied Cassie, tersely.

"On what?" asked Colwyn, blue eyes intense with interest.

"On whether there's a brain somewhere behind the sword or just a lot of brawn," drawled Cassie, dryly.

Colwyn threw his head back and laughed in delight. "Fair Lady Cassandra," he spluttered. "Are all the women in your world so minded, or do those men who are merely brawn go without the comfort of a wife?"

"Oh no," retorted Cassie. "There's plenty of brainless women too, who think so long as a man has lots of rippling muscles it doesn't matter what's going on up top."

"But not you?" enquired Colwyn, suddenly serious.

"No," agreed Cassie. "Not me."

Delmar, who had been listening to this exchange with a fascinated knowing smile on his face, stiffened, head flung back as his eyes pulsed blue.

"Ruby!"

At the lake's edge, Ruby had finished filling the flagon and was staring at the black waters. She turned at the alarm in Delmar's voice as a white, worm-like tentacle snaked out from beneath the still surface and grabbed her ankle in a vice-like grip. Yanking hard, it pulled, and Ruby crashed heavily onto the sharp stones.

Delmar was already running towards her, Cassie and Colwyn struggling to their feet in bewilderment when Ruby's scream of terror split the night air.

"Help me!"

The tentacle jerked her towards the water's edge. Ruby's back scraped over rough stones, her fingers scrabbling uselessly trying to find something, anything, to hang on to.

"Ruby!" cried Cassie, racing after Colwyn as he overtook Delmar and ran full tilt into an invisible wall, being thrown back with such force he knocked into Delmar.

"A barrier?" he yelled, jumping to his feet, thrusting his sword at the air in front of him.

"We have to get through it!" demanded Cassie, beating her fists ineffectively on the invisible shield. "Ruby!" she called. Ruby looked at them in despair as she twisted and fought to get free of the lake monster's grip.

Yes-s-s. The voice was cold and alien. It hissed like a snake writhing through her mind. *S-s-ee how the bea-s-st struggles. We will not allow it to harm u-s-s.*

"What are you?" sobbed Ruby, clawing at the tentacle with her nails as it slowly dragged her closer to the water's edge.

"Let me go!" she begged, projecting her thoughts as if she were communicating with Cora. "Please, don't hurt me."

There was silence. The tentacle stopped pulling. Ruby felt the surprise in her mind.

What nature of bea-s-st are you? Do you intend harm?

"My name is Ruby. I'm human. No, I don't mean to harm you in any way. Please, let go, you're hurting me. If you drag me under the water, I'll die."

Ruby's thoughts tumbled urgently over themselves as she tried to project her sincerity to the creature.

Not the beast? Not harm us-s-s?

"No," agreed Ruby, sobbing with pain as the grip on her ankle tightened. "I'm not the beast, I don't want to harm you, please, please, let me go!"

For a second, the creature hesitated. There was a strange, tickly buzzing in her mind, then mercifully the tentacle uncoiled. Ruby snatched her foot back, rubbing at her throbbing ankle.

"Who are you?" she thought.

The still waters parted, and a strange, white creature arose from their depths, Ruby gaped at the part human, part octopus, part fishlike thing that confronted her.

Its torso was human-shaped. Instead of limbs, it had six long tentacles with fronds at each end, which fluttered delicately as if tasting the air. Ruby could see gill-like openings down the side of its throat, and its face, if it could be called a face, was draped with more fronds which hung around a wet gaping mouth and framed a single eye in the centre of its forehead, gazing sadly at Ruby.

We are, we exi-s-st, we live, yet the beast harvests u-s-s.

"What beast?" asked Ruby, "Do you mean the Sleskeritt?"

There was churning and broiling under the water at her words. Ruby sensed the fear and apprehension of many minds crowding through her mind.

S-s-he names it, she names the bea-s-st. The slithery thoughts panicked, Ruby fought to calm them with soothing feelings until the water stilled, and the creature stared mournfully at her. *Yes-s that is the beast.*

"What do you mean, it harvests you?" Ruby asked, curiously. A horrific image was put into her mind of a great, ravaging, unimaginable beast striding into the lake, savagely snatching up the lake creatures, throwing them into its huge mouth, crunching and ripping with a brutally callous disregard, oblivious to their screams and pleas as it devoured young and old alike.

"Do you mean it eats you?" whispered Ruby shakily, appalled at the graphic images of genocide flashing through her mind.

Yes-s-s, came the hissed answer. *It harvests us.*

"That's awful," gasped Ruby, a wave of compassionate sympathy flooding through her mind.

You feel, you unders-stand.
"Yes," replied Ruby, sadly. "I understand." She looked back at the barrier, at the horrified, anguished faces of the others. Delmar had a hand flat on the barrier, Ruby could see his eyes pulsing blue as he fought to punch a hole through it.

"How are you making the barrier?" she asked. An image was put into her head of all the creatures joining together to create a force field around the lake. "I don't understand," said Ruby puzzled. "If you can create such a powerful barrier, how does the Sleskeritt manage to get through?"

A further thought was placed in her mind of the sheer effort it took to maintain the barrier, that whilst making it, the creatures could do nothing else.

"I see," said Ruby. "So, while you're joined together creating the barrier, you can't swim or feed?" She felt the affirmative, then curiously asked. "What do you eat?" and smiled at the picture of seaweed and shellfish being eaten with relish by the creatures.

"Let down the barrier," she ordered. "I promise my friends won't hurt you, not when I explain it to them." She sensed the creatures' hesitation, adding firmly. "You must let me go. We're on an important quest. We're here to defeat the Sleskeritt and find the crystal heart."

At her words, there was great consternation amongst the creatures. Ruby clutched her hands to her temples as the excited chattering and buzzing reached pain levels in her head.

"It's true," she cried. "We must find the crystal heart. The whole of Erinsmore may be destroyed if we don't."

What is-s Erins-s-more?

"It's the world," cried Ruby, in surprise, "Your world."

No, this-s-s is our world.

Ruby saw the lake, and the beach surrounding it, and realised to try and explain any further would be pointless. The creatures didn't have the mental capacity to grasp the existence of anything beyond the lake.

Is thi-s-s crystal heart important to you?

"Yes," she replied. "It's very important to me." There was silence, and then the creature in the lake sank beneath the waters, leaving barely a ripple to show it had ever existed.

"Ruby!"

She turned as the others reached her, Cassie pulling her away from the lake's edge. Colwyn and Delmar stared out over the flat still water.

"What was that thing?" demanded Cassie, examining the red welt around Ruby's ankle, then surprising them both by clutching Ruby to her in a fierce hug.

"They live in the lake..."

"They?" enquired Colwyn, turning to look at her.

"Yes, there're lots of them," explained Ruby. "They're gentle and want to be left alone, but the Sleskeritt eats them. That's why it grabbed me, why they put up the barrier. They were afraid I was going to do the same."

"How do you know all this?" interrupted Cassie.

"It told me."

"How? We didn't hear it make any sound at all?"

"In my head," Ruby looked at Delmar in confusion.

He knelt beside her. "Show me," he said, gently placing a hand on her forehead. Ruby closed her eyes and replayed the whole encounter with the creature in her mind, looking up when she finished to see his eyes fading from brilliant blue to their usual brown.

"I understand," he said, looking at Colwyn. "We have nothing to fear from these creatures, but the Sleskeritt is indeed a beast which will not hesitate to kill us. I suggest we rest tonight. In the morning we proceed with caution."

"We will need to be on our guard," declared Colwyn in concern, "lest it attacks during the night."

"No need," replied Delmar. "I will construct a barrier of our own around the camp. Nothing will pass through it. Tonight, at least, we shall be safe."

Cassie helped Ruby to her feet. Hobbling slightly, with many backward glances at the lake, Ruby allowed her to lead her back to the camp.

Chapter Eight

The Caves
of the Sleskeritt

uby opened her eyes. It was morning. Through the tent flap, oozed the cold light of dawn. Beside her Cassie still slept, curled in a heap beneath her covers, and Ruby envied her sister for her ability to sleep anywhere. Sitting up, Ruby hastily pulled on her clothes and slithered from the tent.

The air was fresh and chilly; the morning sun still too weak to do any more than illuminate. Ruby quickly pulled on her jumper and sat on a rock to do up her trainers, her mind still full of bizarre dreams of lake creatures and strange beasts.

Looking around, she saw Colwyn sitting on a large boulder at the edge of the camp, methodically sharpening his sword. Crunching on stones, Ruby made her way over to him and he looked up at her approach, flashing a warm welcoming smile.

"Good morning, Lady Ruby. I trust you slept well?"

"Sort of, I had dreams," Ruby confided.

Colwyn nodded sympathetically, sliding his sword back into its scabbard. Ruby thought how much it was a part of him, like another limb.

"Does Lady Cassandra still sleep?" enquired Colwyn.

"Yeah," grinned Ruby, "Cassie sleeps for Britain. At home, it drives Mum nuts. She's always yelling at her to get her lazy backside out of bed."

"Your world," began Colwyn. "It is very different from ours. I think, mayhap, when Gwnhyfar returned with Mark it was not so much. Now, your world has changed and left us far behind. It has lost its magic. It seems to have faith in nothing."

Ruby bit her lip, aware of so much being left unsaid. On an impulse, she touched his arm. "Don't let Cassie wind you up."

Colwyn looked puzzled. "Wind me up?" he repeated.

"She gets uptight about stuff," continued Ruby. "She's big on women's rights and equality, never does know when to keep her mouth shut."

"A true warrior does speak out to right injustice," muttered Colwyn. Ruby frowned, unsure that was what she'd meant. There was movement behind them, Delmar crawled from his tent as Cassie also emerged, grumpily wiping sleep from her eyes, hair tangled into a bedhead bird's nest.

"Good morning, Lady Cassandra," chirped Delmar brightly. Cassie stared at him with dislike. "Huh?"

Delmar beamed. "Isn't it a delightful day? Truly, a day fit for our adventure."

"Oh please," groaned Cassie, stumbling over to sit on a rock. "Save me from perky morning people." Pulling on trainers, Cassie shot him a nasty look with bleary, still asleep, eyes.

"My Lady Cassandra?" enquired Delmar, plainly puzzled.

"Ignore her, Delmar," Ruby laughed at the young mage's wounded puppy expression. "She's always like this until she's drunk her first coffee."

"Coffee?" asked Colwyn, amused by Cassie's bad mood.

"Yes coffee," snapped Cassie waspishly, "One of life's essentials which, unfortunately, along with hot showers and flushing toilets, doesn't exist in this world."

Delmar knelt before her, placing a hand on her forehead. "Think about coffee," he ordered. Cassie stared at him. "Imagine drinking it, the taste, the texture," he continued.

Cassie closed her eyes. Colwyn and Ruby watched intrigued, as Delmar's eyes pulsed blue. On the rocks at Cassie's feet, appeared a large goblet full of a rich brown liquid which steamed invitingly. Her eyes snapped open in surprise, gaze flying wildly from his face to the goblet.

"Is that coffee?" she gasped, incredulously.

Delmar shrugged. "I truly hope so, Lady Cassandra," his tone was almost mocking. "For all our sakes, I truly hope so."

Gingerly, Cassie picked up the goblet and sipped cautiously, her expression changing to one of absolute bliss.

"Oh yes," she murmured. "This is more like it. Delmar, you can make me coffee any time you want." she grinned at him. "All you've got to do now is invent indoor plumbing."

The sun was beginning to burn with the heat of the day as they approached the darkly yawning mouth of the Sleskeritt's cavern. They paused, glancing nervously at each other.

Keeping close together, they entered the tunnel, the light from outside gradually growing dimmer the further in they travelled. Delmar muttered words under his breath, and four glowing globes of light appeared which he gave to each of them.

"You're quite a handy guy to have around, aren't you, Delmar," smiled Cassie gratefully.

Delmar flushed, looking pleased, and Ruby was reminded of a computer geek in Cassie's class. It used to make Ruby laugh how easily Cassie manipulated him; a smile, a casual thanks, and he nearly fell over himself to help her in computer workshop.

Deeper and deeper into the mountain they travelled, Ruby breathless at the thought of the sheer tons of rock above their heads. Delmar led the way. Each time they came to a fork in the tunnel he would pause, close his eyes, homing in on the crystal heart's signal before choosing which way to go. Ruby was relieved to see Colwyn also carefully marking the route on the tunnel walls with a stubby charcoal pencil.

"In case we get separated from Delmar," he explained. "We would stand no chance of finding our way out alone."

The sisters shivered at the thought, and Ruby was grateful when Cassie reached out a hand, taking hers in a firm grasp.

They walked for hours, time losing all meaning in the flickering light cast by Delmar's magical torches. Cassie stopped, nose twitching.

"Eweogh," she exclaimed. "What is that smell?"

The others stopped and sniffed. Ruby couldn't smell anything but knew how sensitive Cassie's nose was, so believed that her sister could smell something awful.

"Oh, that's disgusting," gasped Cassie. "Can't you smell it?" she demanded, as they resumed walking.

Colwyn shook his head, paused, and sniffed again. "There is something," he murmured, looking at Cassie with respect. "In truth, Lady Cassandra, you have the nose of a hunter."

They walked some more, Cassie still muttering and sniffing. Soon, they could all smell it, whatever it was, and Ruby almost gagged in disgust as it grew ever stronger. It was rotting, death and decay; it was like nothing Ruby had ever smelt before and hoped would ever smell again. She tried breathing through her mouth but could taste the smell, clamping her hand to her mouth and nose as if her fingers could act as a filter.

"May the Lady preserve us," muttered Colwyn in revulsion, leading them into a large cavern that echoed back his words. He held his light high, and the full horror of the cave was revealed.

Bodies, and bits of bodies, lay heaped; severed tentacles and dismembered torsos glistened palely in the dim light.

"What is that?" Cassie gasped in horror.

"They're Lake People," replied Ruby flatly. "Or rather, what's left of them. This must be the Sleskeritt's larder."

Cassie made a noise in her throat and stepped closer to Colwyn, putting out a hand to him.

"Those poor people," she whispered, almost tearfully. Colwyn pulled her close, looking around the cavern with a tightly grim expression.

"Over here," called Delmar. They hurried to where he knelt on the far side of the cavern. Half a dozen crude tanks had been fashioned out of the rock wall, each one containing a lake creature submerged in water, chains weighing down their fragile bodies, staring at them in unblinking terror.

"We have to get them out of there," exclaimed Ruby. "The Sleskeritt must be saving them to eat later."

"Try to talk to them, Ruby," ordered Delmar. "Tell them we mean them no harm, that we are trying to help them."

Nodding, Ruby tried to project into the mind of the helpless, terrified, creature. "We're here to help you," she thought, feeling the coldly alien presence of the creature as it dragged itself back from the brink of unconsciousness.

Help us-s-s?

"Yes, help you," repeated Ruby firmly, glancing at Delmar as his eyes pulsed blue and he touched a finger to the chains. There was a spark, and the chains fell away from the creature's body. Quickly, Ruby reached into the tank and pulled it to its webbed feet, Colwyn helping her lift it from the tank.

You s-s-ave us from the beast. It harvests u-s-s, consumes all, even our young.

"I know," thought Ruby. "We're here to kill it if we can."

"Ask if they can find their way out of the caverns," ordered Delmar, "as we do not have time to guide them out."

Yes-s-s, hissed the creature. *Can s-s-mell home, can feel it calling. We go, we find, we are grateful.*

Delmar had now released all the creatures. Quickly, hissing in air awkwardly through their gills, they shuffled from the cave. Ruby hoped they'd manage to reach their home.

"Can we get out of here now, please?" begged Cassie.

Delmar briefly closed his eyes before pointing to a narrow passageway leading from the back of the cave.

"The crystal heart is that way," he declared. "It is very close now."

Edging their way down the dark tunnel, Ruby swallowed as it narrowed, forcing them to go in single file. Colwyn led the way, with Cassie and Ruby following, Delmar bringing up the rear. They stopped as a roar echoed in the darkness behind them. Savage and bestial. Ruby heard the beast's rage.

"I guess it's found dinner has legged it," murmured Cassie. They started moving again, Colwyn going as quickly as he could over the uneven floor. They turned a corner. There was a faint gleam of light up ahead and Ruby became aware of noise – a roaring, rushing, crashing noise, which grew louder and louder the closer they got to the light.

Shockingly, they emerged blinking into the sunlight. Ruby looked around, eyes frantically trying to adjust, realising they were standing in a vast echoing cavern with walls towering hundreds of feet, reaching up to where the roof had collapsed at some point in the past so that now bright glorious sunshine flooded through.

"The crystal heart," gasped Delmar. Ruby looked where he was pointing. A waterfall crashing into the cavern through an opening over a hundred feet up the wall was the source of the noise. At the base of the fall where it divided over a large oblong-shaped rock to smash into a pool below, sparkling brightly in its position on the rock, was the crystal heart.

Ruby gasped aloud at its raw powerful beauty. Not knowing what to expect, she'd had a picture in her mind of a small heart-shaped crystal, not this great jagged chunk of shining iridescence reflecting dazzling beams of light into every corner of the cave. Tempting, beckoning. Ruby could feel its pull and saw by the dazed longing look on Delmar's face it was having an even greater effect on him.

A roar sounded behind them, frighteningly close. They jumped away from the tunnel entrance as a huge scaly head thrust itself through the opening. Snapping and snarling, it attempted to force its way after them.

"Keep back!" yelled Colwyn, as the Sleskeritt managed to wrench away part of the tunnel wall, sending a shower of rocks and earth spinning off the cliff edge to land with a splash in the pool below.

A colossal scaly arm snaked through the gap. They hurriedly moved further along the edge. Its gigantic, razor-edged claws raked the air, a red eye glared balefully at them.

Ruby could smell its hot breath, fetid and rank, and fear clutched her chest. Colwyn drew his sword.

"No," yelled Cassie, clutching at his arm. "You wouldn't stand a chance."

"She's right," agreed Delmar, calmly. "Those claws could easily disembowel you before you'd got within sword range." Colwyn reluctantly sheathed his sword and looked at the beast frantically clawing and thrusting, obviously trying to reach them down a tunnel too small for its bulk.

"Delmar," he snapped, spinning to face his mage. "That tunnel, can you collapse it on top of it?"

"I could," confirmed Delmar, "I risk bringing the whole wall down on us as well."

"We have to do something," snapped Cassie. "That thing's going to force its way through in a minute."

"Do it," ordered Colwyn. "There is no other option."

Delmar's eyes pulsed a now-familiar brilliant blue, his hand outstretched towards the tunnel. There was a rumble deep underground, small stones rained down on the Sleskeritt's head. It roared and twisted, desperately trying to release itself, obviously stuck fast. The rumble grew louder. With a great splitting and crashing, the segment of cliff above the beast's head collapsed in an immense pile of boulders and rocks.

Coughing and spluttering from the dust, they waited, hearts pounding with anticipation. Gradually, the dust settled. Ruby gasped with relief. The entrance to the tunnel was demolished, vanished under a pile of rubble. Of the Sleskeritt there was no sign. They looked hopefully at each other, unwilling to believe it could have been that easy.

Ominous grumblings and rumblings began in the cave walls, and the earth trembled under their feet.

"Cave-in," groaned Delmar. "Just what I was afraid of. Quickly everyone, down here." He led the way to the lip of the ledge, where a narrow rocky path wound its way down to the pool and shallow beach below.

Hastily the others followed as the shaking and trembling grew, struggling to stay upright while the ground quaked and shook beneath them.

"Look out!" screamed Ruby, glancing back in time to see a massive boulder crash onto the steep pathway and begin rolling its way towards them.

"Jump!" ordered Colwyn, grabbing Cassie's arm, and leaping off the pathway with her. Ruby heard Cassie's scream, high and scared, and then Delmar clasped her hand, dragging her over the edge to freefall into thin air.

Ruby had a split second to take a deep breath before they hit the water, and its icy coldness closed over her head. For a moment she panicked, thrashing furiously in the dark, before remembering all those swimming lessons Dad had insisted on and kicked strongly, forcing herself upward.

Her head broke the surface, narrowly missing being hit by a piece of falling stone. She saw Delmar, his face covered with blood, slipping back under the water. Taking a deep breath, Ruby dived and managed to grab him. Desperately pulling him to the surface, fighting to keep calm, she turned him on his back and struck out for the shore, dragging his unconscious body behind.

After what seemed an eternity, Ruby crawled wearily onto the small rocky beach using all her strength to heave Delmar's lifeless body behind her. Frantically, she placed an ear to his chest, hearing with relief the regular thump of his heart. A jagged gash ran across his forehead. Ruby pulled off one of her socks and used it to gently wipe away the blood to reveal a long deep wound that she hoped wasn't too serious.

Painfully, her shoes having been lost somewhere in the water, Ruby hobbled to its edge anxiously scanning for any sign of the others. The earthquake was subsiding now, the tremors fading away, and no more rocks fell.

"Ruby!"

To her enormous relief, Ruby saw Cassie staggering along the beach, her jumper torn, and her hair matted, blood dripping from a scratch on her cheek. She ran to her, and Cassie grabbed her in a fierce hug.

"Are you okay?" she demanded.

Ruby nodded. "Delmar's hurt," she replied, and led Cassie to where he lay, still and white on the ground. Cassie dropped beside him, examining his wound.

"I think he's been knocked cold," she finally decided. "Hopefully, he'll wake up soon," she paused, looking around. "Where's Colwyn?" she asked.

"Don't know," Ruby stared at Cassie with rising fear. "Last time I saw him, he was with you?"

"We got separated after we hit the water," explained Cassie. "I haven't seen him since. Oh no, Ruby..."

"I'm sure he's fine," interrupted Ruby, sounding more confident than she felt. "I mean, he's Colwyn, he's tough... nothing could have happened to him, could it?" Cassie shook her head, staring at Ruby in white-faced shock.

"What do we do now?" Ruby asked, voice quavering, and watched as Cassie visibly pulled herself together, jumping to her feet and stalking to the water's edge.

"There's not much we can do, not until Delmar regains consciousness and Colwyn finds us. We wait, that's all. I mean, we can't carry Delmar, and we certainly can't leave him, so we don't have much choice, do we?"

Ruby shook her head dumbly and sank onto the ground, hugging cold wet denim-clad knees to her chest as Cassie paced up and down the water's edge. Eventually, she stopped, moved to Ruby's side, and sank onto the sand beside her.

A long silence stretched as the girls waited.

"I'm sorry."

Ruby looked at Cassie in surprise. "What for?" she asked.

"For the way I behaved, in that other place ... home. When Dad lost his job, and everything had to go, I knew ... I knew what a tough time you were having, how hard you were finding it to adjust, how difficult things were for you at school. You needed me, and I wasn't there for you. So, I'm sorry ... for being such a complete bitch."

Ruby shrugged, taken aback by her sister's words, unsure how to respond. "That's okay," she eventually murmured. "It was hard for all of us."

"It was like, all I could think about was not letting anyone see how much I minded, how scared I was, so I took it out on everyone, including you. It was unfair of me."

"That's okay," Ruby said again. "I understand."

Restlessly, Cassie examined Delmar's wound again, removing her jumper to make a pillow for his head. "I hope he wakes up soon," she said. "Or that Colwyn appears..."

"You like him, don't you?" Ruby couldn't help asking. This time it was Cassie's turn to shrug, feigning nonchalance, yet Ruby saw spots of colour flame onto her sister's cheeks.

Cassie paced down to the shoreline, and peered anxiously into the water, studying the opposite beach and the cliffs towering above them. The crystal heart sparkled in the reflected glow of the waterfall.

"I think I could reach it from here," she stated.

"What?" Ruby scrambled to her feet.

"The crystal heart," Cassie spun to face her in excitement. "I could get the heart. Then when Colwyn finds us and Delmar wakes up, we could get the hell out of here."

"Are you sure?" Ruby stared doubtfully where the crystal sparkled, so far above them. "It looks a long way up."

"No probs," stated Cassie confidently. "You stay here with Delmar. I won't be long."

Before Ruby could protest, she set off along the beach. She watched, in dry-mouthed trepidation, as Cassie reached the base of the waterfall and began to scramble up the rocks, heart banging into the back of her throat when she slipped on wet rocks and almost fell.

Slowly, steadily, Cassie climbed until she was at the base of the rock on which the crystal heart twinkled, so tantalisingly close, but still out of reach. Taking a deep breath, Cassie stepped through the waterfall and was lost to Ruby's sight. She waited anxiously, gasping aloud with relief as Cassie reappeared behind the crystal, painstakingly hauling herself up and onto the rock.

Pushing her wet hair, which glowed purple in the heart's eerie light out of her eyes, Cassie stepped forward. Hesitantly, reverently, she picked up the crystal heart. Holding it out and up to the light, her eyes gleamed as it sparkled and dazzled, a million prisms of radiance dancing across the water.

"Yes!" screamed Ruby and did a little victory dance. "Way to go, Cassie."

High above, Cassie waved, tucked the crystal into her backpack and disappeared down behind the rock, emerging long minutes later through the waterfall, stepping from its curtain of water like some sort of nymph.

A movement, a sound, had Ruby's head turning to see a scaly arm snaking around the corner of a boulder, inches away from Cassie's feet as she edged her way down the rocky terrain.

"Cassie!"

Her sister's head whipped around. A massive, fanged, scaly face arose from behind the rocks, roaring its displeasure. Staggering back, Cassie moved quick as lightning through the waterfall, around the crystal heart rock, dashing through the twin fall of water on its other side.

Heart thumping, Ruby watched in horror as her sister scrambled desperately up the rocks on the other side, climbing, always climbing, as the Sleskeritt heaved its ponderous bulk up the cliff face after her.

Cassie had one advantage in that she was small and nimble and could wriggle through gaps which the beast had to go around. As Ruby stood there wringing her hands in helpless despair, she could see Cassie's energy beginning to fail, her foot slipping time and again on the wet, slippery rocks.

Cassie reached a fork in the rocks and hesitated, unsure which way to go. An ear-splitting roar galvanised her into action and she scrambled up the left path. Ruby howled with disbelief. From her vantage point far below, she could see what Cassie couldn't.

The way her sister had chosen led to a broad shelf carved into the cliff, but apart from the track her sister was now scrambling up, it was a complete dead end. Once Cassie reached it, she would be trapped, with the Sleskeritt right behind her.

Cassie heaved herself onto the shelf, quickly realising it was a trap. Ruby saw her turn as the Sleskeritt crawled over the rim, and roared its anger, huge scaly tail thumping down sending rocks and boulders flying, knocking Cassie off her feet over the edge of the shelf.

Ruby screamed. Her sister fell, body slamming and bouncing off ridges and rocks to land, wedged into a crevice. Her backpack had been ripped off. It rolled and tumbled before coming to rest on the edge of an overhang, jutting out over the bubbling, churning waters of the falls far below.

Cassie lay still. To Ruby's frantic relief, she raised her head, as the Sleskeritt howled with rage and began lumbering its way back down the cliff. Glancing up, Ruby's heart jumped as a familiar figure emerged from a tunnel above where Cassie lay.

"Colwyn!" she cried, watching as he assessed the situation in a heartbeat, then began climbing swiftly down.

"Get the backpack!" screamed Cassie as soon as she saw him. "Over there," she ordered. "It's got the crystal heart in it."

Colwyn hesitated. The Sleskeritt roared above him, slowly but surely manoeuvring its ponderous bulk to where Cassie lay, trapped and helpless. Ruby knew Colwyn didn't have time to save both the heart and Cassie. He glanced from the backpack to Cassie and made his choice. Surefooted and swift, he climbed down to Cassie, helped her up, and half carried, half dragged her, back up the cliff face towards the tunnel.

Ruby squirmed in agony as the Sleskeritt slowly began to catch up with them, scrabbling and scratching over rocks, great fangs dripping glistening ropes of drool as it bellowed.

Colwyn and Cassie had almost reached the tunnel entrance when the Sleskeritt lashed out with its front claws, raking down the back of Colwyn's legs. He yelled with pain. The beast clung and began to pull him backwards. Colwyn shoved Cassie towards the tunnel with the last of his strength before the Sleskeritt plucked him from the rock face and hurled him through the air, to crumple on the opposite shore far below.

Screaming with triumph, the Sleskeritt jumped down after him, bounding from rock to rock in its haste to finish him off. Ruby heard someone sobbing, and realised it was herself, as she saw Colwyn's body lying so still and broken. The Sleskeritt slobbered and snarled, lifting its claws high to stab and slash and kill.

"Oi! You bully! Pick on someone your own size!"

Ruby's head snapped up in disbelief. The Sleskeritt howled in annoyance as her incredibly brave, incredibly stupid, sister hurled another rock at its spiny head, and Ruby realised she was trying to goad the beast away from Colwyn.

"Leave him alone, bog breath!" she screamed, snatching up rocks and throwing them at the Sleskeritt. It snarled in irritation, and hesitated, claws raised over Colwyn as he lay, still and unmoving.

Cassie threw another rock, a larger one, which hit the beast on the top of its head and bounced onto its chest. Cassie crowed with triumph and did a little mocking dance. Incensed, the Sleskeritt disregarded Colwyn and started up the cliff after Cassie, who continued to throw rocks, seemingly oblivious to her own safety.

"Cassie!" screamed Ruby. "Run!" The beast was almost upon her. Cassie turned and fled towards the tunnel as it lashed upwards with its tail, knocking her sideways to the ground.

"No!" screamed Ruby.

The beast roared in victory, rearing up over Cassie, beating its chest in a savage display of power only to freeze, as its wicked talons were slicing down towards her sister.

Ruby blinked.

The Sleskeritt remained still.

Cassie uncurled from her defensive ball, looking up in stunned amazement at the colossus seemingly turned to stone above her.

"Ruby."

At the weak breathless whisper behind her, Ruby turned to see Delmar, hand outstretched, eyes pulsing blue, and realised it was his magic that had frozen the Sleskeritt before it could deliver its killing blow.

"Ruby," gasped Delmar again.

Ruby saw the strain written across his pale face. On his forehead, the wound dripped blood into his eyes, and she knew the effort it was taking to hold the beast back.

"Help me," he pleaded. Ruby rushed to support him, feeling his strength draining away. "Can't ..." he muttered, his head lolling. "Can't hold it much longer..."

Desperately, Ruby looked up. To her horror she saw the Sleskeritt twitching, trying to break free of Delmar's spell.

Delmar groaned, his head falling forward. The spell broke, and the Sleskeritt reared up. Cassie collapsed to her knees, her terrified face flashing white in the sunlight. Ruby screamed, half-covered her eyes, unable to watch her sister being ripped to shreds.

There was a twang from the rocks below. The Sleskeritt turned, and an arrow penetrated its eye, burying itself deep into the beast's brain.

Chapter Nine

The Crystal Heart

or an instant the Sleskeritt didn't move, as if it hadn't realised it was dead. Then it swayed, and fell, its great bulk crashing to the ground with an awful, terrible sound.

Toppling over the edge of the cliff, it plunged with an almighty splash into the pool below.

Colwyn stood, bow in hand. Even from a distance, Ruby could see the grim determination on his face before he crumpled to his knees and collapsed to the ground.

"Help me to him, Ruby," ordered Delmar.

Ruby struggled to obey, half leading, half carrying him down the beach, splashing through the waterfall to reach the shore where Colwyn lay, lifeless and unmoving.

Cassie was scrambling down the cliff as fast as she could. Ruby saw the horrific scrapes and bruises which covered her from head to toe and heard her anguished sobs as she raced across the beach, dropping to her knees beside Colwyn's motionless body.

"Colwyn," she cried. "Please, oh no, no, no."

Ruby swallowed as she looked at Colwyn's poor, battered body, realising nobody could survive such injuries, that it had been sheer willpower alone that had forced him to his feet long enough to shoot the arrow and save Cassie's life.

"Delmar," pleaded Cassie in despair. "Do something, please, you've got to do something, help him."

"I will try," stated Delmar. "I fear my powers are much diminished by my injuries, I do not know if I have the strength."

"Can we help?" asked Ruby.

Delmar drew his brows together, thoughtfully.

"I am unsure," he began. "It might be possible. Place your hands on my shoulders, I will attempt to heal his injuries, drawing upon your strength – should my own fail me."

Quickly, the sisters stood behind him as he knelt by Colwyn and held out a hand over him.

Frantically wiping away tears, Cassie clamped her hand onto Delmar's right shoulder, Ruby taking up a mirror image stance on the other side.

A piercing blue light emanated from Delmar's outstretched hand. It pulsed and flickered, bathing Colwyn in an eerie unearthly light.

Fascinated, Ruby watched as a gaping jagged break in his ribs began to knit together; a broken leg began to mend; cuts and bruises faded.

"I cannot." Delmar's head fell forward, and the light faded. "Too much needs doing. His injuries are many, there are ruptures within, I need more energy, do not have enough."

In despair, Ruby forced herself to project mental strength into Delmar, feeling Colwyn's life force slipping away through his link with the young mage, and Delmar's anguish as he fought to hold onto the small, rapidly fading, spark of existence.

The bea-s-st i-s-s dead. We are free.

The lake creatures' thoughts buzzed in her head.

"Not now," Ruby snapped angrily in her mind. "The man who killed the Sleskeritt is dying. We must try and save him."

We cannot let thi-s- happen, not the one who s-saved us-s-s.

Unexpectedly, an explosion of pure energy, strong and powerful, surge through Ruby's mind and into Delmar's.

He gasped, his body snapping straight, and light blasted from his hand again shrouding Colwyn in its brilliance.

Ruby felt bone knit together, veins close and refill with necessary, life-sustaining blood.

A ruptured spleen was repaired, broken ribs mended, Colwyn's heart, hovering on the verge of death, began to beat, strong and true.

He stirred.

His life force young and hopeful.

Still, the lake creatures sent energy. It bounced back from Colwyn and repaired Delmar's fractured skull, chasing away the concussion, mending cuts, and bruises.

The energy moved onto Cassie, mending, and repairing until her face was as beautiful as ever, the broken wrist which adrenalin had prevented her from being aware of, was whole again.

Finally, the lake creatures diverted their attention onto Ruby. There was a white-hot pulse of energy as her various ailments were soothed and repaired.

"Thank you," thought Ruby, gratefully, and heard the answer clear in her mind.

You saved u-s-s. The beast will no more harve-s-st us. We are grateful.

Then the lake creatures were gone. They were left staring at each other, feeling refreshed and renewed.

Cassie cried with relief as Colwyn stirred and opened his eyes. His expression was puzzled as Cassie buried her head in his shoulder.

"You're alive," she sobbed, voice muffled in his shirt. Colwyn's eyes widened with disbelief.

He gazed up at Delmar and Ruby's grinning faces; awkwardly wrapping an arm around Cassie's heaving shoulders.

"I am?" he queried, grinning. "In faith, perhaps I should die more often if it means awakening to find fair Lady Cassandra weeping in my arms."

"Oh," huffed Cassie in disgust, pulling away. "Right, make a joke of it, typical man."

Colwyn laughed and sat up. His face sobered as he cupped her face gently in his hands.

"That was one of the bravest things I have ever seen anyone, man or maid, do," he said seriously. "You distracted the beast long enough for me to gather my wits and draw my bow. Once again, I owe you my life, Lady Cassandra. Once again I thank you for it."

"Oh, yes, well," stuttered Cassie, eyes unable to meet his, she twisted away from his touch. "You saved my life two or three times today. I think we're probably quits. Anyway, if anyone saved lives, it was Delmar. Without his magic, you'd be dead."

"Then I am in your debt, my mage," began Colwyn.

Delmar shook his head.

"It was not I, my Lord, or rather, it was not I alone. My injuries were such that I did not have the strength to keep you in this life. The Lady Ruby, somehow, provided me with energy the like of which I have never experienced before."

"It was the lake people," explained Ruby. "They were so grateful to us for killing the Sleskeritt that they joined minds and sent enough energy to heal us all."

"I hate to burst this happy bubble," said Cassie, tersely. "Where's the crystal heart?"

As one, they looked towards the overhang where the backpack had come to rest, staring at each other with dismay as they saw it was gone, realising when the Sleskeritt crashed down the cliff and into the pool, it had taken the heart with it.

"Oh no," cried Ruby, turning to Delmar. "Before," she exclaimed, "you could feel the heart. Can you still feel it? Do you know where it is?"

Delmar drew a deep breath, closed his eyes, and shook his head in despair. "If the heart is close by it is shielded in some way."

"So, what do we do now?" asked Cassie, looking close to tears. Ruby knew how she felt.

They had risked so much, gone through so much, all for nothing.

"There is little we can do," replied Colwyn soberly, "except, leave this place and make camp. Mayhap, after a good night's sleep, Delmar can try again in the morning."

Reluctantly, the others agreed, following Delmar in silence as he unerringly picked his way around piles of rubble, and through miles of dark tunnels, before they finally emerged, tired and heart weary on the shores of Lake Minwarn.

They made camp and sat around the fire as Colwyn cooked a trout-like fish he'd caught in the lake. Nobody was in the mood for talking.

After dinner had been eaten, Cassie and Ruby crawled into their tent and fell into a deep exhausted sleep of bitter disappointment.

We come. We are here. S-s-see us-s-s. Ruby sat bolt upright, instantly awake, the cold slithery thoughts of the lake people whispering through her mind.

"What is it?" she thought. "What do you want?"

Come to u-s-s. The voices insisted.

Puzzled, Ruby slipped silently from her covers and crawled out of the tent. It was dark, but the moon's bright luminosity flooded the landscape with a yellowy light, and Ruby picked her way easily to the water's edge.

"I'm here," she thought. "Where are you?"

There was a second, then the waters moved, and hundreds of lake creatures emerged, glistening palely in the moonlight, tentacles gently rippling, all eyes fixed solemnly on Ruby.

You saved u-s-s. You killed the bea-s-st. We are grateful.

Every lake creature bent its head as they paid homage to Ruby. Tears leapt to her eyes at their sincere and humble thanks. The creature at the front stepped forward, holding out its tentacle.

It i-s-s important to you, s-s-o we find and bring.

Ruby gaped.

Clasped in its tentacle, gleaming brilliantly in the moonlight, was the crystal heart.

"Oh, thank you," she cried, taking the heart in her hand, feeling its unexpected weight, its smooth warm surface, the hint of power buried deep within.

"Thank you," she said again, "You've no idea what this means. This could save everyone."

We s-s-s-ense great s-s-struggles lay before you. It i-s-s important you do not falter from the s-s-hining white way. You mus-s-t not leave the s-s-hining white way.

"What?" asked Ruby, confused, "What do you mean?"

Farewell, Ruby of the human-s-s. We shall always-s-s honour you.

They sank beneath the waters, leaving Ruby staring in wonder at the crystal, holding it aloft, admiring its pure beauty before turning back to the camp to wake the others.

The next morning, with light hearts and happy faces, they set out to make the two days walk back to the barrier so Delmar could take them home.

Two of the treasures had been recovered. Spirits were high as they marched through the rocky terrain.

When they finally reached the protective perimeter, they huddled close to Delmar as he worked his magic and took them safely back to Lady Ninniane's Sanctuary...

... and far away in a darkened room, deep within a forgotten tower, Lorcan stirred. His dark eyes glowed as he felt ... something ... it flashed, pure white and radiant, and his soul shrank away from its power.

"The crystal heart ..." he murmured.

The other occupant of the room turned in alarm and hurried to his side.

Pouring wine into a goblet he offered it to the dark one, his master, waiting with bowed head for his lord to speak.

"It has been found, taken from its resting place."

"My Lord?"

"The crystal heart is in the hands of Ninniane," Lorcan spat, anger flashing from his eyes. "She now has two of the ancient treasures. She must not be allowed to find the others."

"What do you want me to do, my Lord?"

"Bring me more souls to feast on. My strength is still not enough to defeat her."

"It is difficult, my Lord, I can only take so many without arousing full-scale panic, and the skraelings consume whatever they find."

Lorcan leaned back wearily in his chair. It had taken much strength to escape from his bonds, strength he needed to replenish, and this fool was worrying about scaring people.

"I will give you an army then," he purred silkily. "An army the like of which this land has not seen for a millennium. I shall awaken the Gilmesh."

"The Gilmesh?" breathed his minion in awe. "I thought them but a legend."

"They exist," pronounced the dark one. Evil shone in his eyes at the suffering, pain, and death about to be unleashed on this accursed land.

"They exist to do my bidding. They shall bring me more young souls to feast on. Soon, I will be stronger than before, then nothing shall stand in my way, and I will crush the house of the dragon lords forever. Erinsmore shall be mine."

"Yes, my Lord," gasped the other, eyes greedy for power. "And I shall rule under you as your faithful and loyal servant."

"Of course," agreed Lorcan smoothly, hiding a smirk behind long sharp fingers. "I have promised you shall be rewarded as you so deserve. First, we must stop Ninniane from collecting the treasures. Attend closely; this is what you must do..."

Returning to the Sanctuary as heroes was an amazing feeling, thought Ruby that evening, leaning back in her chair and watching the dancing with pleasure.

Next to her, Delmar was deep in conversation with Samson, telling him of their adventures. Ruby listened in wonder, hardly recognising them in the tale of bravery and loyalty being spun.

A group of youngsters descended on her, laughing, pulling her from her chair. Ignoring her claims of being unable to dance, they dragged her onto the floor, good-naturedly pushed and guided her through the complicated steps, until they were all breathless with laughter at her ineptness.

Finally, Ruby escaped from their well-meaning high-spiritedness and dreamily left the banqueting hall in search of a moment's silence and some fresh air.

It was a beautiful starlit night, and Ruby found herself on a broad balcony overlooking one of the small, inner courtyard gardens.

Quietly, she leant on the stone balustrade, gazed down at its formal flower beds and gently tinkling waterfall, enjoying being alone.

There was movement below, Cassie stepped into the garden, followed an instant later by Colwyn.

"I tell you, my Lady Cassandra, it is easy," he teased.

Cassie walked backwards away from him, shaking her head, and laughing.

"It's too hard," she retorted. "I'll never be able to learn all the steps. It's all right for you, you were probably taught in your cradle or something."

"Come," he replied, hand outstretched. "Let me show you."

Cassie placed her hand in his, allowing him to position her in the centre of the walk.

Ruby watched while he gently, patiently, taught her one of the dances Ruby herself had been led through.

Faltering, brow creased in concentration, Cassie slowly began to learn until they moved in harmony together, a beautiful, slow, stylised dance which viewed from above, Ruby could see formed a rhythmic pattern of steps.

The music from the banqueting hall stopped. Colwyn bowed to Cassie, who hesitated, then swept down in a graceful curtsey.

"Cassandra," murmured Colwyn.

Stepping forward, he pulled Cassie up from her curtsey. He placed his arms around her, his head bent to hers. Ruby knew he was kissing her.

Ruby heard her sister give a deep sigh, before she gently pulled away, disappearing inside in a rustle of blue silk, leaving Colwyn standing alone in the moonlight, and Ruby wondering what effect this latest turn of events would have when the adventure was over, and it was time to return to their world.

During breakfast the next day, she carefully watched them. They seemed unchanged. Cassie still snapped at Colwyn, and he took great delight in teasing and goading her. Ruby wondered if she had imagined that moment of intimacy.

Later, she wandered the castle, unsure what to do. Everyone was busy, too busy to talk, although eyes softened when they saw her, and all bowed or curtseyed.

At last, Ruby found herself on a wide balcony overlooking a long green sweep of lawn, where she found Lady Ninniane and Delmar in huddled conference over a large parchment map spread on the table before them.

"Ah, Ruby," exclaimed the Lady. "Please, come and join us." Delmar leapt to his feet and pulled out a chair, which Ruby settled into, looking with interest at the map she assumed to be of Erinsmore.

There, plainly marked, she saw the vast expanse of the sacred forest, the shining turrets of the Sanctuary, the tall forbidding spikes of the Carnethen Mountains, and even the great blue disc that was Lake Minwarn.

Her eyes roaming further over the map, Ruby saw the wide arc of blue water which surrounded Erinsmore on three sides, small, interesting-looking islands dotted about in its blue expanse and there, right in the centre of the land, was its capital, Dragonswell.

She listened with interest as Lady Ninniane and Delmar talked of faraway places, of plans and strategies, and saw Cassie and Colwyn walk out onto the lawn far below, Colwyn carrying a straw-stuffed archery target.

Ruby watched as Colwyn patiently showed Cassie how to hold the bow. Standing close behind, his arms around her, he helped her draw back the string and shoot an arrow towards the target.

Faintly, she heard Cassie's cry of delight, as the arrow flew true to land with a thwack in the centre of the target.

Colwyn stepped back and let Cassie try alone, his rich laugh ringing out as Cassie managed to send the arrow a mere foot before it struck the ground.

Pouting, Cassie watched as Colwyn took the bow and drew back the string. Ruby smiled as Cassie, with a wicked grin, trailed her hand idly down Colwyn's cheek.

The arrow lurched into a nearby flowerbed. Cassie took one look at Colwyn's face, picked up her skirts and fled, her shrieks echoing up to them as Colwyn chased after her and she disappeared around the corner of the castle with Colwyn in hot pursuit.

Ruby looked up to find the Lady watching with a fondly indulgent smile.

"It is somewhat disconcerting," she began, "to see history repeating itself."

Ruby frowned, wanting to ask the Lady what she meant when a sudden caw interrupted them. Cora landed on the back of her chair, solemnly dropping a long, shining black feather into Ruby's lap. Ruby picked it up, staring at its glossy perfection.

Delmar quoted softly under his breath. "You must carry close to you a gift that appears nothing yet is given freely by a dark friend who is not human."

"Oh," exclaimed Ruby. "Thank you."

She sent the words to Cora who looked pleased and rubbed her great beak softly against Ruby's cheek, before flying up high into the sky, circling twice, then disappearing into the distance.

"You are honoured," said the Lady softly. "Cora does not give her feathers lightly. You must keep it with you always, Ruby, for a tail feather from the great raven is said to have magical powers."

"I will," agreed Ruby, looking at the feather with wonder.

"Hold!" demanded the Lady, eyes pulsing a vivid blue.

"I hear it!" cried Delmar, Ruby saw his eyes also change colour. "What is it, my Lady?"

The Lady clamped her hands to her head, face a mask of anguish. Then, Ruby heard it.

A great wailing, screaming howl of agonised suffering, knifed through her thoughts, sending her to the floor with a cry of pain, clutching her temples, curling into a ball as the sound seemed to curdle her very soul.

As abruptly as it had begun, it stopped.

Ruby slowly took her hands away from her head, and struggled back into her seat, seeing Delmar's shocked expression as his eyes returned to normal.

"What was that?" she sobbed.

Delmar shook his head. "I do not know, Lady Ruby," he looked to the Lady. "My Lady?"

Lady Ninniane took her hands away from her face, tears spilling gently from her eyes to slide down her perfect cheeks. "It was suffering," she replied quietly, "Great, great suffering."

There was the sound of running feet, and Cassie and Colwyn burst upon them, eyes wide, shock all over their faces.

"What was that?" cried Colwyn. "My Lady?"

"Colwyn," the Lady turned to face him, great sorrow in her eyes. "The greatest evil imaginable has been released upon the land. Lorcan has awoken the Gilmesh."

"Gilmesh?" cried Cassie. "What are the Gilmesh?"

"Things from nightmares, from myth," said Colwyn. "They do not exist, they cannot. My Lady?" In despair, he turned to Lady Ninniane, who shook her head sadly.

"They did exist, Colwyn, long ago. When Lorcan threatened the very existence of Erinsmore, he called upon ancient wraiths of evil. They had lain dormant for eternity. Somehow, he found the old words of power and awakened them. For five days and nights, they ravaged our land, slaughtering all they found, destroying everything in their path, before Lorcan was imprisoned and the Gilmesh banished back to the dark realms they inhabit."

"So that sound, that scream," Cassie shuddered in memory. "That was the Gilmesh?"

"Would that it was, my child," replied the Lady, bleakly. "No, it was the sound of hundreds of souls being ripped from the bodies of the innocent people of Erinsmore."

"No," cried Colwyn in horrified disbelief.

"This is Lorcan's doing," stated the Lady. "To escape from his bonds must have taken all his strength. The Gilmesh are soul eaters. They have the ability to cleave a person's soul from their body and store its power. That is why Lorcan has awakened them. They are collecting the souls for him. That is why he ensured all heard their suffering. It is a direct challenge to us, to me."

"What can we do to stop him?" demanded Delmar.

"We must go to Dragonswell immediately," stated Colwyn decisively. "My father will have need of us."

"Okay," agreed Cassie. "When do we leave?"

"No," Colwyn shook his head. "By us, I mean Delmar and myself," he paused, taking Cassie's hands in his.

"I am sorry, Cassandra, we do not know what perils we face. It will be too dangerous for you both, I might not be able to protect you. You must stay here. I will return for you, I promise."

Ruby winced, waiting for the explosion. To her complete astonishment, Cassie nodded.

"Take care," she murmured. "Both of you," she added, her look including Delmar.

"Have no fear, Lady Cassandra," reassured Delmar, rising to his feet and crossing to Colwyn's side. "I shall endeavour to keep him out of harm's way."

"See that you do," smiled Cassie, then gasped as Colwyn picked her up in a fierce embrace.

"I will return," he promised, his voice low and intense in her ear. Then they went, their boots ringing on the stone flags of the terrace.

Ruby gaped at her sister in bewilderment, wondering if the Erinsmore air had completely addled her brains.

The sickly-sweet smile remained plastered on Cassie's face until Colwyn and Delmar were lost to sight, then abruptly snapped off as Cassie rounded on the Lady and growled.

"I don't care what you say, or how we get there, we're going to Dragonswell. Stay here where it's safe like good little women, hah! Why that male chauvinist..."

"I agree with you, Cassandra," interrupted the Lady, mildly.

"Thinks he can go swanning off and leave us here. Over my dead body! He'll find he can't order me around ... what?"

Cassie looked at the Lady.

"What did you say?"

"I said, I agree with you," repeated the Lady, in amusement.

"Oh," said Cassie, lamely. "Well, then, good, umm, how shall we get there?"

"I will take you myself," stated the Lady, rising gracefully to her feet.

"It is time," she declared, her hair streamed back in the gust of wind which rushed across the terrace, rippling up the corners of the map, rustling the sister's silken skirts.

"It is time," she repeated softly, and they arrived in Dragonswell.

Chapter Ten

Dragonswell

uby blinked. Having braced herself for the stomach-churning experience that travelling with Delmar was, the smooth instance of their journey from the Sanctuary to Dragonswell was disorientating, to say the least.

So silent was their arrival, that the occupants of the room in which they'd appeared remained unaware of them for a few moments, giving Ruby a chance to look around and try to gain her bearings.

It was a large stone room. A warming fire crackled in a huge hearth, and rich tapestries hung from every wall. In the centre of the room was a long wooden table spread with maps and rolled up parchment, around which huddled four men.

The first was thin and tall, his lean body clothed in a long blue robe, so like Delmar's Ruby guessed he was Colwyn's father's mage, Siminus. Another man was leaning over the table examining the maps, a frown pulling at his roughly handsome face. Everything about him screamed soldier and Ruby wondered if he was Colwyn's father.

A third man sat in a carved wooden chair at the head of the table. As he raised his head and noticed their presence, Ruby realised from his piercing blue eyes and resemblance to Colwyn, that this was Reutghar, Lord of the Dragon Throne, King of Erinsmore.

He rose sharply. "My Lady," he gasped, his voice holding shadows of Colwyn's in the richness of its tone. "Thank the stars you are here. Evil has beset the land."

"I know, Lord Reutghar," interrupted the Lady, stepping forward and raising her hand to him. "We heard the screams of the innocent, Lorcan has awoken the Gilmesh."

All the men in the room, seasoned warriors though they were, blanched at her words. Ruby noticed the fourth man step closer to Reutghar to protect him. She wondered if he was the King's bodyguard, he certainly looked big and strong enough.

"They attacked a nearby village early this morning before the villagers were awake," continued Reutghar. "Most were slaughtered in their beds. The Gilmesh took the youngest to the market square, and there they ..." he paused, swallowed.

"We rode to aid them as quickly as we could, but by the time we reached the village, it was too late, Lorcan's foul work had been carried out. All that was left was for us to bury the dead."

"I am sorry, my Lord. Were any saved?"

"Nay," he replied, bitterly. "The whole village was lost."

"We must take steps," the Lady said, her voice firm with resolve, "to ensure this does not happen again. Every innocent soul Lorcan consumes will increase his strength to a degree against which even I will be unable to resist."

"Aye," agreed Reutghar. His gaze turned to the sisters. "I apologise for my tardiness in greeting you, my Ladies."

"My Lord Reutghar," began Lady Ninniane. "May I introduce Lady Cassandra and Lady Ruby." Reutghar made a stiff bow to them. Hesitantly, Ruby and Cassie dipped into wobbly curtsies.

"They have come from the other world to aid us," continued the Lady, "and brought the Prophecy Stone with them."

"The other world?" Reutghar's dark brows rose in surprise. "Then you have indeed travelled far, my Ladies. I am sorry you visit Erinsmore during such troubled times," he paused. "I do not suppose you happen to know the whereabouts of my son, my Lady. He and his mage have been missing for many weeks now."

"Why yes," replied the Lady casually, settling herself into a chair at the end of the table. "They, and the Ladies Cassandra and Ruby, have been on a quest to recover the crystal heart." With a graceful gesture from her long white hand, she indicated Cassie and Ruby stand on either side of her chair.

She smiled gently at Reutghar. "They should be arriving at any moment. Ah," she held up her hand at the sound of urgent footsteps in the corridor outside. "I believe that this is them now," she continued, smiling conspiratorially at Reutghar. "You may find this rather interesting, my Lord."

There was a knock on the door, it was flung open, and Colwyn and Delmar entered, bristling with importance at their mission.

"My Lord," exclaimed Colwyn. "We came as fast as we could and are ready to help defend the people of Erinsmore against Lorcan's ..." His eyes fell upon the three women at the far end of the table, and Ruby swallowed a laugh at his stunned expression.

"Cassandra?" he snapped, ignoring all others, and striding to her side. "What are you doing here? You promised to remain at the Sanctuary."

"I promised no such thing," retorted Cassie, hotly.

"It is dangerous for you here. I wished to know you were safe at the Sanctuary."

"Where I could mend a few shirts for you while I was waiting, I suppose." Cassie's eyes flashed angry fire.

Colwyn's face was tight with irate concern. "You will return to the Sanctuary now."

"No."

"Cassandra, you will do as I say."

"Oh, let me see, no, I don't think so," she replied calmly. Colwyn growled in frustration. Looking around, Ruby saw amused grins on the faces of the other men.

Reutghar's expression was knowing as he raised his brows at the Lady. "Very interesting, my Lady," he murmured, then cleared his throat. "Welcome back, my son," he said. Colwyn turned, distracted, to greet his father.

"My Lord," he replied and bowed.

"Colwyn," began his father. "I fear I have grave news for you. The Gilmesh attacked one of the outlying villages and its hall early this morning. None survived."

"The village?" enquired Colwyn, his face taut.

"I am sorry, Colwyn," his father paused, sadness etched into his face. "It was Aransvale." Colwyn turned away, his distress plain to see. Instinctively, Cassie stepped forward and placed a comforting hand on his arm.

"It was the village where my uncle and his family lived," Colwyn explained, in answer to her unspoken question. "My cousin, he was my age, we were as close as brothers. He only married last year. He and his wife now have a babe, a little girl." He paused, raising haunted eyes to his father.

"Did none survive?" At his father's headshake, he swallowed, then pulled himself together. "My Lady," he turned in despair to Lady Ninniane. "Do you not agree it is too dangerous for them to remain here? That they must now return to the Sanctuary?"

"I am very sorry for your loss," said Cassie, before the Lady could reply. "But we're not going back."

"They cannot go back," continued the Lady. "It is their destiny to be here."

Colwyn looked like he wished to argue the point further, but a warning glance from his father made him think better of it.

He subsided into silence, shooting a look at Cassie which let her know it was far from over.

"These Gilmesh creatures," began the tall soldierly man. "What nature of beast are they? Do they have any weaknesses that may be used against them?"

"My Lady," began Reutghar. "You remember Lord Darius, my second in command."

"My Lord," said the Lady, inclining her head gracefully. Darius bowed, then snapped to attention awaiting her reply. Ruby thought how like a coiled spring he was, ready to leap into action at a second's notice.

"The Gilmesh are ancient and powerful beings and as such are practically indestructible." Darius and Reutghar exchanged concerned looks. "However," she continued, "there are two ways in which they can be destroyed. One is by fire; the other is by cleaving their heads from their bodies with one stroke."

"This is valuable information, my Lady, I thank you for it. My Lord," Darius turned to Reutghar. "With your permission, I will see this knowledge is passed amongst the troops."

"Of course," replied Reutghar.

Darius inclined his head and bowed to Lady Ninniane, Cassie, and Ruby. "My Ladies."

The Lady inclined her head gracefully, and the sisters found themselves instinctively dipping into curtsies, as he turned on his heel and left the room.

"I will order rooms prepared for you," said Reutghar, then indicated the silent giant of a man at his shoulder. "This is Garth. Whilst you are within these walls, he will be responsible for your safety. I believe you already know my mage, my Lady."

Again, Lady Ninniane inclined her head. "It is a pleasure to see you again, Siminus."

"My Lady," said the older mage, bowing deeply. "My Lord, if you will excuse me, I have much to attend to." He bowed to Reutghar, who dismissed him with a wave of his hand.

"Delmar." The young mage snapped to attention with a guilty look. "Attend me please, you have been absent from your studies for too long."

With a sidelong look at Colwyn, Delmar dutifully followed in his mentor's wake, the door closing firmly behind them.

"My Lady." Reutghar pushed a map closer to Lady Ninniane. "I would be grateful for your counsel. Where do you believe the Gilmesh will strike again? Skraelings too have been terrorising villages, yet we have been unable to determine from whence they are coming."

Lady Ninniane bowed her head over the maps. Cassie and Ruby wandered away, feeling slightly superfluous.

"Cassie," murmured Ruby out of the corner of her mouth.

"Hmm?"

"Colwyn's dad, have you noticed how much he looks like…"

"The latest James Bond, oh yeah," Cassie rolled her eyes at Ruby. "Noticed that one straight away."

"I pray, Lady Cassandra, what did you notice straight away?" Colwyn appeared silently at her shoulder.

Cassie started, laughed, and replied unthinkingly. "How much of a hottie your dad is."

Colwyn's eyebrows wandered over his face in bewilderment, Cassie flushed, and Ruby tried hard not to laugh.

"I fear, sometimes I am at a loss to understand your words, my Lady Cassandra," he finally said.

Cassie cast an amused glance at Ruby. "Probably just as well," she murmured. Ruby spluttered with laughter, sobering as she saw Colwyn's hurt expression. "It was nothing," reassured Cassie. "Just a silly joke, it's not important."

"Colwyn," Reutghar glanced at them. "Why not take the Ladies on a tour of the castle? I will send someone when their rooms have been prepared."

"My Lord," replied Colwyn stiffly, bowed to Lady Ninniane. "My Lady," he said. He turned to the sisters his manner correctly formal. "If you will follow me, my Ladies," and he led them from the room.

As Colwyn showed them around the vast stone castle, which was his home, Ruby knew by his set expression and stiffly polite manner he hadn't forgiven them for being there.

He led them up and down stairs, showing them a huge banqueting hall, and the training yard where men-at-arms were engaged in various activities, Colwyn being hailed and greeted by many.

Ruby saw the genuine pleasure on the faces of the men at his safe return. She also saw the discreetly curious gazes and knew they were wondering who they were.

Finally, Colwyn led them to a charming rooftop terrace tucked away in a secluded corner of the castle. Although small, the space had been formed into a silent green oasis. Roses perfumed the air and small cosy seats big enough for two were placed in each corner.

Correctly interpreting a 'get lost' signal from Cassie, Ruby wandered over to the far end of the garden. Leaning on the balcony overlooking the dry moat, her gaze drank in the activities taking place in the bustling marketplace below. Dragonswell appeared a thriving, happy town, and Ruby was content to merely watch.

"Why are you so cross with me?"

Colwyn turned from surveying the garden at her words, looking at Cassie as she sat down on one of the benches. She spread her skirts neatly, gazing expectantly at him. He sighed, moving to sit next to her on the bench.

"This was my mother's garden," he began.

"It's lovely," replied Cassie. "How old were you when your mother died?"

"I had reached my fifth birthday. I do not remember much of her, merely her soft hands, the smell of her perfume, the sound of her laugh, impressions that linger in my memory."

"How ..." Cassie paused, unsure whether to speak. "How did she die?"

"My father was on a voyage to the Far Isles when his ship was beset by pirates. My mother was accompanying him. During the battle, she was slain by an arrow fired from the pirates' ship."

"Oh, Colwyn ..." Cassie shook her head in horror. "That's terrible, I'm so sorry."

"Now do you understand why I wanted you to remain safe at the Sanctuary?" Colwyn turned to face her, gathering both her hands in his. "These are dark times, Cassandra; I may not be able to protect you. All I want is for you to be safe."

Cassie's face softened at his anguished expression. Leaning forward, she placed a soft kiss on his lips.

"I know," she murmured, resting her head for a moment on his shoulder. "We'll be all right," she reassured him. "With all these fit men all over the place, we're probably safer here than at the Sanctuary."

Colwyn sighed, and slid an arm around her, pulling her closer. They sat, enjoying the nearness of the other and the harmony of the moment.

"Cassandra?"

"Hmm?"

"Does fit – mean what I think it means?"

"Probably," laughed Cassie.

"To arms!"

The loud shout shattered the moment. Colwyn leapt to his feet, rushing to the balcony as Ruby ran back to them, her face pale and scared. A bell began clanging urgently.

"We're under attack!" came another cry, "To arms! To arms!"

"Come," ordered Colwyn.

Silently, the girls rushed after him, down steep staircases and along stone corridors echoing with the cries and shouts of the men who hurried past, buckling on sword belts, faces grim and set.

"Where is Lord Reutghar?" Colwyn demanded of one.

"I believe on the outer walls, my Lord," replied the man, before being swallowed up in the growing tide of firm-jawed, steely-eyed soldiers.

"Garth." A familiar figure appeared at the end of the passageway, and Colwyn hurried them towards him. "Take the Ladies to safety, I must join my father."

"No, we want to stay with you," began Cassie.

"Take the Ladies to safety," repeated Colwyn firmly. With a last look at Cassie, he turned on his heel and hurried off, leaving the sisters with no choice but to obey.

Garth led them deep into the castle, closing vast metal-bound doors behind them, barricading each one as he did. Ruby knew from the look on Cassie's face she was thinking about Colwyn, outside those protective doors, defending them from whatever evil creatures Lorcan had sent against them this time.

Colwyn finally found his father in the armoury, supervising the distribution of weapons. He turned at Colwyn's entry, his piercing blue eyes heavy with worry.

"Colwyn, did Garth find you? I sent him to escort the Ladies to safety, although, in faith, I think he was disappointed not to be facing the enemy."

"Yes, he is taking them to the keep despite her protests."

His father shot him a curious look but remained silent as the last soldiers ran from the room. Taking a shield, Colwyn followed Reutghar into the courtyard where men waited, all eyes turned to the watchers on the wall.

"Skraelings!" came the cry, "Attacking the south wall."

"It will hold," murmured his father beside him. "I personally checked every point of entry, there is no way for them to gain admittance."

Colwyn nodded, his grip tightening on his sword. Around him, tension arose like a tidal wave from the men.

"The wall is breached!" came the hoarse shout from above, "Enemy within!"

"How is that possible?" demanded Reutghar, disbelievingly, at the bloodcurdling howls and yells. "Defend the castle!" he shouted, and then the skraelings were upon them, pouring into the courtyard, wave after ravaging snarling wave of them, and the men of Dragonswell fought desperately for their lives.

Deep inside the castle, Garth's head lifted as the alarm bell rang again. Dark eyes glinting, his nostrils flared almost as if he could smell the enemy.

"The castle walls are breached," he declared flatly. The sisters glanced at each other in fear. "Do not worry, my Ladies," he reassured, seeing the look. "They shall not penetrate the keep."

"What about the others?" demanded Cassie, "All those men outside, in the courtyard, what about them? What about Lord Reutghar and ... and Colwyn?"

"I pity the enemy then," Garth replied with a grim smile. "There is no finer swordsman in the land than Lord Reutghar – unless it is Lord Colwyn. I should know, I taught them both."

The fighting in the courtyard grew fiercer. Colwyn lost sight of his father in the swirling melee of soldiers and skraelings. He saw a man go down, overwhelmed by two skraelings who attacked at once. Colwyn leapt over the body of one he'd slain, hacking at one of the beasts as it went for the jugular of the fallen man.

It died howling under his sword. The soldier twisted on his hip and brought up his sword, skewering the second beast as it savagely gripped his shoulder in its razor-sharp teeth. Colwyn pulled the man to his feet, seeing by the blood flowing down his arm and his glazed expression that the wound was serious.

"Go and find one of the mages," he ordered. "Get that wound seen too."

"My Lord," protested the soldier. "'Tis not my sword arm, I can still fight."

"Go," repeated Colwyn. "A wound from such a beast will likely fester."

He helped the man to the steps of the castle, fighting off skraelings at every turn, seeing with alarm a few had broken through the lines of soldiers and were sniffing around the great wooden door. Colwyn blinked in disbelief as a portion of the door seemed to ripple and disappear, leaving a pathway clear for the skraelings. They loped through the opening, which then closed shut behind them.

Horrified, Colwyn thrust the wounded man at another soldier. "Take him inside," he ordered, and ran to the great door, banging on the place where he'd seen the skraelings enter, but it was solid.

"What is amiss?"

His father appeared behind him, clothing splattered with blood, skraeling blood, his eyes fierce with the light of battle.

"Skraelings are in the castle. This door, it melted away to allow them access."

"Magic," stated his father grimly, heaving at the wooden door. "Come, they must not be allowed to penetrate the keep."

Garth led them up a broad flight of steps. Ruby gasped as a tall figure, clothed in a long blue robe, stepped out in front of them.

"My Lord Siminus," exclaimed Garth. "What news? How goes the battle?"

"Very badly, I fear," replied the King's mage, grey eyes concerned. "Skraelings have entered the castle. Lord Reutghar has sent me to find you and the Ladies. He has need of the sword."

"My Lord," began Garth, frowning in confusion. "I cannot draw the sword, nor can you. How does the Lord Reutghar intend us to carry out his request?"

"Do you question his orders?" snapped the mage.

"No, my Lord..."

"Then follow me," ordered Siminus. He stalked off without glancing back to see if they were following, leading the way to a pair of ornate wooden doors, again carved with the likenesses of the dragon and the raven.

Placing his hands on the doors, Siminus murmured some words under his breath. They swung open to reveal a large empty room, bathed in a warm golden light. Puzzled because the room had no windows, Ruby twisted her head to find the source of the light and saw ... *it.*

At one end of the room stood a large, roughly hewn chunk of stone. Set deep into the stone was the sword. It glowed with a brilliance that made Ruby's eyes hurt, lighting up the entire room with its radiance, and she had an almost overwhelming urge to touch it. Glancing at Cassie she saw the dazed longing on her face and knew she must be feeling it too.

"That sword," gasped Cassie. "It's ... it's beautiful."

"'Tis the sword with which Arturius defeated Lorcan," explained Garth. "It cannot be drawn from the stone by any without royal blood in their veins. Should any with evil intent in their heart touch it, they will be bound forever, a prisoner in chains of purest magic."

"You have got to be kidding," drawled Cassie. "The sword in the stone? Excalibur? You mean it exists?"

"I know not this Excalibur of which you speak," Garth frowned. "Yet, this is the sword in the stone, to be used in times of darkest despair." He turned to Siminus in confusion. "Are you certain Lord Reutghar called for the sword?"

"Do you doubt my word?" The ice in the mage's voice could have frozen an ocean, and Garth stiffened.

"Of course not, my Lord, I am merely ... concerned ... as to how you intend us to draw and carry the sword."

Siminus turned his fathomless grey gaze onto the sisters, and Ruby stepped backwards under the intensity of his stare.

"Lady Ruby or Cassandra, either can draw it."

"Us?" queried Cassie. "But ... we're not royal."

"The royal blood of Mark, king of the West Country in your world, and the blood of Gwnhyfar, princess of the Far Isles, runs through your veins. As their heirs, you may touch the sword."

Cassie stared at him speechlessly, turning to Ruby. "What do you think?" she murmured.

Behind them, Garth shifted uneasily. "My Ladies," he began. "If Lord Reutghar has called for the sword, it must be for the direst of reasons. The sword has never been drawn in my lifetime. I can only believe, mayhap, Lorcan has joined the battle. If this is so, we must not delay. To do so, could make the difference between victory, and defeat."

"All right," said Cassie. "If you think it's the right thing to do."

Taking a deep breath, she walked to the stone slab. Gently, reverently, she laid a shaking hand upon the hilt of the sword. Instantly, the glow emanating from the sword increased, bathing Cassie in a shroud of glory. She paused, straightened her spine, reached into the stone, and plucked the sword from its depths.

Turning, she held the sword aloft and Ruby almost fell to her knees in the face of such splendour, such magnificence. Light poured from its golden surface, danced in the gemstones decorating its hilt, and reflected beams of light onto every surface.

"Good," Siminus nodded his head with satisfaction. "Now we must take the sword to Lord Reutghar as quickly as possible."

Colwyn and his father raced along the passageways, desperately seeking the skraelings, unsure if they were going in the right direction until yells and the rough sounds of fighting had them gripping their swords with fierce determination. Rounding a corner, they found guards at the top of a flight of steps engaged in a furious battle with the pack of skraelings and rushed to their aid.

"Lady Cassandra," began Reutghar casually, spitting a skraeling on the end of his sword and throwing it roughly away. "She seems an uncommonly feisty young lady."

"Aye, feisty is one word to describe her," agreed Colwyn bitterly, slashing a skraeling as it attempted to hamstring him. "As is outspoken, self-opinionated, obstinate, and stubborn ... stubborn as a mule. In faith, I have never met a woman who so vexed me."

His father bellowed with laughter, leaping to neatly decapitate a skraeling. "For all that, I do believe you are rather taken with fair Lady Cassandra," he insisted.

Colwyn snorted, casually despatched another skraeling, kicking its body down the steps. "She is fair," he conceded, reluctantly. "And loyal and clever, and her bravery is unsurpassed. Were it not for her quick wits and valour when we faced the skraelings and the Sleskeritt, I would not be alive to tell you the tale."

His father grunted, pivoted on one foot, and sliced at a skraeling. "I confess to being curious," Reutghar began, nonchalantly slashing the skraelings throat, which collapsed in a howl of blood. "The purple hair, is it hereditary?"

"No, I believe it is a tribal dye that young women in her world frequently use."

His father nodded, jumping to avoid the slobbering jaws of another skraeling.

"The world she comes from is very different from ours," Colwyn frowned. "I fear the fair Lady Cassandra has no comprehension of the rightful place of a woman."

"Oh?" enquired his father, innocently. "And where is that?"

"A place of safety. Not to be forever seeking out danger, as if she is as able as a man." Colwyn stabbed at the last skraeling, surveying the litter of fallen bodies with satisfaction, before turning to face his father earnestly.

"Do you not believe it is a woman's duty to support her husband from the security and Sanctuary of the home? To be his comfort and his solace?"

"Is that what you truly believe, Colwyn?" Reutghar asked, suddenly serious.

"Of course," replied Colwyn, puzzled.

Reutghar sighed, shook his head, and knelt to wipe clean his sword on the fur of one of the fallen skraelings. Looking up at Colwyn with a wry grin, he said dryly. "Remind me someday to tell you the story of how I met your mother."

Cassie gripped the sword tightly, casting disbelieving looks at it, as its radiance lit a shimmering path for them. Abruptly, she stopped.

"No," she said.

"My Lady?" Garth turned to face her.

"Come along," urged Siminus. "There is no time to delay."

"No," repeated Cassie. "I don't buy it." She looked at Garth. "This sword is like a uber sword, right?" At his frown of incomprehension, she added. "I mean, it's important."

"Indeed yes," agreed Garth. "This sword symbolises the house of the dragon lords, its value is without measure. It is the only weapon we know has the power to entrap Lorcan."

"Exactly," said Cassie, firmly. "So, I ask you, would Lord Reutghar entrust it to two young girls he'd only just met?"

"Are you claiming to be unworthy to carry the sword?" asked Siminus, eyes darting over her in irritation.

"No," shrugged Cassie, "I find it hard to believe he'd send you to get the sword, hoping you'd find us along the way, and we'd conveniently be able to pull the sword from the stone for you."

"My Lord was confident your royal blood would satisfy the sword's requirements."

"And that's another thing." Cassie snorted and shook her head. "How did you know about our royal blood? I mean, we've only just found out ourselves, so, how did you know?"

Siminus stared hostilely back at Cassie, his grey eyes narrowing to serpentine slits. She swallowed under his gaze yet lifted her chin and stood her ground.

Garth frowned and gazed from one to the other. "In faith, my Lord, you are Lord Reutghar's mage, I would gladly lay down my life for yours, but Lady Cassandra's concerns are valid."

My Lord?

Ruby heard the mage's voice in her head and realised he was communicating with someone else, the way she talked to Cora and the lake people.

My Lord Lorcan, what do I do now?

They must bring the sword to me.

Ruby gasped as the silkily evil tone of Lorcan boomed through her mind. Siminus' head twisted in her direction; his expression dismayed.

Fool! roared the voice. *She is an empath!*

"It's him," cried Ruby. "He's a traitor! He's making us take the sword to Lorcan."

A change came over Siminus. He seemed to grow taller, his eyes darkening, and when he spoke, the voice of Lorcan echoed in the stone passageway.

"Kill them! Kill them all!"

Garth drew his sword. A fierce growl sounded behind them. Spinning round, the girls gasped as a skraeling slunk around the corner, its eyes red and malevolent. It paced closer, and Garth moved to shield them, his gaze never leaving the beast.

Ruby's eyes snapped back to Siminus, to see his eyes pulse black and a glowing dark ball of energy form in the palm of his hand. He hurled it furiously in their direction. It spat and hissed, increasing in size as it raced towards them, a black cloud of foulness that Ruby knew would kill them should it touch them.

"Cassie, look out!"

At Ruby's shriek, Cassie twisted, eyes widening. Instinctively, she brought up the sword, its golden brilliance cutting into the darkness as it reached and engulfed them.

Time slowed to a standstill, vision became acute, sharpened almost to the point of pain. Ruby saw her sister's face yelling under the strain of holding aloft the sword.

Saw its brightness spread to form a protective bubble around them.

Saw the skraeling frozen in mid-leap at Garth.

Saw the instant of shock and surprise on his face, as he too stilled into an unmoving statue, his sword raised, his body poised to fight.

Ruby was dragged, stretched almost into infinity, then crushed and compressed into the smallest point imaginable.

She heard herself scream, long and drawn out, matched by the screams of the others.

The world exploded in a glittering starburst of hot white blinding light.

Then everything went dark.

Chapter Eleven

Home

uby stirred, moaning under her breath. Everything hurt. Her head felt like a giant in hobnail boots was jumping on it, her eyelids like heavy sandbags were attached to each one. She shifted uneasily, feeling something cold and wet under her cheek. Confused, she splayed the fingers on her right hand which lay by her face and separate strands moved between them.

Grass, she was lying on grass. Judging by its dampness it'd been raining, or the grass was dew drenched. Trying to remember why she came to be lying face down in wet grass made her groan from the effort, and an answering groan came from inches away. Making a supreme effort Ruby forced her eyelids open and saw Cassie lying nearby, face creased with pain, clutching a golden sword tightly to her body.

A sword? Ruby frowned as memory came flooding back. Of course, the sword in the stone, Excalibur, the shock of discovering Siminus was a traitor, the dark spell he'd thrown at them, and Cassie's defensive strike with the sword. Slowly, carefully, Ruby struggled to sit up.

"Oh, what?" moaned Cassie. Eyes fluttering open, she focused painfully on Ruby. "What happened? Where are we?"

"Dunno," mumbled Ruby, heard rustling as Cassie sat up.

"No." Ruby heard the despair in Cassie's voice and curiously followed Cassie's gaze. "No, oh no, please no." There, no more than twenty feet away, stood their parents' car.

"No, no, no," Cassie scrambled to her feet, looking around wildly at the chilly, grey, pre-dawn landscape, at the car parked on the side of the road. "Come on," she ordered, gripping the sword tightly. Ruby followed as she plunged into the sparse strand of trees which lined the roadside.

Desperately, they pushed through to emerge on the edge of a wheat field. In the distance, they could see a farmhouse and outlying buildings and could hear the roar of the nearby motorway. Ruby realised the way back to Erinsmore was gone.

"We have to get back, we have to," insisted Cassie tearfully. "We must warn them about Siminus and give the sword back to Lord Reutghar. It's the only thing that can defeat Lorcan."

"I know," agreed Ruby. "I know, but ... how, Cassie, how?"

"I don't know," whispered her sister bitterly, scalding tears splashing onto her cheeks. Ruby hugged her sister tightly, her chest heaving with unshed tears.

After a while, Cassie's tears ceased. She wiped a grubby hand across her face, silently took Ruby's hand and led her back to the car. Quietly, she opened the boot, taking warm jeans, jumpers, and trainers from their cases. Speedily, the sisters changed into everyday clothes which felt somehow wrong compared to their silk dresses.

Cassie wrapped the sword in her dressing gown, pushed it to the bottom of her case and gently closed the boot. Then they climbed into the back of the car and waited for their parents to awaken and take them home.

It seemed so strange, being home again. Everything was the same. Everything was different. The world had changed, although Ruby suspected it was rather that they had changed. Endlessly discussing it, they went over and over every detail of their adventure.

Always, the same question burned – how did they get back?

Of the two of them, Cassie seemed the most affected by their experiences, at least on the outside. The day after their return, she went to meet Sean and was back within the hour, pale but determined, informing them she'd broken things off with him. Refusing to give a reason, she left the room. Ruby shrugged at her parents' puzzled faces before following Cassie upstairs.

"I felt so mean," sobbed Cassie, lying on her bed with Ruby softly stroking her hair. "He stood there asking me why, and I couldn't tell him. I had to do it, didn't I, Ruby? I mean, it wouldn't have been fair to keep seeing him, not when I ..." Her voice trailed away. Ruby knew she was thinking about Colwyn.

The next day, Cassie asked Mum if she would lend her some money. Mum looked up, coffee cup in hand, frowned and asked why.

"I want to go to the hairdressers and get my hair taken back to its natural colour," explained Cassie.

Mum thumped her cup down and stared, open-mouthed. "Now that," she eventually said, "I don't mind paying for."

So, Cassie went back to her natural, soft brown, and Ruby noticed how she stopped constantly fiddling with it. Instead, she left it loose, although braided strands of it on either side of her face in a parody of Colwyn's hair.

She stopped wearing so much makeup. Ruby thought how much prettier and mature Cassie looked. The permanently sulky expression was gone from her face, to be replaced with a thoughtful one. Ruby overheard their parents comment to each other about how grown-up Cassie was becoming.

That opinion changed, however, when Cassie set the cat amongst the pigeons by calmly informing everyone she wouldn't be going to university. Instead, she'd be studying ancient history and archaeology at the local college, taking on a part-time job to fund her studies and allow her to contribute to her living expenses.

All that day and the next, the argument raged, with Cassie cool and collected in the eye of the storm, unmoving and adamant. She wasn't going away, and that was that.

Eventually, Mum stormed off and Dad sat before Cassie, his eyes concerned. "Give me a reason, Cass, that's all I'm asking. I want to understand." Cassie shook her head, nervously fiddling with her pendant. "What's that?" asked Dad. He lifted the pendant and gazed at the dragon. "Is it new?" he asked. "I've never seen it before, and yet, it looks familiar."

"Someone gave it to me," replied Cassie, looking at Dad intently. He frowned. Ruby watched as he seemed to struggle with long-forgotten memories, memories deeply buried.

"I can't go away from home right now," Cassie said, quietly. Dad's eyes flicked up to her, then back to the pendant. He seemed fascinated by it, nodding distractedly.

"I've thought this through," she continued. "It's the right thing for me to do, Dad. I'm sorry if you're disappointed about uni, but it's my life after all."

"What?" Dad dragged his attention reluctantly away from the pendant, "Oh, yes, all right, I suppose so, if you're sure."

The girls escaped to Cassie's room, leaving Dad to talk to Mum. "It's Dad, isn't it?" Ruby burst out excitedly. He's descended from Mark and Gwnhyfar."

"I thought it must be him and not Mum," nodded Cassie.

"Why?" demanded Ruby.

"Well, think about it, Ruby. I mean, what's our surname?"

"Of course," breathed Ruby. "Markson."

A month passed. Cassie celebrated her eighteenth birthday, astounding their parents by requesting riding lessons as a present. Spending long hours at the stables, she exchanged labour for extra lessons, eager to learn as much as she could about horse care and riding. She persuaded Ruby to have lessons too. Soon, both girls were at the stables frequently, their skill around horses growing rapidly.

When she wasn't at the stables, Cassie was at the gym working out on the weights, Ruby quietly watching as Cassie pushed herself daily, struggling to get fitter and gain muscle.

The eating habits of both girls also changed – much to Mum's surprise. The day after their return from Erinsmore, frazzled from a day of nonstop unpacking and washing, Mum slapped a plate of pizza and fries in front of them, and Ruby recoiled from the bright plastic appearance and unappetizing smell of the food.

"I can't eat this," Cassie stated quietly.

Mum bristled angrily. "Don't get picky with me, Cassie," she warned. "Not after the day I've had."

"It's okay, Mum," reassured Cassie. "I'll get us all something healthy to eat." She rummaged in the fridge, assembling, and competently cooking steaks, potatoes, and salad.

Food tasted different. It was all so bland and dull compared to the simple, delicious meals they'd eaten in Erinsmore. Here, everything tasted the same – grey and boring, colourless, and flavourless – until Cassie took over the shopping and cooking, and eventually, the family's eating patterns changed, with mealtimes becoming something to look forward to.

Mum and Dad seemed to change too. Released from the stresses of cooking, which she'd always hated, Mum had more time for herself. That led, in turn, to a relaxation in her attitude, especially towards Dad.

Things improved when urged on by Cassie, Dad applied for and got the job of manager at the local supermarket. Undeniably a step down from his previous position and salary, it was, nonetheless, a job.

Ruby observed with delight the profound effect it had on his self-confidence and demeanour; to be earning again, to be contributing to his family's needs. As his attitude relaxed, he seemed gentler with Mum, not so ready to criticize and find fault over every tiny detail.

He remained fascinated by Cassie's pendant which she wore all the time, his gaze drawn irresistibly towards it, as ancestral memories bubbled in his subconscious.

The sword, which Ruby couldn't stop calling Excalibur even though Cassie informed her its name should be Caliban – the actual sword in the stone, Excalibur being the sword from the lake – Cassie wrapped in an old blanket and pushed far under her bed. Still beautiful, its radiance seemed diminished in this world, and Ruby wondered if it missed its home.

September came. Ruby went back to school. Cassie started her part-time college courses, sandwiching her studies around working at the stables, gym sessions, and the part-time job she managed to get in a local bookshop. She was rarely home, and Ruby knew Mum and Dad worried she was overdoing it.

One cold, foggy evening in late October, Ruby was travelling home on the bus. Staring morosely through the grimy window at the dirty, rain-drenched streets of the city, she thought how distant Erinsmore now seemed.

Ruby sighed, rubbed at the condensation on the window with her sleeve, peering out as the bus shuddered to a halt at a stop. Abruptly, she straightened, taking a second look as Cassie walked by on the pavement below.

Something about the furtive set of her hunched shoulders, her downcast eyes, had Ruby jumping from her seat, hurrying down the steps and off the bus before it could pull away.

Ruby followed her sister as she left the main road and threaded her way through deserted back streets. Finally, she turned into an alleyway and stopped outside a large, derelict-looking building. Cassie cast a glance up and down the alley, pulled on the beaten metal door, and vanished inside.

Ruby ran down the path, glancing up at the building in confusion. What was this place? Why was Cassie here? A battered sign beside the door read Mick's Gym, but Ruby had the feeling no ladies in leotards would ever frequent it.

Cautiously, she pulled open the heavy door and slipped inside, blinking in the gloomy hall which led to another door opposite. She eased the door open a crack, wide enough for her to peer into the room beyond.

It was a large, dimly lit cavern of a room filled with all manner of weights and other gym equipment, complete with a boxing ring. It was also full of men. Ruby's nose wrinkled as fresh sweat prickled at her nostrils, realising all the men were standing and gaping at Cassie, who was nose-to-nose with a short, muscular man, his expression one of annoyance.

"I've told you, go home, I can't help you," he snapped.

Cassie's jaw lifted. "Please, I can pay; I've got money to pay."

"I don't want your money," he growled. "This is no place for a woman. There are plenty of gyms where you can work out."

"I don't want to work out," persisted Cassie. "I want to learn how to fight."

"Why?" demanded the man. Cassie hesitated, eyes shifting away from his interested glare. Automatically, her hands went to her pendant, pulling it free from her jacket and rubbing it nervously between her fingers.

Ruby saw how the man's eyes were drawn to it, widening slightly, then narrowing with speculation. An expression of almost recognition passed over his face; before his brows crowded together in a frown and he shook his head fiercely.

"Go home," he said firmly, turning away. "I can't help you."

His dismissal acted as a cue for the others who turned back to the equipment, ignoring Cassie who stood, shoulders slumped, in the middle of the room. Finally, she sighed, pulled her bag on her back, and started towards the door.

Ruby scuttled out into the street followed moments later by Cassie, who let the door bang behind her in a flash of temper.

"Cassie?"

Cassie jumped, peering at her sister in the gloom. "Ruby? What the hell are you doing here?"

"I could ask you the same thing," retorted Ruby. "What were you doing in that place? I heard you telling him you wanted to learn how to fight. Cassie, what's going on? Mum and Dad would go ballistic if they knew you were here."

"Well, they're not going to know, are they?" demanded Cassie, then sighed. "Come on, let's go home, it's getting late."

Silently, they walked, Ruby, casting furtive glances at her sister, eventually turning into the park which was a shortcut home. It was deserted due to the miserable weather, and Ruby trailed unhappily after Cassie, bumping into her when she stopped, head snapping up to listen, expression alert.

"What's up?" Ruby asked.

"I thought I heard ..." Cassie began.

Both girls froze, as a familiar howl split the night.

Ruby's heart clutched with fear. "Skraelings?" she gasped in horror. "But ... how...?"

"Never mind," snapped Cassie, grabbing her hand. "Run!"

It was like a black and white horror film, thought Ruby in despair, her heart pounding, her muscles burning with the effort of keeping up with Cassie. The fog rolling over the bare dripping trees, the deserted landscape of the park and somewhere behind them in the dark, terrifyingly close, a maliciously evil creature from another world pursuing them.

She heard it crashing through the undergrowth, gaining on them, always gaining. She imagined its great, snarling jaws, ripping, and tearing at her legs, pulling her down, attacking and killing her without a second thought.

Desperately, the sisters ran, Ruby realised that in the dark and fog they'd stumbled off the main path which led to civilisation and people and help and were now heading across the broad expanse of grass where, in the summer, children came to play football. Glancing back, Cassie saw the loping shape gaining on them, howling as it picked up their scent.

"Run Ruby!" she screamed. "Run!"

They ran, chests heaving with exertion, crashing through the undergrowth, any logical thought of finding the path and the way out fleeing from their terrified minds.

Cassie screamed with fury as she ran headlong into the high railings of the park's perimeter. Turning in despair, she barely had time to push Ruby behind her and snatch up a fallen branch from the ground, before the skraeling crashed through the undergrowth and was upon them.

Yelling with fear and rage, Cassie struck it with all her might. The branch snapped in her hands. The skraeling hit the ground, rolled over, and scrambled back to its feet, growling.

Keeping Ruby behind her, Cassie frantically looked around for another weapon. The skraeling crouched, red eyes gleaming with vicious intent in the glow of a nearby streetlight, jowls pulled back showing rows of jagged, razor-sharp teeth.

The undergrowth rustled. A man leapt out behind the skraeling, sword raised, his massive chest and shoulders bunching with muscles as he ran the skraeling through the heart before it even had time to turn and face this new enemy.

For a split second, there was total silence. He knelt to wipe his sword on the skraeling's body, then looked up, his face clearly seen in the streetlight.

"G-Garth?" stuttered Cassie, in shock.

"My Lady Cassandra," he replied, face tight with concern. "Thank the stars I was in time," he rose to his feet. "I lost your track when you left the path, then heard your screams and came as fast as I could."

"Where did you come from?" asked Ruby.

"Mick alerted me to your presence. I was following you when the skraeling picked up your scent and began its pursuit."

"Mick?" Cassie queried. "You mean the guy from the gym? You know him?"

"He is a friend and by way of being my employer."

Cassie shook her head in confusion. "I don't understand. How did you meet him? Is that where you've been since we all crossed over three months ago?"

"Three months ago? How I wish that were so, my Lady. Nay, I have been waiting for some sign of you these last two years."

"Two years?" squeaked Ruby. "That's impossible, it's only been three months for us. How can you have been here so long, and where did the skraeling come from?"

"I am uncertain," began Garth with a frown, surveying the crumpled body at his feet. "I believe it to be the skraeling that crossed over with us."

"So, why did we all cross into separate times?" asked Ruby, in confusion.

"I do not know," replied Garth. "It is a question, one amongst many, to put to the Lady upon our return."

"You know how to return?" began Cassie, eagerly. "How? How do we do it?"

"Nay, my Lady," Garth looked perplexed. "I assumed you to have that knowledge, as it was your magic which removed us from the evil intent of that most false mage."

"No," responded Cassie bitterly. "We don't know how to return either. If it was because of me we crossed, I don't know how I did it or how to do it again."

Garth's face darkened, and then he shrugged as if pushing the problem to one side to be dealt with later. Holding out a hand over the skraeling, he mumbled a few words. Its body shimmered, then vanished.

"How did you do that?" gasped Ruby.

Garth glanced up, surprised. "Tis only a basic vanishing spell, my Lady," he explained. "Even one as limited in the ability as I can manage it. Come," he sheathed his sword. "I will take you to a place where we may talk privately."

On shaking legs, they followed him across the park down the dark and deserted back streets until they reached the gym. Entering through a side door, they found Mick sitting in an office adding up a cashbook, whilst a football game played silently on a muted TV.

"Oh good," he said, looking up at their entry, bulldog-like face relaxing into relieved creases. "You found them."

"Aye," confirmed Garth, "May we make use of the office? We have much to discuss."

"Make yourselves at home," ordered Mick, with an expansive wave of his hands. Garth ushered them next door where a battered leather sofa took up most of the space, along with a scratched wooden desk, and a tall cabinet displaying various trophies and medals. Dazed, the girls sank onto the sofa staring at Garth in bewilderment.

"I arrived almost two years ago," he began, "on a dark and stormy night. At first, I was confused, unsure where I was and what had happened, then realised Lady Cassandra must have used powerful magic to remove us from the reach of Siminus." Garth paused, face darkening with anger.

"I still struggle to comprehend such treachery," he continued. "And I am deeply concerned as to how much damage he has caused in our absence."

"You and me both," said Cassie soberly.

Garth nodded. "To return to my tale ... attempting to gain my bearings, I heard raised voices. Stealthily, I advanced, unsure of friend or foe in this strange world. I saw a man, surrounded by many, armed with stout cudgels and daggers. It was clear these men intended to kill him. It was plain this lone man, strong as he looked, was vastly outnumbered. The dishonourable situation angered me, so I drew my sword and advanced to defend him. We fought, side by side. By the time we had finished not one remained standing."

"Do you mean you killed them all?" gasped Ruby, appalled.

"Nay, my Lady," Garth shook his head. "Most ran away. But I will cut a long tale down to size. The man I rescued was Mick.

For reasons I do not fully understand, he had angered a colleague who dispatched those cowards to dispose of him. He was most grateful when I foiled their plans. Upon learning I was newly arrived and alone, he graciously offered me a room in his home and employment as his bodyguard. I have been here ever since, and we have become true friends."

"Does he know?" Cassie asked seriously.

"My Lady?"

"Does he know where you've come from? Does he know about Erinsmore?"

"I have told him only what I had to, my Lady. Namely, I have travelled a great distance and cannot return to my homeland. I believe he suspects a great deal more, indeed, sometimes he struggles to remember, and I wonder if his ancestor was amongst those brave warriors who came to our world."

"It's possible, I suppose," Cassie nodded.

"Then, tonight," continued Garth. "He came to me in great excitement, told me of your visit and of a pendant which had stirred long-buried memories. I set out to follow you, arriving in time to dispatch the skraeling."

"So, what do we do now?" Cassie mused.

Garth drew himself up. "My last orders were to protect and serve you, and that is what I intend to do, Lady Cassandra."

Cassie stared at him, a speculative gleam entering her eyes. "There is one thing you can do for me, Garth."

"Anything, my Lady."

"I want you to teach me."

"Teach you, my Lady? Teach you what?"

"Everything. How to swordfight, how to use a bow, how to defend myself."

"Such skills are not seemly or necessary for a lady."

"I must learn. You must teach me," insisted Cassie hotly.

"My Lady?"

"Because we're going back," she stated.

"How can you be so sure?" asked Ruby.

"We have to go back," continued Cassie. "We have to go back to fulfil the prophecy, so I have to be ready." Her chin lifted. She looked directly at Garth with a proud, almost regal expression. "You have to help me, Garth, help me to become a warrior maid."

And finally, reluctantly, he agreed.

Chapter Twelve

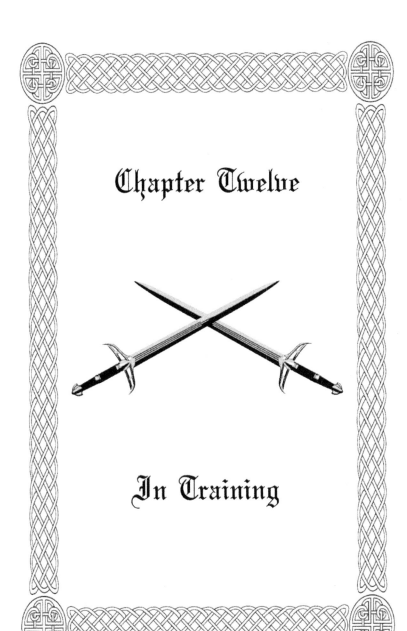

In Training

he arrival of Garth in their lives boosted the girls' flagging spirits, and Ruby began to believe they would return to Erinsmore. Cassie, she realised, had always had faith they would go back, pinning her hopes on the prophecy. Ruby now understood this was why she'd embarked on a programme of self-improvement. She was pushing herself to become the warrior maid the prophecy spoke of.

After his initial misgivings about the unseemliness of a woman warrior, and in the face of her rigid determination to learn, Garth put aside his reluctance to teach Cassie and threw himself whole-heartedly into devising an intense training programme.

Cassie began spending as much time with Garth as she could. When she headed out of the house, bag in hand, their parents thought she was going to the gym; Ruby knew she was off for another training session with him.

Garth pushed her hard, very hard. For the first two months, much to Cassie's disgust, he wouldn't let her even touch a weapon. Instead, he concentrated on her fitness, agility, and strength, forcing her to her limits and beyond.

One evening Cassie limped home, face chalk white with pain. A worried Ruby ran a hot bath, borrowing Mum's aromatherapy oil, and helped her to undress, gasping with horror at the vivid bruises which covered her from head to toe.

"Cass, what on earth have you been doing?"

"We started hand-to-hand combat," Cassie muttered through clenched teeth, easing carefully into the water, wincing at its heat.

"I would have thought Garth would have gone easy on you," stated Ruby, hotly, "considering it was your first time."

"He did," Cassie murmured.

Christmas came. Garth shook his head in wonder at the sheer insanity of a world that squandered its wealth on a mere day, gorging itself into a bloated stupor. Although Ruby noticed his eyes were constantly drawn to the bright decorations and twinkling Christmas trees to be seen in every house, his face creased into a smile at the sound of carols being sung in the cathedral.

In January, Garth finally conceded that Cassie was ready to train with weapons, and Ruby was present at her first lesson in sword fighting. It was Saturday so the girls made excuses they were going to the cinema, then quickly made their way to the large warehouse owned by Mick, which Garth used for Cassie's training.

Garth had acquired wooden practice swords from somewhere, and he proceeded to spend over an hour teaching Cassie the correct way to hold it, how to balance herself, and how to compensate for the weight of the sword in her hand.

Cassie listened intently, amber eyes seriously absorbing every scrap of information. Watching, Ruby reflected how Cassie had changed in the last few months. Not just physically, though she marvelled her parents hadn't commented on her lean and toned physique, and the angled planes of a woman's face completely stripped of a teenager's softness.

No, the changes were more than skin deep. Cassie now moved with tense, coiled alertness. Rather the way Garth and Colwyn did, Ruby realised, as if always on the brink of action. Her newly acquired strength and purpose gave her poise and confidence far beyond her eighteen years.

Ruby knew several boys at college had asked her out. Cassie had rejected them all, her energies directed solely into her training with Garth. Strangely, this single-minded aloofness seemed to add to her appeal, increasing her mysterious allure.

Ruby wondered if the reason she had remained stubbornly single since their return was because of Colwyn. Cassie never mentioned his name, and Ruby was afraid to in case she awakened painful memories.

So now Ruby watched as Cassie begged Garth to let her try to take him on in a sword fight. She winced as Cassie crashed heavily to the ground, Garth's sword at her throat.

"I wasn't ready," complained Cassie crossly, smacking away his sword and scrambling to her feet, bending to retrieve her sword which he'd casually flicked out of her hand.

"Do you think the Gilmesh will wait until you have finished combing your hair, my Lady?" demanded Garth tartly.

"No," she conceded reluctantly, and so the lesson went on. Months passed.

Although Garth was not one to praise, Ruby knew he was stunned at how quickly Cassie learnt. It was as if the skills and knowledge were already there, buried deep within her, Garth's tuition merely bringing them to the surface.

Sometimes, Mick would watch, face crinkling into admiring lines as he observed them fight, bodies glistening with sweat, muscles smoothly flowing as they fought around the large warehouse. Garth always beat Cassie, but Ruby noticed the bouts lasted longer each session as if he had to work harder to win.

"It's amazing," Mick murmured. "The way they fight, it's like something out of the knights of the round table, I've never seen anything like it before, and yet ..." he stopped, his big beefy hand flexing as if remembering the feel of a sword.

Alongside sword training, Cassie was still working hard on unarmed combat and archery. Not such a natural with a bow as she was with a sword, Cassie struggled to learn, and Ruby knew it annoyed her when Garth told her to try harder.

Garth also decided Ruby should learn archery, setting up targets in the warehouse one rainy afternoon, Cassie watched with interest, relieved for once the pressure wasn't on her.

Cautiously, Ruby picked up the bow and something deep within her sighed. Barely needing Garth's instructions on how to position herself or draw the bowstring, Ruby fixed her attention on the target, already seeing in her mind the arrow speeding through the air and burying itself in the bullseye.

Lightly, she drew back the string, then stared in delighted surprise as the arrow landed in the centre of the target with a resounding thwack.

"Beginner's luck," scoffed Cassie.

Garth, brow creasing thoughtfully, retrieved the arrow, making her try again and again until it was clear that whatever it was, it wasn't beginner's luck.

"It's almost as if I think the arrow into the target," Ruby tried to explain.

"Aye," Garth slowly nodded in agreement. "I have heard of such things before. Those within whom the ability is strong are said to be particularly skilled at archery."

As well as physical skills, Garth taught Cassie the hand language used between the fighting men of Erinsmore, explaining how sometimes the ability to communicate silently with each other was a vital necessity.

He tutored her in battle strategies and manoeuvres, once again quietly amazed at Cassie's intuitive grasp, her quickness at summing up a situation, thinking of a solution, and immediately making plans to implement it. He also taught both the dances of Erinsmore, his big burly body somehow fluidic and graceful as he patiently led them through the beautiful steps.

The weeks sped past. Winter gave way to Spring, then to the warmer days of May. Ruby turned fifteen and Garth moved their training outdoors. Mick, an endlessly resourceful sort, arranged for them to use a patch of wasteland to practice and further improve their archery skills, and for Garth to instruct Cassie in sword fighting over rough terrain.

One day, Cassie received a text from Mick stating Garth wished to see them immediately at the warehouse. Concerned, they made excuses and hurried there, using their keys to let themselves in. Finding no sign of Garth, they wandered about its vast interior, echoes calling back as they shouted his name.

"Where do you think he is?" asked Ruby.

"Don't know," Cassie shrugged. "Perhaps he forgot something and had to go back."

"Look," exclaimed Ruby. They'd reached the large open space in the middle of the warehouse. There, lying across a packing crate, was Garth's sword. Puzzled, Cassie picked it up and her face lightened.

"Perhaps he's going to finally let me fight with a real sword," she exclaimed, watching the way the light glinted off the blade.

Ruby stepped back, half admiring, half alarmed, at the sight of her sister with the wickedly efficient-looking sword in her hands.

A low growl from behind made her freeze in terror.

"Cassie," she hissed. Cassie looked up, startled at the panic in her voice. "We're not alone," Ruby gulped.

"What?" began Cassie, confused. Horror flashed onto her face. "Duck!" she screamed.

Instinctively, Ruby hit the deck and air rushed through her hair as a skraeling leapt over her, massive, clawed feet thumping down mere inches from where she lay. With a primal yell, Cassie charged at the beast, sword seeming almost an extension of her arm. Snarling, the beast circled, red eyes glowing with evil malevolence.

Cassie tensed, her eyes never leaving it, slowly manoeuvring round to place herself between it and her sister.

"I'm going to draw it away," she murmured. "When I shout run, I want you to run for the door as fast as you can. Here," she fumbled in her back pocket, tossing her phone to Ruby. "Call Mick. Find out where the hell Garth is and tell him ..." she paused and swallowed. "Tell him I need help."

"Cassie ..." began Ruby, staring in mesmerized horror into the beast's eyes. "I can't leave you."

"You have to," ordered Cassie. She lunged at the skraeling, missing it by inches. Angrily it leapt at her, howling in rage as Cassie brought her sword up and nicked it on the foreleg.

"Run!" yelled Cassie.

Ruby scrambled to her feet and ran, feeling the worst sort of coward but not knowing what else to do, hearing howls and shouts behind her as Cassie fought for her life.

Out of the corner of her eye, Ruby saw the stairs which led up to the office and skidded to a halt. Of course! Garth kept their archery equipment locked in a cupboard up there – Ruby's hands closed over the keys in her hand – a cupboard to which she had the key.

Taking the steps two at a time, Ruby rushed up into the office. Hands shaking, she fumbled with the key, finally getting the cupboard open and pulling out her bow and quiver.

She remembered Colwyn shooting arrow after arrow at the pack of skraelings and how they didn't seem to have much effect. She prayed against one skraeling, if she shot enough arrows into it, it'd be enough to slow it down, perhaps giving Cassie a chance.

Feet clanging on the metal staircase, Ruby charged downstairs, bow in hand, arrow nocked and ready. Following the sound of fighting, she ran down the aisles, heart thudding at the fierce growling and baying. Turning a corner, she saw Cassie ahead of her, still alive and unharmed, her steps nimble and precise as she fought the skraeling.

Positioning herself, Ruby tried to get the dodging, weaving skraeling in her sights. Taking a deep breath, she imagined the arrow penetrating its shaggy pelt and drew back the string.

A muscular hand clamped over her mouth, dragging her behind the stack. Ruby's eyes bulged with shock as Garth set her back on her feet and placed a large finger on his lips.

"What are you doing?" she hissed. "We have to help Cassie."

"Lady Cassandra is in no danger," he assured her, his normally dark eyes pulsing a steady blue.

"That skraeling," Ruby began slowly. "It's not real, is it?"

"It is real enough," he said wryly. "And the Lady Cassandra has no doubt she is fighting an actual skraeling."

Cautiously, Ruby peered around the corner, watching in admiration as Cassie ducked and leapt, the sword moving so fast in her hand it appeared a blur. Time and again the skraeling attacked and Cassie drove it back, even managing to injure the beast which howled with anger when her sword bit into its flesh.

Finally, Cassie staggered back and the skraeling leapt. Swiftly, Cassie's sword flew up and she lunged at the creature's exposed belly with all her strength, the sword burying itself up to the hilt. The skraeling crashed to the ground. Her breathing loud in the sudden stillness, Cassie pulled the sword from the beast's body and wiped the blade on its fur. Then she stood, looking at it in silence.

Garth stepped out, followed by Ruby. Cassie swung to face them, sword springing into readiness until she saw who it was and relaxed.

"Garth," she exclaimed. "Another skraeling crossed, perhaps others have too. We must warn people..."

Garth shook his head and Cassie stopped, confused.

"You fought well," he said, Cassie flushed with pleasure. "It is your first victory over an enemy and for a first attempt you did very well. Yet you let the fight go on so long you risked becoming weary. The trick to fighting skraelings is to despatch them quickly. They usually fight in packs. A warrior needs to conserve his strength to face many."

Cassie nodded thoughtfully, then looked at the skraeling's body and back at Garth.

"Is that ..." the frown deepened. "Is that a real skraeling?"

"As I told Lady Ruby," Garth waved a hand and the body vanished, "it was real enough. More importantly, you believed it was real."

"Ruby?" Cassie noticed her presence. "I thought I told you to get out," she snapped.

"Lady Ruby also showed great courage," said Garth, indicating Ruby's bow. "Instead of leaving her sister to face an enemy alone, she armed herself and came back to assist you."

"Oh," mumbled Cassie, sheepishly. "Thanks."

After that, Garth conjured up many enemies for Cassie to practice against – wild boars, bears, fierce multi-fanged tigers, and of course, skraelings. Sometimes Cassie would win, and her eyes would blaze with triumph. Sometimes she lost, and Garth would sigh, go through the fight step by step, patiently explaining where she'd gone wrong and how she could have fought better.

Gradually, Cassie's abilities developed until even Garth seemed quietly impressed with her. Mick's eyes grew round with admiration on the day Cassie fought Garth to a standstill. Their swords clashing, he gave no quarter but was unable to defeat her.

May slipped into June. It was almost an entire year since Erinsmore. Ruby feared they'd never return. She was worried. Not just what would be happening in the land she had grown to love in the brief time they'd been there, but also about Garth.

He had been an exile in their world for almost three years. Ruby knew how much he missed his home, how out of place he was in theirs, and how deeply concerned he was that Siminus, Lord Reutghar's most trusted advisor, was a traitor working for Lorcan and that they'd been whisked away before having a chance to warn anyone.

There was also Excalibur. In the year since its removal from Erinsmore, its brilliance had faded to a dull gleam. Ruby knew that it too needed to return home.

Getting ready for bed that night, Ruby was in a strangely reflective mood, her spirits low as she thought about Erinsmore and wondered if they'd ever return. A great longing welled up inside as she slipped easily into a deep sleep...

... and straight into a dream. Wandering around the beautiful peaceful landscape, Ruby smiled with pleasure as the warm sun caressed her cheeks, heard the breeze whisper through the saplings, and knew herself to be in the World Between Worlds.

"Ruby."

She turned. Lady Gwnhyfar was there, long auburn hair rippling in the breeze, her green eyes concerned, her beautiful face grave.

"Ruby," she said again.

"My Lady," Ruby dipped instinctively into a curtsey.

"There is no time," Gwnhyfar said. "You must return immediately."

"How, my Lady?" cried Ruby. "We badly want to go back, but don't know how."

"You must journey to where it all began on the shortest night, bring the sacred sword, and be ready at midnight."

"Where?" began Ruby stupidly. "I don't understand, where what all began?"

Gwnhyfar turned as a black cloud of foulness rolled across the land, engulfing the trees, and blotting out the sun.

"Gwnhyfar ..." oozed the cold voice of Lorcan.

"Leave this place," ordered Gwnhyfar, her voice as steel. "You are forbidden to enter its sacred domains."

"There is no law against me entering a child's dreams," he retorted. "And if that child has images of the World Between Worlds placed into her dreams, well then, am I to blame for that? I must confess I am surprised at such blatant interference, my Lady, I thought it was strictly forbidden."

"Ruby," Gwnhyfar placed a hand upon Ruby's cheek. "You must banish this monster back to the shadows where he belongs. Remember what I have told you, act upon it, and tell the others."

"What nonsense have you been filling the child's head with?" demanded Lorcan silkily. "Have you told her how you should have been mine?"

"I would never have been yours," retorted Gwnhyfar, fire flashing in her eyes. "Even if I had not married my Lord, I would still never have been yours. I had been betrothed to Arturius since childhood. Our marriage would have united the houses."

"And after I had killed him and destroyed the house of the dragon lords forever, you would have become my queen, ruling over all the worlds by my side."

"Never!" snapped Gwnhyfar. "I would rather have died first."

"It is of no consequence to me now," Lorcan's voice mocked. "You are long dead and gone, my Lady, you, and your precious

Lord. Even the mighty Arturius is barely remembered, a myth, a childish fairy-tale, whereas I ..." Tension swirled through the air and Gwnhyfar's hair whipped around her face.

"Whereas I am alive and growing in strength each day," he continued. "We shall discover, Gwnhyfar, whether your descendant shares your sentiments; or whether she is more ... shall we say, sensible, of the opportunity being offered her?"

Gwnhyfar's flawless brow creased in confusion, then her eyes widened, and she turned to Ruby in outraged despair.

"You must wake up, Ruby," she ordered. "Tis the only way to stop him. Wake up now and remember all I have told you. Wake up, Ruby!"

Ruby squeezed her eyes tightly shut, trying to obey the Lady's orders. She heard Lorcan's coolly amused chuckle and felt the hot fetid tide of darkness lap at her feet.

"Ruby!"

Opening her eyes at Lady Gwnhyfar's cry, she watched in horror as she was sucked into the black whirling vortex, her hair streaming like a flaming pennant.

"Remember!" The Lady ordered, her eyes pulsed blue, and she vanished. Lorcan howled in anger, his attention turned to Ruby, and she backed fearfully away from him.

"No!" she shouted. "Wake up, Ruby!" she ordered herself. "Wake up!" She stumbled in the darkness, and something grabbed her arms. Seizing her, it shook her like a rag doll, and she twisted, hanging uselessly in its grasp.

"Ruby!"

"No, let me go, no!"

"It's okay, Ruby, it was a dream, you're awake now."

Cautiously, Ruby opened her eyes to the concerned gaze of her sister who sat on her bed in her nightshirt, gripping her arms, her expression managing to be both sleepy and anxious at the same time.

"Cassie? What ... what happened?"

"You tell me," retorted Cassie, with a grin. "You woke me up, you were shouting so loudly. Luckily, Mum and Dad aren't home yet, otherwise, they'd be in here too."

"Shouting?" stammered Ruby, heart jumping around her rib cage with shock. "What was I shouting?"

"Something about remembering, then you started shrieking at yourself to wake up and yelling no, no, no, over and over."

"I had a dream," Ruby began slowly, looking up at Cassie with growing excitement. "No, it wasn't a dream, I was there. I really did speak to her."

"Where? Who?" demanded Cassie, "Ruby, you're not making any sense."

"The World Between Worlds," replied Ruby. "I was there, I saw Lady Gwnhyfar, she spoke to me."

"What did she say?" asked Cassie, suddenly alert.

"She told me there wasn't much time, told me how to do it."

"Do what?"

"Get back to Erinsmore. She told me what we must do."

As soon as it was light, the girls sneaked out and hurried to the gym to find Garth. A sleepy and baffled Mick let them in, directing them to a courtyard at the back of the building where Garth was busy sharpening his sword.

He looked up, surprised, as the sisters rushed at him, both talking at once. He frowned, motioning them to sit at the battered plastic table, carefully re-sheathing his sword before settling gingerly into a rickety, plastic chair.

"Lady Ruby, please tell me exactly what happened. Leave out no detail, however small or inconsequential you feel it to be." His dark eyes grew intense as Ruby complied, finishing her tale with how she'd woken in her bed.

"Return to where it all began, on the shortest night," he mused, rubbing his chin in bewilderment. "I fear it makes no sense to me. Have you any thoughts as to what this Lady Gwnhyfar meant?"

"I'm not sure," began Ruby, then realised what he'd said and stared at him in surprise. "Don't you know who Gwnhyfar is, Garth?"

"In faith, I am afraid not, my Lady. I do remember Siminus saying her blood ran through your veins and realised from his words she was a lady of royal birth, yet I had never heard her name before that day."

"That's strange," said Ruby, in surprise. "If we remember her in this world, even if only through myths and stories, surely she should still be remembered in Erinsmore?"

"Never mind about that now," interrupted Cassie, impatiently. "We must work out what it means. If there's any chance of going back, we've got to try."

"I did wonder," began Ruby slowly, "If she meant Tintagel. After all, that's where I bought the prophecy stone. I suppose it's where it all began for us."

"That's right," Cassie agreed in excitement. "And it's in the West Country where Mark was ruler, and all the Arthurian legends are strongest there."

"I pray you, my Ladies, what is this Tintagel?"

"It's a castle, well a ruin, in a place called Cornwall," Ruby explained. "It's where King Mark ruled, where he and Gwnhyfar lived."

"An ancient site with strong connections to Erinsmore," Garth mused. "In faith, it makes sense a crossing would be more likely to occur in such a place. But what did the Lady mean by the shortest night?"

"Oh," exclaimed Cassie. "Of course, the 21st of June, the Summer solstice, the shortest night. It's also an important date in the Pagan calendar. That must be it. The 21st, that's next Thursday." They stared at each other in rising excitement.

"Just think," said Ruby eagerly. "By this time next week, we could be back in Erinsmore. We've been gone so long it feels almost like it was a dream."

"Where is this Cornwall you speak of my Ladies?" asked Garth. "How many days journey will it take to reach it?"

"It's only about five hours by car," replied Cassie thoughtfully. "I suppose we'll have to try and go by train..."

"No, you won't," a voice from the door said. It was Mick, his rumpled face serious. "No, you won't," he said again. "I'll drive you down. Trains are a nightmare, never on time, never take you where you want to go, so I'll take you."

For the next five days, Ruby swung between frenzied excitement and nerve-paralysing fear at the danger they would be facing on their return. She also worried about their parents.

She watched them going about their normal lives, unsuspecting that their daughters were planning on going to a fantastical other world, a world where they could very easily be killed.

The problem of keeping their parents ignorant of their absence was solved by Cassie, who had the brainwave of booking for them to go for dinner and a night's stay in a hotel. An early wedding anniversary gift, she airily announced to their stunned surprise.

Thursday morning.

The girls left, apparently heading for school and college, but rushing straight to the gym where Garth and Mick were waiting. Excalibur had been smuggled out of the house earlier in the week. Carefully, Cassie picked it up and placed it in the boot of Mick's Mercedes, along with their bows and quivers of arrows, and large holdalls containing clothes Mick had acquired for them, clothes more suitable for Erinsmore.

As they settled themselves comfortably in the car, Ruby wondered at Mick's unquestioning acceptance of all the strange requests Garth had made of him. Refusing to take any payment, his eyes constantly returned to the dragon pendant.

Mick was a fast, competent driver, and his powerful car seemed to eat the miles. Cassie and Ruby exchanged amused looks as Garth visibly winced at the speed they were going, his body tense and stiff, large hands clenched tightly on his knees.

By six, they were sitting in a pub outside Tintagel, enjoying a huge meal, Garth, and the sisters were aware this could be the last hot food they might have for some time. Supplies were packed into one of the holdalls, still Ruby followed Cassie's lead, ordering steak and chips with all the trimmings, piling on ketchup with the zeal of a condemned man eating his last meal.

They stayed in the pub until closing time, drawing curious glances from bar staff and customers alike. Ruby realised what an odd picture they must make. Mick, with his East London accent and flash bling; Garth, muscles bulging even through the conservative shirt and jeans he was wearing; and Cassie, her lithe body, beautiful face, and hair hanging down her back in a long, glossy plait. Ruby thought with a wry grin how she was probably the most normal looking one of them all.

When they went out to the car, night had completely fallen. They drove silently to the village. Ruby directed them to the run-down shop where she had first seen the stone, where it had all begun.

Mick brought the holdalls in from the car and the girls went into the back room to change. Ruby pulled on the long, green, woollen dress, smoothing it over her hips, feeling strangely more at home in it than in her normal jeans.

Fastening a cloak at the neck, she watched Cassie pull on a rough cotton shirt, leather jerkin and leather trousers, tucking them into long sturdy boots, swinging a cloak identical to Ruby's around her shoulders. Both girls slung quivers over their shoulders, slotting bows into carrying positions on their backs. Cassie also buckled on a sword belt, sword sitting low on her hip.

Leaving the room, they found Garth had changed into the clothes he'd been wearing the first time they'd met him, that long-ago day in Erinsmore. He looked comfortable, at ease, and Ruby realised he had never looked right in ordinary clothes.

Mick's jaw dropped as they appeared. His gaze swung from one to the other of them, but said nothing, merely handing them the leather saddle bags, bulging with essential supplies.

"Right," said Cassie. "Where do we go now, Ruby?"

"I'm not sure," Ruby shook her head.

"Well," replied Cassie, picking up Excalibur. "You'd better get sure quickly, it's almost midnight and …oh …!" Her voice trailed away in a soft gasp.

They looked.

They saw.

Excalibur.

Its renewed radiance blazed, illuminating every corner of the ramshackle building. Its jewelled hilt glowed like truth, its finely-honed blade flashing fire as Cassie held it aloft, her stunned face bathed in its glory.

"What is it?" gasped Mick, in awe. Glancing at him, Ruby half expected him to fall to his knees in homage.

"Excalibur," she unthinkingly replied. Mick's eyes nearly bugged out of their sockets.

"This way," said Cassie, and walked from the room, the others hurrying after her.

"How do you know?" gasped Ruby.

"I don't," Cassie shook her head in wonder. "It's the sword that's leading me."

Out onto the headland, they went, into the still, eerily silent night. The only sound was the crashing of the sea on the rocks far below, and the swishing of their booted feet as they followed Cassie and the glorious light that was the sword.

She stopped.

"Over there," she murmured, pointing the sword to a place a few yards ahead, to a patch of darkness which seemed to shimmer and bend away from their gaze.

"Fight well and live long my friend." Garth turned to Mick and clasped his wrist. "There are no words to express my gratitude, no way to repay the debt I owe you."

"You saved my life," retorted Mick. "I'd say that's repayment enough." He turned to the girls. "Take care of yourselves, and of him too," he jerked his head in Garth's direction.

Ruby heard the emotion behind his words and threw her arms around him, surprising him with a firm hug.

"Goodbye Mick," she murmured. "Thanks for everything."

"Yes, thank you, Mick," Cassie echoed.

Mick looked at Cassie, tall and regal in the moonlight, Excalibur casting a golden light onto her dragon pendant which reflected its radiance. Then, he abruptly knelt on one knee, his head bent.

"Take care, my Lady," he said and scrambled awkwardly back to his feet. "You'd better go, it's only a few seconds to midnight."

They walked away from him, a small group of three, as a cloud sailed across the moon plunging the headland into total darkness. When the moon reappeared from behind its screen seconds later, once again flooding the land with its cold light, they'd gone.

Mick started, gazing wildly around the deserted cliff top, then a smile spread across his broad face, and he shook his head in wonder.

"Fight well and live long my friends," he murmured. "Fight well and live long."

Chapter Thirteen

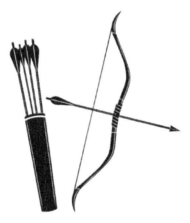

Return to
the Midnight Land

uby pulled the hood of her cloak over her head and hunched deeper into its protective folds, glancing at Cassie who leant against a tree, as still as a statue, staring at the village nestled snugly in the valley below.

Garth had gone to that village three hours ago, ordering them to wait. Ruby shifted uncomfortably from foot to foot, hoping he'd hurry up and come back, chafing her cold hands together and wishing they'd thought to bring gloves.

It had been late summer when they'd left Erinsmore, now it was winter. The cold bit achingly into her cheeks and Ruby could taste the chilly metallic threat of snow. Precisely how long had elapsed during the year they'd been in their world they had no way of knowing. It was winter. Of which year was another matter.

Cassie stirred, becoming alert as a man on horseback leading two more horses left the outlying perimeter of the village and began to climb towards them. Recognising Garth, Cassie busied herself gathering the saddle bags, looking up as he rode amongst the trees and dismounted.

"Well?" she asked.

"Tis the village of Dragonsforge which lays a few hours journey from Dragonswell. We shall be there before nightfall."

"And the date? How long were we gone?"

"Just over three moons, my Lady. The villagers were suspicious and scared. The battle against Lorcan goes badly. Skraelings and Gilmesh have been attacking villages close by and they fear they will be next."

"Did they say anything of Lord Reutghar and … Colwyn?" Cassie's voice shook slightly on his name and Ruby glanced at her in concern, but Cassie's face was still and impassive.

"They both live, although there have been many casualties."

Cassie nodded, running her eyes appraisingly over the horses. One of the reasons Garth had gone to the village, aside from gathering information, had been to acquire mounts for them all using Cassie's pendant as a promise to pay from the crown.

"Will they do?" she asked, patting the nearest horse, and running a hand over its flank.

"Aye, my Lady, they'll do for our purposes. In faith, I did not have much choice." Swiftly, he fastened saddle bags onto the animals' backs, patiently waiting as the girls climbed onto a horse each, helping them to adjust stirrups until they were both comfortably mounted. He then swung into his saddle with enviably fluid ease, turned his horse to face north, and led them away through the trees.

Adjusting herself comfortably into her horse's stride, Ruby silently thanked Cassie for insisting she learn to ride. She steeled herself for hours in the saddle, her heart missing a beat with excitement at how surprised everyone would be to see them. She glanced at Excalibur strapped securely to Cassie's saddle. Surely, now it was back in Erinsmore soon to be reunited with its rightful owner, things would start going better and Lorcan would be defeated.

They rode silently for an hour, the cold increasing until Ruby could feel it nipping through her boots. Her hands rested thankfully on the warmth of the horse's withers, and she was unsurprised when a snowflake danced and twirled its way out of the sky, twisting and spinning in the breeze until it finally settled on her thigh.

Garth glanced up, and frowned at the white sky, increasing the pace until they were trotting. He stopped; his hand held up. Cassie and Ruby pulled their horses sharply to a halt. Ruby opened her mouth to speak then noticed the hand talk, fast and furious, flashing between Garth and Cassie and closed it again, wondering what was wrong.

Garth dismounted and vanished through the trees before them. Cassie glanced at Ruby, placed her fingers to her lips, cupped her hand around her ear, and pointed in the direction Garth had gone. Ruby understood he'd heard something, had gone to check it out, and they were to remain silent.

Moments later Garth was back, his face tight with concern. His hands flew as he communicated his findings to Cassie. Ruby watched Cassie's face pale, her hands falter, and even without understanding them knew her sister was scared.

Obeying Garth's unspoken command to dismount, both sisters shakily climbed down, following Garth's lead as he loosely tethered his horse to a nearby tree and silently led the way through the trees.

Following, watching where her feet trod, scared of making noise, Ruby moved as soundlessly as she could. Ducking behind a row of scrubby bushes, she wiggled after Garth and Cassie as they eased their way through the undergrowth.

On the other side of the bushes, the land fell sharply away to a ravine some fifty feet below. Ruby watched as a group of about twenty or so soldiers went busily about their tasks, watering horses at a small spring and sharing out food.

Ruby's breath caught with relief as the familiar tall figure of Lord Darius strode into the clearing, talking to a man by his side. She wondered why Garth had looked so worried at the sight of his old friends.

Beside her, Cassie stiffened. Ruby followed her sister's gaze to the opposite side of the ravine. There, the land was lower but still considerably higher than the soldiers so she could see what the men below could not.

Things. Strange, grey, vaguely human-shaped things. Ruby realised, with an instinctive clutch of fear that they must be the Gilmesh. Dozens of them concealed amongst the rocks and trees overlooking the soldiers, unseen and waiting. Ruby knew the men below wouldn't stand a chance against such an ambush.

Silently, Garth led them from the undergrowth and began to make his way further along the lip of the ravine, always keeping undercover. Cassie laid a hand on Garth's arm, her hands moving excitedly. His face cleared and he nodded, looking at Cassie in respect. Cassie turned to Ruby and lifted Ruby's skirt, ripping at the long petticoat underneath.

Confused, Ruby grabbed at Cassie's shoulders for balance, wondering if she'd lost her mind. Cassie handed a strip of fabric to Garth who tore it into even smaller strips, pulled his quiver from his back and wound each strip around an arrowhead. Cassie pulled her quiver off and did the same, indicating silently to Ruby to copy. Still puzzled, Ruby did as she was ordered.

"To arms!"

The cry went up from the ravine. Ruby knew the Gilmesh had attacked. Running after Cassie as she plunged through the undergrowth behind Garth, her heart knocked against her ribcage with terror at the thought.

Quickly, Cassie and Garth pulled their bows from their backs and strung them. Ruby did the same, her gaze irresistibly drawn to where Gilmesh were leaping over the edge of the ravine. Their long skeletal arms wielded swords of dull black, and tattered remnants of clothing fluttered giving them the appearance of macabre scarecrows.

Bravely, Darius and his men defended themselves, but Ruby knew they were hopelessly outnumbered. It was only a matter of time before they were completely overwhelmed.

Cassie nocked an arrow. Garth waved a hand over its cloth-bound head which burst into flames. Taking careful aim, Cassie shot the flaming arrow. It flew true, piercing a Gilmesh in the back as it raised its sword to run a soldier through.

The Gilmesh shrieked, a spine-chilling sound which made gooseflesh jump all over Ruby's body, and then it burst into flames, a white-hot column of fire which flared up briefly, before falling to the ravine floor in a pile of grey ash.

Now Ruby understood why her petticoat had been sacrificed but had no time for more than an admiring glance at Cassie before Garth was waving a hand over her arrowhead. Ruby stepped up to the ravine's edge and selected her target.

Arrow after arrow made its way into the Gilmesh. Still more poured over the ravine until finally there were no more arrows left. Throwing down their bows, Garth and Cassie unsheathed their swords. Ruby saw Cassie's quick, nervous swallow before she was plunging down the hillside behind Garth. Clutching her hands helplessly, Ruby watched in agonised worry as her sister charged headlong into her first real battle.

Gripping her sword, Cassie desperately tried to remember everything Garth had taught her. Then they were upon the enemy and there was no time for anything but trying to stay alive.

Slash and stab, leap, and duck, the Gilmesh swords were long and deadly, their dull black surfaces reflecting no light as they rose against the men of Erinsmore. But they were unwieldy, and Cassie realised her speed and agility could be used as a weapon.

Her confidence grew. She began to attack instead of defending, remembering what Lady Ninniane had said. She lacked the confidence in her abilities to attempt to decapitate a Gilmesh, yet she could distract one so a soldier could, so that's what she did.

Taunting and yelling, she set herself up as bait, drawing the attention of a Gilmesh. She attacked it with small, darting forays, manoeuvring until its back was to an ignored and forgotten warrior, then watched in satisfaction as the solder took advantage of that fact and sliced the creature's head off.

They died hard, shrieking, and writhing until their bodies disintegrated into a pile of grey ash. Cassie wondered if that was all they were, dust held together by malevolence.

A soldier, young and fresh-faced, fell before the attack of a Gilmesh, his expression fearful as his sword was knocked brutally from his hand and the creature moved in for the kill.

Desperately, Cassie leapt, and her sword whirled in the air. With disbelief, she saw the Gilmesh howl, clutch its throat, and vanish in a cloud of grey dust. The soldier scrambled quickly to his feet and retrieved his sword, briefly nodded thanks in her direction before they turned to find new targets.

Suddenly, there seemed fewer Gilmesh than before. Wildly, Cassie looked around for Garth and saw him fighting off two Gilmesh at once, his sword swinging confidently in his massive hands as his muscles bulged. Nimbly, he stepped in and sliced once, twice, and two headless bodies shrieked and toppled to the ground, exploding in grey death dust.

Darius was engaged in furious combat with another. This Gilmesh seemed different from the others, taller and larger, and Cassie wondered if it was their leader. Back and forth the contest raged, Cassie sparing a moment's thought for the sheer artistry of Darius's fighting, wondering if she'd ever be as good as him.

Up above, Ruby saw the tide of battle turning. No more Gilmesh were entering the ravine. Darius and his men appeared to be driving back the remaining creatures.

An unheard command seemed to sweep through the Gilmesh. As one, they leapt away from the warriors, rushing up the slopes of the ravine, the soldiers warily watching them go. Shakily, Cassie wiped her sweating sword hand down her trousers and took a deep breath. It was over; she was still alive and had even held her own.

"Skraelings!"

The cry went up as a familiar howl sounded and large, shaggy bodies began pouring over the lip of the ravine. Heart thudding with anticipation, Cassie clutched her sword tightly – skraelings she could fight. With almost gleeful expectation she stepped forward to engage the new enemy.

From her vantage point, Ruby saw the Gilmesh flee up the side of the ravine, and realised, to her horror, they were heading straight for her, were between her and the soldiers.

With a whimper of fear, Ruby picked up her skirts and ran – back to the horses and the only weapon within her reach. With shaking fingers, she swiftly undid the straps holding Excalibur, murmuring reassuring words to the horses as they nickered in alarm.

Trees rustled behind her. Wide-eyed with terror, Ruby swung to face the Gilmesh. Silently, they encircled her, grey, skull-like faces eerily still, yellow lights glowing from hollow eye sockets.

She could smell them, the smell of ancient dust and things long since disintegrated and backed against the horse in fear as they stopped and surveyed her. The largest one, the one she'd taken for their leader, stepped closer.

Well now, what do we have here?

Lorcan's voice, cold and malignant, echoed in her mind. Ruby's panic rose, threatening to overwhelm her. Gulping in air, she raised her chin in defiance, determined not to let him know how scared she was.

Gwnhyfar's little empathic descendant. So, you have returned. How very unfortunate ... for you! Bring her! The command, sharp and compelling, jerked the Gilmesh forward a step.

Crying out in alarm, Ruby unsheathed the sword and held it aloft, its golden brilliance splashing prisms of light around the still wintry forest. The Gilmesh stopped, eyes fixed unerringly on its shining glory, faces impassive.

Ruby sensed their fear, and took a small step forward, relieved when they moved back.

Bring her I said!

She has the sword.

The leader's mouth never moved. Ruby realised that the Gilmesh must also possess the ability to communicate with their minds.

Bring them both.

We cannot touch the sword. It is death to us.

There are enough of you to overwhelm her.

Slowly, Ruby turned, the sword leaving a trail of shimmering sparks as she paced. Again, the Gilmesh retreated, and Ruby's confidence grew.

"If you come anywhere near me," she cried, proud her voice didn't waver. Well – not much anyway! "I'll use the sword and it will destroy you all."

What are you waiting for? Lorcan shrieked. *Bring them to me.*

No. The leader's voice was flat, emotionless. *We are not your slaves, evil one. We serve, only so long as it suits our purpose.*

I brought you back into existence! Lorcan snarled.

Yes, but that does not give you the right of dominance over us. I will not lose any more today. Our numbers are not yet sufficient to sanction unnecessary waste.

The Gilmesh silently melted into the forest, leaving Ruby sagging against the horse with relief. Shakily, she made her way to the ravine holding the sword in front of her, jumping at every sound the forest made.

In the ravine, Cassie knelt, wiping her sword on the fur of the slain skraeling lying before her. Straightening, she surveyed the battle site with satisfaction. Every one of the skraelings lay in untidy, sprawling heaps. Cassie was proud she had despatched at least six of them, hacking and slicing the way Garth had taught her.

Darius finally got a proper look at the two strangers whose timely arrival had saved the lives of him and his men.

"Garth?" he exclaimed; his eyes alight with relieved surprise. "We believed you dead. After the attack, when we could not find you, we feared the worst."

"I would indeed have been dead," retorted Garth, "had not Lady Cassandra used magic to remove me to a place of safety."

"Lady Cassandra?" Darius enquired, eyes nearly popping out of his skull as Cassie strode over to him, sword once more sheathed at her hip, her clothes, hands, and face smeared with skraeling blood. "My ... my Lady?" he stammered.

"Lord Darius, it's good to see you again. We must get back to the castle, it's very important we speak to Lord Reutghar."

"Of course, my Lady," he muttered, then his eyes widened again. "By all that's holy," he gasped.

Cassie turned to see Ruby walking towards them, Excalibur lighting her way through the renewed snowfall like a beacon of hope. Carefully, she made her way down the side of the ravine, face pale, long auburn hair rippling down her back. The warriors stepped back to form a path, murmurs of wonder and awe arising in her wake.

"Lady Ruby?" Darius's tone was that of a man wondering how many more surprises were to come.

Ruby flashed him a wide smile before turning to Cassie. "The Gilmesh came," she said. "They chased me through the forest..."

"Oh Ruby," gasped Cassie in horror. "We left you alone."

"It's okay," Ruby quickly reassured her. "I managed to get to the sword. They were so afraid of it they left me alone."

"The sword," murmured Darius. "Thank the Lady it is safely returned. We must make all speed to return to Dragonswell."

"Before we do, I must speak with you privately, my Lord," urged Garth. Darius gave him a level look, then nodded briefly, before signalling to his men to commence preparing to leave the ravine.

Indicating Cassie and Ruby were to join them, Darius and Garth moved silently away from the general busyness of the soldiers, helping the wounded onto horses, and the grim duty of collecting the dead.

"I beg you, my Lord," began Garth. "Is Lord Reutghar's mage, Siminus, still present within the castle?"

"Of course," replied Darius, plainly puzzled by the question. "He and Lord Colwyn's mage have been labouring long hours to discover Lorcan's whereabouts." Garth and Cassie exchanged glances. Darius's face grew serious. "In faith, Garth," he continued. "I would know what this is about."

"My Lord, during the attack upon the castle by the skraelings," began Garth, "we discovered Siminus to be a traitor."

"Siminus?" Darius's shock was obvious. "Garth, this is a very serious allegation! Are you certain tis so? In faith, I would rather believe myself a traitor than Reutghar's mage."

"I fear it is true, my Lord," Garth paused, his expression grim. "He bade Lady Cassandra draw the sword, assuring us Lord Reutghar had need of it. In her innocence she obeyed, none of us suspecting his loyalties now lay with the dark one. Were it not for the commendable suspicions of Lady Cassandra, and the empathic abilities of Lady Ruby, I am afraid the sword would have fallen into his clutches. As it was, we barely escaped with our lives, for he unleashed the foulest of black magic upon us."

"By the Lady," gasped Darius. "How did you escape?"

"Lady Cassandra used the sword. Its purity was powerful enough to deflect the evil spell, somehow forcing us to cross into their world."

"I am relieved you managed to find your way home, Garth, for we have sore need of a warrior such as yourself. I fear the war against Lorcan goes very badly, losses have been high," Darius paused, expression thoughtful. "I had noticed Lorcan's evil creatures always seemed to have almost prior knowledge of our strategies. If what you say about the mage is true, then that indeed is what they had."

"We need to return to the castle, my Lord," urged Garth. "Siminus must not escape."

"I agree," nodded Darius, bowing his head to Cassie. "I must thank you, Lady Cassandra, for coming to our assistance. I must confess to being surprised at your ability with a sword. Is this a common skill amongst the women of your world?"

"No," smiled Cassie, "Garth taught me."

"Then I am surprised no longer, my Lady, for you have indeed been instructed by a master. Do you require horses, Garth?"

"No, my Lord, we have our own mounts."

"Excellent, then let us ride. It is unwise for any to be abroad after dark."

Retrieving the horses, Ruby returned the sword to its sheath; relieved it had proven so effective against the Gilmesh, shuddering to herself as she remembered their blank, skull-like faces and bony, elongated bodies.

Falling in with Darius and his men, Cassie soberly noted the four shrouded bodies tied securely onto horses. She reflected how much higher the death toll would have been had she and Garth not been there, or if she'd still been weak and incapable of fighting. It made the stresses and struggles of the past year worth it.

They rode northwards through the thickening snow, the only sound the jingle of bridles and the occasional snort as a horse blew warm breath from its nostrils. Shrinking further into her cloak, Ruby wished again for gloves and was relieved when they crested a small rise and the town of Dragonswell lay before them.

It had changed in their short three-month absence. The town which lay beyond the castle walls had been abandoned, and both girls shivered as they rode through deserted streets, past boarded-up homes, and shops.

"The attacks from skraelings and the Gilmesh became so regular it was decided to evacuate all the townspeople to within the castle walls," Darius explained, seeing their faces as they gazed at the emptiness all around.

Speechlessly, the sisters nodded, following Darius and Garth to the great castle entrance, and waiting patiently as the massive drawbridge was lowered, its chains clanking and rattling in the hushed, wintry landscape. They rode over the wooden drawbridge, the horses' hooves echoing off stone walls.

Garth nodded to Darius, then urged both girls to dismount, passing soldiers taking their horses' reins without comment. Silently, the three of them slipped into a side door and up a narrow, winding stone staircase.

"What's the plan?" Cassie murmured to Garth.

"Darius will seek a chance to speak to Lord Reutghar and Lady Ninniane privately and will bring them to us at the earliest opportunity."

"What about Delmar and ... Colwyn?" Ruby heard Cassie's slight hesitation over Colwyn's name, wondering if she was nervous about seeing him again. Garth pushed open a door leading to a small room lined with tapestries. Gratefully, the girls crossed to the roaring fire and held out white, pinched hands to the flames.

"Lord Darius and I believed it would be prudent not to take the young mage into our confidence. After all, he has been Siminus's apprentice for many years. There is a possibility he too is in the service of Lorcan."

"No," Ruby stated firmly. "Not Delmar, he's no traitor."

Garth shrugged his massive shoulders. "Lord Colwyn and his men are patrolling the eastern woodlands."

"Did Siminus know?" Cassie enquired, sharply.

"In faith, my Lady, I do not know," Garth replied. "I would expect as Lord Reutghar's mage he would have complete knowledge of all troop movements..."

"So, Colwyn's walked straight into a trap," Cassie snapped, eyes flashing. "We have to do something, warn them."

"Lord Colwyn left three days ago my Lady. If Siminus did betray them, it is too late to do anything about it." Cassie whirled away in agitation, clenching her hands into fists.

The door opened and Lady Ninniane entered, her lovely face wreathed in a welcoming smile. Ruby had forgotten her beauty and how calming her presence was.

"Cassandra, Ruby," she exclaimed, spreading her hands wide in greeting. "I am truly delighted to see you both safely returned, and you Garth."

"My Lady," he replied, bowing.

"Lord Darius has explained what shocking news you bring. I am deeply concerned Siminus managed to conceal so completely the depths to which his soul has sunk. Come, sit with me, tell me everything that has transpired since last we met."

She gathered them to her, settling onto a carved wooden bench by the fire. Listening silently, her eyes grew angry and thoughtful in turn as the girls told the events of the past year, including the appearance of Gwnhyfar in Ruby's dream, and their eventual re-crossing into Erinsmore with the sacred sword. The Lady's eyes wandered to the wrapped sword still clutched tightly in Cassie's hand. Ruby saw relief flicker across her face.

"Oh, my child," the Lady sighed and patted Ruby's hand. "What an arduous journey you have both made. Yet I fear the road ahead will prove even more dangerous."

The door opened again, and Lord Reutghar entered the room, his face relaxing into a relieved smile when he saw them.

"I cannot tell you how pleased I am to see you safely returned. When we could find no trace of you after the battle, we feared the worst. Colwyn, especially, was deeply concerned for your safety."

"My Lord," interrupted the Lady, smoothly. "I fear we have grave tidings." She nodded at Garth, who clearly and swiftly told Reutghar of Siminus ordering Cassie to draw the sword, their discovery of his treachery, his attempt upon their lives, and Cassie's desperate use of the sword and their crossing into the other world.

Reutghar listened, his face growing darker as the tale unfolded. "Siminus, a traitor? In faith, it would be easier to believe I am one. Siminus has been my mage since we were boys. We are closer than any brothers. Surely, I would have felt such treason through our link?"

Sadly, Lady Ninniane shook her head at the appeal in his voice. "It seems there is no doubt, my Lord. I am as shocked by this news as you, for I too suspected nothing. This explains much that had troubled me, such as how Lorcan's forces always seemed to know in advance where your men were going to be, and any plans or strategies you had devised to overcome them."

"How many lives have been lost due to his treachery?" Reutghar muttered, Ruby heard the steel beneath his words. "What do you advise, my Lady?" he turned to Lady Ninniane.

"He must be approached with caution, my Lord. Siminus is a very powerful mage. If he has the backing of Lorcan, there is no telling how strong he has become ..." she broke off as the door once more opened, and Darius entered.

"My Lord, Delmar is tending the wounded. When I enquired as to the location of your mage, he informed me that four hours ago Siminus was taken ill and retired to his room. Upon our return, Delmar went to see if he had recovered enough to tend the wounded and was surprised to find the room empty. He is deeply concerned as to his tutor's wellbeing, but I suspect Siminus knew he had been discovered and has fled to his master."

"How could he have known?" demanded Cassie.

"Oh, I think that might have been me," began Ruby, slowly.

"Tell us," commanded the Lady. Ruby took a deep breath, told of the Gilmesh, of how she'd held them off with the sword, and how Lorcan had communicated both with the Gilmesh and herself, concluding. "Lorcan knew we'd come back, so..."

"He must have told Siminus to make a quick getaway," finished Cassie.

"It must be as you say, my Ladies. It angers me such a traitor has escaped," Reutghar shook his head, his gaze fastening hungrily upon the sword in Cassie's hand. "I am relieved beyond measure you have returned the sacred sword to Erinsmore, my Lady," he said.

Cassie hastily held it out to him. "I'm sorry," she began. "We never meant to take Excalibur. Siminus tricked us. We've taken good care of it and brought it back as soon as we could."

"You have the gratitude of the people of Erinsmore, my Lady Cassandra, and of its Lord," Reutghar smiled directly at Cassie, his piercing blue eyes so like Colwyn's, warm and generous, that Cassie flushed as he carefully took the sword from her grasp.

"I am curious, my Lady, you called the sword Excalibur?"

"Oh, in the legends of Arthur in my world, one of his swords is called Excalibur," explained Cassie. "We sort of started calling it that." Reutghar nodded thoughtfully.

"I am sure you will wish to rest and refresh yourselves before dinner," commented the Lady Ninniane.

Cassie looked ruefully at her bloodied clothes. "Yes, please."

"Were you injured, Lady Cassandra?" Reutghar frowned.

"No, indeed not, my Lord," broke in Darius, enthusiastically. "Lady Cassandra slew at least half a dozen skraelings. The men are full of praise for her swordsmanship. Without the aid of her and Garth, I doubt we would have made it back alive."

"Is this true?" Reutghar exclaimed. His eyebrows shot up with surprise, and he studied Cassie so intently that she shifted uncomfortably under his gaze.

"Even before we were aware that we were under attack," Darius continued, "Garth and Lady Cassandra were shooting flaming arrows into them, despatching dozens."

"Well, we didn't do it all," mumbled Cassie, embarrassed at Darius's wholehearted championing. "Ruby shot loads too. She's a better shot than me, I prefer the sword."

Reutghar's lips twitched as if something she'd said amused him. "I am deeply grateful to you, my Ladies, and look forward to seeing you later at dinner. Come, Garth, I wish to hear all about your adventures in the other world."

"My Lord."

With a nod and a warm smile in the girls' direction, Garth followed Reutghar and Darius from the room.

"Come," Lady Ninniane arose gracefully from her chair. "I will take you to your rooms. I also would like to question you further but will wait until you have rested."

They trailed after the Lady, making their way down endless stone passageways, passing soldiers, servants, and nobles, all of whom bowed or curtseyed to the Lady, and shot curious glances at the sisters.

"Ruby!"

Ruby turned at the sound of her name and saw Delmar, face alight, hurrying after her.

"I heard a rumour," he exclaimed, "Was afraid to dare hope it might be true."

"Hello, Delmar," Ruby replied, happily.

"You look different," he continued, examining her curiously. "You look ... older."

"Well, it has been a year since you last saw me."

"A year?" he replied, confused. "No, indeed not, my Lady, it is barely three moons since your strange disappearance."

"How is that possible?" Ruby asked Lady Ninniane. "We've been gone a year, yet only three months have passed in Erinsmore."

"Time in both worlds does not run exactly parallel," explained the Lady. "I have heard of instances where a visitor from Erinsmore, who was gone for many years, claimed upon their return to have been absent for less than a week."

"So why was it when we crossed over, Garth and the skraeling didn't arrive at the same point and time as us?" continued Ruby.

"You both had an anchor in your world," replied Lady Ninniane. "Your parents. They dragged you back to the same place in time. Garth had no such anchor. His only contact was his connection to you, hence he crossed two years into your past."

"And the skraeling overshot and went three months into the future," added Cassie thoughtfully, stepping into the light.

Delmar peered at her uncertainly. "Lady Cassandra?" he asked, hesitantly.

"Yes, it's me," Cassie smiled. "I think I've changed too."

"Indeed," agreed Delmar enthusiastically then reddened and blinked owlishly at her. "It is good to see you both alive and well," he continued. "I know Colwyn will be vastly relieved. He was greatly concerned for you ... for both of you."

"Is he well?" Cassie asked hastily. "I mean, can you feel him through your link?"

"Yes, I can feel him, he appears unharmed and is very close," Delmar paused, looking at them in confusion. "Why this concern for him, my Lady?"

"Delmar," began Lady Ninniane gently. "We have news which will distress you greatly. Siminus has been discovered to be a traitor working for Lorcan. I fear he has been betraying all our strategies to him."

"That's why we're worried about Colwyn," broke in Cassie urgently. "Darius and his men had walked straight into a trap. I'm afraid Colwyn might have too."

"I see," replied Delmar, clearly in shock. "Well, I can assure you Colwyn is alive and unharmed. As I said, he is very close to us. In fact," there was a great clanking and rumbling, and Ruby realised the drawbridge was being raised, "I believe that is him returning," Delmar finished and hurried out into the courtyard followed by the sisters.

With a clatter of horses' hooves, Colwyn swept into the courtyard, followed by a troop of grim-faced and silent soldiers. He rode straight to the castle steps where his father and Darius had emerged and wearily dismounted.

"My Lord," he began, Ruby heard the weariness in his voice. "The village of Ladymere is no more."

"Gilmesh?" enquired Reutghar tersely. Colwyn nodded. Ruby thought how much Colwyn had changed in the three months that had passed in his world. His face looked older, more mature, and his mouth was set in a tight line of fatigue and despair. His eyes were shadowed as if he'd seen things that preyed on his heart and soul.

"We had barely left Dragonswell when we met a terrified man on horseback," Colwyn informed his father. "He told us the village was under attack and fighting for their lives. We rode as hard as we could but arrived too late to do any more than bury the dead. Afterwards, we followed the Gilmesh trail for a day until it vanished."

"So, you did not go to the eastern woodlands as arranged?" enquired Darius.

Colwyn shook his head, nodding his thanks as a stable boy ran forward and led his horse away. "No, we had wasted too much time chasing ghosts, so decided to return."

"It is as well you did," replied Reutghar. "We have disturbing news for you. First, come, greet an old friend who is lately returned to us bringing the sacred sword with him."

"Garth?" exclaimed Colwyn in shock. "By all that's holy, where have you been?"

"Tis a long story, my Lord, one best told over a mug of Erinsmore's finest ale, for it has been too long since I last tasted it. But, my Lord, I did not return alone."

He gestured towards the sisters. Colwyn turned, his eyes widening as he saw Ruby.

Cassie stepped from behind Lady Ninniane, her face coolly composed beneath the smears of skraeling blood. Her long, glossy plait spilling over one shoulder, her body relaxed, one hand resting lightly on her sword hilt.

"Hello, Colwyn ..." she said.

Chapter Fourteen

A Woman's Place

or a long moment there was utter silence. Ruby's heart skipped a beat, and tears pricked the back of her eyes at the hope on her sister's face, the smile that waited at the corner of her mouth.

"Lady Cassandra," Colwyn began, and Ruby blinked at his formal tone. "Are you injured?"

"What?" Cassie asked.

"The blood on your face?"

"Oh," Cassie's fingers flew to the marks she'd forgotten were there. "No, oh no, this is skraeling blood, I killed about six of them." An admiring murmur ran through the assembled men.

Colwyn's face darkened. "You, my Lady?" he doubted.

"Are you calling me a liar?" snapped Cassie, waspishly. "A lot has changed. I'm no longer that weak and helpless female, incapable of defending herself."

"You were never that, my Lady," he drawled wryly, and Cassie flushed angrily. "In faith," he continued. "I find it hard to believe that in less than three moons you have gained the swordsmanship necessary to successfully fight skraelings."

"For your information, it was skraelings *and* Gilmesh, my Lord," Cassie's voice dripped with sarcasm.

Looking round, Ruby saw the courtyard silently filling up with more soldiers as word spread of the confrontation.

"We've been gone almost a year," Cassie continued, hotly. "During that time, I've been sweating my butt off nonstop, training and learning. Garth says I'm one of the best pupils he's ever had ..." Her eyes narrowed at his snort of disbelief.

"Tis true, my Lord," Garth's voice was almost apologetic as Colwyn shot an accusing glance in his direction. "Lady Cassandra is a born swordsman or rather swordswoman. I have rarely seen any to match her in agility and speed."

"The Lady saved my life from the Gilmesh today," a voice murmured in the crowd. Cassie flashed a grateful glance at the young soldier.

"Even if Garth allowed you to forget your place and parade around wearing a sword, it does not mean you can compete with men who have spent their entire lives learning."

"Men like you, you mean?" Cassie demanded, eyes flashing amber fire, chin jerking even higher as she faced him down.

"Aye, if you like," Colwyn's angry expression was an equal match for Cassie's. They glared accusingly at each other.

"All right then," said Cassie, slowly. "Prove it, fight with me. If I don't manage to at least draw with you, I'll take off this sword and never wear it again."

"I do not fight women," Colwyn stated, flatly.

With one final glare, he turned on his heel and marched, stiff-backed, into the castle, leaving the soldiers muttering darkly, casting sympathetic glances in Cassie's direction.

Softly, Lady Ninniane drew the stunned, visibly shaken Cassie, back into the side door, and Ruby and Delmar were left looking sorrowfully at each other.

"It's all wrong," whispered Ruby, absurdly close to tears. "They weren't supposed to argue. I thought they cared about each other, even perhaps ..." Her voice trailed away.

Delmar placed a comforting arm around her shoulder, turning her to follow the other women inside.

"He does care about Lady Cassandra," he murmured. "More than he realises. More, perhaps, than he wants to." He paused, looking at Ruby's troubled face.

"When you vanished, Colwyn went out of his mind with worry. He scoured the countryside looking for you. Since then, the fight against Lorcan has gone badly. Colwyn has faced death daily, and that can damage a man's soul. Also, you must appreciate that Colwyn was raised with an ideal of women as delicate creatures who require protection. To be confronted with your sister, not as this ideal, but as a real woman claiming to be capable of defending herself..."

"Cassie's not just claiming it," Ruby broke in hotly. "She can fight, and she really is good. Garth even told her she's better than Colwyn in a lot of ways."

"In faith, that will please him even less," remarked Delmar dryly, and Ruby smiled. "What about you, Ruby, are you returned as a warrior maid?"

"No," replied Ruby, "Although I'm pretty good with a bow."

"Indeed?" smiled Delmar. "Mayhap tomorrow you could show me."

"Arrogant, rude, male chauvinist pig!" raged Cassie, stomping up and down their chamber, boots echoing on the stone floor. Watching from her position of safety on her bed, Ruby sighed, wondering if Cassie was ever going to sit down again.

"He was surprised by how much you'd changed," she began.

"Well maybe he should think about changing too," Cassie snapped. Her face fell, and she slumped onto the bed beside Ruby. "It's not going how I thought it would," she confided.

Ruby patted her hand sympathetically. "I know," she answered. "Though Delmar said when we vanished Colwyn went out of his head with worry and searched for us every day."

Cassie looked thoughtful, and then her expression brightened. "Did he?" Ruby nodded. Cassie looked even more cheerful.

A knock came at the door and a serving maid poked her head in. "Lord Darius sends his compliments and requests the pleasure of escorting Lady Cassandra and Lady Ruby down to dinner."

"Oh," murmured Cassie. "I don't know if we're going..."

"Tell Lord Darius yes, and thank you very much," replied Ruby, quickly. The maid bobbed a curtsey and disappeared.

"I'm not sure I want to go to dinner and have to see Lord Pig Colwyn," snapped Cassie.

Ruby sighed again. "Well, you can do what you want," she replied. "I'm hungry, so I'm going."

Escorted into the vast banqueting hall later that evening, one on each of Lord Darius's arms, the sisters gaped at the sight before them. Like a medieval re-enactment, the hall was crowded with nobility, warriors, and peasants alike. Long tables were heaped with food, jugs of ale and wine. A group of musicians merrily piped away in the corner, struggling to be heard over the roar of conversation and hordes of children darting about at play.

One end of the hall was clearly defined as the province of the nobility. It was to these tables Lord Darius led them. Seeing the richly dressed lords and ladies, Ruby felt desperately out of place in her simple, woollen dress. Glancing at Cassie, she knew by the way her chin lifted, that she was anxious too.

A smiling Delmar moved to make room for them. With a thankful sigh, Ruby sank into the chair next to him, relieved to be out of range of all those judging eyes. They exchanged glances as Cassie sat next to Colwyn and deliberately turned her back on him to study a tapestry hanging on a nearby wall.

"I hear you were issued a challenge today and refused it, Lord Colwyn?"

Ruby glanced up from her meal. The speaker was Lord Barnabus, a thin, nervous man with sparse, sandy hair falling over a high, shiny forehead. He had long, bony fingers which he had a habit of tapping on the table.

"You heard wrong," declared Colwyn flatly. "The challenge was made in jest. I had no option but to refuse it."

"On the contrary," retorted Cassie, raising her head for the first time to look directly at Colwyn. "The challenge was deadly serious." A hush fell over the table, all eyes on Colwyn and Cassie as they gazed hostilely at each other.

"My dear Lady Cassandra, are you seriously claiming to be able to best Lord Colwyn in a sword fight?"

Ruby looked up at the tinkling, amused voice. A lavishly dressed lady had silently appeared behind them, her tiny, bejewelled slippers making no sound on the stone floor, her silken gown swaying beguilingly around her womanly curves.

Gazing at the pretty, dimpled face and ornately dressed hair, Ruby felt a stab of instinctive dislike as all the men at the table, except Delmar, jumped to their feet, falling over themselves to offer her a chair.

"My Lady Melinda," said Colwyn. "I pray you, please be seated." With a flutter of eyelashes and a heave of powdered shoulders, the Lady minced to his chair and delicately seated herself, before bending her gaze once more onto Cassie's flushed, indignant face.

"I don't know about best," replied Cassie. "I certainly think I could hold my own against him."

"My dear child," trilled Lady Melinda, a laugh tinkling from her pouting, red-painted lips. "It is simply not possible," she continued. "Lord Colwyn is famed for being the best swordsman in the whole of Erinsmore. No one can match him, let alone some chit of a girl."

"Well," said Cassie sweetly, "as he's too afraid to fight me, I guess we'll never know."

"It is not a question of being afraid!" snapped Colwyn, snatching up another chair and throwing himself into it. "Men do not cross swords with a woman, it is simply not fitting. Any woman who knew her proper place would not expect him to."

"Her proper place?" asked Cassie, her voice dangerously calm. "And what exactly, in your opinion, Lord Colwyn, is a woman's place?"

"Supporting and aiding her men folk, being mistress of the home, raising the children, as is right and proper."

"I see," replied Cassie. Ruby heard the barely controlled fury in her voice and darted a concerned glance at Delmar who was listening in amused interest to the exchange. "Well, maybe that's so in Erinsmore," continued Cassie. "In my world women are no longer slaves to men. We are free and independent, equal, and in some cases, superior to them. Women in my world know there's nothing they can't do as well as any man."

"What a very strange world," cooed Lady Melinda, eyes carefully watching Colwyn's reaction over the edge of her lace-topped fan.

"Garth has told me of your world," Colwyn responded, slowly. "Of the violence and squalor countless people live in. Of the contempt and disrespect, many men have for women. How the breakdown of the sacred union of marriage is such a common occurrence it goes without comment. That there are even special refuges for women and children to flee to in order to escape the brutality of their husbands and fathers," he paused, shaking his head. "I would not be so quick to boast about the achievements of such a world, my Lady," his voice throbbed with barely concealed sarcasm.

Cassie flushed. "I admit my world's not perfect, far from it, I still believe women have the capacity to be so much more than mothers and housekeepers."

"Of course, they do," snapped Colwyn. "But not by attempting to become men themselves. If you cannot see that I fear we must admit our viewpoints are so vastly different no compromise could ever be reached."

Cassie shrank back as if she'd been slapped, twin spots of colour burning on her cheekbones. Colwyn turned to Lady Melinda, who'd been listening to the exchange with a small smile playing over her perfect mouth.

"My Lady," he said. "Would you grant me the honour of the next dance?"

"Why, certainly, my Lord," she simpered. "It would be my pleasure." Snapping her fan shut, she rose gracefully to her feet and placed a small white hand in Colwyn's, casting a triumphant glance over her shoulder at Cassie.

"My Lady Cassandra," Cassie looked up as Lord Reutghar called her name.

"My Lord?" she said warily, half expecting another lecture.

"Lady Ninniane and I wish to speak with you, privately."

"Of course, my Lord," replied Cassie obediently, and moved to sit next to them.

Ruby looked at Delmar sadly. "What can we do, Delmar? Why is Colwyn being so unreasonable?"

"I believe it is because he is feeling threatened, my Lady. You must understand that Colwyn was raised to be a warrior, to fight to protect the weak and helpless, and in his eyes that means women. His mother died when he was very young. He had no sisters or female cousins to challenge this notion, so I am afraid every time he looks at your sister, he is being torn in two completely opposing directions."

"Which are?" asked Ruby in interest.

"Between what he has always believed to be true and what he feels for her."

"Huh," Ruby huffed. "I'm beginning to think he doesn't feel anything for her."

"Oh, he does," said Delmar, knowingly. "Trust me, he does."

Ruby nodded, watching Colwyn and Lady Melinda dance, their steps precise and measured.

"What about her?" she asked, bitterly. "Where does Lady Malicious fit into all this?"

Delmar spluttered over his mouthful of wine. "Lady Melinda is the daughter of one of Lord Reutghar's most trusted lords. Her family house is very old and noble. I believe it is thought by many that a union between her and Colwyn would be an advantageous match."

"You mean she's his girlfriend?" hissed Ruby in alarm.

"No, no, not in the sense I believe you mean," Delmar hurriedly reassured. "Nothing has ever been said between them. I know Colwyn does not consider her that way, yet I believe the Lady has … hopes…"

"No wonder she was such a bitch to Cassie," Ruby mused, causing Delmar to splutter into his drink again.

"Indeed, my Lady," he gasped, dabbing at his streaming eyes with a napkin.

"Ruby," Cassie appeared behind them, eyes shining, a grin bouncing all over her face. "I'm tired, so I'm off to bed."

"I'll come with you," declared Ruby, eager to get Cassie alone and tell her everything Delmar had told her. Quickly, the girls said goodnight and left the great hall, unaware their departure was being watched intently by the angry, blue glare of Colwyn, and the thoughtful, narrowed gaze of Lady Melinda.

The next morning, when Ruby awoke, Cassie had already gone. Puzzled, Ruby dressed and wandered downstairs to the kitchens in search of breakfast, only to find the castle in an uproar.

"What's going on?" she asked Gretchen, the portly cook, who thrust a hot, buttered scone into Ruby's hands.

"There's to be a duel," she gushed. "Some young lad from one of the villages claims he can best Lord Colwyn. Did you ever hear such a thing? Lord Reutghar has said all who wish to, can watch. Come along, my Lady, you don't want to miss it, do you?"

Ruby followed her to the training arena which was packed with soldiers, servants, and nobility, all craning their necks to see where Colwyn and Garth stood in the centre facing a slender boy. The smoothness of his cheeks betrayed his youth, his rough, homespun clothes his status as a peasant.

"Ruby, over here."

Looking up, Ruby saw Delmar beckoning to her from a platform where Lord Reutghar and Darius were sitting. Climbing into a seat next to him, she looked anxiously around.

"Where's Cassie?" she asked. "I know she wouldn't want to miss this."

"There she is," replied Delmar. Ruby saw Cassie enter the arena from the castle and stand for a moment, blinking in the strong winter sunshine.

"Sit by me, my Lady," commanded Reutghar. Darius moved along to make space for Cassie as she sat between them, waving to Ruby, and looking anxiously at the two opponents as they stood, sizing each other up.

"My Lord," called Garth. "This lad states he is a swordsman to equal Lord Colwyn and claims the right of friendly duel."

"Friendly duel?" whispered Ruby.

"They fight until first blood," whispered back Delmar.

"Do you agree to the duel, my son?" asked Reutghar and Colwyn nodded.

"I do, my Lord, though vow I will go easy on the lad." There was a good-natured chuckle from the audience. Ruby saw the lad's face flush, his grip tightening on his sword.

"I am intrigued by this youth's boldness," stated Reutghar. "I propose whoever wins the duel shall be my guest at a banquet held in their honour. Moreover, at that same banquet, the loser must go down on one knee before the winner and offer up his sword in tribute."

There was a surprised murmur from the crowd. Ruby saw Cassie glance at Reutghar and bite her lip anxiously. Colwyn turned startled eyes up to his father.

"As my Lord commands," he said slowly. "So, do I agree." His opponent merely nodded.

Garth raised his arm. "Let the duel commence," he ordered, dropping his arm.

Both opponents bowed courteously to each other, swords clashed, and the duel began. At first, Colwyn didn't seem to be trying, and Ruby noticed several times the boy almost made it through his guard until Colwyn seemed to realise, that he at least knew one end of a sword from the other.

Back and forth they ranged, swords glinting in the sunshine. Ruby, sitting on the edge of her seat, gripped Delmar's hand so tightly that he winced. Ruby saw Cassie was also watching the duel with rapt attention, her eyes flicking from opponent to opponent.

Faster and faster, they fought, swords blurring and clashing. Their feet flowed and their supple bodies moved with an agility and artistry that almost brought tears to Ruby's eyes. Time ceased to have any meaning. A complete stillness descended upon the audience as they watched, in awed silence, two masters at work.

Unexpectedly, the lad seemed to stumble. Instantly, Colwyn was upon him. Somehow, the boy turned the stumble into an upward thrust which took him under Colwyn's guard and nicked a shallow gash on his forearm.

Colwyn stepped back, stunned, staring at the thin line of blood forming on his arm. The crowd held its breath, a roar of disbelief arising from every throat as Colwyn shook his head, a wry grin spreading across his face. Ruby realised, whatever else he might be, he was at least a good loser.

Colwyn patted the boy on the back. "Well fought," he said.

The boy smiled, flushed and triumphant. "Thank you," he said, in a voice that was all too familiar. The smile froze on Colwyn's face. The lad shimmered, and before the incredulous eyes of all assembled, changed into Cassie.

Gaping in shock, Delmar and Ruby exchanged stunned glances, turning as one to look at Cassie sitting beside Lord Reutghar, only to find she'd turned into Lady Ninniane's maid.

"Tis Lady Cassandra," yelled one soldier. "She did it, she bested Lord Colwyn!" Cheers arose from the crowd.

Colwyn, his face like thunder, stalked from the arena and into the castle. Cassie cast a helpless look at Lord Reutghar and raced after him.

"Colwyn!"

He turned. His expression furiously grim. "What were you thinking, Cassandra?" he demanded. "I could have killed you!"

"Are you in the habit of killing your sparring partners?"

"No, but accidents happen. It was a foolhardy stunt."

"I'm sorry," she stuttered. "It was your father's idea. He persuaded the Lady to cast an illusion over me and her maid, he thought it was a great joke..."

"A joke?" Colwyn stormed. "Aye," he continued bitterly. "A joke is what you made of me in front of my men."

"No," protested Cassie. "Your men hold you in nothing but the highest respect. I really do know how to fight, Garth trained me well."

"Indeed, and I will be having words with Garth about that," snapped Colwyn.

"Don't you blame him," retorted Cassie. "I made him do it, Colwyn..."

"No, Cassandra," he said. "At this moment I am so vexed I do not know whether to challenge Garth, send you to your room, or ... or kiss you."

Cassie's eyes grew huge, a satisfied smile spreading across her face. "Well," she drawled. "I know which option I'd prefer. Please, don't be angry with me anymore, I wanted to prove myself to you, that was all."

Colwyn stared at her. His face softened. Tugging gently on her long plait he pulled her closer and stroked a finger down her cheek.

"Oh, Cassandra," he murmured. "You do not have to prove anything to me. If that is what this is all about..."

"It's not," interrupted Cassie, quickly. "I had to become a warrior to fulfil the prophecy, don't you see?"

"The prophecy?" Colwyn stared in disbelief. "You believe you and Lady Ruby are the ones mentioned?"

"Don't you?" demanded Cassie, earnestly. "I mean, it all fits. So far, everything it said has come true..."

"Colwyn."

They jumped apart as Lord Reutghar's voice echoed off stone walls. He strode down the passageway, followed by Ruby and Delmar. "You fought well, my Lady," he began abruptly.

"Thank you, my Lord," she murmured.

"Do you patrol today?" This was to Colwyn, who gave a terse nod. "Excellent! The Lady Cassandra shall accompany you?"

"My Lord!" spluttered Colwyn. "Tis not safe for a woman."

"Oh come," interrupted his father, heartily. "I think she has proven herself more than capable. If it eases your mind, I too will ride out with you. Delmar."

"Yes, my Lord?"

"You'd better come in case the Lady breaks a fingernail or something." With a last warning glance at his son, he strode off down the passage.

"My Lady," Colwyn bowed to Cassie, once again stiff and formal. "We depart in twenty minutes. If you are not there, we shall leave without you," he stalked off.

"You were amazing," Ruby hugged Cassie, who was looking stunned. "I had no idea it was you. You did it, you beat him."

"Go me," muttered Cassie, smiling weakly. "I'd better get my stuff. Colwyn's got such a bug up his butt I wouldn't put it past him to go without me."

She rushed off, almost knocking down Lady Melinda as she sashayed around the corner, resplendent in lilac silk and lace.

Recovering, the Lady cast a poisonous glance at Cassie's back, before gliding over to Delmar and Ruby. "I pray you, Lady Ruby, have you seen Lord Colwyn anywhere today?"

"Why yes," replied Ruby, with a wicked grin. "He was in the training arena, where my sister beat him in a duel."

"What?"

For a moment Lady Melinda seemed to lose her composure. "Goodness, how... unexpected. He must be in need of having his spirits raised."

"Oh no, Lady Melinda," said Delmar, eyes gleaming. "He is, as we speak, preparing to go out on patrol with Lord Reutghar ... and Lady Cassandra." Ruby watched, fascinated, as Lady Melinda turned a rather unattractive shade of puce.

"I see," she finally managed to say. "Good day to you both." Recovering her wits, she curtsied briefly, then glided away.

"That was evil," murmured Ruby. "You don't like her either, do you?"

"Lady Melinda was confident she could use her winning ways to get to Colwyn through me," Delmar flashed Ruby a grin. "When that failed, she was rather ... abrasive in her comments." Ruby smiled. Delmar patted her arm. "I too must gather my belongings. As Lady Cassandra so elegantly put it, Colwyn does have a bug up his butt. I fear if I am late, he will not hesitate to leave without me either."

Fifteen minutes later Ruby watched a palely determined Cassie swing easily into her saddle. She raised a hand in farewell, before pulling her horse around to follow the others. They streamed over the drawbridge with a great clatter, leaving the courtyard silently empty. Alone, Ruby stood and watched.

The great drawbridge was raised, and the castle went about its daily life. Somewhat adrift, Ruby wandered to her room. She sat on her bed, wondering what to do and how long the others would be out on patrol. There was a tap at the door and the Lady glided in.

"There you are, Ruby. I was wondering if you would care to discuss plans for the continuance of your quest."

"Quest?" enquired Ruby. "What quest?"

"Why to locate the four treasures. Surely you have not forgotten," gently chided the Lady. "You have only discovered two so far, there are still two more to find."

"Oh, of course," cried Ruby. "With all that's happened, I'd almost forgotten about them. What do we look for next?"

"From air the golden griffin, crafted by elfish hand."

"What does it mean, crafted by elfish hand?" asked Ruby.

"Long ago, elves lived in Erinsmore. As the ancient ways were forgotten they retreated further into their lands. Finally, they left Erinsmore altogether and all crossings between this world and theirs ceased. Mayhap, this golden griffin is some artefact crafted by them, for indeed they were excellent craftsman."

"Maybe," agreed Ruby. "But with no starting place to begin looking, I don't see how we're going to find it."

"You must trust your instincts, Ruby, believe events fall out as they are destined to do," she paused, her perfect face composed. "I do not see the feather Cora gave you; I trust you have it safe?"

"It's here," Ruby pulled the feather from under her pillow.

"It should be worn about your person, Ruby," rebuked the Lady, gently.

"I know," said Ruby ruefully. "It's difficult to carry a feather around all the time."

"Let me see if I can remedy that for you, Ruby," smiled the Lady, and waved her hand gently over the feather. Ruby watched, fascinated, as the Lady's eyes pulsed blue once, and a sturdy silver chain appeared with the feather attached.

"Thank you," gasped Ruby, quickly fastening the chain around her neck so the feather dangled almost to her waist.

"You must keep the feather with you at all times," advised the Lady earnestly. "For Cora does not give them lightly, nor, I believe, would Gwnhyfar have told you to do so unless it was of some immense importance."

"I won't take it off again," promised Ruby, then sighed and wandered over to the window. "I wonder where they are now," she mused. "I hope Cassie's okay."

Chapter Fifteen

Ambush!

assie, to her astonishment, was rather enjoying herself. The temperature had risen, and the sun was warm on her face as she cantered with the rest of the patrol, looking around the unfamiliar landscape with interest.

Pure white snow sparkled in drifts and a great surge of joy arose within her. They'd done it. They were back in Erinsmore. Back with the people she'd longed for all year. She glanced at the stiff, implacable back of Colwyn and sighed a tiny sigh, some of the bloom rubbing off the day.

"My Lady." Her young soldier friend cantered up, pointing towards a hill on the left. Squinting against the snow glare, Cassie saw a flicker of movement. She gasped as a large stag, proud and magnificent, lifted his head to watch them pass.

Flashing the soldier a delighted grin, Cassie urged her horse on until she reached Colwyn and Darius, riding side by side, deep in discussion. As Cassie's horse drew alongside, both men stopped talking and looked at her, Darius with a welcoming smile, Colwyn with an ill-tempered scowl.

"Lady Cassandra," he began. "I beg you. It is unfitting for you to be here. What will the men think of a woman who insists on riding patrol? Will you not return to the castle?"

"Umm." Cassie pretended to consider it. "No," she said with a sweet smile.

"My Lady, it will be viewed as extremely unfeminine."

"Do I look bothered?" enquired Cassie, in her best Essex girl accent.

"Cassandra," snapped Colwyn. "Return to the castle."

"Shan't," retorted Cassie childishly.

Colwyn looked pained. "My Lady, I am accustomed to my commands being obeyed."

"Well, I guess you'd better get used to disappointment then."

There was a snort from Darius. Colwyn glared at his suspiciously straight face, before obviously deciding to try a different approach. "Lord Darius," he began.

"My Lord?"

"Did you perceive how very beautiful Lady Melinda looked last night?"

"My Lord?" repeated Darius, plainly puzzled, and shooting an uneasy glance in Cassie's direction, who was watching Colwyn with narrowed eyes.

"Why yes," enthused Colwyn. "Her hairstyle, her gown – were they not the very model of womanhood?"

"Umm, quite my Lord," mumbled Darius, uncomfortably.

"Apparently, she cooks divinely," continued Colwyn, with a fleeting look at Cassie. "And is it not true that through his stomach is the quickest way to a man's heart?"

"No," retorted Cassie cheekily. "It's through his rib cage with a sharp sword!" She touched her heels lightly to her horse, cantering away to ride next to Lord Reutghar and Delmar, leaving Colwyn gaping and Darius chuckling.

"Is she not the most fascinating of creatures, my Lord?"

Colwyn glared furiously at Darius, who was gazing after Cassie admiringly.

"Darius."

"My Lord?"

"If I challenge you to a duel, I will win, and I will hurt you."

"Yes, my Lord."

Still giggling, Cassie arrived beside Reutghar and Delmar, who both smiled to see her in such high spirits.

"We shall soon reach the small village of Corrinshill, Lady Cassandra," Reutghar informed her. "We will halt there to refresh ourselves, and to enquire if they have had any encounters with skraelings. Tis unlikely, this far north of Dragonswell, but we shall again offer to escort them should they wish to evacuate to the safety of the castle."

"Why didn't they go before?" Cassie asked.

"They are a proud and strong village," answered Reutghar. "Many of the men are retired soldiers, even the women are noted for their bravery and courage."

"I didn't think it was allowed for women to be anything but weak and helpless?" muttered Cassie, bitterly.

Reutghar's expression softened. "My son's opinions are not shared by all, my Lady. In faith, I do not think he believes them himself, mayhap he only needs the right woman to show him he is mistaken."

Cassie blushed at the meaning in Reutghar's warm gaze, averting her eyes in embarrassment. They crested the brow of a low hill and saw a neat village laid out in the valley below.

"Strange," Reutghar frowned. "The village is in the habit of posting look-outs, we should have been greeted by now."

They rode towards the outlying houses. Something about the eerie stillness of the place made Cassie's flesh creep and her heart quicken. Looking around, she saw a bundle of rags lying on the ground, gasping in shock as she realised it was the body of a man.

Suddenly alert, swords were drawn as they advanced cautiously into the village. It quickly became apparent, valiant as the men and women of Corrinshill had been, it had not protected them from the Gilmesh.

Bodies lay heaped everywhere, all bearing massive hack wounds inflicted by those deadly black swords. Cassie's eyes grew wide with horror at the awfulness, but it was nothing to the nightmare awaiting them in the village square.

The village children, from babies to teenagers, lying sprawled in various poses of death, clothing ripped away to reveal a large, dusty grey handprint on each chest.

Stumbling from her horse, Cassie clutched the reins tightly, staring in numbed revulsion. "Why?" she mumbled, through teeth that chattered. "Why did they do this? Why the children? What are those handprints?"

"It's where the Gilmesh extracted their souls," replied Colwyn, bleakly. "They take the souls of the young because they are the strongest, the purest." Cassie groaned, tripping over the body of a little girl whose eyes now stared at nothing. Alarm crossed Colwyn's face as he noted her green complexion.

"Wilfric!" he snapped.

The young soldier jumped to attention. "My Lord?"

"You and six others escort Lady Cassandra to the edge of the village. Stay there with her whilst we bury the dead."

"Yes, my Lord."

"And stay alert. We do not know how far away the Gilmesh are." Gently, the young soldier half led, half carried, Cassie away from the carnage, guiding her until they reached a small stream which burbled and rushed its way past the village.

Falling to her knees, Cassie closed her eyes in despair, her forehead clammy and hot. Behind her eyes floated the small faces of the babies and children. She groaned, leant forward, and to her extreme mortification proceeded to lose her breakfast in the stream.

Long painful moments later, a silently sympathetic Wilfric handed her a beaker of water and a damp cloth, and Cassie gratefully washed her face and hands.

"I remember when I saw my first Gilmesh victim," he said. "In faith, it made me sick to my stomach."

"Aye, I remember it too," remarked another soldier, dryly. "You ruined my best pair of boots." Cassie managed a small weak smile at the soldiers' attempts to raise her spirits, then pressed her hands to her eyes in despair.

"Lady Cassandra," began Wilfric, hesitantly.

"Yes?"

"I was wondering. That cunning move with which you defeated Lord Colwyn this morning, could you show us how it is done?"

Cassie lowered her hands. She stared at the small band of soldiers. Instead of the scornful derision, she expected to see, there was only admiration and interest on their faces.

Her spine straightened and her chin rose. "I will show you later," she murmured. "First, there's something we need to do."

Colwyn looked up in surprise from the grisly task of laying the bodies into the large grave they had dug as Cassie strode back into the square, followed by the small group of soldiers he'd sent to protect her.

"What are you doing, my Lady?" he demanded.

Cassie bent, tenderly lifted the body of a small baby, and laid it in the grave. "Helping you bury these poor people," she stated. Colwyn watched as she gently wiped the handprint from its chest, straightened its clothes, and passed a hand over its eyes to end that dreadful blank stare.

Finally, the grim duty was complete. Cassie stood with the men of Erinsmore as they silently bent their heads over the graves of the brave villagers of Corrinshill. Faces bleak and set, they re-mounted to resume their patrol and to spread the news of this latest atrocity, to persuade a nearby village to pack up their belongings and travel to the relative safety of the castle.

At the dread tidings, the next village hurriedly agreed to go, Colwyn ordering a small group to stay and escort them back to Dragonswell. They rode on, Cassie silently amazed that Colwyn had not insisted she return with them to the castle.

When the sun began to set, they stopped to make camp beside a rugged cliff face, and the soldiers busied themselves with their appointed tasks. Cassie wandered over to sit by herself on a fallen boulder, in shock at a day begun in triumph with her victory over Colwyn but ended in death and despair.

"May I join you, Lady Cassandra?" Lord Reutghar towered above her, a beaker of steaming liquid in each hand.

"Of course, my Lord," she murmured. Reutghar settled himself on a boulder and handed her one of the beakers which Cassie sipped at cautiously. "Coffee?" she exclaimed.

Reutghar grinned. "Delmar told me of your liking for this drink. Being of a curious nature, I ordered him to conjure some up for me. Much to my surprise, I found it to be a most agreeable potion, although, in faith, have learnt to my cost not to drink it too late in the evening else I seem unable to sleep."

"Coffee will do that," smiled Cassie, sipping with pleasure at the reviving liquid.

"I came to enquire as to your wellbeing, my Lady. When I ordered Colwyn to allow you to accompany us, I did not expect the experience to be so odious, and for that, I apologise."

"I made such a fool of myself at the village," Cassie muttered bitterly. "Maybe Colwyn's right. Maybe women should stay at home and sew, or something."

"Now, you do not mean that my Lady."

Cassie grimaced and shook her head. "At the village, seeing those poor people, it made me sick. I was a liability."

"I did not see a liability, my Lady," stated Reutghar, firmly. "I saw a brave and compassionate young woman who faced her fears and overcame them. Nobody would have thought any less of you for staying outside the village, yet you came back to help bury the dead. That to me was a worthy and admirable act."

"Colwyn didn't seem to think so," mumbled Cassie.

"Sometimes," Reutghar sighed. "I believe my son requires a good shaking..."

He rolled his eyes heavenward, and a shocked look of alarm leapt into them. Grabbing her roughly, he threw her away as an avalanche of rocks and boulders crashed onto them.

Cassie hit the ground and rolled. Instinctively drawing her sword, she sprang to her feet, seeing with horror, Reutghar lying half-buried beneath a pile of rubble. Frantically, she dropped her sword and knelt by his side, pulling rocks away to expose a deep gash across his forehead which was bleeding profusely. His eyes were closed. With shaking hands, she felt for a pulse in his throat, finding one with a moan of relief.

"Cassandra!" At Colwyn's shout, Cassie turned to see men rushing towards her from all directions.

"Hurry," she called. "Your father's hurt." She turned back to Reutghar, removing rocks as fast as she could. His eyes remained closed, and Cassie thanked heaven he'd insisted on Delmar accompanying them.

A muffled curse had her head whipping round to see Colwyn bounce off thin air, landing heavily on the ground.

"What is it? What's the matter?" she cried.

Colwyn jumped to his feet, advancing cautiously, arms outstretched. "Some kind of barrier," he called, hands feeling along the invisible wall. "Find a way through," he shouted. The soldiers spread out in a line, probing, and pushing.

"Delmar!" cried Colwyn, as the young mage arrived, breathless, from the other side of the camp. "Get through it, Lord Reutghar is injured."

Delmar nodded, and placed a palm flat to the unseen barricade, eyes pulsing blue as he tried to force a way through. "I'm not sure I can, my Lord," he gasped. "I have never known such power, except … it is like the barrier the lake people of Minwarn rose against us, but I do not see how it can be."

"Keep trying," snapped Colwyn. "We must get through."

"My Lord!" yelled a soldier in alarm. "Gilmesh, up on the cliff." Looking up in panic, Cassie saw the familiar grey skeletal figures creeping down the sheer cliff face towards her. Her heart juddered with fear.

"Get this barrier down, Delmar!" ordered Colwyn.

"I am trying, Colwyn, I need more energy."

"Take it from me," retorted Colwyn, clamping one hand onto Delmar's shoulder. His eyes flickered blue as Delmar reached down their link, drawing upon Colwyn's strength and vigour.

"Colwyn!" cried Cassie, watching those awful ghoulish figures creep ever closer.

Colwyn turned to Darius. "Have the archers shoot at the Gilmesh, mayhap the barrier does not go very far up."

Darius indicated to the soldiers to draw their bows. A dozen arrows were released, only to bounce harmlessly away into the evening sky as they struck the invisible wall.

Sobbing in terror, Cassie clawed at the rock pile, tossing them to one side to uncover Lord Reutghar's battered body. His eyes flickered, and he groaned.

"My Lord!" cried Cassie, using her cloak to wipe away the blood. "Reutghar, please wake up, the Gilmesh are coming!" His eyelids fluttered; Cassie bent closer.

"Cassandra!"

At Colwyn's yell, Cassie looked up as a Gilmesh lunged for her, bony fingers clutching at her hair. She screamed and ducked. Grabbing her sword, Cassie pivoted on one hip, slicing blindly upwards with the blade, neatly severing its head from its body. Screaming, it fell to the ground, writhing and thrashing as it disintegrated into fine grey dust.

"Delmar!" yelled Colwyn, pounding on the barrier in despair.

"I need more energy, my Lord."

"Take what you need."

"I cannot. Colwyn, it could kill you."

"Just do it!"

Staggering to her feet, Cassie watched in dumb terror as they climbed nearer and nearer, their hollow eye sockets glowing yellow. Clutching her sword, she knew she stood no chance. They would kill her, whilst the others trapped on the other side of the barrier would be powerless to help.

Perhaps they would extract her soul like the children of Corrinshill. An image of their tiny empty bodies flashed into her mind, and a white-hot tide of anger welled up inside her. A growl broke from her throat. The horrified soldiers stared aghast as Cassie raised a hand, and fire shot from her palm to turn her sword into a blazing shaft.

Barely aware of what had happened, Cassie embraced the still quiet heart of the flame, her body lightly flowed into position, and she met the first Gilmesh as it reared over the prone body of Reutghar. Her blade sang its song, slicing with almost delicate precision through the thick bony torso which burst into a column of fire, the Gilmesh shrieking and disintegrating into dust.

Spinning, Cassie confronted the attacking Gilmesh, their blades met and locked, the radiant beauty of Cassie's sword sparking along the dull black edge of the Gilmesh weapon. With a flick of her wrist, Cassie sent the massive sword flying, dispatching its owner with a thrust of fire.

Silence fell over the watching soldiers, gaping in wonder.

Stepping lightly, Cassie moved so quickly she seemed a blur, and two more Gilmesh fell to her blade. She was death, both terrible and beautiful to see. Her eyes pulsed blue as she dispensed justice, swift and final, for the people of Corrinshill. For all the people of Erinsmore who had died hideous and violent deaths at the hands of the Gilmesh.

Time slowed to a heartbeat. Colwyn sank to his knees, the drain on his energy taking effect, watching with numb hope as Cassie whirled to face another Gilmesh. Her lithe beauty edged with fiery steel as she drove her sword home, and one by one, the Gilmesh screamed and died.

Finally, the last Gilmesh fell and with it, the barrier. Cheering, the soldiers surged forward. Cassie slumped exhausted to the ground, her eyes and flaming sword returning to normal.

The soldiers pulled the last of the rocks from their Lord and Delmar rushed to him. Cassie shakily got to her feet, stumbling to where Colwyn knelt. Silently, she helped him up, bracing herself to take his weight, supporting him as they staggered to where Lord Reutghar lay encased in a blue glow with Delmar working to heal his wounds.

Finally, Delmar pulled back. Darius helped Lord Reutghar to sit, blinking in confusion at the circle of relieved faces around him. "What happened?" he asked, concern leaping into his eyes. "Is the Lady Cassandra unharmed?"

"Aye, my Lord," replied Darius, soberly. "She saved you both. How, is a miracle I am still trying to understand."

It was a sombre and silent group who returned to the castle the next day. Running to the courtyard, Ruby watched in alarm as they filed over the drawbridge, her eyes searching until with a hot jolt of relief she saw Cassie riding safely beside Lord Reutghar. Wearily, Cassie dismounted.

Ruby rushed to her. "What happened? Are you all right?"

"Later," murmured Cassie. "Tell you everything later, I want to have a bath, go to bed, didn't sleep last night, so tired." Ruby hovered, concerned, as Cassie shuffled into the castle.

"Come with us, Ruby," Delmar said gently. "We must see the Lady, and it will be easier to only have to tell the tale once."

Ruby sat, stunned, her mind struggling to understand what she'd been told. She cast a quick look around the table at the others, Lord Reutghar, Darius, Colwyn, and Delmar, then turned to look at Lady Ninniane sitting at the head of the table, her flawless forehead creasing in a thoughtful frown.

"Although I am truly grateful Lady Cassandra discovered she had the ability in such a dramatic and timely fashion," began Lord Reutghar, "I am puzzled as to how one not born of Erinsmore can possess it."

"Well, we do have Erinsmore blood from Lady Gwnhyfar," Ruby reminded him.

"Lady Gwnhyfar?" enquired Reutghar, frowning. "I am unfamiliar with the Lady."

"She was betrothed to Arturius but married King Mark of our world. She returned with him and the other warriors who fought to defeat Lorcan."

Reutghar shook his head, his frown deepening.

Ruby stared in surprise. "I don't understand," she began. "Garth has never heard of Gwnhyfar either, yet she's such an important part of Erinsmore's history we've heard of her in my world. Why does no one here remember her?"

"When someone leaves their own world behind, it is as if they never existed," explained the Lady. "Thus, when Gwnhyfar chose to return with Mark, all trace of her life in Erinsmore was erased."

"But ..." stuttered Ruby. "Garth lived in our world for three years and everyone here remembers him."

"Because in his heart Garth never truly left Erinsmore, never stopped considering it his home, believing one day he would return. When your heart resides in another world, it becomes your home, and your lifeline in your former world ceases to be."

"Oh," said Ruby. "I see."

"Well," sighed Lord Reutghar. "I must visit the admirable Gretchen in the kitchen and give orders for tonight."

"What's happening tonight?" enquired Colwyn.

"Why the feast, my son, had you forgotten?" boomed Reutghar, a wicked twinkle in his eyes, "The feast to celebrate Lady Cassandra's victory over you."

He laughed, and Ruby turned away to hide her smirk at Colwyn's expression.

Peeking in on Cassie, Ruby found her deep in the sleep of pure exhaustion, so crept away and went to find Delmar instead. Going to the training arena, the obliging soldiers set up an archery target, and Ruby demonstrated to the interested men her ability with the bow.

"Remarkable," Delmar exclaimed, as the men moved the target further and further away, cheering as Ruby hit the bullseye every time. "It is truly remarkable how you have both discovered your abilities."

The soldiers clustered around, wondering at her skills. Over again, Ruby heard the tale of the wondrous Lady Cassandra and her stunning victory against the Gilmesh. The tale became more fantastical with each telling, and Ruby grinned to herself, realising Cassie was quickly on her way to becoming a legend.

When the shadows in the courtyard lengthened, Ruby went to their room to get ready for the banquet to find Cassie, awake and grumpy, sitting in front of the mirror, surveying her hair all crinkly from the plait, and tousled from sleep.

"It's no good," she exclaimed on Ruby's entry and tossed her hairbrush down. "I can't go, that's all."

"Not go?"

"To dinner! I've nothing to wear and my hair's a mess."

"You've got to go," stated Ruby firmly. "It's a banquet in your honour. Colwyn's going to go down on one knee before you and hand you his sword."

"He is?" Cassie stared.

"Yes, don't you remember? Before your duel, Lord Reutghar said the loser would have to bow before the victor and give them their sword."

"Well, then I definitely can't go," snorted Cassie. "I mean, look at me. How can I stand there in front of ... everyone, looking like this? And I bet Lady Melinda will be there in some fabulous dress that makes her look, oh so feminine," Cassie snarled at her reflection, "Model of womanhood, hah!"

"What?"

"Never mind."

"It's so unfair," declared Ruby hotly, "You're tons prettier than she is, you just need a stunning dress."

"Yeah," drawled Cassie. "And precisely where do you suggest I ...?" Her voice trailed away, and a thoughtful look settled on her face. "Go and get Delmar," she snapped. "Tell him it's life or death, and really, *really* important I see him."

"Why?"

"Please, Ruby, just do it."

Rushing from the room, Ruby saw a passing servant and requested that Delmar be found and sent to Lady Cassandra's room immediately on an urgent matter.

Ten minutes later there was a knock on the door and Delmar pelted in, breathlessly concerned.

"Lady Cassandra," he gasped. "I came as quickly as I could, what is amiss? Are you unwell?"

"No, no, I'm fine," Cassie brushed away his concerns. "Delmar, that trick you did with the coffee when I thought about it in my mind and you were able to conjure it up, does it work with just drinks, or could you magic up anything?"

"What is it my Lady requires?"

"A new dress," explained Cassie.

Delmar frowned. "I can certainly arrange for the court seamstress to visit you, but I fail to see..."

"No," interrupted Cassie, impatiently. "There's no time, I need the most stunningly amazing dress, and I need it now."

"Lady Cassandra." Delmar looked pained. "I do not think it appropriate to use my ability for the creation of a gown."

"Please, Delmar," Cassie's eyes turned into pleading pools of amber liquid, her lips quivering into a pout. Ruby watched, fascinated, as an expert in the art of manipulation who could give lessons to Lady Melinda, sidled up to Delmar and caught his hands in her own.

"I can't go to the banquet without a dress. You wouldn't want me to be sitting in my room all evening, alone, whilst everybody else was down there having fun, would you?"

Delmar reddened and swallowed. "You must attend the banquet, my Lady, it is in your honour."

"Exactly," cooed Cassie, clutching his hands to her chest. "So, you see, it is your duty to help me."

"My ... duty...?" stuttered Delmar dazed. Ruby felt almost sorry for him.

"Yes, your duty," simpered Cassie, fluttering her eyelashes.

"Very well, my Lady, I will help you."

"Delmar, you're the best," squealed Cassie, dropping his hands and pressing a quick kiss to his flustered cheeks. He reddened even more, stammering and spluttering. Ruby knew at that precise moment he'd have cheerfully walked through fire for Cassie if she'd asked him to.

"Fix an image in your mind, my Lady, of the type of gown you wish to be wearing, picture it. The material, the fit, the colour. The more detail you can imagine, the easier it will be to make."

Cassie closed her eyes. Delmar gently placed his hand on her forehead, his eyes pulsing blue. Ruby watched in amazement as Cassie shimmered into a column of light which engulfed her body. When it faded moments later, Cassie was wearing a dress.

Scarlet. She'd chosen the colour scarlet. Ruby realised it was a colour she'd not seen anywhere in Erinsmore. Out of all the rainbow-coloured assorted gowns present at dinner the other night, not one had been of this particular shade.

The gown was long, its full skirt rustling in silken folds to a lace-trimmed hem. The sleeves were long and tight to the elbows, then frothed and foamed in folds of lace to Cassie's slim wrists. Lace-trimmed the neckline and swept down to her waist. It was undoubtedly beautiful and yet ... Ruby put her head on one side, surveying the dress, something was not quite right.

There was a knock at the door. It opened to reveal Lady Ninniane and Lord Reutghar, the latter holding a small, ornately carved wooden chest.

"I came to offer my services with acquiring gowns for you to wear to the banquet tonight," the Lady began, stopping with a frown as she took in Cassie's appearance. "I see you have already made your own arrangements."

"What do you think?" asked Cassie, in excitement.

"It is a very beautiful dress, and what a stunning colour," declared the Lady. "You have done excellently well, Delmar."

"Thank you, my Lady," he grinned. "I pray you, do not speak of this to anyone or else all the ladies of the castle will be requiring my services, and the guild of the seamstresses will be baying for my blood."

"It is a lovely gown," mused the Lady, thoughtfully. "And yet, may I be permitted to make a few alterations." Cassie nodded. The Lady waved her hand gently, and again Cassie was bathed in light. When it faded, Ruby gasped in delight.

Every scrap of lace was gone. The skirt was not so full and flowed suggestively over her hips. The sleeves were tight, ending in elongated points over the back of Cassie's hands, showcasing her smooth, well-toned arms. The bodice was longer, tapering to a narrow point to emphasise her slender waist. The neckline was slightly lower and squarer, the dragon pendant glinting on her collarbone.

"There, that is much better," declared the Lady, satisfied. "Sometimes," she continued, "it is better to go for stunning simplicity and stand out from the other ladies, rather than blindly follow court fashions. Now then, what shall we do with your hair? Oh yes, how about something like this..."

Once again, she waved her hands. Cassie stared in speechless amazement at her reflection and the cascade of corkscrew curls reaching almost to her waist.

"Now it is your turn, Ruby," said the Lady, with a smile. Much to Ruby's delight, a moment later she was clad in a gown almost identical to the moss green one she'd worn at the Sanctuary and loved so much.

"Thank you," she gasped, running her fingers over her long auburn hair, now glossy and shining as if she'd stepped from the trendiest of salons.

"My Ladies," started Reutghar gruffly. "None will match you tonight at the banquet in beauty, nor in valour. It is of the latter I have come to talk with you, Lady Cassandra."

"My Lord?" Cassie looked puzzled.

Reutghar held out the wooden casket. "I owe you my life, my Lady. I am grateful for your courage and your swordsmanship. Not only yesterday. I have been reliably informed by Lord Darius, that without the bravery and skill of you, Garth, and Lady Ruby, he and his men would have been extremely unlikely to have survived."

He opened the casket, removed a string of pearls, and handed them to Delmar.

"Please place these around Lady Ruby's neck as a token of our esteem." Beaming, Ruby lifted her hair so a gently smiling Delmar could fasten the clasp. Softly, she stroked the glowing pearls, which were warm and alive to her touch.

"And for you, Lady Cassandra," Cassie's eyes rounded as Reutghar drew a magnificent tiara from the casket and handed it to the Lady, who gently placed it on Cassie's head.

"Oh, my Lord, thank you," gasped the sisters, admiring their gifts in the mirror.

"They belonged to my wife. I feel she would be delighted to know they are now yours. Now then, my Lady, Delmar, we must away to open the feast. Might I suggest you Ladies bide here for a while, then enter the hall by the great staircase," his eyes twinkled. "You will make more of an entrance that way."

When the door closed, Cassie and Ruby stared joyfully at each other, then Cassie dived for one of her saddle bags and pulled out a small bag.

"What's that?" asked Ruby, curiously. Her jaw dropped as Cassie pulled makeup from the bag. "I thought you said we could only bring essentials?" she demanded.

"These are essentials," murmured Cassie, expertly smudging eyeliner, stroking mascara carefully onto lashes. A blush of colour to emphasise her cheekbones, a smear of soft pink lip gloss and she was ready. Ruby had never seen her sister look more beautiful.

The banquet was in full swing, and still, she had not come. Colwyn stared morosely into his goblet of wine, trying to define exactly what his feelings were for the stubborn, headstrong, infuriatingly alluring, Lady Cassandra.

"My Lord Colwyn," Lady Melinda, resplendent in lemon silk, lace, and emeralds, hovered at his shoulder, poised to receive his compliments.

"Lady Melinda," he rose to his feet. "You are looking very fine this evening."

"Thank you, my Lord," she simpered, snapping open her fan with an expert flick of her wrist. "I have been reflecting on your words, on how right you are. A woman should concentrate on what is appropriate; should accept her place in life."

"Really?" Colwyn glanced at her. His face impassive. "And what place would that be, Lady Melinda?"

"Why, behind her lord and master, of course," she breathed huskily. Colwyn frowned and was about to reply when the music abruptly stopped. A hush fell over the hall.

Cassie and Ruby stood on the steps. Two sisters, radiantly beautiful in their own way, yet Colwyn only had eyes for one of them. Behind him, one lady muttered to her companion. "Where did she get that gown? Observe the colour."

"I do not know," was the murmured reply. "But I desire one just like it."

The silence dragged on. Unsure, Cassie lifted her chin in defiance of the shocked stares. Then a muttering began, which quickly grew into a chant. Louder and louder rang out the soldiers' voices, as men who had been on patrol with her and watched her fight the Gilmesh; soldiers whose lives she and Garth had saved, and others who had merely heard the stories and admired, joined in.

"Cassandra. Cassandra. Cassandra!"

Swords were rattled, and fists were banged on tables. Cassie smiled in delighted wonder at the full-throated homage being paid to her by the warriors of Erinsmore.

All thoughts of Lady Melinda instantly banished from his mind, Colwyn strode through the crowd, across the dance floor. He dropped to one knee before Cassie. The chanting stopped immediately.

"My Lady," he began. The silence was absolute as all strained to see and hear. "I kneel before you in honour of the fairest of ladies. One who not only bested me in a friendly duel but has consistently displayed such acts of valour and bravery her name will be forever synonymous with courage. You have all heard how Lady Cassandra saved the life of our beloved Lord Reutghar, my father. How the whole of Erinsmore now owes her a debt beyond repayment."

Cassie blinked back tears as Colwyn unsheathed his sword. Eyes never leaving her face, he held it up to her in both hands.

"I offer you my sword, Lady Cassandra, and my pledge that whatsoever you command, so shall I obey."

There was a stunned silence, so thick Ruby could almost hear it. All eyes flicked to Cassie. She stepped gracefully forward, taking the sword in both hands.

"My Lord Colwyn," she began, voice husky with emotion. "I accept your sword and pledge, and the honour that you have shown me. I hereby return your sword with a pledge of my own. Neither my sister nor I shall rest until Lorcan has been defeated, and the people of Erinsmore avenged for the foul atrocities visited on them by this most evil of tyrants."

Bending, she returned the sword to Colwyn's grasp and held out her hand, which Colwyn took and kissed, before rising to his feet and turning to face the crowd.

"All hail Lady Cassandra," he cried, and the cheers nearly lifted the roof.

Later, much later, Ruby sprawled contently in her chair and thought what a wonderful evening it had been. The food had been superb, and she'd drunk more wine than Mum would approve of. The dancing had begun, and Ruby smiled to see Colwyn and Cassie on the floor, eyes only for each other, moving together with precisely elegant steps.

Undoubtedly, it had been Cassie's evening. Delmar and Ruby exchanged smugly satisfied glances at the expression of bitter resentment on Lady Melinda's face every time she looked at Cassie seated between Colwyn and Lord Reutghar.

Stifling a yawn, Ruby wondered if anyone would notice if she crept off to bed. The evening was showing no signs of ending, and Ruby was tired, worn out by the events of the past three days.

"Are you wishing to retire, Ruby?" Ruby smiled, sleepily nodding at Delmar. "Come, I will escort you to your room," he offered, and gallantly helped her from her chair.

Lord Darius also rose. "I will escort Lady Ruby to her room," he said. "I must check on the changing of the watch, so can see the Lady safely back to her room on the way."

"I'm quite capable of going on my own," murmured Ruby.

"Indeed, you are, my Lady, yet it is no trouble for me to escort you," insisted Darius. Ruby nodded, murmuring sleepy goodnights to Delmar and Lord Reutghar. Lady Ninniane had already retired some time previously.

Leaving the hall, Ruby realised how empty the rest of the castle was, grateful Darius was there, feeling safe in his company. As they made their way up steps and along corridors, Ruby shivered in the chilly air which gusted down the passageway making the flames in the sconces flicker, casting eerie shadows on the walls.

At the strange, whispering, tickling sensation in her mind, Ruby rubbed uneasily at her forehead and Darius glanced at her in concern. "Are you feeling all right, Lady Ruby?"

"I'm not sure," replied Ruby. "I feel a little odd, as if..."

Gilmesh were upon them.

Ruby screamed in utter shock. Darius pulled his sword and dragged her back.

"Run!" he commanded.

Ruby fled down the passageway. Glancing back, she saw his blade flash, the sparks fly, as it clashed with the black sword of the lead Gilmesh. Crying out in horror, she ran, headfirst, into another group of Gilmesh coming the other way along the passage. Cold, grey, skeletal hands gripped her tightly. Ruby felt a wave of revulsion at their touch, kicking and screaming in their clasp.

"Let her go!" ordered Darius, desperately fighting three Gilmesh at once.

Good evening, Ruby. The cold, silky tones of Lorcan echoed in her mind. *Do not struggle and you will not be harmed.*

Let me go! Ruby screamed in her mind.

Delmar's head snapped up and he leapt from his chair. In her bed, Lady Ninniane awoke abruptly from her sleep.

Bring her, commanded Lorcan. The Gilmesh lifted Ruby over one bony shoulder, carrying her like a sack of potatoes.

"Ruby!" yelled Darius, slicing frantically at a Gilmesh, who disintegrated into dust.

What about him? The voice of the Gilmesh was indifferent.

Take his soul, ordered Lorcan.

Frantically, Ruby screamed and thrashed, kicking in frenzied despair as the Gilmesh carried her off. The last thing she saw was Darius being forced to the ground by half a dozen Gilmesh, who ripped hungrily at his shirt.

"No!" sobbed Ruby. There was a rush of frigid air and she realised they were outside the castle, that there was no one coming to help Darius or her. A bony hand pinched a nerve at the back of her neck, and Ruby knew no more.

Running desperately down echoing stone passageways, Cassie heard a scream of despair which bounced off the walls and turned her blood to ice. Gathering up her skirts even further, she lengthened her stride, trying to keep up with Colwyn, Delmar and Reutghar ahead of her.

Turning the corner, they saw the Gilmesh savagely holding down a frantically struggling man, who twisted and writhed in agony as a Gilmesh thrust a grey bony hand onto his chest.

Yelling with rage, Reutghar and Colwyn drew their swords and fell upon the Gilmesh, whilst Delmar calmly released fireballs into them. Unarmed, Cassie yanked a torch from the wall. Brandishing it before her, she waded into the battle, snarling as she thrust it into the Gilmesh, reducing them to grey dust.

Finally, none were left. Delmar dropped to his knees beside a still Darius. Anxiously holding out a hand, he engulfed him in a blue, shimmering haze, until Darius coughed and groaned, rolling over and struggling to get to his knees.

"Easy now, my Lord," ordered Reutghar.

Darius thankfully sucked in air, eyes focusing painfully on Cassie. "I am sorry, my Lady," he croaked. "There were too many of them, I tried but was overwhelmed by their numbers. I was unable to stop them from taking her."

"Taking who?" demanded Cassie, a cold fist closing around her heart. "Where's Ruby?" she shrieked. "Where is she?"

"I am sorry, my Lady," Darius bowed his head in shame. "They took her."

"No!" denied Cassie wildly, tears pouring unchecked down her face. Instinctively, she turned to Colwyn who placed an arm around her shoulders, his face drawn with horror.

"They'll kill her," she whispered, images of the dead children of Corrinshill swimming past her eyes. "They'll take her soul, oh no, Ruby!"

"If that was all they were planning," came Lady Ninniane's cool voice behind them, "they would have done that here and now. No, they have taken her to Lorcan, although for what purpose I cannot imagine."

"They have not had much of a start," declared Reutghar. "To horses! We will track them, forever if we must. My Lord," he turned on Darius. "Are you able to ride?"

Darius staggered to his feet. "To find Lady Ruby, yes, my Lord, I am able."

"Good," Lord Reutghar hurried away. "Colwyn, come. We must be after them before the trail grows too cold."

Gently, Colwyn handed the sobbing Cassie over to Lady Ninniane, then cupped her face in his hands. "I will find her for you," he promised. "I will find her."

"Colwyn!" roared his father, and Colwyn had to go, his farewell the wild sobs of Cassie as she wept for her sister.

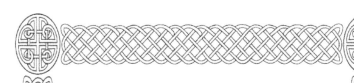

Chapter Sixteen

Ruby! Ruby! Ruby!

oftness beneath her cheek. Somewhere, beyond her eyelids, Ruby felt the heat of a fire, smelt wood smoke, and heard the crackle of logs shifting and burning.

Cautiously, Ruby opened her eyes. She was lying on a bed. A huge comfortable bed, heaped high with cushions and velvet throws, topped with a magnificent canopy draped in purple velvet.

Slowly, she sat up, head throbbing, and looked around. She was in a large, pleasantly proportioned circular room with stone floors and walls. Many thick brightly patterned rugs and exquisite tapestries hung on the walls and covered the floor. The fire she'd heard glowed merrily in a large hearth, flickering shadows around the dimly lit room.

To her relief, she was alone. Tentatively, Ruby swung her legs over the edge of the bed and stood up, the pounding headache threatening to remove the top of her skull. Memory flooded back. Ruby swallowed hard, tears pricking, as she remembered Darius being forced to the ground by the Gilmesh.

She examined the room. The door she presumed was the exit was firmly locked. No amount of pulling made any difference. A small door on the other side of the room led to a side chamber containing a washstand and commode. Gratefully, Ruby poured a little of the water from the pitcher into the bowl, and washed her face and hands, drying them on a soft towel.

Back in the main room, a small round table stood before the fire, a chair pulled up invitingly to it, a covered tray on its polished surface. Removing the cover, Ruby found soft rolls enfolded in a snowy damask napkin, still warm, with a pot of butter. Cheese wrapped in paper and a selection of fruit was also on the tray, along with a small jug of wine and a larger jug of water.

Ruby stared at the tray, wondering whether she dare eat or drink. Perhaps it was poisoned. Eventually, she reasoned if her abductor wished her dead, they could easily have done so whilst she was unconscious, and she risked a little water, the headache easing as she gulped thirstily at the crystal-clear liquid.

Revived, Ruby continued the exploration of her prison. Drawing back the sumptuous velvet curtains, Ruby found doors leading onto a stone balcony. Trying the doors, she was surprised to find them unlocked. Heart pounding, she stepped into the chilly air, shocked it was mid-morning. She must have been unconscious for hours.

The balcony wasn't large, and Ruby rushed eagerly to the balustrade, hoping to gain a clue as to her whereabouts and maybe discover an escape route. She peered over, reeling back in stunned, nauseated shock. She was high, so very high. The ground was a mere far away smudge, and wisps of clouds pressed against the tower below.

Sinking down onto the balcony, Ruby realised why the doors had been left unlocked. There would be no escape that way. Nothing but certain death awaited anyone foolish enough to try and climb down the sheer walls of the tower.

Fighting extreme vertigo, Ruby edged to the balustrade and looked over again, the ground swimming dizzily before her watering eyes. Quickly, she looked skywards to survey the turreted rooftop stretching above her into the snow-laden sky, realising her room was the highest in the whole tower. The perfect prison, she thought bitterly.

A noise, the sound of a key, had her hurriedly turning. Lorcan, the evil presence from her dreams, stepped into the room followed by a young, thin, dark-haired girl, dressed in simple peasant clothes, her eyes bent firmly onto the floor.

He seemed bigger than in her dreams, looming more menacingly. Ruby swallowed nervously as he looked her up and down, thin lips curling into a cold, bloodless smile, his mane of pure white hair gleaming in the fire light.

"Good," he purred, voice smooth as silk. "You have awoken. I trust you are well and not experiencing too many side effects from your journey."

"Where am I?" demanded Ruby. "What do you want?"

"All in good time," he purred. "Firstly, this miserable creature," he gestured to the girl, "is to be your servant. She exists to cater for your every need. She is to obey your commands, unless, of course, they contradict my own. Her name is Nerrisa. If she does not suit, I shall dispose of her and acquire another for you."

"Dispose of her?" stuttered Ruby, disbelievingly.

"The Gilmesh enjoy feasting on the souls of the young," he informed her. Nerrisa's eyes met Ruby's, terrified and pleading.

"No, no, I'm sure she'll be fine," stammered Ruby quickly, and saw the grateful relief before the girl lowered her eyes once more to the floor.

"Go," Lorcan dismissed her with a wave. "Your mistress will summon you when she has need of you." Bobbing a curtsey, Nerrisa scurried from the room. Lorcan silently surveyed Ruby, before moving to the table and pouring a goblet of wine.

"Drink," he ordered, pouring a second goblet which he held out to Ruby.

"I don't want any," retorted Ruby.

Lorcan's face darkened. "When I give you an order," he boomed, "you will obey it! You live only so long as I deem you should. The slightest excuse, my Lady, will suffice to make me give you to the Gilmesh, and that pathetic child will not be the only one they feast on."

Terrified, Ruby silently reached out a hand and took the goblet, taking a tiny sip of the full-bodied and utterly delicious wine. She turned wide eyes back onto Lorcan, who smiled, his good humour restored.

"Do not attempt to leave this room, my Lady, Gilmesh guard the door, and you have already discovered that escape from the balcony is impossible. Every morning, you and your maid will be escorted to the roof terrace for fresh air and exercise. Every evening, you will join me for dinner. Do not even contemplate trying to escape, Gilmesh guard the tower at every level. You would not get more than two steps before being apprehended."

"Where is this place?" demanded Ruby.

"This is the last elfish building left standing in Erinsmore. Protected by a magical force field, none know of its existence. So put all thoughts of rescue out of your mind. Your sister and Reutghar's muscle-bound son will never find you."

"Why?" whispered Ruby. "Why have you brought me here?"

"It was to be your sister," he mused, sipping at his wine, black eyes glinting maliciously. "Somehow, she managed to destroy the Gilmesh I sent to fetch her. I was, I must admit, surprised at her level of ability. I had believed, other than your powers, nothing had been passed to you from Gwnhyfar."

He smiled. Ruby's flesh crawled.

"Upon reflection, I find myself strangely relieved that destiny intervened to make your sister an untenable choice. Being older, and of such a forceful nature, it was more desirable for her younger, more malleable sister to be the one."

"One?" stuttered Ruby. "What one?"

"Why the one to reign Erinsmore at my side. I was trapped for millennia. I became lonely, Ruby. I desire companionship."

"What?"

"Rejoice in your good fortune, my Lady, for I have chosen you to be my queen."

"No," the goblet slipped from Ruby's numb fingers, ruby red liquid splashed like blood onto the rug. "Never!" she gasped.

Lorcan smiled. "So, like her," he mused. "I find it … pleasing. Not only do you resemble her greatly, but your spirit is also strong. It will make it such a challenge to crush it."

"I don't understand," gasped Ruby, mind spinning. "Who do I resemble?"

"Gwnhyfar," he snarled, cruelly handsome face twisting into a sneer of frustrated rage. "She should have been mine."

Ruby stepped back from the fury in his voice.

"I told my fellow mages I desired her for my wife. They refused to countenance it. Dared to lecture me … me … on the unfairness of immortals marrying mortals, that Gwnhyfar was betrothed to Arturius, a betrothal they were not prepared to break." He paused. Ruby saw the madness in his eyes.

"Imagine my rage when I escaped my imprisonment to discover her betrothal *had* been broken, after all, broken so she could marry Mark and accompany him back to your world. The insult was too much to bear, my Gwnhyfar, given to the man responsible for my capture."

"She was never your Gwnhyfar," denied Ruby, hotly. "She would have rather died than marry you … so would I!"

"You will change your mind," declared Lorcan, smiling thinly. "When Reutghar and his band of fools are destroyed, the Lady stripped of her power, you will appreciate what it means to be the queen of a great and all-powerful ruler. Imagine, Ruby, I will control this world and other worlds besides. With you by my side, we could breed a dynasty of demigods that will rule forever, and never be defeated."

"No," whispered Ruby numbly, backing away. "I will never agree, never."

"Oh, you will, eventually ... perhaps when I drag your sister before you and offer you a choice. Become my queen or watch whilst the Gilmesh slowly wrench her soul from her tortured body." He shrugged, draining his goblet dry. "I shall leave you to reflect, my Lady, and will send your maid to you later to prepare you for dinner." With a swirl of black cloak, he left.

Her knees buckled. She sank to the floor. The tears that she'd successfully held in streamed, unchecked, down her face, and Ruby gave in to despair.

Colwyn knocked gently on the door to Lady Ninniane's chambers, rubbing at eyes gritty through lack of sleep. A moment later it was opened by Moll, Ninniane's lady-in-waiting, who put a finger to her lips and stepped back to allow him entry.

"How is she today?" Colwyn whispered.

Moll shook her head. "About the same, my Lord, she slept fitfully, if at all. I managed to coax a little porridge into her. In faith, it is the first food she has eaten in days."

"May I see her?" Colwyn asked hopefully.

Moll pursed her lips. "She is sleeping, my Lord...."

"Of course, do not awaken her," agreed Colwyn, disappointment etched into his face. "Will you tell her I was enquiring after her?"

"Of course, my Lord," agreed Moll, ushering him to the door. "Colwyn?"

Colwyn's heart lurched at the pale, stricken figure standing in the doorway, clad in a long white robe, her hair loose and spread over her shoulders like a shawl.

"Cassandra," he breathed. Taking her hand, he led her to a chair by the fire. "Come, sit," he urged, sitting opposite.

"Is there any news?" Cassie's voice was breathless with hope, hope which Colwyn despised himself for having to crush.

"I am sorry, my Lady," he replied gently. "We have searched the countryside for miles around, there is no sign of her." Cassie's face fell. Colwyn saw her eyes brighten with unshed tears. Desperately, he reached for her hand.

"Oh Colwyn," she sobbed. "It's been weeks. We're not going to find her, are we?"

"There is always hope, my Lady," he replied, hoping his voice did not betray his true convictions. "And I will not stop searching. You have my word on that."

"My Lady?" Ruby looked up from the book she was reading to find Nerrisa peering anxiously at her. She realised from the lengthening shadows and gathering gloom, that it was getting late. Once again, it was time to dress for dinner.

She sighed, marked her place, and put the book regretfully down. Watching Nerrisa scurry around the room, building up the fire and lighting lamps, she was reluctant to move from her armchair to face her nightly ordeal.

In the weeks since her abduction, Ruby's life had settled into a mundane, almost boring routine. She slept late; being awoken by Nerrisa with breakfast long after the sun was up.

Once she had eaten and dressed, they would be escorted up to the terrace which clung to the steeply turreted roof. They would be allowed to remain there for exactly two hours, after which time they were escorted back to her room for lunch.

On those first visits to the terrace, they'd frantically searched for an escape route. Nerrisa watched out for the Gilmesh guards, whilst Ruby risked life and limb clambering up steep tiles, heart leaping into her mouth every time her foot slipped. The girls quickly realised if they were to escape from the tower, it would not be from the terrace with its breathtakingly terrifying view to the ground, hundreds of feet below.

After lunch, Nerrisa had to perform other chores around the tower and Ruby was locked in her room. Following her complaint of boredom, Lorcan sent her books. At first, Ruby read them simply as something to do, but quickly became fascinated by the ancient legends of Erinsmore and other worlds, recognising, to her surprise, some from her world.

In the late afternoon, Nerrisa was released from her duties to attend to Ruby and prepare her to dine with Lorcan. Ruby dreaded the evenings. The nightly ordeal of facing Lorcan down a long highly polished table, eating exquisitely prepared food, each mouthful disintegrating like sawdust in her mouth as he talked to her as if they were old friends.

Only once had Ruby rebelled and refused to attend. Nerrisa woke her next morning, livid bruises marring her small face where she'd been beaten by the surly cook on Lorcan's orders. A horrified and guilty Ruby never disobeyed again.

Every evening, Lorcan would ask if she'd reconsidered his offer. Every evening, Ruby would swallow down her fear, and resolutely shake her head. Lorcan would smile at her over the rim of his wine goblet.

"You will," he'd purr. "You will."

The only bright point for Ruby was the time she spent with Nerrisa. At first shy and scared around her, the young girl soon realised Ruby was a prisoner, like her. Under the grim circumstances in which they found themselves, a deep friendship quickly formed.

Now, Ruby leant back in her chair, watching as Nerrisa busied herself with laying out one of the many sumptuous gowns Lorcan insisted she wear.

"Nerrisa," she enquired. "How did you get here? Were you kidnapped by the Gilmesh too?"

"Aye, my Lady," replied Nerrisa grimly, choosing a deep green velvet gown from the wardrobe and spreading it on the bed.

"What happened?" asked Ruby interested.

"I was gathering firewood, my Lady. I probably should not have been, what with the skraeling and Gilmesh attacks, but they had all happened south of Dragonswell. The opinion was they wouldn't come as far north as my village. I was in the forest when those monsters were all about me, and one grabbed me. Next thing I knew, I was here."

"I'm sorry," murmured Ruby. "He only brought you here to look after me."

"It is all right, my Lady," reassured Nerrisa, with a quick smile. "It was not your fault; I know you do not want to be here anymore than I do."

"I'll say," agreed Ruby, wryly. "What was your village?"

"Corrinshill," replied Nerrisa.

"Oh, Nerrisa," Ruby stared at her in horrified dismay.

Nerrisa's face tightened with fear. "My Lady?" her voice quavered. "What is it? Why do you look at me like that?"

"Oh Nerrisa," said Ruby, again. "I'm so sorry."

"My Lady?"

"Corrinshill was attacked by the Gilmesh the day before I came here."

"Do you know how it fared, my Lady?"

"There were no survivors," Ruby whispered, hurrying to hold Nerrisa as her face crumpled and she began to cry.

"All?" she gasped, "All dead?"

"I'm so sorry," murmured Ruby, Nerrisa's slight body shuddered in her arms. "My sister was out on patrol with Colwyn and Reutghar. They arrived too late. The Gilmesh had already ... well, they had to bury the whole village."

"My family," whispered Nerrisa, and Ruby's heart ached.

Grimly, Colwyn swung himself into his saddle, preparing to lead his men out. After weeks of fruitless searching for clues as to Ruby's whereabouts, constant ongoing skirmishes with the skraelings, and frantic chasing of the elusive trail of the Gilmesh, at last, there was a purpose to their patrol.

There was a surprised murmur amongst the men. Cassie strode from the castle, sword at hip, a saddle bag slung over one shoulder.

"My Lady," he began, as a groom led out her horse and Cassie busied herself with buckling saddle bags to its back. "Do you ride with us today?"

"Delmar told me you think you've found the skraelings lair?"

"That is correct. At least, we have pinpointed the location from whence all the attacks seem to originate."

"Then I want to be there." Cassie swung into her saddle, wheeling her horse around to face him. "I want to be there when we destroy them." Touching her heels to her horse's flanks she led the way out of the castle and over the drawbridge, the soldiers following, spirits rising at her presence.

Colwyn felt unease creep up his spine. Something about the grim set of her jaw, the steel he'd heard beneath her words, alarmed him. He couldn't help but wish she'd stayed behind.

They journeyed for two days. Days of hard, non-stop riding, of early starts and late endings. Cassie seemed lost in her thoughts. If any man considered talking to her, one look at her pale, closed face soon ended the notion.

Every evening when they'd made camp, Cassie insisted Colwyn train with her. The soldiers watched, fascinated, as they fought around the campsite, swords flashing in the firelight, Cassie struggling to regain strength and agility in muscles grown lax from weeks of inactivity.

Finally, each duel ended in a draw, and the admiring murmurs of the men grew into full-voiced compliments. Sometimes she fought the others, her determination and skill quickly disarming them, leaving them slack-jawed with shock. Still, Colwyn watched and worried. It was as if Ruby's abduction had left a gaping hole, a hole Cassie seemed determined to fill with revenge.

On the third day, they noticed changes in the landscape which left them muttering uneasily, hands constantly straying to sword hilts. The complete lack of wildlife indicated to Colwyn they were in the right location, his eyes becoming silent and watchful.

Colwyn turned in the saddle, hands communicating to the man behind they were to spread out, advance silently, and stay alert. Nodding, the man relayed the message. Soon, the two-hundred-strong patrol was in formation, progressing through the trees onto the rim of a plain bordered on one side by a low-lying series of hillocks dotted with dozens of openings.

Suddenly, skraelings were upon them, snarling and savagely attacking. With the primal instinct to protect their homes and young whipping them into a rabid frenzy, they launched themselves at the mounted soldiers.

Chaos ensued as the warriors grimly fought back, using the hack and slash technique which had proven the most effective way to fight the shaggy creatures. Fighting off two of the beasts, Colwyn saw Cassie heel her horse and spur it onwards and knew with a sinking heart she was heading for the dens.

"Cassandra, no!" he shouted, despatching two skraelings with savage hasty stabs, urging his horse to follow, watching Cassie calmly lean from her saddle and lop a skraeling's head off as it leapt to snatch at her leg. Heart in his mouth, Colwyn saw her almost fall from the saddle, claw her way back on, and bend low over her horse forcing it on ever faster.

Behind him, he heard victory cheers as the patrol began to overwhelm the skraelings. He realised it had never occurred to the skraelings' limited intelligence that anyone would be foolish enough to come looking for them. They had underestimated their enemy and left themselves vulnerable to attack.

Cassie reached the first of the hillocks, swinging at the skraeling which poured from the dens with a calm detached air, almost as if she were swatting flies. Waves of skraelings rushed from all sides. Cassie's horse went down under a pile of shaggy-coated beasts. Colwyn saw her sword flash as she hacked her way up through the bodies, her horse's death screams abruptly silenced as skraelings ripped out its throat.

With a howl of rage, Cassie emerged from the melee. Long plait whipping around, she waded amongst the skraelings with a casual disregard for her own safety, screaming and slashing at the skraelings which continued to attack.

Reaching her, Colwyn held out his hand. "Grab hold."

Cassie flicked him a glance. "No," she yelled, running another skraeling through the heart.

"Cassandra, come on," Colwyn shouted in disbelief.

"I'm going to kill them all," she snarled. Colwyn fell back in horror from the glazed, fanatical gleam in her eye, and knew from the savagely ruthless way she was carving a path through the skraeling, that there'd be no reasoning with her.

Thundering hooves behind told him the patrol had successfully dispatched the last of the skraelings and had followed them to the dens. Soldiers were everywhere, slashing and killing. Taking his eyes off Cassie for one moment, Colwyn turned back to see her scrambling to the mouth of the nearest den. His heart stopped as she crawled in.

Leaping from his horse, Colwyn raced up the slope, fear giving his feet wings at the frenzied snarling. Reaching the mouth of the den, he saw Cassie facing a litter of terrified skraeling pups huddling at the back of the burrow, their eyes still closed, whimpering piteously for their mother whose body lay at her feet.

"Cassandra, do not," he gasped. She glanced over her shoulder with a coldly defiant stare before her sword swung in the cramped burrow and the pups whimpered no more.

"My Lord," Wilfric panted up behind him. Dazed and sickened, Colwyn gladly turned to him. "All the adult skraelings have been despatched, my Lord. None are left, save a few mothers protecting their young. What are your orders, my Lord?"

"Kill them," said Cassie softly. "We must kill them all."

"My Lady?" gulped Wilfric, eyes widening at the sight of the tiny dead bodies.

"Skraelings grow quickly," declared Cassie, wiping her sword on the mother's fur. "In a few weeks they will be old enough to start attacking and breeding, and all this will have been for nothing. They must be wiped out, completely exterminated."

In his heart, Colwyn knew she was right, yet it seemed so cold, so inhumane, so wrong, to hear such words coming from her mouth.

"My Lord?" Wilfric questioned. Slowly, reluctantly, Colwyn nodded, and the soldier ran to obey his orders. Cassie started forward, but Colwyn caught her by the arm, the blood-drenched shirt bunching beneath his fingers as she turned.

"Not you," he said.

Cassie's lip curled with disdain. "What? Let me go," she snapped in disbelief.

Colwyn shook his head. "No, my Lady," he said gently. "There has been enough killing for you today."

"It will never be enough," she snarled, pushing his hand away. "I need to do this, and you can't stop me." She shoved past him.

Colwyn grabbed her shoulders. "It is enough, Cassandra. This will not bring her back."

"Maybe not," she panted, fighting his grasp. "It helps..."

"Does it?" he asked, gently.

Cassie stared at him for a long, silent moment. Her face crumpled, tears sliding down her blood-splattered face.

"No," she whispered, "it doesn't, oh Ruby."

She collapsed into his arms, sobbing and he held her tightly, the sounds of genocide echoing all around them.

Another month slipped by. Ruby began to despair of ever getting free from Lorcan's clutches. She and Nerrisa discussed it endlessly, trying desperately to think of a way in which to escape. It seemed hopeless.

Nerrisa would avidly watch and listen while going silently about her chores. Ignored, and for the most part, forgotten about, she gathered every scrap of information she could. Ruby knew Siminus was in the tower somewhere, although she had yet to see him. She wondered what evil the pair of them were planning.

Every evening, Nerrisa would carefully dress her for dinner. Ruby would sit opposite Lorcan, trying to hide the loathing in her eyes, carefully watching him and weighing every word before she spoke, fearful of his unpredictable mood swings.

For Lorcan was mad, Ruby did not doubt it. Perhaps it was long centuries trapped with only evil thoughts for company. Perhaps it was the sheer burden of foul deeds which weighed heavy. Perhaps the seeds of insanity had always been there, each act of depravity forcing him deeper into megalomania. Whatever had caused it, Ruby feared him but tried to hide it, sensing any sign of weakness would make him less inclined to keep her alive.

As it was, her show of bravado and coolly contemptuous attitude seemed to amuse him. Sometimes, Ruby even fancied she saw a spark of admiration in his eyes when she refused to be cowed by his threats.

One afternoon, Nerrisa had come as normal to prepare her for dinner. The girls were idly chatting as Nerrisa stood behind her at the dressing table brushing Ruby's hair. Both looked up, shocked, at the rattle of keys at the door. It crashed open. Lorcan erupted into the room, anger sparking from his eyes.

"My Lord?" stammered Ruby. Nerrisa backed away from him, clutching the brush to her chest in trepidation.

"You will agree!" he ordered, his usually implacable face twisting with fury.

"No," Ruby replied firmly. Maintaining a calm demeanour, she was far from feeling, she turned back to her reflection in the mirror, indicating to Nerrisa that she was to continue brushing her hair. With a growl of frustrated anger, Lorcan thrust out his hand and the mirror shattered, glass showering onto the table.

"You will agree, my Lady!" he snarled.

Ruby saw black flames of madness flare deep within his eyes.

"What is it?" she asked, slowly. "What's happened?"

"What has happened, my Lady?" he repeated, sarcastically. "What has happened, is your sister and that ignorant offspring of Reutghar have today located my skraelings dens and butchered all they found there, the young and their mothers. It will take months for stocks to rebuild to previous levels."

Ruby and Nerrisa exchanged quick, hopeful glances. Ruby couldn't help the small smile which twitched her lips.

"Does it amuse you, my Lady?" stormed Lorcan.

Ruby instantly smoothed her face back into its impassive mask. "No, my Lord," she murmured. Lorcan's expression darkened, his eyes flicking to Nerrisa as she placidly brushed Ruby's hair. A speculative gleam crossed his face.

You have become very fond of your little maid, have you not, my Lady? His voice whispered silkily in her mind, and Ruby turned, startled, as the voice continued, smooth and oily. *You will agree to bond with me, my Lady.*

Never! Ruby thought back fiercely, and Lorcan smiled a thin, cruel smile.

Then you will watch, whilst the Gilmesh take her soul.

What? No, you can't!

Oh, I can, my Lady, I can, and I will. You have a choice. Agree wholeheartedly to become my queen or I will give her to the Gilmesh. I will order them to make her suffer such torment it will haunt your dreams for eternity. You have one hour to decide!

The pressure in Ruby's skull increased as his mind held her, trapped and defenceless, feeling for the first time the full extent of his power. She cried out, hands flying to her temples, pressing in useless agony as pain bored through her, crushing and subduing. With a contemptuous flick, he released her to fall to the ground, sobbing with anguish, huddled in Nerrisa's arms.

"One hour," he said, and whirled from the room, the door slamming behind him.

Shaking all over, fighting dizzying waves of nausea, Ruby allowed Nerrisa to help her onto the bed where she lay in stricken horror. Nerrisa hurried to fetch a damp cloth and laid it gently over Ruby's poor throbbing forehead and eyes.

"Oh, Nerrisa," sobbed Ruby. "I have to agree to marry him."

"You must not, my Lady," stated Nerrisa firmly. "Have we not both agreed he has some use for you other than simply desiring a queen? That there is some purpose to his demand you agree to this union?"

"Yes," agreed Ruby, desperately, "But you don't know. You didn't hear..."

"You are not the only one with empathic ability, my Lady. I heard what he said."

"Then you know I have no choice Nerrisa, I have to…"

"Hush, my Lady," ordered Nerrisa gently, stroking her hair back from her face. "Take a moment to rest. You have an hour, so can spare a few minutes to recover."

Drained, Ruby lay unresisting on the bed, listening to the small soothing sounds Nerrisa made as she moved quietly about the room, the squeak of the wardrobe door, the rustle of clothing as she spread a dress over a chair.

"I have laid out your green silk, my Lady," she stated. "I have always thought it suits you the best."

"I won't let him kill you, Nerrisa," replied Ruby, firmly. She heard Nerrisa sigh.

"Rest, my Lady," she murmured. Too tired to reply, Ruby struggled to think of a solution, of a way out, but there was none. To save Nerrisa's life she had to agree to Lorcan's demands.

A rush of freezing air made her frown behind the cloth, and she put up a hand to remove it, hearing the creak of the balcony doors.

"Nerrisa?"

Struggling to sit up, she saw Nerrisa standing on the balcony staring sadly back at her.

"Nerrisa, what is it? What are you doing?"

"There is always a choice, my Lady," she said.

Ruby went cold at the finality in her voice.

"There is always a choice … Ruby … and this is mine."

She turned, and climbed onto the balustrade…

"No, Nerrisa, no!"

… and jumped.

Chapter Seventeen

The Golden Griffin

n hour passed. Ruby heard, with dull resignation, the sound of the key in the door. Lorcan hesitated when he saw her huddled on the balcony where she'd been ever since...

"My Lady?" he enquired. "Have you come to a decision?" Ruby merely looked at him. Something in her eyes made him pause. With a frown creasing his brow, he looked around the room.

"Where is your maid, my Lady?" he demanded.

"She's dead," muttered Ruby, brokenly. "She jumped."

"Jumped?"

"Yes, she jumped. Rather than be used by you as a weapon, she sacrificed herself."

Lorcan faltered, trying to understand such an alien concept. "My Lady ..." he began.

Ruby's eyes narrowed into dangerous slits. "Leave me," she snarled. "Leave me alone!" Much to her surprise, he did.

Colwyn, feeling the need to briefly escape, retreated to the haven of his mother's rooftop garden one afternoon. Enjoying the peace that he found there, he sat on a bench to mull over his constant, ever-present, concerns about Lady Cassandra.

Ever since the destruction of the skraelings, that short, intense moment of vulnerability when she sobbed in his arms, Colwyn had felt her drift further and further away from him.

That evening, during the banquet, all talk had been of courageous Lady Cassandra, her daring dash right into the heart of the skraeling dens, and her fearless attack even after her horse was slain under her.

Colwyn listened, amused how each telling increased the number of skraelings by a hundredfold. Lady Melinda, ignored by her usual ardent admirers all praising and discussing Lady Cassandra's exploits, appeared to have been sucking too many lemons, he thought, so sour was her expression.

Cassie remained apart from it all, detached and silent. Face closed, she'd picked at the food on her plate, refusing to be drawn into the discussion. Finally, she excused herself on grounds of tiredness and retired early, Colwyn and Delmar exchanging concerned glances as she passed them.

Now, Colwyn closed his eyes wearily and sighed, a heavy sigh of frustrated despair, now she all but ignored him, refused all requests to accompany him on patrol, practice with him, or even walk in the castle gardens with him. Eventually, hurt, and baffled, Colwyn left her alone.

Hearing footsteps and a rustle of clothing, he opened his eyes. She was before him, face still and composed, hands clasping a small leather-bound item.

"I've been looking for you," she murmured.

"For me, my Lady?" he enquired, cautiously.

"Yes, I'd forgotten, I brought you a present from my world."

"A gift? For me?"

"Yes," she replied. "I wanted to bring you something, something I thought you'd appreciate. With everything that's happened, I forgot about it until this morning. So anyway, here," she thrust the leather pouch into his hands.

Bemused, Colwyn opened it, gazing uncomprehendingly at its contents. "I thank you, my Lady, but must admit am perplexed as to its purpose."

"It's a pair of binoculars," Cassie explained. "Here, I'll show you." She crossed to the balcony, Colwyn following. "Look, see those two guards, way over on the furthest watchtower?"

"Aye, I do, my Lady."

"Who are they?"

"Who are they?" repeated Colwyn, baffled. "By the lady, Cassandra, how am I supposed to tell from this distance?"

Cassie took the binoculars back and peered through them. "It's Wilfric and Gunther," she declared and grinned at him, almost as she used to.

"In faith," said Colwyn, uncertainly. "Are you sure?"

"Here," she replied, handing them to him. "See for yourself."

Doubtfully, Colwyn raised the strange contraption to his eyes and peered suspiciously, almost dropping them as the distant figures swam into focus and he saw they were indeed Wilfric and Gunther. So close, he could see the colour of Gunther's kerchief as he brought it to his mouth to stifle a sneeze, and Wilfric's mouth move in some silent remark.

"My stars!" Amazed, he stared with awe at the innocuous device. "How remarkable. Why, with these, what did you call them, binoculars, you could see the enemy long before he was within striking distance."

"Yes," agreed Cassie. "They're also great for bird watching."

"Bird watching?" said Colwyn, puzzled. "Why would you wish to watch birds?"

"Never mind," smiled Cassie, shaking her head. "Anyway, they're for you. Something to remember me by when I'm gone."

"Gone?" Colwyn's head snapped up his new toy forgotten. "Where are you going, my Lady?"

"Well," Cassie seemed flustered by his question. "When this is over and Lorcan's been defeated, I'll be going home, and I'll tell you something," she continued grimly.

"I hope the rule about ceasing to exist in your own world if you choose to stay permanently in another applies if you're dead. Because I can't even begin to imagine how I'm going to explain to Mum and Dad about Ruby..."

In the days following Nerrisa's death, Ruby fell into a fit of despair. A heavy, black mood wrapped around her like a blanket, smothering and choking, until she felt she might suffocate from all the heavy layers of guilt.

Nerrisa was dead because of her. Whichever way you looked at it, there was no getting away from the fact she had died to prevent Ruby from being forced to agree to Lorcan's demands.

As days trickled by, Ruby began to wonder if Nerrisa had had the right idea, if maybe she should end it all, quickly and easily. One jump and it would all be over.

Then she would pull herself together, something inside her recoiling from the thought. She would dress in her finest gown, brush her hair until it shone and dine with Lorcan. Her face a mask to hide her true feelings, her eyes watchful, and her mind busily thinking, always thinking, of how she could escape.

One afternoon, Ruby was in her room alone, as usual. Bored, unable to settle to any of her books, she wandered about the chamber, a wave of sorrow and self-pity welling inside threatening to swamp her.

Blinking back tears of desolation, Ruby opened the balcony doors and stepped into the cool air. During her captivity, the harsh grip of winter had eased and there was a scent of spring in the breeze.

Leaning against the doors, Ruby closed her eyes, almost choking on the lump of despair in her throat. There was a rustle of wings, a soft chirp, and a small brown bird perched on the balustrade, surveying her, head cocked to one side.

Ruby stared back at the bird, envy at its freedom burning behind her eyes. Suddenly, she was looking back at her own body, its eyes blank and staring.

She was flying, free and wild in the clear blue sky, diving and twisting, heart beating madly with sheer exhilaration.

Shocked, her mind jolted and she was back in her body, heart pounding from the experience, mind buzzing with questions. Of the bird, there was no sign.

Slowly, Ruby went back into the room, and sank into a chair, considering what had occurred. It must be something to do with her empathic ability, of that Ruby had no doubt, but what exactly had she done? Could she do it again? If she could, what did it mean? The questions pounded.

Excited, Ruby closed her eyes, deliberately sending her mind out, questing, probing, searching...

Instantly, she sensed the minds of the Gilmesh guards outside the door, cold and detached. She quickly pulled away before they could become aware of her and went further, dipping into the minds of the kitchen staff, the surly mistrust of the cook; the unimaginative pettiness of Lorcan's manservant, stealing his master's wine and living in constant fear for his life.

Further, she went, examining with interest the strong, honest mind of the young boy who did all the heavy jobs in the tower, his fear of Lorcan, his sorrow and regret at Nerrisa's death, and his pity for the lady locked in the highest room.

Further and further, she went, retreating in fear when she intruded into the thoughts of Siminus, scurrying back to her own mind at his dawning awareness of something being amiss.

Breathless, Ruby opened her eyes in the relative safety of her room and smiled for the first time in over a week. She was stunned at her ability, unsure if it could be used as a means of escape but feeling that somehow the tide had finally turned.

In the days that followed, during her long hours of solitude, Ruby practised her newfound skill, learning and discovering the limits of her ability. Scared she might accidentally blunder into the mind of Siminus, or worse, Lorcan, Ruby avoided contact with the minds of the people within the tower, instead, probing the minds of the animals living in and around it.

Sharing consciousness with birds was by far the most exciting and enjoyable. Ruby lived for the hours she could spend as a bird, flying far away from her captivity, soaring wild and free. Gradually, she experimented with controlling the animals with which she was temporarily sharing a mind.

The smaller the animal, the easier it was to control. Ruby found large creatures, such as the stags or wild boar which roamed the forest below, couldn't be controlled at all. Once, she entered the mind of a great, eagle-like bird, and discovered a coldly logical intelligence. It tolerated her presence but would not allow her even the slightest degree of control over it.

So, Ruby confined herself to small birds; to the mice and rats that existed in vast numbers in the tower, finding their small brains malleable and open to her orders. Scurrying around, seeing everything from their secretive viewpoint, Ruby built up a picture of the tower in which she was held captive.

Its sheer scale shocked her, as did the sophistication of its fixtures and fittings. The problem of climbing hundreds of stairs every day was solved by using a basic, very effective, lift controlled by a series of weights and pulleys.

As Ruby gained strength in her abilities, she discovered she could range further and further with her chosen bird, viewing the landscape below, searching, always searching, for something familiar, for a way back to the castle.

Finally, one day, her patience paid off. Ahead of her, she saw the turrets and towers of Dragonswell. Mind humming with excitement, Ruby directed the frantically flapping bird to the castle, where she made it search the grounds and peer through windows, looking for her sister, Lady Ninniane, Delmar, anyone to connect with.

Ruby swooped through an open window into the vaulted throne room, seeing through the bird's eyes the giant figures of Reutghar, Garth, and much to her relief, Darius. They were huddled around a long table, faces serious, studying a map.

"By the lady," gasped Darius as she landed on the table and strutted boldly onto the map. "Whatever ails that bird?" Ruby felt the bird's natural terror and struggled to stop it from flying away as the men looked on with baffled surprise.

"Is the creature ill, do you think?" asked Reutghar, lightly stroking its downy beige chest. The little bird's heart thumped madly with blind terror. The connection snapped, Ruby reeled back into her own body and knew the bird had died.

After that, Ruby travelled many times to Dragonswell, becoming familiar with the aerial route to its beckoning security. Confined within the mind of a bird she saw Cassie, her heart aching at how thin and drawn her sister was, the lines of sadness etched in her face. She sorrowed her presumed death had driven a wedge between her and Colwyn.

Time and again, Ruby tried to touch the mind of one of her friends, to leapfrog from the mind of the bird she was occupying. Each time, her consciousness bounced back to her body in the tower. Eventually, she gave up, having to accept this limitation on her ability.

One evening, Ruby dined with Lorcan as normal, giving her usual answer to his usual question, his mouth thinning at her refusal. Escorted back to her room by her Gilmesh guard, she sat before the fire, drowsy, but oddly reluctant to go to bed. Dreamily, she stretched her mind out and contacted a small mouse scurrying behind the walls of the dining chamber.

Lorcan was still sitting at the table slowly sipping from a goblet of wine, eyes narrowed thoughtfully over its rim. There was a knock at the door, and Siminus entered. Ruby watched with interest as he bowed and was waved to a seat by Lorcan.

"My Lord," he said, settling himself into a chair and helping himself to wine. "What answer did she give this evening?"

"The usual," snapped Lorcan, peevishly, draining his goblet and thrusting it abruptly at Siminus who filled it from the jug.

"How much longer can we wait, my Lord?" enquired Siminus, face concerned.

Behind the wall, Ruby overrode the mouse's instinctive reluctance and crept nearer, straining to hear.

"She will agree, she must," growled Lorcan, anger snapping in his eyes. "I thought my plan to wait until she had become attached to her maid would work. Who would have thought such a pathetic child so capable of so noble a gesture?"

"Indeed, my Lord," murmured Siminus, grey eyes fixed on Lorcan's face. "I am curious, my Lord, could you not manipulate her mind to agree to the union?"

"No," replied Lorcan, regretfully, Ruby tensed with interest. "She must agree wholeheartedly to the union. If her mind is clouded by magic the link will not work, I will not be able to use her to gain control of the World Between Worlds, and thus have access to other worlds and timelines."

"A pity, my Lord," murmured Siminus, and Lorcan nodded.

"I must confess, I had thought she would have submitted by now. I am surprised by her strength. It makes her even more … interesting."

"Interesting, my Lord?"

"Her levels of empathic abilities are stronger than I suspected. She has no idea what she is capable of. I find her fascinating, the way she opposes me, it has made me re-think my plan of using her ability to my own ends and then destroying her."

"What plans do you have for Lady Ruby now, my Lord?" Siminus leant forward, cruel grey eyes gleaming with interest.

"I plan to keep her alive, Siminus, make her my queen and begin a dynasty. After all, I cannot be expected to rule all the worlds at once. The thought of strong, loyal sons ruling under me has a certain appeal."

"Indeed, my Lord, as long as they do remain loyal."

"Oh, I have ways to ensure that, Siminus, never fear."

There was a silence in the room for a moment. Both sipped thoughtfully at their wine, Ruby was about to return to her own body, when Lorcan spoke again. The tiny body of the mouse jerked with Ruby's shocked response to his words.

"Tell me, how do plans for the castle's capture progress?"

"Very well, my Lord, we should be ready to proceed within the next six days. The Gilmesh troops are almost up to full complement. Although the loss of the skraelings is a blow, I am confident we shall succeed even without them."

"It was inspired of me, do you not think Siminus, to have you hide the portal stones throughout the castle, long before your position there was compromised?"

"It was, my Lord, they have proved themselves to be in perfect working order, as we saw when you were able to successfully transport a pack of skraeling within the castle walls, and when the Gilmesh were able to abduct Lady Ruby."

"Imagine their surprise," stated Lorcan in satisfaction, "in the middle of battle, whilst their attention is diverted to defending the walls, the Gilmesh appear in the keep. Think of the panic as the Gilmesh attack from behind, not stopping until every living thing in the castle has been destroyed."

"It will be a magnificent victory, my Lord," Siminus agreed, voice oozing with sycophantic approval.

"You must instruct the Gilmesh to locate Lady Ruby's sister and bring her to me unharmed. She will make the perfect bargaining weapon, should our Lady still be resistant. She will do anything to save her sister's life."

"What will you do with Lady Cassandra once you have achieved your goal of domination over the World Between Worlds?" enquired Siminus, with a casual intensity which had Lorcan narrowing his eyes suspiciously, then laughing in disbelieving scorn.

"Why Siminus, I do believe you desire the Lady," his voice dripped with sarcasm, and Siminus flushed angrily. "I was unaware you were seeking a wife."

"I am not, my Lord," denied Siminus, bitterly. "I have a grudge to settle with fair Lady Cassandra. When she used the sacred sword to deflect my spell, it … damaged me. I would have my revenge upon her."

"Damaged you?" Lorcan leant across the table in interest. "What do you mean?"

Siminus hesitated then undid the buttons on his robe to reveal his chest. Mouse Ruby recoiled in horror at the livid red and purple scar slashing horizontally down his body, pulling the skin into a jagged mountain of twisted, tortured flesh.

"Why not heal yourself?" Lorcan asked curiously.

Siminus's face darkened in anger. "I cannot, my Lord, my spell was a potent one. When it combined with the purity of the sword's protective charm, it created such a powerful vortex I was lucky to escape alive."

"Very well," Lorcan waved his hand expansively. "Once Lady Ruby has submitted to me you may have her sister. Do with her what you will."

"Thank you, my Lord."

Ruby shuddered at the evil smirk on the mage's face.

"I grow weary," stated Lorcan, his voice bored. "Leave me."

"Yes, my Lord." Siminus rose, bowed, and left the room. Ruby returned to her own body and climbed wearily into bed, where she passed a restless night tossing and turning, her mind throbbing with the enormity of what she'd overheard.

Finally, at dawn, she slipped into the carefree mind of a small bird as it swooped and dived in the clear skies above the tower. Its tiny body pulsing with the joy of being alive. Ruby was soothed by its uncomplicated needs and desires.

A shadow loomed. Looking up, Ruby saw a kestrel, talons extended, cruel eyes gleaming. Heart shuddering with fear, the bird dived into the lee of the tower, swooped under a large, weathervane, twisting in the breeze on the highest turret.

Perched on a loose tile, safely tucked away under the vane, the bird waited until the kestrel, with a disappointed cry, flew away towards the sun. The tiny bird crept out and landed on the weathervane to recover from its brush with death.

Idly, Ruby looked at the vane, at the lion-like creature rearing up, and was dazzled as the rising sun hit its surface, bathing it in a warm, golden glow. The bird flew away. Ruby slid into her own body and dream-filled sleep.

She saw Cassie being tortured by Siminus, his cold eyes alight with pleasure at her suffering; Dragonswell under attack from Gilmesh, thousands of them, who appeared magically in its heart, slaughtering every living soul.

Finally, she dreamt of Delmar, his face serious. "It is all a matter of perspective. Sometimes a familiar thing can look very different when viewed from an unlikely angle," he said.

Ruby awoke with a gasp, sitting bolt upright in bed.

"Of course," she murmured, casting outwards with her mind until she found another bird, wanting to be sure, to be certain. Finding a wren-like creature, she forced it upwards until she could look again at the weathervane. A thing she'd seen dozens of times over the past week, yet never looked at, so had never really seen.

A creature like no creature she'd ever seen, its strong lion-like torso thrusting upwards from mighty, outstretched wings; its long tail lashing upwards; its smooth, golden surface glinting in the early morning sun.

Stunned and energized, Ruby snapped back into her own body. "From air the golden griffin, crafted by elfish hands," she muttered, placing a hand to her chest, feeling the rapid thump of her heart as it pounded with excitement.

The weathervane must be practically the highest point in Erinsmore so you couldn't get much closer to the air if you tried, she reasoned to herself. The creature could be a griffin, she was unsure what one looked like, but it was made of gold, and Lorcan had told her the tower had been built by elves.

After breakfast had been delivered by the sour-faced cook, Ruby waited impatiently for the Gilmesh to take her to the roof terrace, relieved that after Nerrisa's death there'd been no change in her routine.

As soon as the tower door closed behind her escort, Ruby quickly stripped off her heavy ermine-lined cloak and velvet gown, and carefully tucked up her full-length petticoat into a thick leather belt she had fastened around her waist when she'd dressed that morning.

Removing her stockings to leave her legs and feet bare, better equipped for climbing, Cora's feather tickled her chest when she bent over. Briefly clasping it for luck, her heart jumped into her mouth as she looked at the almost sheer rooftop rising above her.

Climbing onto a stone bench, Ruby managed to get hold of the edge of the guttering, and carefully pulled herself up and over the edge of the roof, easing her way on hands and knees, searching for the easiest route to the top.

Slowly, painstakingly, she climbed ever upwards, creeping over the uneven roof tiles, using them as hand and foot holds, until finally, triumphantly, she reached the uppermost point of the turret. Thankfully straddling the broad, flat capping tile, she hugged the vane tightly as she got her breath back and tried not to look down.

Wonderingly, Ruby stroked its smooth golden surface, gazing in awe at its beauty, tracing a finger over its noble features and wondering how to remove it from its perch.

Seeing a small bolt at its base, Ruby carefully twisted it and found to her surprise it came out quite easily. The whole vane lifted gently and smoothly from its bracket, and she marvelled at its lightness. Holding it aloft, the morning sun drenched it in glorious golden light, and a sensation of absolute peace and serenity bathe Ruby's entire body.

She smiled as the light of the griffin entered her eyes and her heart, hearing its song, low and beautiful, resound around the rooftop. The glow faded. Ruby was left wondering exactly how she was supposed to get it down.

Clutching it to her body, Ruby reluctantly swung her leg back over the relative stability of the capping tile, heart lurching as she slid several feet down the tiles, feet and fingers scrabbling desperately to catch hold. The griffin, light though it was, unbalanced her. Ruby realised she should have brought a bag or something to hold it.

Panicking, imagining herself falling, beads of sweat breaking out on her forehead, she managed to climb down a few feet, the griffin hanging precariously from her fingers.

Then disaster struck. Her petticoat came loose from the belt and Ruby slipped on it, feeling the material snag and rip on a rough piece of tile. Desperately clutching at the roof, the griffin slipped from her fingers, bounced, and fell, striking the edge of the guttering before falling with a clatter onto the terrace several feet below.

Ruby climbed down, and hung from the guttering edge, probing with her scratched and bleeding feet until they found the security of the stone bench. She fell onto its comfortingly solid surface, her breathing ragged and hoarse, and her heart pounding in fear and exertion.

Shivering with cold, Ruby picked up the griffin and examined it, relieved to see it appeared undamaged. She struggled back into her clothes, barely having time to hide the griffin behind her back as the roof door opened behind her.

Shocked, Ruby watched Lorcan step onto the terrace, eyes alive with speculation as they flicked around the empty terrace and rested on Ruby.

"Where is it?" he demanded.

"Where's what?" Ruby stuttered, feeling the smooth, warm surface of the griffin as she clutched it tightly behind her back.

"I felt such a surge of power, the like of which I have rarely known before. It came from up here where you happen to be, my Lady. So, I ask again. Where is it?"

"I don't know what you're talking about," Ruby backed away from his madness.

"What do you have behind your back?" he demanded. Ruby felt with a shocking thrill the cold edge of the terrace's railing behind her back and realised she had nowhere else to go.

"Show me," he ordered, his eyes black.

Against her will, Ruby's arm moved, and the griffin emerged, shiningly glorious in the bright spring sun.

"The Golden Griffin," he gasped, his expression shocked and awed. "Give it to me," he commanded.

Ruby's body gave an involuntary jerk forward as she fought against the authority in his voice.

"No," she cried, clutching the griffin with both hands, struggling to hold herself back. "You won't have it," she cried.

His mind crept into hers, demanding, ordering, controlling. "You cannot resist me," he gloated. Ruby's foot wrenched forward a reluctant step.

What is your will, my child? The voice was rich and kind, old beyond time. All-knowing, all-powerful, it flooded through Ruby's mind, Lorcan's will being overwhelmed by its strength.

Who are you? She thought in unafraid wonder.

I am time, I am ages lost and ages yet to come, I am love and strength, I am life reborn from the flames of despair, I hope, when all seems lost, I am hope. Dazed, Ruby stared at the griffin glowing in her hand. *What is your will, my child?*

He mustn't take the griffin. He mustn't reach me.

Very well, it is done, yet the enchantment cannot last for long.

Lorcan and the Gilmesh were trapped behind a shimmering barrier of light, the dark lord releasing bolt after bolt of sizzling black fire, face twisting with impotent rage as each one was absorbed harmlessly.

"The barrier will not last forever, my Lady," he snarled. "You will submit to me."

"Never," cried Ruby, backing away, instinctively clutching the feather.

"Where do you think to go, my Lady? You stand on the edge of the abyss, alone and friendless, there is none to help you. You will be mine. You have no choice."

"There's always a choice," cried Ruby, defiantly.

A memory stirred at his words. A wild hope leapt into her heart. Carefully, deliberately, Ruby climbed onto the broad stone railing, shaking at the distance which gaped inches from her feet.

"You will not jump," snarled Lorcan. "I know you, my Lady, you will not jump. Join me, Ruby, be my queen, for I admire your spirit. Your friends are doomed, accept that, think now of yourself. Submit, there is no other choice."

"I believe in my friends," cried Ruby. "I do have faith, I do!"

Clutching Cora's feather, she stepped backwards, plunging into the abyss which yawned wide and swallowed her whole.

Chapter Eighteen

Reunion

ind rushed past her face. Ruby's hair whipped up. Her body plummeted down, down, down. Going faster and faster. As The faraway smudge of land grew frighteningly nearer, Ruby screamed with terror. Hugging the griffin to her chest, Ruby clutched desperately at the feather in her other hand and her shoes flew from her feet to be lost forever in the abyss.

Cora!

Her mind yelled the word in panic-stricken fear. Closing her eyes to block out the awful view, an image flashed into her mind of Cora circling above her head in the World Between Worlds; of Gwnhyfar, her long auburn hair rippling in the breeze as she gave Ruby the warning; of Lady Ninniane telling her to keep the feather with her always.

Ruby relaxed, a smile curving her lips and went limp with acceptance. Her frenzied downward rush slowed and levelled out. Opening her eyes, Ruby found herself flying away from the tower on the back of something.

Vast golden wings stretched out either side of her, beating through the air with calm steady strokes. Wonderingly, Ruby put a hand down to the sleekly gleaming back on which she was sitting, only to start with shock, almost losing her seat, as her hand passed straight through to encounter nothing.

Sit still, my child, I do not want you to fall. The powerful head of the griffin turned to look at her. Ruby heard its kind, mildly amused words in her mind.

I don't understand, she thought. How is this possible?

Aeons ago, ravens performed a noble selfless deed for the griffin. In gratitude, the griffin pledged their word that should any wearing the dark apparel of those gallant birds ever call for help, we would aid them to the very limits of our powers.

I see, stuttered Ruby. *Thank you, you saved my life. Lorcan was trying to make me bond with him to invade the World Between Worlds and get control over other worlds.*

I have slumbered for countless ages, stated the griffin, *and know nothing of this Lorcan of whom you speak, but the World Between Worlds has always been a refuge and should remain so. Now, choose wisely where you wish me to take you, my child, for my assistance, is yours only for so long as the feather glows darkly.*

Glows darkly? Ruby enquired. She looked at the feather held tightly in her hand and saw it was no longer a solid block of glossy black, that white now tinged its base. As she watched, a hairs width more appeared. Ruby wondered if the griffin would change back into a weathervane when all the black was gone.

That is correct, the griffin confirmed, before Ruby had finished forming the enquiry in her mind. *Where do you wish me to take you, my child?*

Dragonswell. Ruby imagined an aerial map gained from her many voyages there in the minds of birds, experiencing the bizarre sensation of the griffin changing direction beneath her but not feeling anything other than a rush of cold air.

They flew on. Ruby anxiously watched the white creep inexorably up the feather, deciding when the white had almost reached the tip, she would ask it to land, not wanting it to disappear in mid-air.

Finally, as they were cresting a tree-lined hill, Ruby decided she couldn't wait any longer. The feather now gleamed almost entirely white with the faintest trace of black at its very tip. Almost before the request had formed in her mind, the griffin was wheeling in mid-air, bearing her down to a small clearing below.

He landed smoothly. Ruby slid from his back and stood firmly on the ground, relief at being back on Erinsmore soil bringing tears to her eyes. Looking up, Ruby found the griffin watching her, his large patient eyes calm and unblinking.

Thank you, thought Ruby.

The griffin bowed his head. *Farewell, my child,* the words resounded in her head. He was fading, Ruby could see trees through him, tall and solid next to his insubstantial wraithlike form. Ruby sensed his smile and returned it.

Do not forget, the words were a whisper, a ghost in her mind. *There is always hope...*

He was gone. Ruby was alone in the woods, the Golden Griffin once more merely a weathervane lying at her feet. Ruby looked around disorientated, wondering exactly which way she needed to go to reach Dragonswell. She knew it was very close but being unfamiliar with the terrain seen at ground level ... of course. Smiling to herself, Ruby reached out with her mind and entered the consciousness of a small bird swooping high above her in the midday sky, seeing with relief the well-known towers of the castle in the distance.

Returning to her body, Ruby picked up the Golden Griffin and began to walk. Relishing her freedom and blinking back tears, she looked around at the signs of spring visible in the wood, tipping her head back to feel the sun warm on her face as it flickered through the canopy of trees far above her.

Hooves thundering through the wood, close and getting closer, snapped Ruby back to reality and had her dashing to hide behind the nearest bush. Peering fearfully through the leaves, Ruby watched, heart in mouth, as a group of warriors approached with a familiar figure at their head. Relieved, Ruby stepped out and Darius pulled his horse sharply to a halt, his eyes wide and disbelieving.

"Lady Ruby?" he gasped.

"Darius," cried Ruby with a grin. "Am I pleased to see you!"

"The feeling is mutual, my Lady," he replied. "When we could find no trace of you, we feared the worst."

"Lorcan kept me prisoner, I managed to escape."

"I have many questions, my Lady, but Gilmesh frequent these woods. We must get you back to the castle where I know your sister will be greatly relieved at your safe return." He rode closer and held down his hand.

"Yes, I've got to get back to the castle," exclaimed Ruby, taking his hand and allowing him to pull her up behind him. Darius nodded and gestured to the men behind him, whose faces were wreathed with smiles of relief and expressions of shock, at her sudden appearance. Ruby held tightly around his waist and the powerful muscles of the horse bunched beneath her as they broke into a gallop. Breaking free from the trees, they swept down the hillside, heading towards the gleaming towers and fluttering flags of the castle.

Once inside the courtyard, Darius sent one of the soldiers to fetch Lady Cassandra and hustled Ruby into the castle and straight up to the throne room. Barely pausing to knock, he flung the door open and marched in, startling Reutghar, Ninniane, and Delmar, who looked up, surprise at his abrupt entry changing to delight when they saw Ruby.

"In faith, Lady Ruby," exclaimed Reutghar, worry lines on his fiercely handsome face relaxing into smiles of relief. "How...? Where...?"

"Ruby." Lady Ninniane merely opened her arms. Almost sobbing with relief, Ruby rushed into the warm embrace, feeling safe for the first time in months.

Footsteps pounded in the corridor, the door burst open, and Cassie appeared, Colwyn behind her. She paused, eyes wide and unbelieving. A wild cry burst from her throat. She crossed the room in almost one jump and the sisters were in each other's arms.

"I thought you were dead," Cassie sobbed.

"I know," replied Ruby. "I saw you. It was awful, I could see you all but couldn't make you hear me."

"What?" Cassie stared at her "What do mean?"

"Come," the Lady ordered calmly, placing a gentle hand on Ruby's arm. "Let us sit, I shall pour you a drink and you shall tell us everything. Leave nothing out, Ruby, I imagine you have much to report."

Gratefully, Ruby sank into a chair, shaky and tearful, and gulped at the crystal-clear water. Taking a deep breath, she looked around at their expectant faces and began to talk.

There were many interruptions. When she told of the elfish tower, Reutghar pulled the map of Erinsmore towards her, and Ruby attempted to pinpoint its location. When she talked of Nerrisa, of her brave sacrifice to save them all, Ruby had to stop to wipe tears from her face, seeing twin tears in Cassie's eyes, and the silent sympathy in the Lady's.

"Her name will be marked with the dead of Corrinshill," declared Colwyn. "Her bravery shall be forever remembered."

Then, Ruby reached the most remarkable part of her tale. Excitedly, she told of her newly found empathic ability to enter the consciousness of animals, and her many trips to Dragonswell within the minds of birds. Reutghar grunted with humour, exchanging an amused glance with Darius as she spoke of walking on the very map now spread before them.

She also told of the conversation overheard between Lorcan and Siminus, leaving nothing out, voice faltering as she repeated the mage's vow to capture Cassie and make her pay for his injuries.

"I'm glad I hurt him that badly," exclaimed Cassie, hotly. Colwyn's face was tight with anger and concern, and Ruby noticed he moved closer to her sister.

Carefully, trying to remember the exact words, Ruby repeated Lorcan's plan to bond with her, to use her empathic abilities to invade the World Between Worlds and others beyond that. The Lady frowned, shaking her head slightly.

"Is it possible?" enquired Reutghar in alarm. "Could such a scheme have worked?"

"Normally, no. The World Between Worlds has parameters of pure innocence through which none with evil intent in their hearts may pass," replied the Lady. "Yet, if Ruby had bonded wholeheartedly with Lorcan, there may have been a way, using her empathic abilities, to breach these boundaries."

"There's more," interrupted Ruby urgently. "We're not safe here, Lorcan plans to attack the castle in five days using something he called portal stones..."

"Portal stones?" For the first time, Ruby saw the Lady visibly shaken. "Are you sure you heard him correctly Ruby?"

"Yes," insisted Ruby. "That's how they were able to put that pack of skraelings within the castle walls, and how the Gilmesh were able to kidnap me."

"What are these portal stones?" Reutghar turned to Ninniane in alarm. How do we defend ourselves against them?"

"Portal stones are very ancient, powerful devices used for transportation."

"You and Delmar didn't need these stones when you transported us," Cassie said, a puzzled frown on her face.

"Mages as powerful as Delmar, or I, do not need to use them. Yet, even our abilities are limited in that we cannot transport very many at once. Portal stones allow the passage of vast numbers, even whole populations, and their livestock."

"So why aren't these portal stones used now?" Ruby asked.

"They are extremely rare. Only seven have existed since the dawn of time. It was discovered each time a portal stone is used it causes a tiny wrinkle in the fabric of existence to form. Although the wrinkle is small, almost inconsequential, it was feared the cumulative effects could be devastating so it was decided the stones be destroyed. The Council of Mages were unanimous on this matter, and the stones were eliminated."

"Well," replied Ruby slowly. "Either Lorcan has found some more stones or..."

"The original stones were never destroyed," finished Cassie, biting her lip thoughtfully. "How were they disposed of?" she asked the Lady.

"A council member sent them into the heart of the sun."

"Which council member?" Cassie queried.

The Lady shook her head. "I do not know. A blind draw was undertaken to determine to whom the task should fall, I only know it was not me."

"So, there's a chance it was Lorcan?" Cassie stated.

"Yes," agreed the Lady. "Yet this occurred many aeons ago while Lorcan still held true to the beliefs of the council, long before he allowed evil to reign in his heart. I find it hard to believe that even then he was already lost ..." She stopped. Ruby glanced curiously at her, feeling there was much being left unsaid; more Lady Ninniane knew but didn't wish to share.

"Well," remarked Reutghar practically. "It makes no odds precisely where these portal stones came from, only that they are here now and must be found and dealt with. My Lady, will you be able to detect them?"

"Yes," the Lady nodded. "Now I am aware of their existence, I should be able to locate them, although they can disguise themselves as anything to blend into their surroundings and remain undetected."

"We know the approximate locations of two of them," replied Reutghar, "The passage where the Lady Ruby was abducted, and the south courtyard where the skraelings entered the castle. They would appear good places to begin our search."

"Yes," agreed the Lady. "That would be logical. Tell us, Ruby, how did you manage to escape?"

Breathlessly, Ruby told of her final flight within the small bird, its escape from the kestrel, her discovery of the weathervane, the Golden Griffin, and the wonderful irony that it had been over Lorcan's head the whole time.

She told of her heart-stopping climb over the roof to retrieve it, her confrontation with Lorcan and the timely intervention of the Griffin. Cassie gasped and paled when Ruby told of her desperate leap from the tower and the magical flight home. Ruby unwrapped her cloak from the Golden Griffin, holding it up for all to see, its perfect gleaming beauty glinting in the strong afternoon sun streaming through the window.

"Magnificent!" boomed Reutghar.

"So now there is only one treasure left to find," exclaimed Delmar, in satisfaction.

"Indeed," agreed the Lady, rising gracefully to her feet, "But, on to more pressing matters. Delmar, attend me, please. We must attempt to locate all the stones, and I must reflect on a way to destroy them without the powers of the council."

"About that," began Cassie slowly. "I have an idea of a way to turn these portal stones to our advantage."

"Then, by all means, attend us," offered the Lady.

"You're coming too," Cassie stated, clutching Ruby's hand fiercely. "I'm not letting you out of my sight again."

"Okay, can I find some shoes from somewhere first?" Ruby asked, happily. She saw the hopeful expression Colwyn shot at Cassie and the way Cassie ignored him, turning her head away to follow Lady Ninniane and Delmar as they left the room, leaving Lord Reutghar facing his son.

"I see you and Lady Cassandra have not reconciled your differences?" he enquired.

Colwyn sighed, his expression one of irritation. "She is the most infuriating of women," he exclaimed hotly. "I will admit to never having seen her like at swordsmanship, and she is brave and fearless, yet she will not learn her place and possesses none of the traits a man would look for in a wife."

For a long moment, Reutghar stared at his proud, stubborn son, then shook his head, a grin pulling at his mouth. "Mayhap, it is time I told you the tale of how I met your mother," he began.

Colwyn looked at him curiously. His father sat, indicating he should too. "I know she was the sister of one of your most trusted Lords, and that you met whilst you were visiting his family's manor."

"Aye, that is true enough," agreed his father. "There was a little more to it than that. As you know, my boyhood companion was Lord Tyrone. We were as close as brothers, and we both enjoyed hunting to the exclusion of all other pursuits, especially the fierce, wild boar prevalent in the forests around his ancestral home." Reutghar grinned.

"I had not ascended the throne, so was able to indulge my passion. My father had indicated I must choose a wife, but I was resistant. None of the court ladies, accomplished and beautiful as they were, aroused any interest in me."

"I know that feeling well," agreed Colwyn, ruefully.

"Then Tyrone invited me to hunt at his manor. A savage boar had been attacking the village, stealing livestock, and terrorising the villagers so we made it our target, vowing not to return without its carcass. Tyrone had many brothers who accompanied us, including the youngest, a lad tender in years. A lack-beard, he appeared frail and slight of build, but for all that he sat a horse as if his mother had birthed him there." Reutghar smiled at the memory.

"Each time we flushed out a boar, he would be first with the killing arrow. He was a remarkable bowman, better by far than I. It rankled the lad didn't hold back. After all, I was heir to the dragon throne." At Colwyn's raised brows, Reutghar chuckled.

"I was young and arrogant, had not learnt the painful lesson of humility. I digress, finally we picked up the tracks of a large boar. I knew in my heart it was the one we were seeking. He led us a merry chase deep into the forest, but at last, we cornered him, and I raised my bow to despatch him."

"What happened?" asked Colwyn, his eyes interested.

"A pheasant flew up under my horse. He reared, unseating me. I crashed to the ground, and the boar charged. Before he could reach me, someone stepped in his path, an arrow sang from his bow and the beast fell dead. It was the boy who had so annoyed me all day. He saved me from a nasty mauling."

"A brave lad indeed," muttered Colwyn, admiringly. "To willingly step in the path of a charging boar, not many would be so courageous, or so foolhardy."

"I was grateful to the lad and ashamed of my previous manner towards him. I ordered the boar's teeth to be removed and presented them to him, declaring if at any time he desired a favour, he had merely to ask. We then returned to the manor where a grand feast was planned for the next evening when we would consume the noble enemy who had provided us with such sport," Reutghar paused, his expression softening.

"That evening at the feast, the ladies of the household entered, and I saw her for the first time. Her dark hair reached almost to her waist and her face was strong and wild. I had never met Tyrone's sister but knew her to be recently returned from training at the Lady's Sanctuary. Yet as she was led over to be presented, I had the strangest feeling we had met before. She curtseyed, looked at me with eyes that sparkled in mischief and drew a necklace of boars' teeth from her belt, declaring her favour from the Lord Reutghar was the honour of the first dance."

"The young lad was my mother?" gasped Colwyn. "How could her parents, her brothers, allow such a thing?"

"Her mother was long dead. Her father let her run wild with her brothers who were her conspirators in the deception, seeing it as a great joke. Proudly, Tyrone introduced us, claiming his sister to be the best bowman, the most accomplished swordsman he knew. That evening, I realised if a man could best me in the hunting field, he was worthy of my respect. If a woman could, she was worthy of my respect and my love. The next day I asked for her hand in marriage."

"Did you not worry she would be unable to cope with the running of a royal household?" asked Colwyn.

His father shook his head. "I had people to cook, clean, sew, and indeed, oversee castle matters. They were turbulent and troubled times. Pirates were raiding our coastal villages. Brigands who inhabited the Wild Woods to the north were becoming bolder and pushing ever southwards. I believed it more important my wife could defend the castle in my absence and was a lady whom my men could respect and follow."

He placed a hand on Colwyn's shoulder. "The man that wears the crown is a lonely one, Colwyn. He needs a wife who can take her place at his side, one confident and strong enough to cope with adversity, not a mouse cowering in his shadow."

He paused, lips twisting into an amused grin at his son's confusion. "Now," he said. "Shall we enquire what scheme the Lady Cassandra has hatched to defeat the Gilmesh?"

The hunt for the portal stones was going well. So far, five had been located, Ruby and Cassie watching with interest as Lady Ninniane instructed Delmar how to perform a seeking spell to strip the stone of its disguise and enable it to be seen.

Stones had been disguised as a bench in the corridor where Ruby had been abducted, and a trough in the south courtyard. Three others had been located – in the kitchen disguised as a chair, in the sewing chamber as a tapestry, and in the throne room as a gridiron in the great stone hearth. Now they were seeking the sixth stone, following the Lady up to the bedchambers as she cast her mind forth, searching for its energy. At last, they tracked it down in an unused bedchamber, posing as a wooden linen chest.

The Lady frowned, as she tried to locate the final stone. "I can feel its presence within the castle," she said finally, "but cannot pinpoint its exact location. It is constantly moving, never staying in one position long enough for me to determine its whereabouts."

"It could be disguised as something that gets carried about," suggested Cassie, "Maybe a tray or a jug, something like that."

"Perhaps," agreed the Lady. "We must continue to seek it."

"Mayhap we should divide our efforts," suggested Delmar. "I am confident now of my ability to perform the seeking spell."

"The idea has merit," stated the Lady.

"Okay, I'll go with Delmar," Cassie put in quickly. Ruby knew she wanted her to be with the Lady, believing her better able to look after her. "First," continued Cassie, "we should take the stones to Lord Reutghar and put my plan in action, in case Lorcan decides to attack a few days early."

"Why would he do that?" wondered Ruby.

Cassie smiled grimly. "He no longer has you, Ruby, you've spoilt his plans for world domination, and I should imagine he's peed off about that. From what you've told us he's mentally unstable as it is. This could be all it takes to push him over the edge."

Lorcan glared as the Gilmesh leader strode into the room, its eyeless sockets gleaming yellow, grey tattered clothing streaming behind it. "Well?" he snapped, impatiently.

We searched, for many leagues in all directions, we searched. Finally, we followed a faint scent trail to a wild boar's den and found this. Casually, he dropped a shoe onto the table. Lorcan poked at the savaged and chewed item, his frown turning thunderous.

"You found nothing else?" he demanded.

The Gilmesh shook its head. *Nothing, but boars are known to consume every morsel. We were lucky to find this. She could not have survived the fall. The boar must have dragged her body back to its lair and feasted on it.*

"She was pivotal to my plans," Lorcan growled with savage disappointment, sweeping the shoe off the table, and turning on Siminus who stood quietly to one side.

"Without her empathic abilities, I will be unable to enter the World Between Worlds."

"What shall we do, my Lord?" enquired Siminus.

"We shall advance our plans," declared Lorcan. "Assemble your troops," he ordered the Gilmesh leader, "You move at dusk. They will be at dinner and will not suspect an attack."

"My Lord," began Siminus. "All the Gilmesh have not yet returned..."

"Do you dare question me?" screamed Lorcan. "We have enough to overcome them. They will be powerless to stop the Gilmesh. I will laugh at their screams as their souls are ripped from their bodies. Do what you like with them." He turned to the Gilmesh leader. "There is to be none left living within the castle by morning, except the Ladies Cassandra, and Ninniane. I want them brought to me alive and unharmed. I have ... plans for them," he stated, and even Siminus flinched at the madness in his eyes.

Standing on the battlements, Ruby shivered and drew her cloak closer. The sun was on the verge of setting and a chill wind was whistling over the castle ramparts.

"My Lady?"

Ruby looked at the young lad standing beside her, gratefully accepting the goblet of warming mulled wine he offered. "Thank you," she murmured. The boy grinned cheekily, before turning to give Delmar a goblet too.

"My thanks, Hobbs," he said. "Please locate Lords Reutghar and Colwyn and request their company on the battlements."

"Of course, my Lord," replied the lad, and ran briskly down the steps.

"I don't remember seeing him before," said Ruby.

"Hobbs? Oh, he's an orphan. His parents were killed in a skraeling raid and Siminus picked him out to serve him. He cleaned his quarters and ran errands. He was at a loss when Siminus left, so I took him on with the notion of training him to assist me."

"That was kind of you," replied Ruby. Delmar shrugged, opening his mouth to reply when the arrival of Lord Reutghar and Lady Ninniane stopped him.

"Where are the stones?" Lady Ninniane asked. Ruby pointed over the battlements to the dry moat many feet below.

"Down there," she replied.

Reutghar peered curiously through the deepening gloom as Cassie and Darius joined them. "In faith, Lady Cassandra, will you not enlighten us as to your cunning plan?" enquired Reutghar.

Cassie grinned at Ruby. "Just call me Baldrick," she quipped, and Ruby smiled.

"My Lady?"

"Never mind. The stones are in the moat in the middle of a bonfire of wood, covered in all the pitch and lamp oil we could lay our hands on. That part of the moat is a positive ocean of highly combustible material now, and if you look along the edge of the moat, there will be a 24/7 watch mounted."

They all did so, and Ruby saw a platoon of archers filing into position along its lip. Cassie continued, "the second anything tries to come through those stones, bam! We turn the moat into the towering inferno."

"My Lady," began Reutghar, admiringly, "you are indeed a most cunning tactician." He looked at the Lady Ninniane. "Have we yet located the seventh stone?"

"No, my Lord," Ninniane's face was drawn with concern. "It never stays still for one moment and defies all my attempts to locate it. Siminus chose this stone's disguise well."

Ruby started, a thought flashing through her mind. "Oh," she said slowly. They all looked at her. "The stone," she continued. "It can be disguised as anything, right?"

"That is correct, Ruby."

"Even a person?"

"I have never heard of a stone being disguised thus," replied the Lady. "When a portal stone is activated it releases a powerful burst of energy. Any life form being used would be destroyed."

"What if someone didn't care about that?" Ruby pressed with growing excitement. "What if all they cared about was disguising the stone as completely as possible, and didn't particularly mind what happened to the disguise?"

"Then yes, it would be possible for the disguise to be a person," replied the Lady. "It would certainly explain why the stone appears to be constantly moving."

"There are over a thousand people within the castle walls at the moment, Lady Ruby," declared Reutghar in a worried tone. "How do we determine who it is?"

"I think I know," exclaimed Ruby, turning to Delmar. "You know who it is too. Think Delmar, someone who was introduced to the castle by Siminus not long ago, someone whose job as a servant means he's always on the go."

"By the stars," breathed Delmar. "Hobbs."

"Is that skinny lad a traitor?" said Reutghar, incredulously.

"It is entirely possible he is innocent of any knowledge of this," replied Lady Ninniane. "We must find him quickly. If a seeking spell is used before the stone is activated, there is a good chance his life will be spared."

"We'll split up again," Cassie declared, taking charge with a casual ease which surprised Ruby. She realised how much her sister had changed since their return. "Delmar, you search the bed chambers again, I'll check the living quarters."

"What about me?" enquired Ruby. "Where shall I look?"

"I want you to stay close to the Lady," ordered Cassie. "I know we've found six of the stones, but that still means there's one in the castle somewhere. Until it's found, we can't run the risk of you falling into Lorcan's hands again."

"Come with me, Ruby," urged the Lady gently. "We shall search the kitchen. It is the most likely location for Hobbs, especially as it approaches dinner time." They all hurried into the castle intent on their search, knowing the lives of all of them depended on their success at finding one skinny serving lad.

Hurtling through the corridors and chambers of the castle, all deserted as the nobility were busy dressing for dinner and the servants busy preparing it, Cassie's frustration grew as she looked in empty room after empty room with no sign of Hobbs.

Running down an empty passageway, boots echoing on the stone-flagged floor, Cassie wondered how the others were doing before the breath was knocked from her body as she ran headlong into Colwyn rushing the other way.

"My stars, Cassandra!" he cried, clutching her arms to steady her. "Where are you going in such haste?"

"We have to find the serving boy, Hobbs!" Cassie gasped. "We think he might be the seventh stone."

"I have just left him," Colwyn exclaimed. "I was obeying a message he delivered to join Delmar on the battlements."

"Come on!" yelled Cassie, charging down the corridor. "We have to find him."

They rounded a corner, emerging into a cloistered inner courtyard and there, at the far end, was the slight figure of Hobbs.

"There he is," cried Colwyn.

"Hobbs!" yelled Cassie.

The boy stopped and turned, confused, and alarmed at the urgency he heard in her voice.

"My Lady?" he called.

Then, with an awful cracking, tearing, grinding sound, a thin line appeared down the centre of his body. He screamed as light poured forth. Painfully blinding, it forced the split open until Hobbs vanished in a blast of raw, wounding energy, which knocked Colwyn and Cassie to the ground.

Staggering to their feet, they saw in horror the tall, looming figures of the Gilmesh pouring through the hole, and knew they were too late.

The invasion of the castle had begun.

Chapter Nineteen

In the
Heat of Battle

nstinctively, Cassie drew her sword preparing to engage the never-ending flow of Gilmesh pouring through the jagged hole in existence whose edges burned with a fierce light.

"No, Cassandra!" cried Colwyn, dragging her away. "There are too many, we must sound the alarm." Together, they ran from the cloisters, hearing the guttural cries of the Gilmesh as they followed.

High on the battlements, Darius climbed shakily to his feet, stunned and half deafened by the force of an explosion that seemed to blast the moat apart

"My Lord, the stones!" cried Darius, peering over the battlements. "The Gilmesh are emerging. To arms!" he called to the archers staggering drunkenly to their feet. "Bowmen!" Urgency sharpened his voice. "Engage the enemy."

A few soldiers responded and sent flaming arrows shakily into the moat, where the pitch and lamp oil ignited in a flaming curtain of fire engulfing the ranks of Gilmesh marching through the blazing portals. Shrieking and twisting, the Gilmesh dissolved into piles of grey ash.

Encouraged by this, more soldiers shot randomly into the moat, then more, until the moat was indeed a towering inferno filled with writhing, screaming, dying Gilmesh. Still, they came, hundreds of them, marching endlessly into oblivion. Darius realised the advancing Gilmesh on the far side of the portal could not be aware of the fate awaiting them.

The alarm bell clanged with desperate urgency from within the castle and Reutghar and Darius looked at each other in dismay. "The seventh stone," stated Reutghar. "The Gilmesh are inside the castle. You stay here, make sure none make it out of the moat alive."

"My Lord," agreed Darius, and Reutghar ran from the battlements, unsheathing his sword and preparing to defend his castle to the very last.

In the kitchen, the muffled boom of the explosion shook the walls making them totter uneasily on their feet, and pots and pans shudder from shelves. "What was that?" gasped Ruby, as the kitchen staff huddled close to the Lady in alarm.

"The portal stones have been activated," declared the Lady calmly, then stiffened, her eyes pulsing blue. "The Gilmesh are within the castle, arm yourselves," she ordered the servants. Obediently, they picked up meat cleavers, knives, and anything that could conceivably be used as a weapon.

"Follow me," commanded the Lady. "We are needed."

"What about Cassie?" asked Ruby, fearfully.

"She is alive, although scared."

After ringing the alarm bell and hearing the answering shouts echoing within the castle, Colwyn grabbed Cassie's arm, dragging her out of the path of the advancing Gilmesh.

"Garth!" he cried. A familiar figure had appeared in the corridor ahead, face grim as he buckled a long, lethal-looking sword onto his hip. "Gilmesh are inside the castle, call all men to arms. We must protect the keep."

"Aye, my Lord," agreed Garth, and hurried off, yelling orders to the growing numbers of soldiers spilling out into the hallway, faces set and determined.

The heat from the raging hellhole in the moat forced the rows of bowmen back from the edge. Still, they continued to shoot blazing arrows into its midst, Darius arraying a line of archers high along the battlements to also shoot directly down into the seething mass of shrieking Gilmesh.

To his relief, Darius realised Cassie's plan was working. Not one Gilmesh was going to make it alive from the moat. He wondered how things were faring elsewhere, hearing with concern the sounds of battle emerging from the castle.

"Edwin!"

"My Lord?" the hawk-eyed soldier snapped to attention.

"Maintain the bombardment. See to it none escape."

"My Lord." Nodding in satisfaction, Darius unsheathed his sword and bounded from the battlements in search of the fight.

Rounding a corner, Colwyn and Cassie ran into a small group of Gilmesh busily hacking their way through a group of terrified servants. Yelling, they charged, swords flashing as they engaged the enemy. There was no more time for thinking or talking, there was only the instant of the fight and the fury of battle.

Grabbing a petrified servant by the arm and bodily hauling the sobbing woman out of the way, Cassie was nearly decapitated by a Gilmesh, ducking frantically as its evil black sword hissed over her head, missing her by inches.

Beside her, Colwyn was fighting with two Gilmesh at once, his blade whistling as it sliced through the air with a speedy precision so refined and practised, two headless Gilmesh were writhing and dying on the floor before Cassie could blink.

"Head to the battlements!" Colwyn ordered the servants as the last Gilmesh fell.

The small group hurriedly lifted the wounded and staggered away down the corridor. Cassie and Colwyn raced further into the castle, hearing screams and cries ahead.

Emerging into the banqueting hall a chaotic melee of desperate defence and death met their eyes. Gilmesh swarmed, and the people of Erinsmore, soldiers, nobles, and servants alike, fought for their lives and their castle.

Horrified, Cassie followed Colwyn into the heart of the fight, and it was no longer glorious or intoxicating.

It was real; horrifyingly, frighteningly, sickeningly real.

As Cassie fought, she saw all around people she knew, people she cared about, men she'd patrolled with, fought alongside, and laughed with, now falling, and dying.

She scrubbed frantically at the bitter tears which soaked her cheeks, mingling with blood, sweat, and snot to cake her face in a grubby mask.

Managing to finally slice the head off her opponent, Cassie tripped over a body on the ground, recognising Lord Barnabus, elegant even in death, lace collar and cuffs drenched in blood, eyes wide and staring.

In the far corner of the room, Cassie saw Gunther, that dryly amusing soldier whose boots had been ruined by Wilfric, go down under a tide of Gilmesh. Before she could reach him, she saw the blades flash black, and knew she was too late.

She tried to stay close to Colwyn, but the pressures of combat soon forced them apart. It was with relief when now and then, through a gap in the fighting, Cassie would catch a glimpse of him and knew he still lived.

A serving lad desperately shielded a terrified, sobbing lady. Cassie noted with admiration, his defensive thrust with a candelabrum brightly lit with a dozen candles and leapt to despatch the Gilmesh as it attempted to slice the lady in two.

"Get to the battlements!" she ordered them. Grimly, the lad nodded, gripping his makeshift weapon in his hands. "Take as many with you as you can, fire's the only thing that stops them, hurry, go!"

Cassie briefly hoped they made it, before turning to face yet another Gilmesh.

Deep within the castle, Lady Ninniane halted, her hand held up to stop the small party following them, a group swollen with the addition of other terrified servants they'd encountered along the way.

"What is it?" Ruby whispered, then jumped as a group of Gilmesh seemed to appear from nowhere before them. Calmly, the Lady held out her hand, her eyes pulsed blue and a giant flaming fireball rolled down the passageway consuming and destroying every Gilmesh it touched.

"We must hurry," stated the Lady. "Many are dying." Once more the little band hurried through the castle, following the sounds of battle.

Hands slippery with sweat and blood, Cassie fought on adrenalin only, heart pounding, legs shaking. Still, the battle raged, the tide of Gilmesh never-ending. Cassie prayed her plan had worked, that the Gilmesh emerging into the moat were being destroyed.

She saw a Gilmesh leaning over the terrified body of a wounded maid. Ripping at her bodice, it pressed a skeletal hand on her chest. The girl's body bucked; an anguished scream ripped from her throat as the Gilmesh feasted.

Enraged, Cassie sliced blindly at it. The Gilmesh ducked. Flailing one long arm upwards it sent her sword spinning from her numb hand, knocking her breathless to the ground.

Howling with rage, Cassie felt its weight on her frantically kicking legs. She screamed in terror as it clawed at her shirt, empty eye sockets glowing yellow with anticipation, icy bony fingers grasping her wrists and forcing them over her head, its other grey hand clamping coldly onto her exposed chest.

"Cassandra!"

On the far side of the room, Colwyn yelled desperately. Through eyes swimming with tears of pure terror and pain, Cassie saw he was hemmed in by at least a dozen Gilmesh, sword flashing as he recklessly tried to reach her.

At the sound of her name, the Gilmesh hesitated, but its instincts to feed were stronger than any orders. Once again, there was the pressure of his hand and Cassie screamed as something tore and ripped deep inside.

The Gilmesh exploded into a howling column of flame. Cassie shoved and wriggled out from under, watching with disbelief as the lit sconce clattered to the ground, along with the grey death ash of the Gilmesh.

Looking up, she saw the scared face of Lady Melinda as she clutched the edge of the minstrel's gallery, and realised she'd been the one who'd thrown the sconce. Their eyes met.

"Look out!" screamed Cassie.

Melinda turned, crying out in fear as a Gilmesh lumbered into the gallery, black sword raised over the terrified woman who backed away, trapped, Cassie watching in helpless horror. Abruptly, the Gilmesh exploded into flames and Delmar erupted onto the gallery, pulling Melinda to her feet.

"Are you injured, my Lady?" he enquired urgently.

Melinda fell sobbing into his arms. "You saved my life!" she cried, clutching at him.

"And in turn, you saved Cassandra's," he retorted. "Your bravery was so ... unexpected, my Lady."

A look passed between them, an intense, meaningful look that had Cassie thinking – as she rolled to retrieve her sword and leapt to face the next Gilmesh – hello, what have we here?

The battle raged on.

Time ceased to have any meaning. Existence narrowed to single moments. Specks of time in an endless sea of blood, death, and tears.

Were they making any difference? Cassie was unsure. Then came a point when the Gilmesh appeared less. Then there were none. Slowly, the survivors lowered their swords and gazed at each other in wide-eyed disbelief, hoarse, ragged breathing the only sound.

Striding through the bodies, Colwyn reached her and placed his arms around her. For a moment Cassie was grateful to lean into his strength, relief at their survival and shock at the loss of so many making her tremble in his embrace.

"Are you harmed?" his tone was urgent.

Pulling back, Cassie saw his eyes go to her ripped shirt and exposed chest, where the faint outline of a grey handprint could be seen. She shook her head, speechlessly. Fiercely, he gripped her again.

"My Lord!"

Darius strode into the hall followed by a small band of soldiers, their faces stern and bloodied.

"Darius, what news?" demanded Colwyn.

"Lady Cassandra's plan worked, my Lord, no Gilmesh will escape the moat. I assume you did not reach Hobbs in time?"

"No," Colwyn shook his head. "The stone activated as we found him, I fear the lad was the first casualty of the battle."

"Not the last, my Lord," Darius's eyes were grim.

"Have you seen my father?" asked Colwyn, "Or the Ladies Ninniane and Ruby?"

"Lord Reutghar was rallying soldiers to assist him in defending the keep, my Lord," replied Darius. "I fear I have not seen the Ladies, although I know Lady Ninniane to be more than a match for any number of Gilmesh," he added hastily, at Cassie's concerned look.

Were it not for the bodies they encountered at every turn, Ruby might almost have been enjoying herself as they hurried through the castle, the Lady destroying with casual ease any Gilmesh which dared to stand in their way, and Ruby became aware for the first time of the Lady's powers.

Not as blatantly obvious as Lorcan's, Ruby had considered the Lady a wise and gentle advisor only. Watching in stunned admiration as she coolly and calmly destroyed the enemy, Ruby now realised she was a force to be reckoned with and felt safe in her presence.

Rallying together the survivors of the battle of the banqueting hall, Colwyn organised a group with Delmar at its head, to assist the wounded to the battlements.

Cassie noticed Lady Melinda stayed close to the young mage's side, eyes constantly straying to his with a gaze of adoration, making Delmar straighten and give orders with a new tone of authority.

Following Colwyn and Darius, Cassie hurried with them towards the keep, worrying about Ruby, taking heart from the fact she was with the Lady.

They rounded a corner and found Gilmesh surrounding a small, but determined, group of soldiers defending a terrified huddle of court ladies.

"My Lord, shall I assist?" enquired Darius, with a gleam in his eye.

At Colwyn's nod, he ordered half their force to follow him, and they charged to relieve the beleaguered group.

Hurrying by Colwyn's side through dimly lit passageways, Cassie wondered wildly what time it was.

Time had ceased to have any meaning.

Night would never end.

Morning would never come.

They paused at the top of a broad flight of steps and saw Reutghar and Garth, together with a band of soldiers, their backs to the final door to the keep, holding off what looked like the entire Gilmesh army.

Bodies littered the floor.

Casualties had been high.

Cassie swallowed hard, and wiped her sweaty palm, sticky with blood, down her side, gripping her sword tightly.

"We shall attempt to surround them," Colwyn ordered his men. "Form a pincer to trap them between us and Lord Reutghar's men. Cassandra ..." he began.

"I will fight by your side," she declared fiercely, chin rising, Colwyn hesitated and grinned.

"Indeed, my Lady," he replied. "There is no other place I would have you."

For a heartbeat, they gazed at each other.

Cassie's senses hummed.

Ignoring the knowing looks and quiet chuckles of the soldiers surrounding them, she grabbed a handful of his shirt and pulled him to her, planting a fiercely possessive kiss on his shocked lips, smiling in feminine satisfaction at the dazed look on his face.

"Now," she said firmly. "Let's go kick some Gilmesh butt!"

With wild yells and battle cries, they surged onto the enemy. Reutghar's forces cheered with relief at the sight, their arrival boosting flagging spirits, and Cassie almost danced for joy as she met, engaged, and despatched in a grim yet oddly beautiful dance of war, Colwyn never far from her side.

In a nearby passageway, Lady Ninniane stopped, eyes pulsing vivid blue as she sent out with her mind, seeking, probing. Ruby followed suit, briefly touching on minds, feeling with relief the chaotic thoughts of her sister and Colwyn.

Then she found the Gilmesh, thousands of cold emotionless minds pouring through the seventh portal, intent on the total annihilation of the castle.

"What shall we do?"

Snapping back into her body with a jerk, Ruby clasped at the Lady's sleeve.

"What shall we do, my Lady? There are too many of them..."

"The portal must be destroyed," Lady Ninniane declared.

"But how, how?" cried Ruby wildly.

"There is only one way. We must fetch the sacred sword."

Finally, there were no more Gilmesh, their remains little more than grey death dust which clung to their boots. A tidal wave of relief arose in the soldiers as Reutghar strode over and clasped his son tightly, before engulfing Cassie in a hug that lifted her off her feet and left her breathless.

"We did it," declared Reutghar in satisfaction.

"My Lord!"

At Darius's urgent cry, they turned to see him rush down the steps.

"The Gilmesh still come through the stone and have headed to the battlements."

At his words, despondency and despair crept over Cassie. There were so many, too many, and she was so tired, they all were.

How could they carry on?

How could they continue to fight when they had already been fighting forever?

"Colwyn," snapped Reutghar. "You and Cassandra take your troops around to the south side of the battlements. We shall head to the north. We fight on. Lorcan shall see the men and women of Erinsmore do not give in. For Erinsmore!" he yelled, raising his sword, and the soldiers cheered.

"For Erinsmore!"

The journey to the sword room had been eerily uneventful. Ruby knew from the mutterings of the servants that they too were unnerved by the castle's quietness.

"Where are they all?" murmured Gretchen.

"They head for the battlements," replied Lady Ninniane. "We must get the sword before enough come through to completely overwhelm the castle."

They entered the room. Once again, Ruby gasped in awe at the sword's pure, blinding brilliance, the servants' mutterings rising to excited chattering.

Swiftly, the Lady pulled the sword, its beauty momentarily sheathing her in radiance.

"Sword of Erinsmore," she declared, voice ringing with authority. "I, Ninniane, last of the Council of Mages, awaken you from your slumber. The land is under attack from the forces of evil. Your King, and your people, need you."

A sound, sweet and perfect, resonated through the room. A wild dart of hope and happiness pierce through Ruby and she beamed at the smiling faces of the others.

"Come," Lady Ninniane glided past, sword held aloft. Silently, they followed her.

They'd barely started towards the battlements when Gilmesh fell upon them. Once more, Cassie found herself caught up in the wild madness of battle.

They were many, so many. Cassie wouldn't – couldn't – allow herself to think of numbers. Instead, she dealt with them one by one.

Cut, hack, slash, thrust, her individual conflicts taking her further and further from the main battle.

Finally, she realised in alarm that apart from the Gilmesh she fought, she was alone in a gloomy corridor.

Apprehension gave her strength and she jumped and slashed, reducing the Gilmesh to dust, then rushed back down the passageway.

The Gilmesh was huge, the biggest she'd ever seen.

It stepped from the shadows and threw her to the ground. The wild thought occurred as she crashed to the floor with a cry of pain, that it must be their leader, the one Ruby had described.

Hands on hips, the Gilmesh surveyed her, its empty eye sockets glowing yellow with satisfaction as three more Gilmesh joined it.

You are the one I have been seeking. You are the one Lorcan wants.

It stepped forward, knocking her sword from her hand, and hauling her up. Slinging her over its shoulder it set off down the corridor, its massive strides taking her away from all help.

"No!" she screamed, desperately fighting its steely grip.

"My Lady!"

Wilfric ran down the passageway after them. Casually, the Gilmesh cast her to the ground. Stepping over her winded body, it lifted its great black sword as if it were a javelin and threw it.

Cassie saw in slow motion the panic in Wilfric's eyes before the sword embedded itself in his stomach, and he crumpled to the floor.

"Wilfric!"

Cassie cried and ran to him, cradling his body in her arms. His eyes opened, struggling to focus.

"My Lady," he said, almost apologetically.

Then that sweet young soldier, her friend who'd comforted her after the slaughter of Corrinshill, died in her arms. An uncontrollable, wild rage boiled and churned deep within Cassie's soul.

Bring her, ordered the Gilmesh, and its escort bent to lift her. Cassie turned, eyes blazing a brilliant blue, Wilfric's sword in her hand, its length a roaring column of fire which moved, once, twice, three times.

The Gilmesh guards fell, shrieking and twisting, flames consuming them. She stepped towards the leader, hatred burning in her veins.

It fled, grey bones rattling as it ran, Cassie in hot pursuit, holding her blade aloft, its glow lighting up the dark passageways.

She reached the cloistered courtyard and saw the Gilmesh leader leap through the portal, which glimmered with a savage light, still disgorging dozens of Gilmesh in a constant stream.

A roar erupted from her throat.

She snatched up a sword from a dead soldier. It too exploded into flames, and she was truth, and she was vengeance.

All-powerful, she danced into their midst, her twin blades dispensing death and justice.

Erupting into the courtyard, Colwyn shielded his eyes from her glory, relief at seeing her alive tempered with fear for her survival as she cut a swathe through the grey, tightly packed mass of Gilmesh.

Reutghar and Darius pounded into the courtyard on the opposite side, the soldiers who followed them cheering on the Lady Cassandra and falling upon the flanks of Gilmesh with renewed vigour.

"My Lord."

Lady Ninniane and Ruby entered the courtyard, the sword held aloft, and the Gilmesh parted at their approach, fear of the sword sending them scurrying.

"My Lady?" enquired Reutghar.

"The portals must be closed," she declared. "The sword is the only way."

"Then let us waste no time doing it," he exclaimed heartily. "Whilst Lady Cassandra is doing such an excellent job of distracting them."

"There is a problem, my Lord," she said. Reutghar moved closer to listen.

On the other side of the courtyard, Colwyn was fighting his way to Cassie's side, hacking at the shrieking, fleeing Gilmesh with something almost approaching glee, and he realised they were on the run, terrified of Cassie and her swords of might.

Out of the corner of his eye, he saw his father listening to the Lady, his face serious, then saw him pull back and gaze levelly at her before taking the sword.

Reaching Cassie, Colwyn saw his father approach the portal. An inexplicable foreboding gripped him.

"Father, no!" he yelled in sudden fear.

His father paused, cast a regretful glance at his son, and then held the sword aloft, words of magic powerful on his lips.

A wave of pure light swept outwards through the courtyard, crumbling every Gilmesh into dust. Then, Reutghar simply stepped through the portal. It shimmered and snapped closed behind him.

An eerie, unnatural silence fell.

Cassie stared in horrified disbelief. The power left her eyes and her swords clattered to the ground. A thin finger of dawn crept over the battlements.

Somewhere, a bird sang to welcome it.

Chapter Twenty

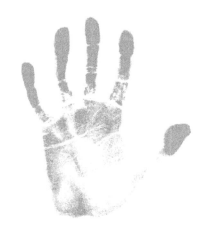

Beneath the Centre
of this Land

orning. The people of Dragonswell moved about their violated castle, tending their wounded and counting their dead, of which there were many, too many.

Colwyn, their new Lord, walked silently amongst them, his face bleak and etched with tightly controlled grief.

"Why?" he'd howled at the Lady.

"The portal could only be closed from the other side," the Lady replied, eyes gentle with sympathy. Colwyn turned away in bitter understanding, knowing his father would have accepted the price for saving his castle and his people.

Understanding the reason could not soften the blow of loss. The people of Erinsmore mourned their king, sorrow binding them together in the chill early light as they went silently about their grim tasks.

Shocked and disbelieving, Cassie wanted to be with Colwyn to comfort him. She was gently, but firmly, snubbed by a man grown into a king, bowed down by duty. Eventually, she gave up and miserably went to find her sister.

She found her in the banqueting room helping Lady Ninniane and Delmar tend the injured, noticing with a brief twist of ironic amusement that Lady Melinda was still by Delmar's side.

Her exquisite hair was matted, her silk gown ripped and bloodied. The petulant expression on her face had been replaced by a quietly thoughtful one. Her gaze resting often on Delmar as he ably healed and comforted, Cassie thought she'd never seen the other woman look so beautiful.

"Cassandra," Delmar glanced up at her approach and smiled. "How is Colwyn?"

"I don't know," Cassie shrugged, ridiculously close to tears. "He won't talk to me or anything ... I don't know what to do."

Delmar shook his head, eyes clouded with concern.

Lady Melinda placed a hand on his arm and looked directly at Cassie.

"He is grieving deeply, Cassandra," she murmured. "He is trying to come to terms with the fact he is now the Dragon Lord, a role he did not expect to assume for many years. Give him time, he knows your feelings. Very soon he will have need of your strength, for now, you must bide your time."

"You're right, he needs time to grieve." Cassie paused, looking steadily at Melinda. "Thank you," she said. "For everything."

Melinda inclined her head gracefully, knowing it was not just the advice for which she was being thanked.

"My Lord."

The serving lad who'd so ably held off the Gilmesh with a candlestick came rushing up, panting with exertion.

"What is it, Adam?" asked Delmar.

"Lord Colwyn asks that you, Lady Ninniane, and the Ladies Cassandra and Ruby join him at the moat."

Clattering onto the drawbridge, Melinda still close to Delmar's side, Ruby wondered why they'd been summoned. Colwyn was pacing by the side of the moat. He looked up, relief at their approach flashed onto his face and he pointed into the moat.

"What do you make of that?" he asked, and they all turned to look. The moat was deep, extending downwards many feet below even the dungeons of the castle. Ruby wondered if at some time in the distant past it had ever held water, then noticed something odd in the side of the moat where the portal stones had been contained, and the Gilmesh destroyed.

The inferno had reached such extremes of temperatures all the grass had burnt away. Even the top layer of soil had partially melted, and Ruby saw beneath the earth the glint of some type of bronze material.

"What is it?" murmured Cassie.

Colwyn frowned. "I do not know. The rest of the soil needs to be cleared away, yet the ground is still too hot to walk on. Delmar, could you...?"

"Of course," finished Delmar.

Holding out a hand, his eyes pulsed blue, and a warm glow emanated from his fingertips bathing the side of the moat in a shimmering haze. When it cleared, a large round door was revealed, its smooth surface shining in the morning sun.

"A doorway," breathed Melinda, eyes wide with curiosity. "How very strange. Where do you think it leads to?"

"I have never seen or heard of it before," stated Colwyn, turning to Lady Ninniane. "My Lady?"

"It is the gateway to the labyrinths which lie far below the city," she replied, her expression thoughtful. "I had heard a way to them once existed, yet it has been unknown for millennia and I assumed it had been destroyed."

"The fourth treasure we're looking for," exclaimed Ruby. "Isn't that supposed to be buried deep underground somewhere?"

"By the stars, yes," cried Colwyn in excitement. "From fire the D'raiqwq, 'neath the centre of this land. Do you not see? From fire?" The others looked back at the gateway standing proud amongst the charred and blackened ground.

"Fire did indeed uncover it," agreed the Lady.

"We have to get to it, see if it can be opened," insisted Colwyn. The Lady waved her hand and a shimmering bridge appeared spanning the moat, ending in a flight of steps leading down to a platform before the gateway.

With rising excitement, they crossed in single file, carefully climbing down the stairs until they all stood before the gateway.

"It's huge," breathed Cassie, craning her neck up. "How do we open it?"

"There is no lock or handle," agreed Delmar, running his hands lightly over its surface. They all looked, examining every inch for any clue as to how to gain entry.

"Look, what is this?" Lady Melinda exclaimed in excitement, running her fingers lightly over a depression in the smooth bronze.

Ruby squinted, trying to make sense of the shape. "It's a dragon," she cried. "Look, it's the shape of a dragon."

"Lady Cassandra, your pendant," began Melinda. "Would it not fit exactly?"

"Do you know," agreed Cassie. "I think it might."

With hands that shook she unclasped the chain and pressed the dragon into the gateway. It slotted exactly into the gap, fitting so perfectly that no join between it and the surface of the door could be seen.

For a moment nothing happened, then a network of fine gold lines shot out from the dragon writhing over the gateway, and an ominous grinding sound echoed from underground.

"Keep back," ordered Colwyn as the door rumbled and rolled over to reveal a long, dark passage stretching away and down.

Cassie picked up the dragon pendant which had fallen from the hole as the door opened.

"Are we going in?" she asked.

Colwyn peered into the darkness. "Yes," he stated firmly. "Yet someone needs to remain and tell Darius where we have gone. We cannot vanish without a trace. It would alarm the people."

Delmar nodded, Ruby knew Colwyn was thinking about his father, and his abrupt disappearance through the portal to certain death at the hands of Lorcan.

"I will remain," declared Melinda. "I would only be a liability to you. I have no great level of ability, nor am I able to protect myself, or others, if the need arose."

"Oh, I don't know," murmured Cassie. "You did pretty well last night.

"Nonetheless," replied Melinda, flashing Cassie a grateful smile. "I shall remain and await your safe return."

"Thank you, my Lady," said Colwyn.

Delmar took her hand in his. "We shall return as quickly as possible, hopefully with the fourth treasure with which we can put an end to Lorcan and recommence our lives. Then, my Lady…"

Melinda hastily put her hand to his lips.

"Upon your return, my Lord, we shall see what fate has in store for us. Until that moment, I pray you all go safely and return soon."

She walked away across the bridge and onto the drawbridge, pausing to glance at them, before turning back into the castle. Delmar watched her go, his face dazed and confused.

Cassie and Ruby exchanged glances.

"Well," Ruby exclaimed dryly. "I guess this means you like her now?"

"My Lady?"

Delmar stared at Ruby and Cassie's smirks. A blush spread across his face, he coughed and shuffled his feet awkwardly.

Colwyn frowned at them all, then swiftly seemed to understand, and grinned.

"By the stars, Delmar, you and Lady Melinda? I am amazed. How did this occur?"

"My Lord, I … I …" Delmar stuttered.

"It was when Melinda saved my life, and then Delmar saved hers," interrupted Cassie, with an evil grin at Delmar. "That's when they fell in lurve."

"My Lady!" protested Delmar.

Colwyn laughed, clapping him on the back. "I wish you every joy, Delmar, for the Lady is fair."

"Come," ordered Lady Ninniane, already several paces into the tunnel.

Their faces sobered from the moment of much-needed humour, and they followed the brightly glowing ball of light the Lady set to guide them into the darkness.

They walked for a very long time, always the tunnel heading steadily downwards. Ruby wondered if it would ever end, or if it would keep going down and down forever until they reached the centre of the world.

Finally, something glinted in the darkness ahead and their pace quickened, until they stood before a circular door, a twin to the one at the tunnel's entrance.

Once again, Cassie placed her pendant into a dragon-shaped depression set in the door, and once again the door radiated a starburst of light and rolled open. Walking through, they found themselves in a stone-clad chamber with no other doorways. It was a dead end.

"So now what?" Cassie enquired, fastening her pendant back around her neck.

"I know not," the Lady shook her head. "The labyrinth was lost, almost forgotten about, long before I was born. All I know are scraps of knowledge from legend and myth."

"Oh," Ruby started, confused. "You were born?"

She stopped, embarrassed, wondering if she'd offended the Lady. Ninniane smiled gently.

"Of course, I was born, Ruby, though many centuries ago, tis true. I was born in the normal way and had a family as you do, yet the ability was extremely strong in me. When I was tested, it was discovered my powers were such I was destined to join the Council of Mages and become eternal."

"My Lady."

During the conversation, Colwyn had wandered around the chamber examining the walls. Now he beckoned them over to where a set of five handprints were set into the wall.

"Do we place our hands within them?" enquired Delmar.

"Yes," nodded the Lady. "I can see no other option." Stepping up to the wall, she placed her right hand into one of the smaller prints. Delmar immediately followed suit.

Hesitating for a second, Colwyn pressed his right hand into the largest of the handprints.

Ruby glanced at Cassie, who shrugged, and then both girls did the same, placing their hands into the final two prints.

Immediately, a bright light flooded the chamber. A voice, terrible, ancient, and all-knowing, boomed through their minds.

"Who comes, after so long, who comes?"

A beam of light played over each one of them. Ruby struggled to free her hand from the wall but was gripped fast. Looking around, she saw the others unable to escape as the light examined and probed each one of them.

"The two seekers of prophecy, finally they come with their three champions. As there must always be balance in Erinsmore, each champion must face its equal. It must be, so it is..."

The last word echoed through their minds, their hands were free, and they were ... somewhere else...

Cassie spun around wildly, clutching at Ruby.

"Where are the others?" she cried, eyes darting around the small, circular chamber in which they'd found themselves. "Where are they?"

"I don't know," replied Ruby, voice trembling.

With mounting desperation, the two girls searched every inch of the tiny, though lavish space, pulling aside ornate tapestries to examine the solid stone walls, hoping to find another dragon-shaped hole, there was nothing.

At last, they flopped down on the great canopied couch heaped high with fur throws and velvet cushions.

"What do we do now?" asked Ruby, fear choking her words.

"Do not despair, child," said the voice. The sisters clutched one another in shock.

"Who are you?" cried Cassie. "Where are you?"

"I am the keeper of the secret. I have been waiting millennia for the seekers of the prophecy of old."

"Why can't we see you?" asked Cassie, slightly calmer now.

"You perceive with the limitations of your species. You cannot see me because I do not exist in corporeal form. I am energy and I am life; its force can be felt. It cannot be seen with mere vision, only its effects are visible."

There was a pause, then a dusty chuckle from the voice. "Ah yes," it continued. "You are correct, my child, like the electricity you have in your world."

"Can you read my thoughts?" asked Ruby.

"You are a powerful empath, my child, but have much to learn about controlling which thoughts you wish to project, and which you desire to keep secret."

"What about our friends?" demanded Cassie.

"You wish to observe your champions as they battle for your right to proceed?"

"Battle?" cried Cassie. "What do you mean? Where are they?"

"It is your right to do so," continued the voice, as if she hadn't spoken. "Consider the pool of knowing..."

The girls slid onto the floor, leaning over the stone bowl of dark water which was placed in the exact centre of the chamber. The water rippled as if a gentle breeze were blowing across it, and they saw...

... a great cavern, columns of twisted rock thrusting upwards to the ceiling many feet above. From somewhere came the sound of running water. Somehow, the whole cavern was brilliantly lit, like a floodlit football stadium.

It was a bizarre sensation. It was as if they were in the cavern, but Ruby knew they were still in the chamber, could feel the cold stone rim of the bowl as she leaned over it.

"Colwyn!" exclaimed Cassie in alarm, clutching her arm. Ruby saw Colwyn standing alone, far away in the centre of the chamber, looking around him with wary caution, his hand on his sword hilt.

"Colwyn, look out!" Cassie screamed. Colwyn gave no indication he could hear or see them. The girls could only clasp hands in agony, watching Colwyn turn, instinct making him draw and roll to one side as the Gilmesh leader, its massive black sword already drawn, charged at him from behind a pile of rocks.

Their swords clashed.

Colwyn fought for his life.

Already tired from the long night of battle, it was plain to the sisters he was at a disadvantage. As the fight ranged all over the cavern, he was always defending, whilst the Gilmesh leader attacked, again and again.

"He's so tired," Cassie murmured beside her. Ruby saw her face was pinched, drawn with anguish, and realised how much Cassie cared about Colwyn.

Heart hammering, a film of exhaustion across his eyes, palm slippery with sweat, Colwyn knew he was failing. He could feel his strength and determination draining away as the Gilmesh leader forced him backwards, raining hammer-like blows with its powerful sword, blows Colwyn was hard-pressed to deflect, shockwaves jarring his sword arm until it felt ready to snap.

The inevitable happened – Colwyn stumbled.

The Gilmesh leader with a contemptuous flick, sent his sword flying to lie many yards away on the cavern floor. Colwyn fell heavily to the ground. The Gilmesh leader paused, sword drawn back to deliver the killing blow, its lipless mouth curled in a snarl of disdain as it surveyed the fallen man.

Know this, oh mighty prince, with your death ends the reign of the dragon lords. As I took your father's life, so shall I take yours. Its voice was cold steel in his mind.

Colwyn closed his eyes in despair. 'Oh Father,' he thought. "Cassandra," he whispered her name, a soft farewell.

Ah yes, the Gilmesh sounded almost amused. *The beautiful Lady Cassandra, I am to take her to the mage, he has plans for her. It is as well you die now, Colwyn, last of the dragon lords, than be forced to watch whilst the mage slowly strips your Lady of every inch of flesh, until finally, she begs him for death, and only then be allowed to join you in the afterlife*

"No!" howled Colwyn.

Vivid blue fire flashed into his eyes.

His sword shot through the air into his waiting hand, flames leaping along its length as he pivoted on one hip and thrust upwards with the blazing blade.

"You will not touch her!" he snarled.

The Gilmesh leader twisted, howling in the flame's deadly embrace, before collapsing into a pile of grey dust. Colwyn staggered to his feet, gasping with exertion, the fire leaving his eyes and his sword. He stirred the mound of death dust with the toe of his boot.

"I have avenged you, Father," he declared. He raised his head, eyes widening as the girls became visible to him, though faint and ethereal.

"Cassandra?" he gasped, then vanished, snatched from the cavern, and hurled through space, to reappear, breathless and stunned on the floor of the banqueting hall.

"My Lord?"

Lady Melinda looked up in shocked surprise from tending the wounded and ran to support him as he shakily tried to sit.

"What happened? Where are the others?"

"I do not know," he replied in concern, staring into her apprehensive eyes. "In faith, my Lady, I do not know..."

... Back in the chamber, the girls hugged each other, tears of relief in their eyes. "He did it," murmured Cassie. "For a moment there, I thought ... but he's okay, he did it, he won."

"Your first champion has indeed proved himself worthy," came the eerie, disembodied voice. "It is time to see if your second champion is as able."

The waters shimmered again.

Once more, they found themselves in the underground cavern, only this time Delmar stood there looking around in interest, his keenly intelligent eyes narrowing as Siminus stepped out to confront him.

"Why?" he asked.

His former tutor's thin lips twitched into a sardonic smile. "Am I here?" he asked. "Or do you mean, why did I choose to support Lord Lorcan?"

"You were the King's mage," snapped Delmar, keeping a wary distance. "He trusted you ... I trusted you. Why did you betray us all?"

"Since Lorcan's capture, my family have been his staunchest secret supporters. Finally, I was born. When it was realised my level of ability would set me apart from all other men as a great mage, my father prepared me to take my rightful place at the dark lord's side."

"So, it was you who aided his escape from the chains that held him?" stated Delmar and Siminus smirked in agreement.

"It was so pathetically easy. I was above suspicion. My Lord Lorcan's gratitude when he gained his freedom ensured my place as ruler under him when the house of the dragon lords was finally crushed forever."

He paused, swiftly turned, and flung out his hand. A ball of dark, sizzling energy shot from his palm.

Just in time, Delmar's hand launched a counter strike of pure white light, exploding the dark material into a thousand shards of black which fell harmlessly to the ground.

"Your skill has improved," conceded Siminus, reluctantly. "Yet you are still no match for me. Join us, Delmar, for you have the potential to become a mighty mage, and I know my Lord will value your loyal service."

"Never!" snapped Delmar and spun a web of steel strands that engulfed Siminus from head to toe in a cocoon of light. With a contemptuous shrug, Siminus vanished from within the web to reappear several feet away, brushing the last strands from his long dark robe.

"You cannot defeat me," he sneered, cruel grey eyes gleaming with scorn. "I am invincible, none can harm me."

"The Lady Cassandra injured you sorely," taunted Delmar, bounding sideways through the air in a mighty leap to avoid a mushroom cloud of poisonous gas Siminus flicked at him from his fingertips.

"That she-wolf!" The older mage's face darkened in a scowl of rage. "My Lord has promised I shall be revenged upon her. I will make her beg. When her beauty is gone, her body twisted with the scars of my making, she will grovel at my feet for the sweet release of death."

"That will never happen," exclaimed Delmar. Fire spat from his hands to swirl around Siminus, solidifying into a barrier of shimmering light.

"And who's going to stop me?" laughed Siminus, examining the barrier with interest. "You? That muscle-bound oaf Colwyn? Lady Ninniane? You are none of you a match for my Lord or me." He touched the barrier and recoiled as sparks flew.

"This is familiar," he smiled almost proudly at Delmar. "Ah, I see you copy the barrier with which I trapped Lady Cassandra. I am delighted to see you learning from your experiences, Delmar, but you cannot think to trap me with a device of my creation."

A hum of pure energy travelled up his body, shattering the barrier and throwing Delmar to the ground.

"A neat trick," he mused, as Delmar writhed in agony. "I, in turn, was inspired by your tale of the barrier erected by the creatures in Lake Minwarn. And now," he continued, grey eyes cold with purpose. "I grow weary of this sport. It is time to end it."

Lightning crackled from his hands encasing Delmar. His body bent double, and screams of pain were wrenched from his throat.

"Such a pity," sighed Siminus. "You showed such promise, Delmar, I am almost sorry to have to kill you, however..." he sighed again, releasing another blast of energy into the young mage's twisted form.

The watching girls cried out in horror, powerless to help their friend slowly dying before them.

Struggling against the tide, feeling his life force draining away, Delmar forced open his hand. With his last remaining shreds of power, he opened a doorway as Lady Ninniane had taught him.

There was a shimmer of light. Ruby saw a flicker of the World Between Worlds. Delmar hurled himself through, dragging Siminus behind him still connected by ropes of crackling energy.

For a second, the older mage was suspended on the threshold, then a blood-chilling, heart-stopping scream was ripped from his soul as his body dispersed into a million fragments and were scattered throughout eternity.

Delmar fell backwards to land with a thud on the cavern floor, his laboured gasps echoing in the stillness.

"Delmar!" cried Ruby. "You did it, he's gone."

Delmar painfully raised his head, eyes focusing on their blurry forms.

"Ruby?" he asked, and then he too vanished. The girls found themselves alone in the circular chamber again.

"Your champions have so far proved worthy, most worthy indeed," mused the voice, and the girls clutched at each other with relief. "Yet now comes the final, hardest confrontation of all. Your champion must be victorious, or all will be lost."

The waters shimmered.

The girls found themselves again in the now-familiar cavern, watching silently as Lady Ninniane stood calmly, hands folded neatly on her skirts, blue eyes watchful and unsurprised as Lorcan stepped towards her, his long sweep of white hair a negative reflection of her glossy black tresses.

"Ninniane," he stopped, dark eyes glinting with unfathomable emotion.

"Lorcan," her voice was low and sweet.

"So, it has come to this then," he said, "Just us, facing one another, alone."

"As it was in the beginning," Ninniane stated, "so shall it be again. Since the instant we first drew our newborn breath, mere minutes apart and shared our mother's milk, it was destined this moment would come ... my brother."

Chapter Twenty-One

The Dark Path

uby stared at Cassie in bewilderment. "Twins? They're twins?"

"Sshh," urged Cassie, her attention on the occupants of the cavern who faced one another in calm contemplation.

"There is still time for you to change your mind," said Lorcan. "Think, Ninniane, we could rule eternity. It would please me to have my sister once more by my side."

"Oh, Lorcan," replied the Lady with a small sad smile. "You know that cannot be. I have chosen my path and you ... how did you get so lost, my brother? I have been reflecting on the past, trying to understand why you opened your soul to evil."

"It was the portal stones," Lorcan replied. "I was the one chosen to destroy them, yet when I held them in my hand, felt their power, something stirred deep inside. I could no more obliterate them than I could myself. I kept them safe, shielded them from the rest of the Council, and tested their power. Even I was surprised at the forces of nature I could unleash with them, the destruction I could cause throughout time."

"The tidal wave," Ninniane stated. "That was caused by you?"

"Wasn't it magnificent?" Lorcan demanded, almost proudly. "When you think of the irony. It was I who used a portal stone to rescue the survivors, never suspecting it would be my future self who would create the shock wave that would travel back in time to wreak such havoc."

"All those innocent people killed," Ninniane said. "Alys..."

"Ah yes, your little lady-in-waiting. It does not do to become attached to mortals, Ninniane, in the end, they always leave you. Although I am curious. Your man Samson, how is it he still lives? What witchery did you use to grant him long life?"

"That is none of your concern," stated Ninniane, firmly.

Lorcan shrugged uncaringly, pacing around her, eyes animated as he continued his tale. "Years passed. I grew dissatisfied with the measly crumbs of authority handed us by the other mages."

"We were the youngest," stated Ninniane firmly. "It was right and proper we be trained by those older and wiser than ourselves."

"Older maybe," exploded Lorcan. "Wiser? Come ... we had more ability in our little fingers than they had in their ancient bodies. They were blind fools, they deserved to die."

"They trusted you," retorted Ninniane. "They believed your loyalty was absolute and perished for that trust. Whereas I..."

"Yes, you, my sister, my twin, you were beginning to suspect something. For all your perception, Ninniane, even you had no concept of the depth of my ambition."

"It is true," began Ninniane slowly. "I did not wish to consider my soulmate could be anything other than good. I was naïve. I kept my concerns to myself rather than take them to the Council, and four innocent and wise mages died at your hands. Erinsmore was plunged into war and so many perished, savaged by your skraelings and the Gilmesh."

"Ah yes, the Gilmesh," Lorcan mused, eyes glinting with amusement. "I must admit their ferocity surprised even me. Their thirst for souls, any souls really, but particularly those of the very young, made them unpredictable allies."

"Is that why you bonded them to you?" enquired Ninniane, blue eyes steady and enquiring. "That very bond proved their downfall. When you were imprisoned, they too were trapped in ancient vaults where they remained until..."

"Until I escaped and once more released them," Lorcan finished, smiling. "Let it not be said I do not learn from my mistakes. This time I did not bond with them, merely formed an alliance of mutual need. They needed fresh souls. I needed the people of Erinsmore to learn the taste of terror."

"You did not bond with them?" For the first time, the girls heard shock in Ninniane's voice. "That means..."

"That if I am captured or killed the Gilmesh will remain free. They will not stop until every man, woman, and child in Erinsmore is slain."

"This is madness!" stated Ninniane. "Why would you wish such a thing? These are our people, Lorcan, why do you bear such malice towards them?"

"Because it was always you. You were the one our parents loved most, the one the Council of Mages wanted. Oh, don't try to deny it!" he snapped, as Ninniane's eyes clouded with confusion. "I know the only reason I was asked to join the Council and was granted eternal life was because they knew you would not join without me, for we were inseparable."

"You were my other half," Ninniane agreed softly, stepping towards him. "Brother," she said, her voice low and pleading. "There is still time. Help me stop this madness. Together we can destroy the Gilmesh and mend this broken land."

Lorcan hesitated, Ruby fancied she saw a longing in his eyes before madness crowded it out and his handsome face twisted scornfully.

"Oh, you would like that, would you not, sister," he spat disdainfully. "To see me reduced to nothing whilst your precious dragon lords rule a world that by rights belongs to me. No, Ninniane, the time for talking is over. If you will not join me, be prepared to die."

"You cannot kill me, brother," Ninniane replied.

"You think not, sister?" his mouth twisted into an ugly sardonic smile. "Let me assure you, your death will not cause me to lose even a moment's sleep." He held up a hand, his eyes throbbing a deep fathomless black as clouds of foulness oozed from his palm, seeping over the floor to Ninniane.

"Oh, my brother," she whispered sadly. "Do not do this, for you will harm yourself more than you harm me." Deliberately, she stepped into the black oily cloud, walking slowly but surely towards him whilst the filth flowed upwards over her, laying a patina of dark as it crept over her body.

"Stay back," he ordered. "Stay back, Ninniane, don't make this harder than it needs to be." Lorcan paused, face twisting into anguish. "You have been infected with the darkest of magic, there is no escape from the enchantment, my sister. Stand perfectly still and your death will at least be relatively painless. The more you move, the more painful death will be for you."

"Oh, Lorcan," Ninniane was moving more slowly now. The girls could see her flawless skin rippling as if something alive was crawling beneath it. They watched in fascinated horror. The wrinkles spread and deepened as the ages of centuries past claimed Ninniane's body. She opened her eyes, their now black depths regarding Lorcan sadly.

Her hands twisted into wizened crone's paws, and she lifted them painfully to gently cup Lorcan's face. "My dear brother," she whispered. Gold trickled from her fingertips into his temples. He flinched, as though ants were biting at his flesh, closing his eyes to block out her final moments. She fell towards him with a wordless cry, his arms automatically catching and cradling his sister.

"Ninniane." Her name was a caress on his lips. When he opened his eyes, they were the kind and steady blue regard of his sister. Peace settled on his face. He lowered her carefully to the ground and sat with her, holding her gently as shudders wracked her feeble body, and then she lay still.

"No!"

The sisters held each other, faces wet with tears, as Lorcan's cry of denial echoed through the cavern. He clutched Ninniane's body to his chest, as great wild sobs were wrenched from his throat.

"Ninniane, I am sorry, I did not mean ... No! I did not want this. Not this!"

He bent his head over her disintegrating remains and gave an almost inhuman moan of despair. Before the girls horrified, disbelieving eyes, a golden cloud of sparkling dust emanated from within him. Engulfing and consuming, it grew denser and denser until it imploded. When it cleared, both Lorcan and Ninniane had disappeared.

Ruby blinked. They were back in the circular chamber staring at each other in stunned disbelief. "What happened?" she whispered. "Where did they go? If Ninniane is ... dead," her voice stumbled over the words, "what happens to us now?"

"How unexpected," the voice said. "Still, it says nothing in the rules about what happens should your champion die whilst slaying the enemy..."

"Slaying the enemy?" interrupted Cassie. "So, does that mean that Lorcan's..."

"Dead, oh yes," finished the voice. "Although, as I said, in a most unexpected fashion. I do not believe this has ever happened before. Still, death of the enemy is death of the enemy, so I suppose you must now proceed."

"Proceed?" asked Cassie, warily. "Proceed where?"

"Why, onto the dark path of course. Hurry along now, there's not much time," the voice insisted, fussily. A portion of the wall slid open to reveal a long tunnel stretching down into the darkness.

"Where ... where does it go to?" Ruby whispered nervously.

"To that which you seek."

"We're not sure what we're seeking," replied Cassie.

"Well then, even more reason to hurry," snapped the voice waspishly. Before the girls could argue any further, a gust of impatient wind blew them through the opening and the door slammed shut, leaving them standing in pitch darkness.

"Cassie," Ruby whimpered, and Cassie took her hand.

"It's okay, I'm here."

"What do we do now?"

"Well, I guess we go on."

"Where to? We can't see where we're going." There was a pause, and Ruby almost heard Cassie thinking, considering.

"This will not defeat me," she muttered, then came the sound of her sword being drawn, a faint hum of power, and light exploded into the darkness.

Ruby looked at Cassie, saw the blueness of her eyes, and realised she was using her ability to illuminate her sword.

"I thought you had to be angry to do that?"

Cassie grinned in the eerie light cast by the sword. "Let's just say I'm not very happy."

They looked around. Beyond the glow from the sword, darkness stretched in all directions, endless, fathomless.

"What do we do now?" Ruby asked again.

"Look," said Cassie. "Look at the ground."

A row of pebbles led away from them, small smooth white pebbles which shone brightly. A memory leapt from Ruby's mind. "The shining way," she murmured.

"You what?"

"The shining way, that's what the Lake creatures said," Ruby tried to remember their exact words. "They told me after they'd given me the crystal heart, that they sensed great struggles ahead and I was not to falter from the shining way."

"Okay," said Cassie, her sword held down to illuminate the stones. "I guess that's as good as it's going to get. Come on."

"They could lead anywhere," whined Ruby, knowing she wasn't being very grown-up or brave, but feeling so scared and shocked she couldn't help it.

"Do you have a better plan?" snapped Cassie. Ruby fell silent, shaking her head in the gloom. "Well then," Cassie continued, "we follow them. Let's go."

They walked for what seemed like forever, progressing slowly, as they kept their eyes firmly on the pebbles. Occasionally, they would come to a crossroads or a junction in the passage, and Cassie would pause, swinging her sword until they found the pebbles again.

Ruby peered down the passages they passed, wondering where they led, wondering if they led anywhere, imagining being lost down here forever, roaming helplessly until they died of exhaustion or thirst, or went mad.

"Cassie," said Ruby, trying to divert her mind from the thought.

"Hmm?"

"Now Lorcan's dead, why do we need the fourth treasure?"

"You heard what he said. Even if he's dead, the Gilmesh will kill and take souls until no one's left alive. Maybe the treasures will make a weapon powerful enough to stop them."

"Oh, right," agreed Ruby, uncertainly.

They walked on in silence.

"Ruby," this time it was Cassie who spoke, and Ruby grunted an affirmative. "Did he say this was the dark path?"

"Erm, yeah, think so," replied Ruby. "Why?"

"Doesn't it say something about the dark path in the prophecy?"

"Does it?" Ruby tried hard to remember, it seemed so long since she'd last read it. "I think it does," she said slowly, "Something about two walking it?"

"Well, there's two of us and we're walking it," replied Cassie. "Do you remember the last line of the prophecy?" she asked casually, Ruby thought she heard something in her tone.

"No," she said. "Do you?"

"No," came the quick reply. Ruby knew she was lying and tried to remember what was in the prophecy to make her brave sister sound so afraid.

It was later, much later, although how much time had passed it was impossible to tell. Ruby was stumbling along blindly in Cassie's wake, fantasising about sunlight when Cassie stopped, and Ruby cannoned into her.

"What's the matter?" she hissed, rubbing at her bumped nose.

"Don't go another step," Cassie ordered.

"What? Why?"

"Something's changed. Our voices, do you hear how they're now echoing?"

"Yes, why..."

"Wait," barked Cassie, dropping to the ground and wiggling forward on her belly, pushing the sword along in front. Ruby waited, wondering if her sister had finally gone mad. Cassie stopped, peering at something on the ground.

"Look," she ordered tersely. "Come here beside me, but don't go any further."

Carefully, Ruby crawled beside Cassie, trying to see what had worried her. "What am I supposed to be looking at?"

"That," Cassie held the sword aloft, pointing down. For a moment Ruby saw nothing, then realised nothing was all there was to see.

"Where's the ground gone?" she gasped, instinctively moving back from the gaping hole which yawned before them.

"A sheer drop," murmured Cassie, feeling around for one of the many chunks of fallen rock that littered the path. "Let's see how far down it goes." She tossed the chunk over the edge. The girls waited and waited – nothing.

Ruby clutched Cassie's arm. "It's bottomless," she cried.

"No, that's impossible," Cassie replied. "The bottom's there all right, just so far down we can't hear it."

"What do we do?" Ruby tried to stay calm, the quiver in her voice betraying the panic rising in the pit of her stomach.

"We follow the stones," Cassie said casually. Ruby realised that far from leading them straight over the edge, the stones did a sharp right-hand turn taking them alongside the precipice. Carefully, the girls followed them, staying well clear of the edge.

"There!" Ruby heard the relieved triumph in Cassie's voice, "A bridge." The pebbles turned left, stretching away into the darkness, apparently suspended in mid-air over the sheer drop. Cassie held high her sword, cautiously shuffling closer.

In the light, Ruby saw there was a bridge. A high delicate span of ancient brickwork barely more than a metre wide. In places, she could see gaps where the bricks had crumbled away into nothing.

"You're not serious?" she demanded. "Call that a bridge? We can't cross that!"

"We have to."

"I can't..."

"Do you want to go back?"

"No."

"Well then, we have to cross it." Ruby swallowed down her fear, following Cassie closely as she stepped gingerly onto the bridge, testing its weight-bearing abilities.

"Step where I step," she ordered. "And don't look down."

It was the stuff of nightmares. Eternal dark gathering beyond the feeble sword light; the thought of endless passages stretching behind and ahead of them; the even scarier thought of the sheer drop into nothing, mere inches below them.

Ruby shuffled behind Cassie, watching where she placed her feet and standing in her sister's footprints, heart fluttering with fear.

"You're doing great, Ruby," Cassie's voice floated back over her shoulder. "We're halfway across now. Keep going."

"Do I have a choice?" Ruby muttered, sarcastically.

"Wait," Cassie paused, holding up a hand. "What's that?"

"I don't hear..."

"Sssh, listen."

Ruby listened. She heard the soft moaning of the wind through the tunnels, but that sound had been with them since the start of their journey. She didn't think Cassie would be drawing her attention to it now. She opened her mouth to speak, stopped, listened, and felt the faintest of vibrations beneath her feet.

The bridge trembled, then settled. From behind them, back in the darkness at the beginning of the bridge, stonework groaned, moved, and rumbled.

"What's happening?" she whispered, afraid of the answer.

"The bridge is collapsing," cried Cassie in horror. "Run!"

They ran, feet skidding on the slippery bricks as the rumbling grew louder, echoing down into the chasm below. Bricks dislodged, fell, and cracks ran away beneath their hurrying feet.

Ruby's stomach lurched as the bridge rocked sideways.

"Cassie!" she screamed.

"Hurry," yelled her sister. "We're nearly there! We're nearly at the other side." The sword bobbed ahead of Ruby. Desperately she fixed her eyes upon its comforting light, saw Cassie safely reach the other side, jump onto firm ground, and then turn to help her sister. Ruby stretched out a hand, their fingers brushed ... and the bridge collapsed beneath her.

"Ruby!"

Desperately, Cassie threw herself forward and grabbed a handful of Ruby's dress – pulling sharply and stumbling backwards as the whole cavern shook and rumbled, the edges of the precipice crumbling beneath their feet.

Still, she held on, staggering backwards, until her feet reached firmer ground, boots scrabbling for purchase on the ever-shifting bricks. She dropped the sword, grabbed Ruby's hand, and pulled. They were finally safe, sprawling onto the ground as the world behind them fell away into oblivion.

"No!" shrieked Cassie, lurching forward, fingers outstretched. Too late. The sword slipped, blazing in response to Cassie's rage, illuminating its way as it plunged and fell into the chasm, leaving them gasping for breath, huddled together in total darkness.

The darkness was absolute. Ruby heard someone sobbing, realised it was herself and tried to stop; to regain control.

"Ruby, it's okay." Her sister touched her face and Ruby was comforted a little by her presence, but still, the panic rose.

"What are we going to do?" she gasped. In the darkness she heard a rustle as her sister moved closer, putting an arm tightly about her.

"We do what we were doing. We follow the shining path."

"Without the sword? How can we? We don't even know where the pebbles are."

"Well, right now they're pressing into my bum," Cassie shifted uncomfortably, took Ruby's hand, and guided it down to the ground. "Here, feel."

Under her probing fingers, Ruby felt the row of protruding pebbles. "We can't see them. How can we follow them?"

"We feel for them with our feet," stated Cassie firmly. "Come on, up you get."

"But ... but ... it's dark..."

"I know Ruby," Cassie hugged her. "I know how you feel about the dark. You must trust me; we'll get through this. I promise you. We'll reach the end of the path."

"Perhaps there is no end. Perhaps it goes on forever and ever, leading us deeper and deeper underground."

"I don't believe it," Cassie stated firmly. "There is an end. We must stick to the path, that's all, okay?"

"Okay," Ruby agreed weakly.

If their progress had been slow before, now it was snail's pace. Cassie walked softly and carefully; the soles of her boots pressed firmly onto the pebbles. Ruby clutched her hand, also feeling the reassuring bump of the pebbles beneath her shoes.

Deliberately, inch by painstaking inch, they edged their way forward. All around them the darkness seethed, pressing against their eyelids, creating imagined sounds which in turn placed images in their minds.

They sang to help dispel the creeping terror. Nursery rhymes, pop songs, Christmas carols, anything to keep their spirits up. It was midway through Cassie's version of The Twelve Days of Christmas, a particularly filthy version which had Ruby giggling with disbelief, that Cassie's voice stuttered, and abruptly stopped.

"Go on," urged Ruby. "What did he give her on the next day?"

"Sssh," hissed Cassie urgently. "Listen."

"Cassie! Ruby!" A voice, joyously familiar, echoed down a nearby passageway.

"Colwyn?" called Cassie in disbelief. "Is that you?"

"Yes," came the reply. "I'm so relieved I've found you."

"Where are you?" shouted Cassie. "It's so dark we can't see anything."

"Over here, I've found the way out. Follow the sound of my voice, Cassie."

Cassie moved, but Ruby gripped her arm. "If we leave the pebbles, we may never find them again."

"So?" cried Cassie. "Colwyn's there waiting for us. He can lead us out of here."

Something else was niggling at Ruby. "This isn't right," she insisted. "In every book, I've ever read, in every legend, the hero is always tempted from the path he should take. What if that's what's happening here?"

"It's Colwyn," Cassie insisted. "I'd recognise his voice anywhere."

"And another thing," Ruby insisted. "Since when did he start calling you Cassie, not Cassandra? And no way would he say I'm or I've. The real Colwyn would say I am, and I have."

She felt her sister's hesitation. In the darkness, Colwyn spoke again. "What are you waiting for? Shift your butts you two."

"You're right," Cassie gasped. "Colwyn would never say such a thing. If you *are* Colwyn," she called aloud, "come here and show yourself." There was silence; then the softest whisper of a breeze and the voice spoke no more.

"You were right," murmured Cassie. "If it hadn't been for you, I'd have led us away from the path and we'd have been lost forever."

Ruby took her sister's hand, and without another word, they started following the pebbles again, the dark seeming, if possible, even denser than before.

Long hours later, Cassie stopped, touching Ruby gently on the shoulder. "Can you see something?" she asked.

Ruby stared in the direction of her voice. "Have you completely lost the plot?" she demanded.

"Up ahead," demanded Cassie. "The black doesn't seem so ... black." Ruby squinted, the velvet darkness pressing heavily on her eyes.

"Not sure, maybe" she conceded. They walked in silence for a few more eternal minutes before Ruby tugged on Cassie's hand. "You're right," she exclaimed in excitement. "It's not so dark."

With renewed energy, the girls stumbled towards the light, until finally, the tunnel ended in a solid wall of rock. Above their heads, a shaft stretched up. Dim light filtered down, and they saw a rough ladder carved into the rock.

"Do we go up?" asked Ruby.

"What other choice do we have?" enquired Cassie. She let go of Ruby's hand, stretching up to grab the first rung of the ladder. Swinging herself nimbly onto it she began to climb, leaving Ruby to follow her.

Climbing more slowly, disadvantaged by having neither Cassie's height nor a year of intense, physical training behind her, Ruby cast nervous glances downwards at the dark pooling at the base of the ladder. The thought of a hand reaching up to grab her ankle popped unnervingly into her head.

Luckily for Ruby, the climb was short. It wasn't long before Cassie was pulling her over the rim of the rock face, and they were standing in a small chamber facing a pair of vast, ornately carved wooden doors, resplendent with fierce-looking dragons whose great wings were opened in flight.

Hesitantly, Cassie reached out a hand and gently pushed on the doors. They opened instantly. Casting nervous glances at each other, the girls slipped quietly through them and into the cave beyond.

It was vast, so massive, they could hardly make out the other side, its soaring cavernous roof arching up hundreds of feet above their heads. Feeling small and insignificant Ruby followed Cassie further into the cave, eyes glinting in the dim light as her head swivelled this way and that.

"What do you suppose these are?" Cassie stopped at one of the huge crystal mounds that spaced the cavern in long regimented rows, cupping her hands to its surface, trying to peer into its distorted depths.

"Don't know," said Ruby, doing the same, then jumping back in shock as images beneath the crystal realigned themselves to form a giant, scaly, closed eye, crested with a brow of emerald ridges leading down to a spiny back and a pair of shiny, folded wings...

"They're dragons!" she exclaimed, backing away from the mound. "They're all dragons! Cass, this is like some sort of giant dragon graveyard."

"Except they are not dead, merely slumbering..."

Squeaking with fear, Ruby clutched at Cassie and both girls spun round.

A dragon ... huge and powerful, its scales glimmering resplendent indigo.

A dragon ... surveying them with unblinking dispassionate eyes.

A dragon ... a wisp of smoke curling from its saucer-sized nostrils.

A dragon ... a dragon ... a dragon...!

Chapter Twenty-Two

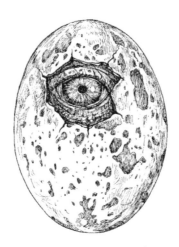

The Song
of the Dragon

uby gulped, legs quivering beneath her. Breathlessly, she leant against her sister who stared back at the apparition, apparently unafraid.

"Why aren't you sleeping as well then?" Cassie asked.

The dragon regarded them. "I am the guardian," it stated. Its voice was rich and low, and for a mad instant, Ruby was reminded of the voice of Simba's dad in the Lion King.

"It was my task to await the seekers, so my slumber was light. I was awoken when the gatekeeper allowed you onto the dark path." It paused, an almost grudging note of respect creeping into its voice.

"You showed great courage," it continued. "Many have simply wandered from the path to roam forever in the bowels of the earth."

"Why are they sleeping?" Cassie asked.

The dragon looked almost ashamed.

"Long ago, the race of dragon and man co-existed in peace and harmony. One strong family were bonded to us. Together, we ruled Erinsmore."

"The house of the dragon lords," breathed Cassie, fingering her pendant.

"Yes," agreed the dragon. "Yet one of our number betrayed his lord. In shame, the dragons placed themselves under a spell, vowing they would slumber until the hour of Erinsmore's darkest need until the seekers came to awaken them."

"It's obvious," said Cassie slowly, turning to Ruby. "Not Dragonswell, but dragon spell. Over the years the name has changed. People forgot what it meant."

"Are you the seekers?" the dragon demanded.

"Yes," replied Cassie firmly, stepping away from Ruby. "We are. We seek the D'raiqwq. Erinsmore is in its hour of darkest need, the time has come to unite the four ancient treasures."

The dragon bowed its magnificent head. "And are you prepared to pay the price?"

Cassie nodded. "We are..."

"Hold on," Ruby interrupted, prickles of fear dancing up her spine. "What price? What are you talking about? Cassie...?"

"Be quiet, Ruby," said her sister firmly, and looked directly into the dragon's iridescent, turquoise eyes. "We are," she repeated, and the dragon bowed again.

"Follow me," it said and led the way to a small crystal mound. Gently, it blew a column of fire; the crystal shimmered and melted, revealing a beautiful smooth golden orb about a foot in length.

"The D'raiqwq," announced the dragon.

The girls stepped forward in wonder, hardly daring to reach out and stroke its beckoning surface.

"And now," boomed the dragon, rearing up on its back legs and unfurling its leathery wings to their full span. "You must decide," it declared.

It swung its massive head around to look at Cassie.

"I see the decision has already been made," it said flatly.

"Yes," replied Cassie. "Ruby, my sister, she is the gemstone who will unite the treasures, and I … I will pay the price."

"Cassie," cried Ruby in growing dismay. "What do you mean? What price?"

"The prophecy," whispered Cassie, sadly. "Remember, Ruby, two shall walk the dark path and one return alone. I knew. In a way, I think I've always known…"

"Known what?" demanded Ruby shrilly, sweat breaking out down her spine, her heart beginning to pound wildly.

"That I wouldn't be going back," said Cassie flatly.

Ruby's jaw dropped.

"Cass," she began desperately. "Please, don't do this, let's forget about the treasure, we'll find another way, there must be another way, Cassie, please!" she cried, as Cassie shook her head.

"The choice is made!" roared the dragon. "There can be no going back. Take the D'raqwq!"

"No, wait, please, Cassie!" screamed Ruby.

"Pick it up!" bellowed the dragon.

"But…"

"Pick it up!"

Flustered and shocked, Ruby grabbed the orb, staggering under its weight. The dragon belched a cloud of golden flames at her. Ruby cried out in fear, yet they didn't burn, instead, the cavern shimmered and began to fade.

Ruby had one last glimpse of her sister. She saw the fear in Cassie's eyes as she watched her go, her face impassive. The dragon pendant glinting around her neck, she raised her chin and faced the dragon, awaiting her fate...

...then Ruby was dropping to the cold, hard, stone floor of the battlements, hearing Melinda's cry of shock as she fell, and kept on falling into darkness.

Moments later, she opened her eyes to a ring of concerned faces. Still clutching the orb, Ruby looked up at them and began to cry, wild desperate sobs. She clutched at Delmar's blue robes as he knelt and gently helped her to sit.

"Ruby, where are the others? Where is Lady Ninniane?"

"She's dead," Ruby sobbed. "Lorcan killed her, then he died, I don't know why, I don't understand what happened. The gatekeeper said they were dead, he made us walk the dark path, so we did, and we found a giant cave full of sleeping dragons."

"Dragons?" exclaimed Colwyn, exchanging a shocked glance with Delmar.

"There have always been myths, legends," he muttered. "Yet I never thought ... what happened then, Ruby?"

"This dragon, it gave us the D'raqwq, then ... then, it said a decision had to be made, that a price had to be paid ... and Cassie ... she ... she..."

Ruby broke down in a fresh storm of weeping. Through her tears, she saw Colwyn's face turn ashen.

"Where is your sister?" he demanded through clenched teeth. Crouching beside her, he grasped her shoulders and shook her almost painfully.

"Where is Cassandra?"

"She's dead," whispered Ruby miserably, hearing Melinda gasp. "I'm sorry," she cried, as Colwyn shrank away from her.

"She said she'd always known she wouldn't be coming back because of the prophecy; Colwyn, I'm sorry, please..."

Colwyn turned away. Swiftly, he climbed the steps to the ramparts and stood at the parapet, back rigid, fists clenching and unclenching at his side.

"I'm so sorry," sobbed Ruby. "By the time I realised what she meant, it was too late, she'd already decided. The dragon said the decision had been made and sent me back here."

"Oh, Ruby," sighed Delmar, hugging her close as Lady Melinda patted her on the arm.

For a moment, Ruby allowed herself to be comforted by her friends while Colwyn stood alone and apart. Melinda gently passed her a lace-trimmed handkerchief, which Ruby gratefully used to mop up her tears.

"Come, let us take you to your room," offered Delmar, gently helping her to her feet. "You need to rest and then..."

"There's no time to rest," Ruby interrupted. "It's not over yet."

"I thought you said Lorcan was dead?" exclaimed Delmar.

"He is," agreed Ruby. "He told the Lady he hadn't bonded the Gilmesh to him this time, so if he was captured or killed, they would go on and on, killing everyone, until no one was left alive."

There was a stunned silence. They all stared at Ruby, even Colwyn turned to face her, his expression carved from stone.

"But ... without the Lady, without the sacred sword," stuttered Melinda, "how are we supposed to fight them?"

"Cassie said we had to unite the treasures," sobbed Ruby, the lump in her throat at the thought of her sister choking her. "She said it might be the only way to stop them."

"We only have two of the treasures here," cried Colwyn. "This," he nodded his head at the golden orb still clutched in Ruby's arms, "and the griffin."

"Then, I must go to the Sanctuary and retrieve the other two," stated Delmar firmly. Reluctantly, Colwyn nodded.

Taking a deep breath, Delmar's eyes pulsed blue. Ruby stepped back expecting him to disappear.

Nothing happened.

"What is amiss?" demanded Colwyn.

Delmar shook his head confused. "I know not. It is as if something is preventing me from transporting, yet I..."

"Enemy approaching from the north!" the cry went up from the sentry on the turret above them.

"Enemy approaching from the west."

"From the south."

"From the east."

The cries of the sentries on the battlements rang out. They shot despairing glances at each other, before rushing up the steps to stand beside Colwyn who had snatched Cassie's binoculars from his belt and was studying the horizon in horror.

"By the stars!" he cried, handing them to Delmar who also exclaimed in dismay. Straining her eyes, Ruby could make out a dark smudge stretching in an unbroken circle as far as the eye could see, surrounding the castle.

"Gilmesh," breathed Colwyn. "Thousands of them," he turned to Delmar. "Do you think they are somehow stopping you from travelling?"

"Undoubtedly," replied Delmar.

The two men exchanged a long level look, which Ruby saw and understood. It was a look which said it was over, against so many there was no hope. She slid to the floor in sudden total exhaustion.

"It's hopeless," she cried. "Cassie died for nothing. It's all completely hopeless."

"Now, now, Ruby," gently chided a familiar voice. "Have you learnt nothing? No situation is ever without hope."

"My Lady!" breathed Colwyn, in relief.

Ruby stared in dazed disbelief. Lady Ninniane smiled at her, as young and beautiful as ever, Samson beside her, craggy features creased into an almost gleam of welcome, the prophecy stone and the crystal heart held firmly in his grasp.

There was a caw, and Cora circled down from above and landed before Ruby. Strutting up to her, she laid her head on Ruby's arm, lovingly rubbing her beak on her hand, projecting images of pleasure at seeing her, and sorrow for the loss of her sister.

"I don't understand," began Ruby, rubbing at her eyes in wonder. "You're dead, I saw you die!"

"In a sense you did," agreed the Lady. "Yet Lorcan failed to understand the ancient laws of magic. Sometimes, the willingness to be sacrificed to save others is enough. I took the dark from his soul, so I had to die, its burden was too great for me to bear. Once the evil had been purged from him, Lorcan became again my soulmate. Great remorse gripped him and this, combined with my essence which I placed into him at the last, was enough to undo his spell."

She paused, and Ruby remembered the gold leaving her fingertips as she'd caressed her brother's face.

"Enemy approaching," the cries went up again. They looked at each other in concern, the Gilmesh army having been momentarily forgotten.

"What do we do, my Lady?" cried Colwyn. The alarm bell began to clang wildly inside the castle. "There are so many, how do we defeat them?"

"It is time to reunite the treasures," the Lady smiled at Ruby.

"But … I don't know how to do that," stuttered Ruby, backing away from their expectant, hopeful eyes. "I'm sorry, I don't know what to do."

"Come," the Lady held out her hand, helping Ruby to her feet. Silently, they made their way to the throne room where the golden griffin rested in solitary splendour on the table. Gently, Samson placed the prophecy stone and the crystal heart next to it. Ruby finally laid the orb down, arms aching from its weight.

"What do I do?" she asked, glancing at the Lady in concern.

"Whatever you feel is right," Ninniane replied.

Sighing, Ruby sat before the treasures and stared at them, hoping for inspiration. Behind her, the Lady gently dropped her hands onto her shoulders, her eyes lightly pulsing blue.

"From earth, the prophecy stone, a symbol of patience and endurance," Ninniane murmured. "From water, the crystal heart, shining with the pure unbreakable light of unselfish love. From air, the golden griffin, standing for faith and hope when all seems lost, and from fire, the D'raiqwq which means…"

"Life … reborn and renewed …" finished Ruby, slowly. Her eyes blazed brilliant blue, gold sparkled from her hands onto the treasures, and the orb cracked.

It was beautiful, was the only thought Ruby could manage, so beautiful. The gold cloud shimmering beneath her palms intensified.

Dimly, she saw the prophecy stone, the crystal heart and the golden griffin, meld, joining together in a molten flow of brilliant lava, which swirled into the air in a tornado of light and then poured through the crack into the orb.

"By the stars," gasped Delmar.

"It's so beautiful," murmured Melinda.

The last trickle of light vanished into the orb. They were left blinking owlishly at each other, the world seeming dark. They waited, gazing expectantly at the orb.

It shuddered on the tabletop, abruptly lurching to one side as the crack widened and whatever was inside fought to get out.

With a final push, the orb exploded into fragments and Ruby realised what she should have known all along. The D'raiqwq, that symbol of life reborn and renewed, was an egg.

As the little creature struggled to its feet, stretching out its tiny deep red wings, its long scaly tail frantically lashing the table and attempting to balance, Ruby let out the breath she'd been holding and reached out her hand.

"A dragon," exclaimed Colwyn.

The dragon lifted its small head, staring unblinkingly at Ruby, its jewelled eyes deep and mysterious. It tipped its head from side to side, studying her, considering her.

I am Iliana. Ruby heard the voice in her head, knowing it came from the dragon. *I have chosen you, Ruby.*

Me? Ruby thought back. *What have you chosen me for?*

You are my kinswoman, Ruby. My life is now dedicated to serving you. I am the first dragon to be born in aeons. The wheel has come full circle. The time of the dragon is once more.

We are in great danger. Ruby thought back urgently. *Gilmesh surround the castle, we won't be able to hold them off for long.*

Show me. Iliana ordered simply.

Ruby looked up at the others, silently watching. "Iliana wants us to show her the Gilmesh," she said.

Colwyn frowned. "What does she think to do against so many?" he asked. "The legends all agree dragons are mighty warriors, nothing can stand against them, yet Iliana is newly born, and is so small."

Have faith and trust me.

"I think we must do as Iliana requests," Lady Ninniane murmured when Ruby conveyed her words to the others. "After all," she continued, with a glance at Colwyn, "it cannot harm."

He shrugged and nodded, casting a sceptical look at Iliana who tottered on her clawed feet and fell backwards, as a thud reverberated through the castle and they all staggered, trying to maintain their balance.

Thud, it came again.

Ruby saw the remains of the D'raiqwq judder and rattle on the table, as the castle shook to its very foundations.

"My Lord!" Darius appeared in the doorway; his normal implacable composure visibly shaken. "My Lord, you must come quickly, the Gilmesh..."

Exchanging alarmed glances, they quickly followed him, Ruby cradling Iliana in her arms, feeling a surge of almost maternal protectiveness towards the beautiful, tiny creature.

The castle continued to shake at regular intervals and Ruby struggled to keep her balance as she followed the others, Iliana wrapping her tail around her wrist, hooking curled talons into Ruby's cloak.

Colwyn reached Darius's side. Ruby saw his face register horror, then was at the edge of the ramparts. She looked and saw, her heart sinking. Whilst they had been inside the Gilmesh had advanced steadily and now surrounded the town at a distance of a mile at most.

Forming a solid grey line of hulking, skeletal figures, it was not this alone which struck terror into the silent watchers. Behind the marching Gilmesh came a line of creatures.

The closest description Ruby's panicked mind could provide was dinosaurs – colossal, armour-plated beasts with dense, flat snouts and massive, thick-boned heads.

Looming twenty metres or more above the Gilmesh, they were a terrifying sight. Perfect battering rams, Ruby realised, her heart clutching with fear.

"What are they?" she cried.

"They are kroneals, beasts from the very dawn of time. Lorcan must have brought them to our time before he died," replied the Lady, her eyes filled with concern. "They are practically indestructible and will destroy anything which gets in their path."

Ruby.

Ruby looked down at the whisper. Iliana gazed back unblinkingly.

Do not lose hope.

There are so many and if they can't be stopped...

Do you trust me?

The question rang clear and true in Ruby's mind. She stopped, swallowing down her fear.

Do you trust me? Iliana spoke again, her voice firm and urgent.

Yes, thought Ruby. Her fear vanished, and she straightened her spine. *Yes, I trust you, Iliana. I trust you with my life.*

Then it is time.

Iliana threw her head back. A note, resonant with crystal clarity and purity soared from her throat. Low and sweet, it penetrated every room in the castle, and all who heard it felt hope and strength enter their heart.

On and on, went the note. On and on, throbbing through the very stones beneath their feet, down it reverberated until it reached the cavern of sleeping dragons.

The guardian, Irridian, turned his gleaming indigo head and listened.

"It is time!" he roared. "The gemstone has reunited the treasures. The dragons are reborn. It is time!"

Flames flooded from his great nostrils, bathing every crystal sarcophagus in a white-hot veil, melting the crystal from around each giant slumbering form, warming their silent frozen blood.

"Awaken!" he ordered, voice booming like thunder through the cavern.

"It is time, awaken! The dragon lords summon us. We must answer!"

Iliana bowed her head. The last note of her song hung in the air. Ruby came back into her body, into reality. Looking at the stunned, beaming faces of the others, she realised she hadn't been the only one affected by the song. Colwyn turned, almost expectantly, to look at the Gilmesh.

"They still come," he declared. Ruby heard the disappointment in his voice.

"Look to the skies!" came the urgent cry from the watchtower. They turned, craning their necks upwards.

"What are they?" cried Colwyn, gesturing to the huge, dark shapes swooping up over the horizon, massive wings beat steadily and the skies of Erinsmore once more throbbed with the cry of the dragon.

"Dragons!" declared the Lady. "The dragons have awoken."

Colwyn snatched up his binoculars, training them onto the swarm of shining, jewel-coloured dragons, then gave a hoarse cry of recognition.

"Ruby!" he yelled, holding out the binoculars to her. "Look! On the lead dragon!"

With fingers that trembled, Ruby held the binoculars to her eyes, nearly dropping them as an image swam into focus. An image of her sister, of Cassie, sitting astride the huge, indigo-coloured dragon, mouth open in an unheard yell of pure exhilaration, plait streaming out behind as the dragon dived low overhead.

"Cassie!" screamed Ruby, dropping the binoculars, and rushing to the edge of the ramparts to wave frantically as Cassie and the dragon flew over.

"She's alive!" she shrieked and threw herself into Colwyn's arms. "She's alive!" she cried again and saw the answering joy and relief on his face.

"Thank the stars!" he cried, hugging Ruby tightly, staggering as the castle once more shook to the mighty thud of the approaching goliaths.

Hundreds of dragons were now wheeling and soaring above them, their glimmering, magnificent bodies the stuff of fable, of legend

The people of Erinsmore cheered themselves hoarse as the dragons swept past on another flyover of the castle, then swooped to engage the enemy.

Fire belched from gaping, scarlet maws. They were beautiful and terrible to behold. Gilmesh twisted and writhed. Helpless before the all-consuming hungry flames, their dying shrieks arose until the castle was surrounded by a solid wall of the sounds of death.

The dragons pulled back, and regrouped, diving again to attack the kroneals. Those mammoth lumbering brutes twisted their great blunt snouts skywards, trying to see from whence their attackers came, their challenging, earth-shaking roars ringing out over the death cries of their allies.

Fire rained upon them. The dragons turned their attack upon the kroneals, and they died, falling to their knees before the dragon's awesome might.

Upon the battlements, the people fell silent, Ruby and Lady Melinda turning away with murmurs of distress at the genocide they were witnessing.

Finally, an agonisingly long time later, it was over. The last kroneal crashed to the ground, and a sullen silence settled over the land. The dragons soared upwards, the wind scattering the heaped piles of grey Gilmesh death ash.

"It is done," said the Lady.

Ruby heard regret in her voice. In the end, peace had come at such a high price.

Then Colwyn was dragging her down the steps as Cassie and her dragon swooped to land in the courtyard, sending people scattering out of the way.

"Cassie!" yelled Ruby.

Cassie slid off the dragon's back, using his lifted front leg as a step, hurling herself into her sister's arms to the cheers of the watching crowd.

"You're alive!" sobbed Ruby, desperately patting Cassie all over to double-check that, yes, she was all here, whole, and gloriously, wondrously, alive.

"I thought you were dead, I thought that dragon was going to kill you."

"So, did I," grinned Cassie.

"My Lady..."

"Cassandra..."

Delmar and Melinda reached her. There were more hugs, expressions of joy and relief, then the crowd parted as Lady Ninniane stepped through and Cassie's eyes went huge with surprise.

"My Lady?" she stuttered. "But ... we saw you die!"

"You did indeed," smiled the Lady. "It is a long story, one best left for later. It is enough that we have succeeded. The scourge of Lorcan and his army of skraelings and Gilmesh have been removed from the land. Erinsmore owes a debt it can never repay to the Ladies Ruby and Cassandra who fought so valiantly, both prepared to sacrifice so much to save this land and her people."

Cheers erupted from every throat. Cassie and Ruby looked at each other, flushed with delighted embarrassment, the mighty dragon surveying them all with curious interest.

Colwyn stepped from the crowd. "My Lady Cassandra," he said quietly and bowed.

"My Lord Colwyn," she replied, equally formally. The crowd held its breath. Colwyn stroked a hand down her mussed plait, and Cassie smiled at him, hesitantly.

"I am ... relieved ... you are safe and well," he said.

Cassie briefly rested her cheek on his palm. "So, am I," she replied, flashing him a smile. "I've brought you a present." She indicated the gleaming indigo dragon behind her.

"This is Irridian," she declared, looking into the dragon's bejewelled eyes. "And this," she continued, "is Colwyn, Lord of the house of dragons, rightful heir to the dragon throne of Erinsmore."

"No, he is not," stated the dragon flatly. "He is not the rightful heir to the dragon throne."

Chapter Twenty-Three

Farewell
my Kinswoman

hush descended over the courtyard. All eyes were on the dragon, standing impassively, indigo scales glimmering in the sunshine.

"I'm sorry, what?" The cocky smile fell from Cassie's face.

"He is indeed Colwyn," replied Irridian, "heir apparent to the dragon throne. As such, we offer him all due honour and respect, yet he is not the rightful heir."

There was a puzzled murmur.

Colwyn stepped closer, a wary, fearful hope growing on his face as he held out a pleading hand to Irridian.

"Please," he gasped, voice breaking with emotion. "What do you mean?"

"I mean, the rightful heir of the house of dragons is not present. He is far away in the extreme north-west of this land, attempting to return here."

"My father's still alive," gasped Colwyn, incredulous joy lighting up his face.

"Lord Reutghar's alive!"

The cry was carried in a wave across the courtyard and into the castle until the cheers once more rang out.

"Can you take us to him?" Cassie asked Irridian.

"Of course," replied the dragon, and obligingly held up his foreleg so Cassie could swing confidently onto his back.

"Do you trust me?" Cassie asked as Colwyn hovered indecisively, eyeing the dragon with caution.

"With my life," he replied instantly. Cassie held out her hand.

Hesitating for only a second, Colwyn took it, pulled himself up onto Irridian's leg, and swung himself behind Cassie. He settled gingerly between the wickedly sharp spines on the dragon's back, clasping Cassie firmly round the waist.

"Fasten your seatbelt," yelled Cassie, "cos you're in for the ride of your life. Back soon, Ruby, try to stay out of trouble."

With a whoosh of air, the dragon launched himself into the sky. Colwyn's stomach lurched unpleasantly up into his throat. Groaning, he tightened his hold on Cassie.

Whooping with joy, Cassie threw her head back against his shoulder as Irridian swooped and wheeled in mid-air, catching the exhilarated mood of his passengers, showing off, and generally enjoying the sensation of flying free after so long confined in slumber in a dark, subterranean, cavern.

A convoy of dragons accompanied them, a particular one catching Colwyn's eye. A stunningly beautiful beast of brilliant emerald, it flew steadily beside them, and he couldn't stop glancing at it.

My Lord...

"What? What did you say?" he demanded.

"Nothing," replied Cassie, craning her neck to look at him. "Isn't this like the best thing ever? I mean, it's totally... totally..."

She screamed in terrified ecstasy as the dragons crested a mountain ridge and dived into a valley.

My Lord.

Once more, the voice sounded. Colwyn realised it was in his head. Looking around, he saw the emerald dragon beside him bow its head in acknowledgement.

With a burst of excitement, he realised it was the dragon projecting into his mind.

Is that you?

He tentatively thought, feeling the beast's amusement.

It is, my Lord.

The voice was female and young sounding.

I am Indrina, and I have chosen you as my kinsman. My life is now dedicated to serving you, my Lord.

Emotional connection, warming and fulfilling, swept through Colwyn, and a smile of wonder spread across his face.

I thank you for the honour you show me, he thought solemnly.

He was unsure of the correct protocol to use when addressing an eighty-foot-long dragon offering to serve you all your life but was pretty sure it was a clever idea to be polite.

"Down there!" shrieked Cassie.

Colwyn followed her pointing finger, seeing with a heartbeat of anticipation, a lone horse galloping frantically across the plain below. He felt Irridian shift beneath him.

The mighty dragon changed course effortlessly, gliding down to gently land several feet before the terrified rearing horse and the two figures desperately trying to stay on the frenzied animal's back.

Sliding carefully off Irridian's spiny back, swallowing at the thought of the damage those razor-sharp edges could do to a man, Colwyn saw his father's face as he swung down from the horse, eyeing the dragon nervously.

"Colwyn."

He was embracing his father, feeling for a moment like the child he'd been, desperately clinging to his father and being told his mother was never coming home again.

"My Lord," he stammered, choking on the words. "Father..."

"Well now," exclaimed his father mildly, looking up in unafraid wonder at Irridian.

"What have you got here?"

"My Lord," cried Cassie, full of self-importance. "This is Irridian. He's kind of the leader of the dragons, they've been asleep under Dragonswell for like, well, forever. We reunited the treasures, the dragons woke, and..."

Reutghar held up a hand and Cassie's mouth snapped shut. He stepped up to Irridian's magnificent indigo head and gently laid a hand on it.

He blinked, looking surprised.

His hand flew to his head in wonder.

He nodded to Irridian, and Colwyn realised his father must have experienced the wonder of bonding.

"Tell me, quickly," his father demanded. "How goes the battle? Lorcan...?"

"Is dead," broke in Colwyn quickly. "The Gilmesh are all destroyed by the dragons, Siminus is dead at Delmar's hand, Lorcan destroyed by the Lady. It is over, my Lord, we have won."

"Thank the Lady," breathed his father, and gestured to the terrified lad huddled in petrified wonder on the horse. "This is Merric, I saved him from the tower."

Cassie realised this must be the young boy Ruby had spoken of, the one who'd also been a captive of Lorcan and whose frightened thoughts she'd dipped into.

"We thought you were dead, my Lord," she said. "How did you escape?"

"The last thing the Gilmesh were expecting was for me to burst through the portal wielding the sacred sword." Reutghar chuckled at the memory.

"Before they could stop me, I'd smashed the stones, destroyed as many Gilmesh as I could, and made my escape into the forest where I waited and watched. The next morning, I witnessed a great panic and confusion amongst the Gilmesh, I have no idea why..."

"That must have been when the Gilmesh leader, Siminus, and Lorcan were summoned by the gatekeeper to face us in the cavern," exclaimed Colwyn.

"It seems we both have tales to tell," said his father, blue eyes keenly surveying his son.

"Soon after every Gilmesh left, so I took the opportunity to explore the tower and found Merric in hiding, the other servants had run away. We set out on foot to follow the Gilmesh. On our way, we came across a village the Gilmesh had raided. Obviously looking to increase their energy, they'd extracted every soul," he paused, face grim at the memory.

"It was a difficult thing to do, we left them unburied. We were only two, I was fearful of where the Gilmesh were going and what their intentions were. So, we took the best horse we could find and set off in pursuit. A few hours ago, we found tracks, realised the Gilmesh from the tower had joined with thousands more Gilmesh and were headed towards the castle, along with many giant creatures whose tracks I had never seen before."

"They were kroneal," explained Colwyn. "Great beasts from the dawn of time, Lorcan summoned them to destroy us, but they were all obliterated by the dragons."

"It seems I have much to be thankful for," mused Reutghar, stroking Irridian's scaly neck.

"Now, let us return. Come Merric, you will ride with me upon Irridian."

"My Lord," whispered the boy, reluctantly sliding off the horse and approaching the dragon with obvious trepidation.

"Oh, but ..." began Cassie, stopping as Irridian swung his great head to fix her with a baleful glare.

With a rustle of emerald-green, Indrina landed beside Colwyn, offering up her foreleg to assist him onto her back.

Would you allow the Lady Cassandra to accompany us? Colwyn thought, settling himself onto her shining back.

If she must, came the waspish reply.

Colwyn grinned at the note of jealousy in his dragon's voice.

"Home," stated Reutghar simply.

With a great sweep of multicoloured, bejewelled wings, the dragons launched into the sky.

That evening, the people of Erinsmore gathered in the banqueting hall, scene of the fiercest fighting during the battle, to share a simple meal, rejoice at the miracle of their deliverance, and wonder at the return from the dead of Lady Ninniane, Lady Cassandra, and their beloved Lord Reutghar.

Tomorrow would be soon enough to mourn their dead. Tonight, was the turn of the living. The hall echoed to loud, relieved voices, endlessly reliving their victory.

On the top table, Ruby was explaining to a fascinated Delmar and Melinda the story behind the four treasures, as it had been told to her by Iliana, now curled up in a sleeping red ball on her lap.

"Something happened," she said. "Something so terrible, Iliana won't talk about it. In self-punishment, the dragons sealed themselves into crystal tombs. The last dragon egg to be laid was separated into four parts and scattered throughout the land."

Ruby paused and softly stoked Iliana's scarlet head. The tiny dragon stretched like a kitten, her eyelids flickering.

"The stone, with the prophecy carved on it, represented the endurance and longevity of dragons," Ruby continued. "The crystal heart, their unselfish love and loyalty. The golden griffin, the gift of flight, and the hope and faith no dragon can exist without. And the D'raiqwq was the actual physical body."

"I see," breathed Delmar in wonder. "And all four treasures lay undiscovered for millennia waiting to be reunited and for the dragons to be reborn. Amazing."

"I will tell you what I find amazing," interrupted Melinda. "That Lord Colwyn and Lady Cassandra have sat mere inches away from each other for the whole evening, not betraying by look or word that which we know them both to feel."

"You're right," agreed Ruby, worriedly. "I don't know what's with them. It's like, now it's all over and they can be together, they don't know how to, almost as if they have nothing left to say to each other..."

"Give them time," suggested Melinda, and Delmar nodded in agreement.

"I believe Melinda is right. There is much to come to terms with, much to reflect on, and many changes which have occurred. Perhaps, all they need is time."

Ruby bit her lip, hoping they were right.

Next morning, Ruby was awoken by an urgent pounding on their chamber door. She crawled up from sleep with a painful groan. In the other bed, Cassie muttered and turned over, flinching away from even the thought of waking up.

It had been late, very late, before they'd fallen into bed, and Ruby muttered dark curses under her breath as she fumbled into her robe and staggered to the door.

"Yes?" she snapped.

The servant on the other side flinched.

"My apologies, my Lady," he stammered. "Lady Ninniane requests your presence in the throne room immediately."

"This had better be good," Cassie muttered twenty minutes later, still braiding her hair, as Ruby knocked on the throne room door and opened it.

The girls entered, and Lady Ninniane stood to greet them, her expression serious. Lord Reutghar and Delmar were also present. Over by the window, Colwyn stood, his face closed and unreadable.

"What?" cried Ruby, her empathic senses humming with distress. "What is it?"

"A crossing has opened near to the castle," replied Ninniane. "If you are going to return home, it must be now."

"Home?" echoed Ruby disbelievingly.

Beside her, Cassie gasped. Ruby felt her sister's hand, small and trembling, creep into her own. The sisters stared at each other in silence. Home, they were going home.

It seemed like the whole of Erinsmore had turned out to see them go. As the sisters walked down into the valley, knowing the crossing was somewhere at the bottom, they both dabbed at the tears caused by saying goodbye.

On the rim of the valley, Lord Reutghar, Darius, Garth, Colwyn, Delmar, Lady Ninniane and Melinda, sat on horseback watching the sisters walk away.

"I cannot believe Lady Cassandra is leaving," murmured Melinda, exchanging a glance with Delmar, before sliding a sideways, accusing glare at Colwyn.

"I am curious, my Lord," Delmar continued casually. "What reason did she give for not staying?"

"I do not know," replied Colwyn, through gritted teeth. "I did not ask her to stay."

Six pairs of eyes swivelled to fix incredulously on Colwyn.

"Well, by all that's sacred," exclaimed Reutghar. "Why not?"

Ruby kept glancing curiously at Cassie until finally, she could contain herself no longer. "Why did you say no, Cass?"

"What?"

"When he asked you to stay, why did you say no?"

"I didn't say no, he didn't ask," Cassie glared at Ruby with miserable eyes. "Oh, Ruby, he didn't ask me to stay."

"My Lord," protested Darius, face flushed with emotion. "I cannot believe you are letting Lady Cassandra leave."

"She made her choice," snapped Colwyn peevishly. "So that is an end to it."

"A choice cannot be made if no choice is given," mused Lady Ninniane mildly, and Melinda nodded in agreement.

"You heard Cassandra's views on the subject," protested Colwyn. "In her world, women are independent. She would have no respect for a man who begs a woman to stay with him. They are the ones who do the asking. She did not ask to stay."

"My Lord, I spent three years in their accursed world, and trust me," Garth drawled wryly. "For all their proclaimed independence, it is still the men who do the asking and the women who do the deciding."

"Is this true?" Colwyn turned in his saddle to stare at Garth. "But ... I thought ... do you mean if I had only asked, she may have ... by the stars...!"

To the delight of the others, he drove his heels into his horse's side and tore off down the hillside at a furious gallop.

The sisters walked on in silence a little longer, Ruby hardly daring to look at Cassandra's stricken face, knowing it wasn't right, knowing she should do something about it, unsure what.

"No," she exclaimed, stopping dead, turning to face her startled sister.

"What?"

"No," Ruby repeated. "This isn't right. You must stay Cassie."

"But ... I can't..."

"You must. Think about the prophecy."

"The prophecy, what do you mean?"

"That last line, one return alone. We got it wrong, Cass. You thought it meant you were going to die in the dragons' cave, it didn't. It meant only one of us was going to go home, me. You must stay Cassie, stay here with Colwyn, that's what it meant."

"He didn't ask me to stay, Ruby." Cassie's expression went stubborn.

Ruby sighed in exasperation. "So? Are you a modern twenty-first-century woman or what? He didn't ask you, so what, why don't you ask him?"

"I couldn't," spluttered Cassie, "What about if he says no?"

"He says no, we go home, at least you'll have tried, at least you'll know for sure. If you don't ask, if we go home, you'll wonder for the rest of your life what might have been."

Cassie frowned, and Ruby pressed home her point.

"Answer me honestly, Cass, how does it feel, the thought of never seeing him again?"

Cassie swallowed, bowing her head. "It's killing me," she quietly admitted.

Ruby smiled. "I know, that's why you've got to ask, you've got to give it one last shot."

Cassie hesitated, and then her face cleared.

"Wait for me?" she smiled. Ruby nodded.

Cassie turned back and they saw the horseman galloping towards them, bent low over his horse's neck, urging it on, his hair blowing back in the wind, his face alive with hope.

Cassie took a small step forward, then another, and then she was running as fast as she could.

Colwyn reached her, pulling his horse to a sharp halt. He swung down from the saddle.

As Ruby hurried towards them, she saw Cassie jump into his arms, Colwyn dragging her close, holding her as if he were never going to let go.

"I don't know anything about being a lady," Ruby heard her sister babble as she reached them. "I know even less about being a princess, I'll probably get it all wrong..."

Colwyn grinned. "Do I look bothered?" he asked.

Then, to the full-throated roar of approval from the hundreds of watchers, he claimed her lips in a kiss which made Ruby feel she was going to explode from the sheer romance of it. What a fantastic ending for a film, she thought.

Cassie staggered back, dazed, and flushed.

"Ruby," she stammered. "I don't think I'll be going home with you..."

"I know," Ruby agreed, happily. Then, her face fell with the realisation she was never going to see her sister again.

"Oh, Cassie ..." she began.

Cassie clutched her in a tight hug. "I'll never forget you, Ruby," she sobbed.

"But I'll forget you, won't I?" cried Ruby. "You're choosing to stay, so it'll be as if you never existed, I won't even remember I ever had a sister."

"Cassandra, your pendant," interrupted Colwyn urgently.

Cassie gasped, clutching at the dragon around her neck.

"Of course," she cried.

She undid the chain, pressing it into Ruby's hands.

"It might help you to remember me."

The sisters held each other tightly.

A long while later, Ruby pulled back and found herself being hugged by Colwyn.

"Farewell, my sister," he murmured. "I swear to you, I shall cherish and protect her until my last breath."

"I know you will, Colwyn," Ruby smiled, planting a quick kiss on his cheek.

There was time for one long, last look at her tearful sister, and then Colwyn placed a claiming arm around Cassie's shoulder.

Ruby picked up her bag, turned her back on Erinsmore and walked, quickly and firmly, towards the crossing.

Ruby!

She looked up; Iliana was circling high above her head, scarlet wings aflame in the morning sun.

Farewell, my kinswoman.

The mists of the crossing swirled around her. As Ruby walked slowly into them, she heard Iliana's words of goodbye echoing in her head.

Know this, Ruby, I shall never forget you and we shall meet again. So, it is written in the stars and so shall it be. It is only farewell for now, my friend...

The darkness closed all around her, and Ruby was gone.

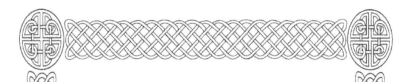

Chapter Twenty-Four

In Loving Memory

ick had reached his car and was fumbling with the lock in the pitch dark when he heard running feet and someone calling his name.

He turned abruptly as Ruby hurried out of the darkness.

"That was quick," he exclaimed.

"Not really," Ruby shook her head. "Time's a bit different there. I'm so glad I crossed over here and was able to catch you."

"Did Garth get back okay?" Mick asked as Ruby threw her bag on the backseat, sliding thankfully into the warmth of its interior.

"Yes. He's so happy to be home," Ruby replied. "And ..."

She stopped, unsure of what she'd been about to say, feeling there was something important she'd forgotten.

"You all right?" Mick enquired, eyeing her anxiously.

"Fine, I'm fine. Mick, it was only me and Garth you brought here, wasn't it?"

"Of course," he replied, in surprise. "Why?"

"Oh, no reason."

Ruby shook her head in confusion. The powerful engine purred into life, and they set off for the long journey home.

Having slept for most of the drive, by the time Mick dropped her home in the small hours of the morning, Ruby was alert and wide awake.

Whispering goodbye to Mick, promising to see him soon, Ruby let herself in, relieved she'd arranged for her parents to be away, and thankful there'd be no awkward questions.

Standing under the welcoming, cleansing streams of hot water in the shower, Ruby couldn't shake the feeling something was missing, that there was something she'd forgotten about, something important.

Pulling on her robe, Ruby left the bathroom. For some reason she found herself pushing open the spare room door, staring around its cluttered interior.

The old double bed with the faded chintz quilt, the broken computer desk in the corner with the ancient Apple Mac Dad used, the awful watercolours Mum had painted at art evening class.

Ruby gazed at it all, frowning, whilst something nagged and pulled at her memory.

Shaking her head, Ruby returned to her room and sat at her dressing table, pulling a comb through her long hair, and staring at her reflection in the mirror.

Her eyes fell upon the bag she'd brought back from Erinsmore. She dragged it towards her and opened it.

On the top, looking like it had been hastily stuffed in at the last minute, was a heavy golden dragon pendant.

Ruby picked it up, frowning.

Colwyn's pendant?

She remembered it being around his neck.

Why did she have it?

Had Colwyn given it to her?

If he had, why couldn't she remember?

The dragon's eyes bored into hers.

Ruby bent closer, staring. The dragon reminded her of Iliana.

As she gazed, closed, and locked doors in her head flew open, and memories begin to flicker through her mind.

A girl laughing, long purple hair shining in the gleam of the crystal heart, a beast rearing up over the girl, and the same girl training with Garth and learning how to sword fight.

She remembered the girl fighting with Colwyn by her side, always by her side.

She saw the girl, radiantly beautiful, being cheered by dozens of soldiers in a crowded banqueting hall, Colwyn kneeling before her, offering up his sword.

She remembered watching her friends fight for their lives against Lorcan and his allies, remembered seeing the girl's set, bravely determined face as she offered herself up as payment in return for the last treasure.

Ruby experienced again the pain when she'd believed the girl dead; the wild joy at seeing her fly over her head on the back of a magnificent dragon, destroying the enemy in a hail of flames.

Ruby remembered the full-throated roar of approval from the ranks of watching soldiers when the girl agreed to stay with Colwyn as his bride and future queen of Erinsmore.

Ruby clasped the pendant tightly to her chest in dazed bewilderment, seeing the reflected tears in her eyes.

In her mind, the girl looked up at her and smiled and the last piece of the puzzle clicked into place.

Ruby swayed, disorientated by the flood of memories, clutching the edge of the dressing table with relief.

"I remember," she whispered thankfully. "Oh Cassie, my sister, I do remember you, I do…"

The End

~ About the Author ~

Julia Blake lives in the beautiful historical town of Bury St. Edmunds, deep in the heart of the county of Suffolk in the UK, with her daughter, one crazy cat and a succession of even crazier lodgers.

She has been writing all her life but only recently took herself seriously enough to consider being published. Her first novel, The Book of Eve, met with worldwide critical acclaim, and since then, Julia has released many other books which have delighted her growing number of readers with their strong plots and instantly relatable characters. Details of all Julia's novels can be found on the next page.

Julia leads a busy life, juggling working and family commitments with her writing, and has a strong internet presence, loving the close-knit and supportive community of fellow authors she has found on social media and promises there are plenty more books in the pipeline.

Julia says: "I write the kind of books I like to read myself, warm and engaging novels, with strong, three-dimensional characters you can connect with."

~ A Note from Julia ~

If you have enjoyed this book, why not take a few moments to leave a review on Amazon. It needn't be much, just a few lines saying you liked the book and why, yet it can make a world of difference.

Reviews are the reader's way of letting the author know they enjoyed their book, and of letting other readers know the book is an enjoyable read and why. It also informs Amazon that this is a book worth promoting, and the more reviews a book receives, the more Amazon will recommend it to other readers.

I would be very grateful and would like to say thank you for reading my book and if you spare a few minutes of your time to review it, I do see, read, and appreciate every single review left for me.

Best Regards
Julia Blake

Other Books by the Author

Black Ice

A magical steampunk retelling of the
Snow White story

The Forest
~ a tale of old magic ~

Myth, folklore, and magic combine in this engrossing tale
of a forgotten village and an ancient curse

The Perennials Series

Becoming Lili – the beautiful, coming of age saga
Chaining Daisy – its gripping sequel
Rambling Rose – the triumphant conclusion

The Blackwood Family Saga

Fast-paced and heartwarming, this exciting series tells
the story of the Blackwood Family and their search for
love and happiness

The Book of Eve

A story of love, betrayal, and bitter secrets that
threaten to rip a young woman's life apart

Eclairs for Tea
And Other Stories

A wonderful collection of short stories and quirky poems
that reflect the author's multi-genre versatility
Includes the award-winning novella – Lifesong

Printed in Great Britain
by Amazon